The Bootmaker of Berlin

OTHER TITLES BY DEBBIE TERRANOVA

Enemies within these Shores

The Scarlet Key

Baby Farm

The Bootmaker of Berlin

People lie, especially the ones you love

DEBBIE TERRANOVA

Please note that this novel is written in Australian / British English. The spelling and meaning of some words may differ from the standard English used in other countries, in particular the United States of America.

First published 2023 by Terranova Publications
PO Box 4144, St Lucia South, Queensland 4067 Australia
Email: terranovapublications@gmail.com
Website: www.terranovapublications.com

A catalogue record for this book is available from the National Library of Australia

ISBN: 978-0-9941700-3-3 (paperback)

Cover design by Elise Terranova

For my family

One

Alexanderplatz: October 2010

Three hours to kill. Kathy Giuliano gritted her teeth and stepped from the overheated *U-Bahnhof* into freezing drizzle. Her bomber-jacket—electric blue with orange trim—was no match for the weather. An arctic wind slashed through the fabric and stabbed icicles into her flesh. Shuddering with cold, she hauled her suitcase-on-wheels across open ground to the entrance of the *Galeria*. From behind a glass windbreak, she turned and scanned the vast concrete plaza.

Figures in Michelin-man jackets dashed between buildings; kids splashed in rain puddles; a busker coaxed tunes from a xylophone made of bottles part-filled with water; teens with dreadlocks swayed to throbbing techno music. Bike bells tinkled; sirens wailed; umbrellas flapped; shoes slapped on the wet pavement.

At one end of the plaza, steam billowed from lunchtime market stalls. Kathy's mouth watered. Breakfast in the transit lounge at Heathrow—rubbery eggs and greasy bacon—had been an age ago. Tempting, so very tempting. But everything outside was slick with moisture one degree warmer than ice. Her travel clothes were not suitable for northern Europe in autumn. The last thing she needed was to contract pneumonia or some other awful disease so far from home. Mentally, she added another item to a growing list of imprudent things she'd done this year. First on that list was making a rash promise to someone she loved, but who didn't love her back. Second was deciding to fulfil that promise unaided and alone.

Turning her back to the plaza, she ventured into the *Galeria*. Amongst the ground-floor displays she found a rack of raincoats. Black, padded, utilitarian. A saleswoman came over, asked her in English if she'd like help. Kathy said that her two requirements were waterproof and warm. Before she knew it, she was trying one on. It fitted, as snug as a wetsuit. The price was outrageous, made worse by the exchange rate. But the coat was a necessity, so that was that. She handed over a good proportion of the Euros that she'd exchanged before leaving home. With insufficient folding money to last the week, she would have to navigate a foreign banking system. A daunting prospect and another item for the kick-me list.

In her new puffy raincoat, she steered the wheelie bag to the market stalls, squinted at the menus and ogled the offerings in the bain-maries. *Knödel, Currywurst, Bratkartoffel, Flammkuchen.*

Up close, the odours of sizzling cooking-oil, vinegar, and mustard were overwhelming. Her stomach did a backflip and her appetite vanished. Like a lost soul, she drifted from stall to stall, seeking comfort food. A simple Vegemite sandwich would have done her nicely, but alas this was Germany. Exhaustion and emptiness pushed her to tears. So very tired, so bewildered, so far from home.

Crammed into egg-carton seats, she'd counted every hour of the thirty-two-hour journey. Sleep, if it came at all, was interrupted by cabin service, turbulence, grizzling babies, the snores of her neighbour—a stranger—whose corpulence oozed beneath the armrest and pooled against her thigh. Throughout the long dark hours over the Middle East, she'd come to hate him. How dare he enjoy blissful slumber while she sat bolt upright and anxious, jammed against the aircraft wall.

What was she thinking? Why had she come here at all? She should have been at home marking assignments, or preparing dinner, or watching the seven o'clock news with Jack. She'd scoffed at her husband's flippant offer to carry her luggage or hold her hand.

'No,' she'd insisted. 'I need to do this alone.'

Eventually a food vendor with passable English sold her a bread roll with warm roast pork and sauerkraut. On a long low step outside Burger King, she took refuge from the squall. Peeling off the wrapper, she chomped into the first edible meal in two days. The bread was crispy; the pork was moist and tender. The salty sourness of the cabbage and the tangy sauce rounded out the symphony of flavour.

Beside her was a group of rosy-cheeked students. Snippets of their conversation whipped past her. Words, but not meanings, caught in her ears. At high school, Kathy had battled *Hochdeutsch* and lost. All those irregular verbs, all those cases, all those noun genders and word endings. On the flight, she'd flipped through a pocket-size phrase book, hoping to brush up. A waste of time, she concluded, and tossed the little book into the seat pocket, where she promptly forgot about it. Now the only link to the language, which had lain dormant in her brain for four decades, was lost. Another one for the list.

In her shoulder bag was the printed-out email from her host. For the umpteenth time she fished it out and reread the instructions.

> *Take the U8 to Franz-Neumann-Platz. Walk 300 metres north. Turn left into Holländerstrasse. At the security gate, enter the code shown below and collect your key.*

A sudden gust almost tore the page from her hands. Her cosy refuge was no longer cosy. Although it was far too early, she decided to push on to Reinickendorf. With this in mind, she towed her wheelie bag into the fog, retraced her footsteps to the U-Bahnhof.

The drift of passengers and the acrid stench of burnt iron-filings led her down to a platform marked U8, deep beneath the city. On one side, trains terminated at Hermannstrasse; on the other at Wittenau. With no knowledge of the transport system, she examined a spidery diagram on the wall. The U8 line was blue and her station was near the top. Minutes later, she boarded an almost-empty train to Wittenau and began to count the stops. At the eighth she got out. A clunking escalator brought her to the surface in the midst of a shopping precinct. The sun glimmered weakly but, after the gloom of the subterranean tunnel system, the brightness was dazzling.

In a coffee shop in a park by a lake, she ordered *Milchkaffee* and a square of *Bienenstich*. After settling in a quiet corner, she consulted the email again. The apartment would be ready at three. One hour to go, give or take. Without a hitch, she'd made it halfway around the world. Solo and for the first time. That itself was worth a pat on the back. Perhaps she should start afresh, with a list of achievements rather than mishaps. She devoured the honey-and-almond slice, sipped the milky coffee, and felt brighter. On the lake, swans glided across the water; red and yellow autumn leaves pirouetted onto the path; a bushy-tailed squirrel bounded gracefully through the grass. Sooner than expected, the hour had passed.

The apartment block at Holländerstrasse stood inside a high metal wall topped with spikes. Following the instructions, she located the key-safe and punched in the code. An envelope with her name held the keys. The entire operation took less than a minute. Cool and efficient. No human contact. No welcomes, no arguments, no emotion. In this modern age of technology, she felt like a Neanderthal.

As she fitted the key into the security gate, she wondered what she'd let herself in for. From the outside the place looked like a prison or a fortress. With a mechanical sigh, the gate swung open and she entered a courtyard of clipped shrubs and neat lawn. The wheels of her suitcase rolled smoothly along the path, a welcome relief after all that juddering over cobblestones.

Her apartment—number 10—was clean and minimalist, and white from top to bottom. White walls, white ceiling, white curtains, white sheets on the double bed. That bed was the only thing she could think about. Within minutes she'd kicked off her shoes, wriggled out of her jeans and given herself up to sleep.

Much later, she woke to the blink of a neon light through the window. The room was in darkness. Her body was half-frozen; her stomach was growling. She reached for her phone; the time was 03:26. Wide awake now, she drew the curtains, snapped on the lamp and dressed. In socks, she padded from the bedroom to the bathroom to the living room. The furniture was simple but practical: one couch, one table, two chairs. No TV. The kitchenette had a mini-fridge, cooktop, electric jug and toaster.

She should have bought supplies. Yesterday she'd passed several food stores and two supermarkets. In her muddled mental state, it had not occurred to her to buy a loaf of bread or some fruit to see her through the night. Doubtfully she opened the cupboard, expecting to see nothing but a few cups and plates. Instead, there were teabags, sachets of coffee and sugar … and a cellophane packet of plain biscuits. Ripping it open, she stuffed her mouth with sweetness.

Sipping black tea, she gazed out the living-room window. The metal wall cast jagged shadows across the courtyard. Beyond the compound, streetlamps blazed over a boulevard which, in the wee hours of a Tuesday morning, was as silent as a graveyard. Low in the sky, a dull glow marked the whereabouts of the city centre. Dawn, it seemed, was yet a long while off.

She amused herself with a ten-year-old Berlin guide book, the only reading material in the apartment. She also speculated on the promise she'd made and the enigmatic man that she'd vowed to track down. Horst Schuhmacher. The surname literally meant 'shoemaker'. That he made footwear for a living was an astonishing coincidence. The clues she'd been given were vague to say the least. Apart from the dodgy-sounding name, all that she had were an equally dubious address—hand-written on a tattered scrap of paper—and a black-and-white photograph taken maybe fifty years ago.

She'd allocated herself one week in Berlin, exactly one quarter of her month-long vacation. Her reward was to be a slow river cruise to Hamburg, followed by ten glorious days exploring the museums and galleries of London. Then, with her obligations fulfilled, she'd return to her comfortable middle-class life with a clear conscience.

How to find this man was the burning question. Before leaving, she'd asked Stephanie to help her with preliminary research. Like most Millennials, her daughter was a whiz on computers and taught her a trick or two. But the findings were inconclusive. On Google Maps, many of Berlin's street-names were not marked. Street View was useless, for entire city blocks were omitted or the images were purposely blurred. It seemed that privacy in Germany was more precious than in Australia, where buildings were shown in broad brassy daylight, and only faces and number plates were blanked out. Neither Horst Schuhmacher nor his curiously-named street showed up in any of the search engines.

At around five o'clock a wave of fatigue rolled over her and, there on the couch, she sank into a deep and dreamless sleep.

Sunshine streamed into the apartment. On waking, her first thought was breakfast. Then she would begin the search for Herr Schuhmacher.

It was clear that he and Alice had once been friends. But, to the best of Kathy's knowledge, her sister had never travelled abroad nor did she speak a word of German. The nature of their relationship remained a mystery. The only evidence that he'd ever existed was the photograph that Alice had given her earlier in the year. More precisely, it was half a photo. The image had been recklessly snipped in two with a pair of blunt scissors. Kathy's half showed a handsome blond man relaxing at the beach. Although she'd searched Alice's room for the other half, it had never turned up. Neither had any letters, postcards, notebooks, or diaries that might shed some light.

Already she was convinced that this week in Berlin would be nothing but a wild goose chase. But she had made a promise, and promises were meant to be kept.

Showered and dressed in fresh clothes, Kathy retraced her route of the previous afternoon. Along Residenzstrasse she passed pharmacies, delicatessens, bakeries, shops that sold Turkish hookahs and shisha, bars that were not yet open. Munching on a salt-bejewelled *Brezel*, she flicked idly through a rack of *dirndl* skirts and *Lederhosen* on sale for *Oktoberfest*.

In the next window was an array of porcelain ginger jars. Smart and sleek and nicely shaped, she pictured a blue one on her sideboard at home. A souvenir of her trip, or proof that she'd been brave enough (or foolish enough) to take on this mission. Scanning the blurb for the price, she stumbled on the word *Einäscherung* and an alarm bell went off inside her head. Looking beyond the jars, she noted the other items in the shop. Brass plaques, sample pieces of marble, polished timber caskets.

Those were definitely not ginger jars. Imagine if she'd gone in; imagine if she'd actually bought one. She began to giggle at the faux pas she'd narrowly avoided. As she mopped tears of mirth and embarrassment, the memories flooded in.

Italian funerals were stupendous affairs. Hundreds of relatives, friends, acquaintances would flock from all over the country. A Requiem Mass would be held at the church, followed by a ceremony at the graveside; then there'd be a feast to which everyone was invited. Already, both her parents had had a traditional Italian send-off. But Alice—being Alice—was determined to be different. Alice wanted to be cremated and to have her ashes released into the ocean. No formalities, no mourners, no fuss. Kathy— ever the dutiful sister—had vowed to follow her wishes to the letter.

Near the cross-roads was a garden shop, bright with potted greenery and colourful flowers. Outside was a small sign. *English spoken here*. Aimlessly wandering the streets was getting her nowhere. If she wanted to find Herr Schuhmacher, then she must trot out her rusty German and ask some of the locals.

She pushed the door open. A bell tinkled; an earthy perfume tickled her nostrils. A woman of Kathy's vintage—beyond fifty—was fitting a spray of baby's breath into an impressive sheath of white roses, white carnations, and white lilies.

Kathy took a steadying breath then launched into unchartered territory. '*Guten Morgen*. Do you speak English?'

'*Hallo*. Yes, a little. Can I help?'

'Actually, I am lost.' Kathy took the scrap with the address from her purse, showed it to the florist. 'Do you know this street? I've looked everywhere and can't find it.'

The woman studied the old-fashioned handwriting, which might have been Horst's, and shook her head.

'I'm not sure it actually exists,' Kathy mumbled beneath her breath as she tucked the paper back into her purse. She cursed herself for believing Alice's made-up stories and committing herself to this ridiculous task.

'*Wie bitte?*' said the florist.

'Never mind.' To avoid further awkwardness, Kathy grabbed a bouquet from a bucket by the counter. 'I'll take these, thanks.'

She hadn't intended to buy, but the blossoms would brighten up her tombstone-white apartment. Symbols of death were popping up everywhere. An omen, perhaps? She had no delusions about how this would end. She thought about the half-photo of Horst. The style of clothing was 1950s. He looked young yet his serious facial expression suggested maturity. Aged in his thirties at the time, perhaps? That would make him beyond eighty now. A smarter idea would be to return to the funeral parlour and inquire there.

The florist wrapped the bouquet, flowerheads and all, in brown paper and fastened it with sticky tape. The package looked like a lopsided balloon on a stick.

'Some streets have different names since the war,' she said.

'Really?' Kathy paid and lifted the cumbersome package. 'How do I find out?'

'*Deutsche Post*. Not far.' She indicated the direction with her hand.

Kathy nodded and thanked her.

'*Tschüss,*' said the florist in a sing-song tone before returning her attention to the white floral arrangement.

'*Tschüss,*' Kathy echoed. A new German word, modern and succinct. The farewell she had learnt at school was *aufwiedersehen*. Forty years was a long time in anyone's language. Her schoolgirl German was probably as outdated as British rhyming slang.

At the post office, Kathy stood in a long queue for a long time. With each minute that passed, her hopes of solving the puzzle of Horst Schuhmacher diminished.

When her turn came at last, the taciturn official did not admit to knowing any English at all. She showed him the address and asked in halting German for directions.

He rattled off a string of incomprehensible words.

Persevering, she asked if the street name might have changed.

His lips curled into a tight smile of schadenfreude. '*Ich kann Ihnen nicht helfen.*'

Summarily dismissed, she raised her chin in defiance and strutted toward the exit.

An elderly woman in the queue caught her by the sleeve. 'I have lived in this neighbourhood all of my life. What is the name of the street?' Her voice was soft but steady and her English was perfect.

'Hermann-Göring-Strasse,' said Kathy.

'I know where it is.' The woman gave a brief account of the history of the street, then sketched a map on the back of an envelope. It was so close that she could walk there in ten minutes.

With a nervous pulse beating in her temple, Kathy thanked her informant and left. Ten minutes was not enough time to prepare. She was carrying a brown-paper balloon, for goodness' sake. No, she must first return to the apartment and think this through. What if Alice's ramblings turned out to be true? Then she'd be faced with an elderly man and a message that would be hard to deliver.

She made a detour to Netto, where she purchased a few provisions. Bread, fruit, orange juice, snacks. In her room, she drank the juice, filled the bottle with water and arranged the flowers. Against the white, they made a delightful splash of colour but they also signified something deeper: a glimmer of hope that the burden of obligation might soon be lifted.

In the bathroom, she examined her reflection. Dark shadows encircled dark eyes; an impressive collection of wrinkles ran down her neck; her tongue was blanketed in cream-coloured fur. She splashed her face with water, brushed her teeth, applied red lipstick, fastened her wayward hair into a messy bun. Before leaving, she downed a cup of strong black tea and practised how she might break the news to her sister's friend.

According to the woman at the post office, Hermann-Göring-Strasse was one of many street names that had ceased to exist after the war. At the Nuremberg Trials its namesake had been found guilty of war crimes and had conveniently chosen to pop a cyanide capsule rather than face the executioner. To compensate residents for having their street named after a Nazi monster, the Council rechristened it Frühlingstrasse after Spring, the season.

The street was short and bordered by plane trees. At the end was overgrown park. The only dwelling was a two-storey cottage with a peaked roof, lead-light windows, and an attic under the eaves. A red-brick section at the front added variation to an otherwise plain façade. Window-boxes of geraniums and an evergreen hedge completed the picture of a quintessential German residence of the early twentieth century.

As Kathy approached the gate, her courage failed. What would she do if he wasn't there and the residents had no knowledge of him?

Procrastination steered her into an avenue appropriately called Herbststrasse. Autumn Street. Golden leaves and spiky shells lay in drifts across the cobblestones. A grey squirrel bounded across the path and raced up a tree trunk. Enchanted, she decided to walk its length.

The buildings on either side were old and decrepit. One, possibly a factory, was boarded up. Strands of ivy crept over the walls; velvety moss framed the brickwork; the gates were secured with padlocks and chains. Above the entrance was a weathered sign. Just one word was legible: *Schuhwerk*. The logo was a little bird perched on a boot. Could it be?

She forced herself on, past apartment blocks with box balconies and vases in the windows. The impromptu sightseeing tour calmed her and settled her nerves.

So what if nobody knew of Horst Schuhmacher? It wasn't the end of the world. She had done her very best and was confident that Alice would rest easy, whatever the outcome.

The brass knocker of Frühlingstrasse Number 2 made a dreadful clatter, loud enough to wake the dead. She waited, heard soft-soled shoes padding toward the entrance. The door cracked open, revealing a tiny desiccated woman dressed in a black cardigan, checked woollen skirt, socks and slippers.

'*Ja?*' She glared at Kathy as if challenging her to a duel. Despite her advanced age, her eyes were sharp and glacial blue.

In hesitant German, Kathy delivered her opening lines. 'I'm looking for an old family friend called Horst Schuhmacher. Does he live here?'

'I know no-one by that name.' She looked Kathy up and down, took in the messiness of her hair, the cheapness of her clothes, the inappropriateness of her light-weight summer joggers. For several moments there was silence. Kathy vacillated, wondering whether to stay in the hope of gleaning information, or turn around and go.

The woman seemed to have reached a decision. Her face softened as she spoke. 'The owners before me made shoes. *Vogel.*' The name was dropped with a certain emphasis, as if living in their former residence was a claim to fame.

Blankly Kathy stared at her, aware that she knew very little about German fashion or history or culture. The only brand names that sprang to mind were a couple of appliance manufacturers and a hairdressing product.

'You *must* know Vogel,' the woman insisted. 'It was famous all over Germany. The factory was just around the corner.' She narrowed her eyes. 'What do you want with this Horst Schuhmacher anyway?'

'It's a personal matter.'

The ancient woman sniffed. 'Well, he does not live here. Never has. Perhaps you will find him at the Swan Café. That's where all the old men go.'

Kathy obtained directions, thanked the woman and left.

Like a cat stalking a bird, the closer Kathy came to the target, the more her body tensed. Adrenaline carried her three blocks to a circular lake where a rustic café nestled by the shore. A feeling of déjà vu came over her but she put it down to jet lag. The customers were indeed all male and none looked a day less than eighty. The place was packed. The men sat in groups talking, reading newspapers, or playing chequers. A country club for octogenarians.

One glance at the display cabinet and Kathy knew why they were there. It was happy hour: everything was half-price. There were pastries with luscious berries, layer cakes oozing with chocolate ganache, slices shimmering with honeyed almonds. As she stood in line for service, she felt dozens of rheumy eyes boring into her back. Her clothing and manner screamed 'tourist'. Here in Reinickendorf, tourists were a novelty. Tourists stayed at Mitte near the museums and galleries, not in this working-class suburb. To them she was an outsider, a curiosity, out of place.

When she placed her order, she also asked about Horst Schuhmacher. The server answered with a shrug. Taking the tray of coffee and cake, she cast about for a place to sit. All the tables were taken. In a corner she saw a spare chair, opposite a fellow with a Santa-Claus beard. His newspaper was open and spread out like a table cloth. He was puzzling over the crossword.

She made a soft cough and he glanced up. His eyes were as blue as the deep ocean.

'*Darf ich hier sitzen, bitte*?' She indicated the vacant chair.

He nodded and folded the newspaper.

Kathy slid the tray onto the table, unloaded the contents, and sat down. The plum cake glistened with a ruby glaze. She cut a morsel and placed it on her tongue. The balance of sweet and sour was perfect. Her eyes closed and she made an involuntary sigh.

'Best café in Berlin,' said her tablemate in accented English. 'I come here often.'

'First time for me. First time in Berlin too.'

'Pardon my curiosity, but I overheard you before. You asked about Horst Schuhmacher.'

'Do you know him?' She put down the fork.

'Horst the bootmaker.' He chuckled. 'I've known him most of my life.'

'Please, tell me about him. He's a family friend. Would you like another coffee? My treat.'

'Thank you, but no. Too much coffee and I'll be up all night.' He leant in as if to share a secret. 'I went to Australia once, a long time ago. Nice country. Almost as nice as Germany.'

'How do you know I'm from Australia?'

'Why, your accent of course.'

She felt her cheeks redden. It had never occurred to her that she spoke English with an accent. Accents were for foreigners. But here in Germany, *she* was the foreigner.

'When were you in Australia?' she said. His face looked vaguely familiar, but she couldn't put a finger on it. Maybe he had a doppelganger on the other side of the world.

'*Ach*, well before your time. It's all ancient history now. Would you like Herr Schuhmacher's address? Yes, of course you would. I'd take you there myself … only my knees.' He made a grimace as he shifted in the chair. 'Arthritis, they say. Should have the joints replaced. It's no fun getting old, let me tell you.'

Kathy produced pen and paper from her handbag.

He took his time writing, then passed it back. 'Now, I must be getting on. Give Horst my regards. It was nice talking to you. *Aufwiedersehen.*' Unsteadily he rose from the chair and limped towards the door.

The old-fashioned farewell sat comfortably. '*Danke schön und aufwiedersehen,*' she called after him, wondering if her Australian-ness was equally evident when she spoke German.

Horst's abode was in a street flanked by amber-leafed oaks. The apartment block was a concrete cube four storeys high with sand-coloured render and white trim. At the security door, Kathy pressed the buzzer of the number that the old man at the café had written.

A husky voice crackled through the intercom. '*Ja? Hallo?*'

She answered in English, for she was sure he'd be fluent. 'I'm looking for Horst Schuhmacher.'

No response. Perhaps she was mistaken. '*Ich suche Horst Schuhmacher,*' she repeated.

An asthmatic wheeze confirmed he was still there. 'Who is this?' he said at length. His tone was wary, as if suspecting she was a Stasi informant.

'Alice Zanetti.'

A gasp. 'Alice? Oh Alice, is it really you?' His voice cracked with emotion.

The raw response surprised her; she chastised herself for deliberately misleading him. 'My apologies, Herr Schuhmacher, I am not Alice. I'm her younger sister, Kathy.'

'Alice doesn't have a sister.'

'Actually, I'm her half-sister. Our mother had me late in life.'

A pause. 'Please, come in. First apartment on the left.' The security door clicked open.

The man who greeted her was as white as her apartment. White hair, white whiskers, white skin. His eyes were a startling blue. Wearing trackpants and a moth-eaten pullover, he was obviously having a quiet day at home. He must have been well over eighty, yet a wiry build made him look younger.

He greeted her formally with a nod and handshake. His hand was warm and firm. After ushering her into the living room, he busied himself picking up newspapers from the couch. 'This room is a terrible mess, Frau Zanetti. I wasn't expecting a visitor.'

'And I didn't make an appointment. By the way, it's Giuliano but please call me Kathy.'

At the sound of her surname, he lifted an eyebrow ever so slightly before recovering his composure. 'And you must call me Horst.'

The room was not at all untidy. Overdecorated, perhaps, but the clutter was arranged tastefully on and around various pieces of vintage furniture. The armchairs were brown leather; the lampshades were burgundy; a rich Persian rug graced the parquetry floor. The vast bookshelf along the wall was filled with titles in English and German. Many were classics by authors that she knew and loved: Dickens, Thomas Hardy, Joseph Conrad, Goethe, Thomas Mann. Afternoon sunlight angled in through a tall tilt-and-turn window. Spacious and comfortable, the place exuded a sedate charm.

'Let me take your jacket. Can I get you coffee? Or schnapps? Oh, I forget, you are Australian. Would you prefer a glass of beer?' He folded the newspapers and shoved them beneath the couch.

'A beer would be nice, thanks.' She shrugged out of her bomber-jacket and he stowed it on a hook by the door.

'Now, make yourself at home.' He disappeared through a doorway.

She wandered to the window and looked out. The central courtyard was a forest of russet trees and yellow shrubs. Beyond the boundary fence was a playground shadowed by a brick structure with a gable roof and clocktower. The time was twenty past three. Children in puffy jackets and red backpacks raced across the asphalt to the gates. Their squeals and laughter reminded her of long ago, when she was a young mother and Stephanie was at primary school. Whatever the language, all kids sounded the same.

He returned, wielding a tray with two brimming glasses and a plate with cheese and crackers. After easing the tray onto a low table, he handed Kathy a glass and claimed the other for himself. They clinked and said *Prost!* before drinking. He sank into an armchair and Kathy sat on the couch opposite. For several minutes neither spoke, each lost in their own thoughts.

Horst was the first to break the spell. 'How is Alice?' he said leaning forward. 'She hasn't written in years.'

Kathy sighed. This was the moment she had been dreading, but it was also the main reason for her visit. She'd promised to tell him in person. A promise made in haste, always the hardest to fulfil. Clearly, he was fond of her sister and the news would come as a shock. Stalling, she lowered her eyes and ran a finger around the rim of the glass.

'Oh, I see. That is why you have come.' He took a swallow of beer. 'I sometimes forget that I am so very old.' His eyes misted with tears.

'She left us in April,' she said gently.

'You must miss her.' He patted her hand like a father. 'Your dear sister and I were very close … when I was in Australia ... during the war ...' His voice cracked and he looked away.

'The war ended long before I was born. Our relationship was complicated; there's a big age difference between us. Our mother was widowed young and remarried.'

'Ah yes, I remember your mother.'

Kathy's eyebrows shot up. 'You knew Mum?'

'I met her once or twice. Always beautifully dressed. A school teacher, I recall.'

'She loved nice clothes, but she wasn't a teacher. Not to my knowledge, any rate.'

'Did Alice say much about me?' His blue eyes drilled into her brown ones.

Kathy shook her head. 'She kept her private life to herself. Near the end she developed dementia. Her daydreams were so vivid that she thought they were real. Her stories became bizarre and confused and I didn't know what to believe.'

Horst seemed crestfallen. 'Did she ever talk about the camp?'

'What camp?'

He drained his beer and placed the glass solidly on the tray. 'Well then, I must start at the beginning. Perhaps I should give you some background first. Stop me if I am … how do you say it … preaching to the converted.'

He settled himself in the chair, his fingertips together like a church steeple while Kathy sat back and prepared herself for a long and convoluted story.

'My country has a difficult history,' he began. 'Our troubles go back centuries. But in more recent times, the Treaty signed at Versailles after the First World War cut us off at the knees. In 1923, the year I was born, our economy fell apart. Mutti told me that she always bought the bread in the morning because, by afternoon, the price would treble. Max, my father, was forced to pay his workers in cash twice a day. Banks could not keep up with demand and the Treasury money-printers worked right through the night. Unless you had gold to sell on the black market or goods to exchange for what you needed, your family went without. I don't know exactly how Max did it, but somehow our footwear business survived.'

'I didn't realise it was so bad,' murmured Kathy. Normally she'd be making excuses to escape, but today she had all the time and patience in the world. Something about this man intrigued her. His knowledge, his life experience, his gentle manner. She might learn much from him if she held her tongue and listened.

'Don't get me wrong,' he said. 'Despite all the setbacks, we lived a comfortable life here in Reinickendorf. When necessity called, people rose to the occasion. During the hard years, the government made land available for people to grow food. Entire forests were felled for firewood. Others went hungry but we never did. I always had warm clothes for winter, I attended school—the one right behind us, in fact—and in the afternoons I played football in the park with the other boys. Childhood is golden and mine was no exception.

'When I was thirteen, the Olympic Games came to Berlin. For me, this was terrifically exciting. Parades through the streets, bunting and the red flags of Nazi Germany flew everywhere. A real carnival atmosphere. Fifty-two nations competed. Television screens were set up all around the city so we could watch the events live. This was a world first, created especially for the Berlin Games. Can you imagine how, in 1936, television sparked a youngster's imagination? A new era had dawned, we thought. *Der Führer*, ever eloquent and passionate, turned our country around. In no time we went from famine to fanfare, and he promised greater things to come.

'The city sprang to life; no expense was spared. One day Herr Koch, a business associate of my father, invited us to the *Olympia-stadion*. The grandstands were packed to capacity. We were guests in a section for senior government officials, for Herr Koch was quite high up in the Party. I will never forget that day. Herr Hitler sat in the section opposite us; the great Olympic cauldron and the flame were to our right; the *Hindenburg* zeppelin glided overhead like a glistening metal balloon. Whenever German athletes entered the arena, spectators in their thousands would stand and chant *Sieg Heil* and make the one-arm salute. It was completely and utterly breathtaking.

'Soon after, Max signed me up for the Hitler Youth, partly to impress Herr Koch, who had shown interest in doing business with our footwear factory. Perhaps Max could foresee what lay ahead. He was keen to pursue government work rather than rely on what he called *fickle fashion*.' Horst paused for breath.

Although Kathy found the story fascinating, sitting on that couch was oh-so-comfortable. Her stomach was happily digesting cheese and crackers, and the beer had made her mellow. The clock in the schoolground chimed four. Her internal timeclock, firmly anchored in Australia, chimed one in the morning. She tried to stifle a yawn but he caught her out.

'I must be boring you. An old man remembering his youth always becomes a long and winding story.'

'No, not at all. I'd love you to continue. Really. Please forgive me. I travelled here non-stop from Brisbane. Between jet lag and almost no sleep, I'm totally spent.'

'Then you must sleep. We will continue tomorrow morning. Come at nine.'

'Perfect,' she said. 'And thank you.'

She gathered her handbag and jacket. At the door they shook hands. Thankfully her accommodation was not far. She went straight to bed and slept soundly until 3:30 the next morning.

Two

Reinickendorf: October 2010

At nine o'clock sharp, Kathy pressed the buzzer of Horst's apartment. Punctuality was a virtue. For Alice, being on time was optional, another point of contention between the sisters.

He opened the door with a smile which instantly turned to a frown. Unprepared for the changeable autumn weather, Kathy had been caught in a sudden shower and was shivering and dripping wet. He bustled her inside, helped her out of her sodden blue bomber-jacket, brought her a towel and one of his pullovers to wear. When she was dry and snug, she gave him a box of pastries that she'd bought at the Swan Café on the way. He made two cups of milk coffee and they settled in the living room to continue the conversation.

She began by asking how he came to be in Australia. What she really wanted to know was what happened to Alice during the war, but she didn't ask any more questions for fear that he'd shut down.

'Do you want the short answer or the long one?' he said.

'I've got all day. In fact, I've got all week.'

'The long one it is then. Also, I would like to show you Berlin. Maybe in a day or two, when the weather improves. By the time you leave, you'll know more about my city than your dear sister ever did.'

She gave a tight smile. 'That wouldn't be too hard.'

'You sound just like her,' he said. 'Direct and brutally honest.' He took a swallow of coffee. 'And so, to Australia. But first, permit me to provide a little context.'

'The stage is all yours. I won't interrupt.' She sat back in the cushions and folded her hands in her lap.

~

When I was fifteen, Mutti and I went to live with Aunt Berry in England. In the autumn of 1938, a brooding atmosphere hung over Berlin. Most nights, the Wehrmacht paraded through the streets of Mitte. Uniformed troops with flaming torches. The city folk turned out in their thousands to line the footpaths and chant *Sieg Heil*. Their faces lit up with pride and wonder. The national flag—scarlet with the black Swastika—hung from every building and flagstaff in the country. We sang patriotic songs that praised *Der Führer* and the Third Reich; we signed off our correspondence with *Heil Hitler*.

But there was also a dark side. In the Jewish quarter, shops and businesses were vandalised and burnt down. Some of my school friends vanished, never to be seen again. I felt sure that Max knew more than he let on; he never talked straight with me. He probably thought I was too young to understand, or that I might blab to someone at school. Herr Koch might have alerted him to the coming war. In any case, Max concluded it was no longer safe for Mutti and me to live in Berlin.

One night he told us to pack the bare essentials and be ready to leave at daybreak. I opened my mouth to argue. I didn't want to leave my home, my city, my friends. His eyes had a wild look about them, as if he was very angry or afraid. He grabbed me by the collar and threw me into my room. 'I said, get packing!' Then I felt scared. He was a strong man with a quick temper but I'd never seen him so agitated. His hands were shaking so hard that he had to swallow two nerve pills then and there. In those days, he carried the Pervitin tube in his pocket … just in case.

Into my school satchel I stuffed winter clothes and boots made by Opa for my birthday. Already they were a little tight, but they were the only ones I wanted. I loved them as much as I loved the man who'd made them. As well as clothes, Mutti took her writing things: a silver pen, spare nibs, and a bottle of ink.

In the morning, she clipped her 'lucky dragon' brooch to her coat lapel and the three of us assembled in the entry hall. No-one spoke. The pendulum clock ticked off the minutes. At six o'clock sharp, a taxi came and took us to the station. Max did not accompany us, saying he did not wish to draw attention to our hasty departure.

Aunt Berry was not a blood relative but an older friend of my mother. She lived in a terrace house in London and we stayed there with her for a year. She also owned a farmhouse in Kent, where we went in the winter of 1939, not long after war was declared. For me it was a relief to leave the dreary greyness of London. In comparison, Kent was paradise. Straight away Mutti placed her writing things on the table overlooking the rose garden. I wondered who she wrote to. Max, probably. She didn't have many women friends. Perhaps she kept a diary. I never found out.

Aunty was a kind woman with sparkling green eyes, silver hair, and cheeks the colour of roses. Throughout the frosty English winter, she cooked cauldrons of bean soup and warmed us with bread-and-butter puddings and baked custard.

In Kent, I attended the local secondary school. I'd studied English in Berlin and was reasonably proficient, or so I thought. School in England was different from what I was used to. My imperfect understanding and the strong Kentish accent of the teachers and students didn't help. But the thing that made my life a real misery was my nationality. At school they called me a *Nazi* and a *filthy Kraut* and the younger boys would throw rocks at me on the way home. I had no friends, no company my own age. Despite this, I was determined to pass the Higher School Certificate, so I buried myself in schoolwork. On weekends I studied instead of playing football. As I sat by the living-room fire, poring over the text books, Aunty would bring me cups of hot cocoa which always made me feel good.

In the spring of 1940, the Wehrmacht hurtled towards Britain, conquering the low countries with little opposition. Mornings and evenings like clockwork, we tuned in to the BBC wireless broadcasts. Nazi Germany was spreading its tentacles at an astounding pace. They marched incessantly, even through the night, covering more ground than anyone thought possible. To the west, to the east, to the south. Unstoppable. One night, Prime Minister Churchill announced on the BBC that all male 'enemy aliens' would be detained immediately. Aunty bit her lip and glanced directly at me. I was sitting at the table, pretending to study.

'Surely they don't mean schoolboys,' she whispered to Mutti, loudly enough for me to hear. I had not long turned seventeen. My skin prickled at the thought of being sent to a prison camp. I had seen what a prison for political dissidents looked like. Once, with my father, when we visited Herr Koch, whose latest promotion made him the Commandant of Sachsenhausen. It was a horrible place. Prisoners were whipped for transgressions as minor as stumbling over uneven ground. No, I did not wish to be sent to a place like that.

Mutti shook her head, vowed they would take me over her dead body. A prescient sentiment, as it turned out. Her reassurances gave me little comfort, for I had witnessed the cruelty that men in uniform could mete out in the name of duty.

The day I lost my youth was 20 May 1940. I arrived home from school to find two burly policemen sipping tea in our parlour. Mutti and Aunty showed brave faces but this was no social visit. My blood turned to ice. As I stepped into the room, the larger man rose and demanded that I tell him my name and date of birth. Of course he would have already known these things, but he was twice my size. I responded without hesitation.

His response was like a punch in the belly. 'All male German nationals, aged seventeen and older, are to be detained by order of the Prime Minister, Mr Winston Churchill. You are hereby under arrest.' Images of Sachsenhausen flashed through my head. I was doomed.

Mutti packed a small bag of clothes and hugged me as if I were a favourite teddy-bear. When Aunt Berry gently pulled her away, my shirt was wet from her tears. Handcuffs were snapped on and I was shoved into the police van. In a blur of fury and fear, I peered out the tiny window. Mutti and Aunt Berry stood trembling at the gate.

Along with a dozen other German captives, I was put on a freight train and taken under guard to Manchester. An army truck picked us up and carried us to an assembly of bleak buildings perched on the banks of a mighty river. Warth Mills. As the name might suggest, it had once been a cotton mill. During the Industrial Revolution the factory would have been modern and impressive. Red brick, arched windows, soaring roofs, majestic smokestacks. But in 1940, it lay derelict and forlorn. Inside, the ancient milling machines stood dark and brooding and swathed in rust. Cotton fibres drifted about like cobwebs. The concrete floor was cracked and oozing with muck. The walls were slimy. The stench of decay made me gag.

We were welcomed with a strip search. Rough fingers explored every fold and cavity of my body. Never had I felt so humiliated. My hands formed fists which I would have gladly used if not for the warnings of my comrades. Luckily, I held my temper.

Satisfied that we had no contraband, the guards issued each of us with two thin blankets and a hessian bag, which we were told to stuff with straw. The old mill building was already crowded and the best sleeping spots had been claimed. The existing inmates were a motley mix of Germans, Austrians, and Jews. Some wore the uniforms of the Wehrmacht; some had side locks, skull caps, and long black coats; others were ordinary civilians like me. At just seventeen, I would have been the youngest.

The main pavilion was vast but built for machines, not men. For all those prisoners there were just two ablutions blocks, one at either end. Twenty toilet pans and twenty washbasins were shared by two thousand. To make up the shortfall, latrine buckets were lined up along a wall. With no proper washing facilities, we grew dirtier and smellier by the day. Our bodies became breeding grounds for lice.

On the first night it rained. Water dripped through the rusted-out roof and streamed across the floor. Our mattresses were soaked. In the morning, guards beat us for damaging army equipment. Breakfast was a pannikin of watery porridge. My anger turned to despair. Were we to remain in this cesspit until the end of the war?

One week passed. After morning rollcall, I was given a telegram. The envelope had been torn open, which meant it had been read by our captors. Retreating to a quiet corner, I unfolded the slip of yellow paper. It was from Aunty. Her address was blacked out but the message was brutally clear.

> *Your dear mother passed away Tuesday. Funeral: Saint Margaret's 4 June, 10am. Deepest sympathy, Berry.*

At first, I thought it was a cruel joke. Who would do such a thing? My tormentors from school didn't know where I was. Surely the policemen who'd arrested me wouldn't be up for that caper. I read the message again and again before its meaning registered. How could it be? Mutti was too young and healthy to die. Numbly I stared at the yellow paper. The room began to spin and the light went dim. I slid down the wall to the floor.

When I came to, an elderly man whom I'd seen the day before was kneeling beside me. He looked a bit like Opa, my father's father and the most wonderful man on earth. 'Are you all right?' he said in German. The accent was Austrian.

I lowered my eyes.

He glanced at the paper in my hand. 'Bad news?'

Tears rolled down my cheeks.

'Do you want to talk about it?'

'Maybe later.'

'Of course. I'm not going anywhere.' The old man patted my shoulder and hauled himself up.

I folded my arms and buried my face so that no-one could witness my grief.

At midday, hunger propelled me into a long queue for a slice of stale bread and a pannikin of black tea. I took my rations to a space between two massive machines. One clique had already claimed it as a dining place. Packing cases were arranged like seats around a central pallet, which was the table. The old Austrian fellow was there and he waved me over.

'Sit next to me, my dear boy. My name is Werner. Are you feeling better now?'

I apologised for my earlier rudeness and tried to explain. The words would not come, so I gave him the telegram to read.

'My deepest sympathy.' He said it as if he meant it.

'How can I go to her funeral when I'm stuck in here?'

'Where is Saint Margaret's?'

'In Kent. Near my aunt's house.'

Werner stroked his chin. 'We are near Manchester, a few hours away. I'll take you to see the Commandant. Under the circumstances, he might grant you leave on compassionate grounds.'

'Could you really do that?' My spirits began to rise.

'No guarantees, but it's worth a try.'

After lunch, Werner arranged an appointment with the Commandant for the following morning. The timing would be tight, for I would have to catch the Sunday night train. I had no idea of the process for getting compassionate leave, but I sensed it would be tricky.

At the appointed time, Werner and I stood together outside the Commandant's office. It was like being back at elementary school, waiting for the headmaster to cane us for some offence. My crimes then were trivial: dipping a girl's plaits in the inkwell; forging Mutti's signature on a sick note. Here I was again, wondering if permission would be granted or whether I'd be punished for asking. I could not help wondering how Werner had such easy access to the British army officer who was in charge of our camp.

As if reading my mind, Werner explained that he was the elected camp leader of the German and Austrian internees. 'The position comes with certain privileges. I can raise any matter of concern directly with our captors. Sometimes I win; sometimes I lose.'

'Why did you choose to help me?'

'You remind me of myself at seventeen. That was the age I lost my mother. My father was already in his grave; I had to deal with it alone.'

The office door opened and the Commandant greeted us with handshakes. 'Now, Doctor Werner, what can I do for you today?'

Werner did all the talking. My role was to remain silent and produce the telegram on cue.

After the interview, which went rather well, I asked Werner if he was a real doctor.

He laughed. 'Last time I checked the medical register I was.'

'You should have said. I meant no disrespect by calling you Werner, not Doctor Werner.'

'Please, everyone calls me Werner. In Austria I was a medical researcher, specialising in the effects of radiation on the human body. Let's just say that no-one would wish to be undertaking research of that nature under the Nazi regime. I know what is going on, and I want no part. That is why I am here and not in Vienna.'

The hours dragged by. No word about my leave. On Sunday morning, I attended the church service, delivered by an Anglican pastor in the 'dining room'. Werner must have had a word in the pastor's ear. At the end of the sermon, he dedicated a prayer 'in memory of the beloved mother of Horst'.

Morning became afternoon and still no news. My spirits crashed through the floor. I had heard that the last train to London would depart at six o'clock. My chances of catching it were slimmer than flying to the moon. It had been a stupid idea to ask for leave in the first place. If our dreadful treatment by the British guards was any indication, denying me the opportunity to attend my mother's funeral was to be expected. I cursed them a thousand curses, then I cursed myself for having been taken prisoner without a fight. As meek as a lamb, I had allowed those policemen to lead me away while Mutti and Aunty wept at the gate. If only I had known that, shortly after, my mother would be committed to the cold hard earth, I would have behaved differently.

When the mill lights snapped on, I realised that I'd missed the evening meal. It was probably the usual: bog-water broth and fossilised bread. It should not have mattered, only my last solid food had been breakfast. My stomach was turning into knots.

The lilt of an Austrian accent echoed through the shadows. 'I've been looking for you.' Werner squatted beside me and passed me a chunk of bread and a mug of soup. His expression was as inscrutable as a gambler with a winning hand of cards.

I asked him if there was any news. He grimaced and looked away. Ravenous, I dunked the bread and shoved it into my mouth. The soup was lukewarm and tasted awful but it settled the rumbling in my guts.

'I have just come from the Commandant,' Werner began.

'And?' I cut in. My heart was thumping in anticipation but I already knew the answer.

'Your compassionate leave has been approved,' he said evenly.

I almost leapt for joy. Those dark angry thoughts about our British captors, I wanted to take them all back. Without inhibition, I threw my arms around Werner and thanked him.

Gently, he peeled me off. 'I'm afraid there's more to it, my friend. A massive military operation is underway at this very moment. Every bus, boat, and train in the country has been called into service. The Wehrmacht has taken France and the Brits are on the run; they are pulling troops out as we speak. So, while your leave has been granted, you will not be able to travel.'

I felt like a football, soaring one minute, kicked into a ditch the next. I was shattered, but I'd never held much hope anyway. Although the Commandant's decision was in my favour, Fate had intervened. Whether I attended the funeral or not, Mutti was gone forever. That was the reality and I would have to accept it.

Three

Reinickendorf: October 2010

The morning passed quickly. Horst suggested lunch at a restaurant nearby. 'Authentic German food is not easy to find these days,' he said. 'Pizzas, kebabs, burgers. A person could be anywhere in the world; it's all the same.'

The Spree Café was down a side street that ran off Residenzstrasse, between a furniture store and a plant nursery. They sat outside in a cottage garden shaded by a linden tree. The meal, which Horst insisted on ordering and paying for, was hearty and definitely authentic. *Schnitzel, Bratkartoffeln, Sauerkraut* washed down with malty local beer. The food was delicious and Kathy ate her fill. The filtered sunshine and easy conversation were so very relaxing. In fact, she could barely keep her eyes open.

From an article she'd read about jet lag, she'd learnt that the human time-clock reset itself by an hour per day. The time difference between Brisbane and Berlin was nine hours. If that theory held true, her misery would last until next week! If only she'd known before making her travel plans. Today was even worse than yesterday.

Stretching she said, 'Do you mind if we walk?'

Horst raised his eyebrows. 'I do not understand this aeroplane disease. It is caused by flying too fast across time zones, am I right? In my day, we travelled by ship. Slow and easy.'

'I've never been on a ship. Seasickness scares me.'

'Believe me, I know about seasickness.' He considered this for a moment. 'Yes, I think seasickness is worse.'

They walked slowly in the direction of the lake. Kathy had her bearings now and recognized the landmarks and the layout of the shopping strip. The florist shop, Deutsche Post, the supermarkets, the four street entrances to the U-Bahn at Franz-Neumann-Platz.

'We will walk around the lake. Have you seen the swans?' he said.

'I know the Swan Café.'

'Ah, yes. Where all the old men go. I do not patronise that establishment … unlike another gentleman I know.' He chuckled at a private joke.

The humour went right over her head and she let it go. Perhaps, when they were better acquainted, little quips like this would make sense.

They came to a concrete path around the shoreline. At the centre of the lake was a fountain, which he said aerated the water to keep the fish alive. Beneath the weeping willows were flocks of waterhen and ducks, and two majestic white swans. The swans of Australia were jet black. A woozy thought crossed Kathy's mind: she was looking at a photographic negative of the lake. Black was white, and white was black. Night-time was daytime, and spring was autumn. She sank onto a park bench before her off-balance brain threw her onto her ear.

Horst sat down beside her. From his pocket he produced a small cellophane-wrapped bar, which he offered. 'In Germany, chocolate cures everything.'

She took it and wolfed it down. In an instant, the sugar snapped her back to life. But she knew it was a reprieve and not a cure.

'Would you like to hear about my voyage to Australia? The story is quite astonishing.'

'I'd love to.' Feeling alert now, she strapped herself in for the next episode.

~

In July 1940, seven weeks after my internment, I was deported from England, along with all the other German and Austrian prisoners at Warth Mills. From the camp, we marched under cover of darkness to the station to board a late-night train. The wartime curfew meant that none of the townsfolk were out on the streets. We'd been promised a beating and solitary confinement if we so much as sneezed on the way. Armed soldiers kept us in line.

In the small hours of the morning, our train arrived at the docks of Liverpool. The ship weighed anchor and departed before dawn. Our vessel was the *Arandora Star*, an ocean liner that had been converted to a troopship and repainted battleship grey. All the cruise amenities—restaurants, bars and the like—had been removed, and she'd been refitted for soldiers and military equipment. Of 1,600 souls on board, three-quarters were internees and one-quarter was crew and guards.

The Italian internees far outnumbered the Germans. They too had come from Warth Mills, where they'd been held in a separate section. Most of the Italians were old and frail and no real threat to the nation. However, Prime Minister Churchill made no exceptions when it came to rounding up enemy aliens. 'Collar the lot', he ordered. The Italians were given quarters deep in the hull, down where there was little ventilation and constant noise from the engine.

Already I had met many of my compatriots. We were a mixed lot with one thing in common. We were refugees, not Nazis or fascists. One was a professor at Leipzig University, whose communist leanings had landed him in a Nazi prison. On release, he'd escaped to Britain. Some were Jews, or the sons of Jews, or former Jews who'd converted to Christianity. Under Hitler, no-one marked with the yellow star was immune from 'racial cleansing', so they'd fled while the gate was open. Others were German or Austrian businessmen, scientists, teachers who were ideologically opposed to the regime. One was my good friend, Dr Werner, who feared that his medical research would be hijacked and turned against innocent people.

As well as civilians, the ship also held a hundred or so prisoners-of-war, soldiers of the Wehrmacht who'd been captured in France and airmen shot down over the Channel.

The British treated us all the same. Ignorant of our differences, the guards randomly allocated us to mid-deck compartments. Nazis and Jews were locked up together. Civilians were locked up with soldiers. Trouble was brewing from the outset.

Throughout the first day of the voyage, Werner and I kept track of our course and tried to guess the destination. America? Canada? Not Greenland, surely. None of us had any idea where we were headed or how long it would take to get there. Initially the steamer chugged north-west, skirting the Isle of Man. Then she turned due north. Along one stretch, lines of blue hills could be seen on either side of the channel. Beyond the reach of land, the *Arandora Star* headed west into the North Atlantic Ocean.

Conditions on board were surprisingly comfortable. At dinner-time we had sufficient food and it was as appetising as British cooks could make it. Afterwards we stood on deck until the last rays of sunlight vanished. Werner said, 'Wherever we are going, my dear boy, I'm sure it will be memorable.' Never were truer words spoken.

With our stomachs content, we climbed into our bunks before lights out. I was on the upper bunk; Werner was down below. Exhausted from raw emotion and too little rest, my head no sooner touched the mattress than I fell into the deepest of slumbers. The gentle rocking of the swell soothed my nerves and freed me from the usual play-list of nightmares.

BAM!

I was rudely tossed from the bunk. As I fell, I collided with others. We landed on top of each other on the floor. The lights were out; the compartment was as black as pitch. Some shouted, some swore, some cried out for salvation. A pair of stray knees crunched down on my ribcage. Utter panic and confusion.

From the passageway came the cry in English. 'Everyone out! Go! Get out!'

Blindly I stumbled out of the cabin into a cloud of fumes and smoke. Wheezing, I found a life jacket and fumbled it on. My ribs ached but there was no time to lick wounds. The place was in chaos. In darkness, I inched along the passageway wall. A crowd had gathered around the ladder to the deck. Everyone was jostling to get a foothold. One fellow slipped and skittled the others below.

Torpedo. The word spread like wildfire. Apparently, our ship had been blasted by a German U-boat. Attacked by one of our own.

'Poetic justice for deserters like us,' mumbled Werner from behind.

Up on deck, pandemonium. The ship was listing to starboard; men scrambled to hang on. The stench of burning oil made me cough, which made my ribs hurt even more. Precious few lifeboats and insufficient life-rafts. I fought to get in, but was beaten back. The second-last lifeboat was about to launch. Standing beside it was Werner. I yelled to him and waved my arms. He didn't hear me. As he was about to climb aboard, the half-empty boat was released and crashed into the ocean.

One lifeboat remained. It was within reach, just a few paces away. Head down, I barged forward. The boat dropped; I launched myself over the railing behind it.

Splash! Into the freezing water.

Five metres from the lifeboat I surfaced and took a few strokes to the side. My body was black with oil and as slimy as an eel. Unseen hands grasped me by the shirt and hauled me in. We took out the oars and rowed away from the stricken ship, away from the flames that licked the stern, away from the ooze of spilled oil. One flying ember and that oil would ignite. And then we would all be incinerated.

When we were clear, we put down the oars and rested. A glow in the east announced the coming daybreak. These were the cold hours, made even colder by drizzle. I scanned the gloomy scene, counted ten lifeboats and thirty-two life-rafts. Survivors in the water were clinging to whatever floated: barrels, boxes, oil drums. Others were bobbing about in life jackets or clinging to the sides of lifeboats. Six were hanging onto ours, which was too low in the water to take anyone more. Even the pull of their desperate hands was destabilising us and threatening to drag us under. Seawater slapped over the side and sloshed about the boards. Our survival hung by a thread. Desperately, I searched for Werner. You see, I had come to rely on him, on his wisdom and optimism. Without him, I was defeated. I was a boy, trying so hard to be a man. That morning, I knew I'd failed.

All I could do was pray. We all did, simultaneously. In three different languages. In that lifeboat were three nationalities: German, British, Italian.

The night lifted and became a miserable dawn. No land was visible, only the sinking ship and the horizontal circle where the murky sea met the murky sky. Two hours on, the men who had been clinging to the side of our boat had succumbed to cold or fatigue and had quietly slipped away. Corpses and flotsam drifted together to form gruesome rafts that dipped and swayed on the choppy ocean. Hundreds of dead were held afloat by lifejackets that would gradually lose buoyancy and, like anchors, drag them down.

An explosion announced the finale. In unison we turned as the *Arandora Star* erupted into flames within a halo of burning oil. The grand lady moaned. As if in slow motion she began to roll, showing her underbelly and the secrets that were normally concealed beneath her plimsoll line. Hundreds who remained on board scurried about like black ants. In awful fascination, I watched them jump and skid and tumble into the flaming ocean. As the ship went into the final death roll, the ones left clinging to the rails cascaded down the precipice like a human waterfall. Screams of anguish echoed across the water. A dying ship of dying men. My eyes were blurry with tears.

The bow reared up out of the ocean. The stern was completely submerged. How many men were trapped inside? It was impossible to know; their remains would never be found. Was it better to drown in a sinking ship, or perish slowly of thirst and exposure on a wide empty ocean? A lifeboat came with no guarantee that the souls inside would be saved.

Momentarily, the bow shot higher. Then the burning vessel slipped, howling and bubbling, down to the bottom of the sea. The displacement of air by water was like the roar of a blizzard. All that remained were clouds of steam and smoke off the oil.

For several minutes we sat in silence. Messy waves slapped against our lifeboat, rocking it from side to side and from bow to stern, a gut-churning motion that had no end. Some puked over the side. Remembering an old sailor's trick learnt from Opa, I fixed my sight on the horizon. Way out there, beyond the bouncing whitecaps, was an illusion of calm.

I remember thinking that these could be our last hours on earth. We had neither food nor drinking-water and the inside of the boat was slopping with brine. On and off, we attempted to bail out using unlikely containers. Hats, boots, cupped hands, a leather jacket. An hour after the sinking of the ship, the clouds parted and the sun blazed through, warming and drying us. My throat was parched; I had no spit to swallow.

One of the Englishmen pointed to the sky. 'Look over there.'

Everyone raised their heads. A tiny dot, black against the blue, was barely visible through salt-crusted eyes. The dot grew into a bird, that grew into a flying boat. The drone of its engine was unmistakeable. The red-white-blue target symbol of the RAF was under the wings. Seen from above, our little rescue vessels would have been pinheads in a million hectares of deep blue. By some miracle, the pilot spotted us. The plane dipped low and released dozens of packages, which rained into the water. One landed about twenty metres away. The oars were refitted and we manoeuvred the lifeboat towards it. Being the lightest, I was elected to retrieve it. With my legs anchored by two men, I leant out and secured our blessing from the sky. Made of waterproof fabric, it was the size of a small tent bag. Inside was a first aid kit, food rations, drinking water, cigarettes, and a message that a rescue ship was on its way.

The aircraft circled for half an hour, waggling its wings as if to reassure us. The sun, nearing the meridian, blazed mercilessly from a cloudless sky. Fair skin turned pink, then stinging red. Yet the sight and sound of that plane was enough to keep our spirits alive. We would be rescued. All we had to do was keep breathing.

Since the sinking, the lifeboats and life-rafts had drifted far apart, making it harder to count the survivors. The hardiest of the hardy were still in the water, clinging to various floatation devices.

Still no sign of Werner.

The flying boat did a final lap and departed at the same time a grey rectangle appeared at the edge of the world. The promised ship, a Canadian destroyer named *St Laurent*, drew closer. We shouted and waved our arms. It hove-to a little removed from the flotilla of floating objects. Two small boats were launched to pick up the solo survivors. The life-rafts and lifeboats were tethered and towed to the side of the warship.

My legs were shaking so hard that I could barely climb the rope ladder. The entire rescue took less than an hour. A headcount established that 868 had been rescued, which was roughly half the ship's complement. The other half had perished at sea.

Safe at last, I picked my way through rows and rows of casualties with lacerations, burns, fractures, sunstroke, dehydration, searching for one man. Would he be there, somewhere on the rescue ship, or would I have to face my worst fears?

Four

Reinickendorf: October 2010

'Well?' said Kathy. 'Don't leave me hanging off a cliff.'

'Below decks, where the casualties had been taken, the cabins had been turned into infirmaries. The place was in turmoil. The sick and injured were crying out and writhing in pain. Blood was everywhere. Werner was in amongst it, using his skills to do wherever he could. My relief was enormous, not only that my friend had been spared, but also that the other survivors, some of whom were in a bad way, were able to get urgent treatment. The *St Laurent* was a destroyer, a ship equipped for war. Amongst the crew was one Navy doctor and a handful of first aid officers. They were completely overwhelmed. Despite being snatched from the ocean minutes earlier, Werner was applying pressure to the stump of a leg to staunch the flow of blood. He glanced up, saw me, called me over to help. I almost fainted, but I did what he said, which freed him up to see others.'

'So, the *St Laurent* took you back to England?' said Kathy.

'Yes. First, we stopped in Glasgow, where the worst cases were taken to hospital. Days later, we were shuttled onto another prison ship, the *Dunera*. It was 10 July 1940, mid-summer in Liverpool. After all we had been through, we were being deported for the second time in a week. We had lost all our possessions—clothes, photos, identity papers—and wore rags on our backs. Boarding the ship was chaotic, done in haste before the tide turned and our departure would have to be delayed. A rollcall of internees from the *Arandora Star* produced so few responses that the guards discarded the list and wrote down the names of the survivors instead. That was the chance I'd been waiting for.

'You see, I was worried about my family in Berlin. I was certain that Max was in thick with the Nazi leaders, which put him in a precarious position. These were business relationships: easy to make, easy to break. I knew that if you went against the Party you'd be punished. I wondered whether my defection to Britain had caused trouble. Had Max or Opa been hauled in for questioning? Had they been put out of business, or imprisoned, or worse? All I wanted to do was protect them. I had no plan, but while I was standing in the queue to board the *Dunera*, an idea came to me. With no identity papers, I could become whoever I wanted.'

'Horst *Schuhmacher*,' Kathy breathed. 'So that explains it. Your occupation became your surname. That's why I had trouble tracking you down. I found your old address amongst Alice's things. The woman who lives there now said she'd never heard of you.'

'My dear, you could pass for Sherlock Holmes.'

'One mystery solved. I expect there will be others,' Kathy said brightly. The thrill of discovery was an antidote for weariness. Horst was an extraordinary raconteur and his shipwreck story was like no other. She could listen to him until midnight. She looked out across the lake. The palette of autumn—russet, gold, orange—made a striking contrast to the cerulean sky and the emerald hues of the evergreens. On the surface of the water, the colours reflected in dots and swirls like an Impressionist masterpiece.

An elderly woman with a brown paper bag came and stood at the edge of the lake. Although a sign warned it was *verboten*, she began throwing crusts to the birds. Bits of white bread littered the bank and the ducks were flapping and squabbling.

'Look at that,' Kathy whispered to Horst. 'I thought you Germans were an obedient lot.'

He waved the comment away. 'Depends on how old and cheeky you are.'

She laughed, feeling closer to this stranger than she cared to admit.

Continuing, he said, 'Today I will finish my voyage to Australia. Tomorrow, you should see the city. Do the tourist things. Visit the museums, the art galleries, the memorials to the Holocaust, the Wall. The day after, I will take you somewhere dear to my heart.'

~

And so, to the second part of my journey. One week after the disaster at sea, we were installed in the transport ship, *Dunera*. Already cramped for space, she had to accommodate an extra four hundred, all survivors of the *Arandora Star*. All told, two and a half thousand detainees plus crew and guards were squeezed onto a vessel built to carry twelve hundred.

This time our compartment was in the bowels of the ship. No portholes, no fresh air, and not a glimmer of natural light. Barbed wire was intermeshed across the doorway to form a barricade to keep us in. The space was shared by fifty men. Each day we were allowed two periods of twenty minutes on deck when we could attend to ablutions and exercise. After lights out, no-one was allowed outside, not even to answer the call of nature. We slept in four layers like herrings in a tin. Uppermost were hessian hammocks tied to the rafters; next came timber benches which were used as tables by day; third came wooden forms which nested beneath the tables. Last was the floor. Nobody wanted the floor, especially not in rough weather. As one fellow put it, 'I broke my knuckles to get a hammock. Now I will gladly puke on all the bastards beneath me.'

Our ship headed north between the coastlines of Scotland and Ireland, following the same shipping lane as the doomed *Arandora Star*. That first night in open waters, the sinking replayed over and over in my mind. Sleep would not come. I was surprised when Werner jiggled my hard-won hammock and I opened my eyes to find that we were alone in the compartment.

'Wake up, Rip Van Winkle,' he said in a light-hearted tone.

I felt groggy and my ribs hurt. 'Where is everyone?'

'Get up. It's our turn on deck.'

We scrambled up the ladders. The rush of morning air ruffled my salt-stiff hair and blew the cobwebs from my lungs. Although no trace of the shipwreck remained, I was certain we were at the spot where she'd sunk. Werner and I looked at each other and heaved a sigh.

'Next stop, Canada?' I said as brightly as I could.

'Who cares. As long as it doesn't end like last time.'

Instead, the ship headed south. Water and supplies were taken on at Freetown and Takaradi on the west coast of Africa. We continued moving south and crossed the Equator, still with no idea of where we were going. It could have been anywhere in the British Empire: South Africa, Ceylon, India, Singapore. After we departed Cape Town, brisk winds sped us east.

Throughout the eight-week nightmare the guards performed regular inspections of our belongings. To ensure there were no illicit items or weapons, we were told. What actually happened was despicable. So-called 'luggage inspectors' would remove everyone's bags and suitcases and upend them on the deck. Then they would sift through the contents and help themselves to any items of value. Fob watches, jackets, currency, cigarettes, medicines. Written material that was not in the English language was tossed overboard. When the inspection was over, we were allowed to retrieve our tangled possessions. Of course, internees like me who had lost everything to King Neptune, had nothing more to lose. But I felt sad for others, whose precious things were stolen or destroyed.

We were treated like animals. Worse, as if we were filth, not worthy of being called human. *Give an ignorant man a uniform and you give him power,* Opa used to say of the Nazi soldiers who strutted about Berlin in their smart uniforms with brass buttons.

On the ship, the British guards wielded their might whenever the whim took their fancy. They went out of their way to be cruel, looted our compartments, withheld all comforts. Even when we suffered dysentery— as we often did from bad food and poor sanitation—the ration of toilet paper remained at two sheets per man per day. They constantly swore at us— *bloody* this, *bleedin'* that—until the decks ran red with blood. Some could barely string a sentence together. *The dregs of the British military,* Werner called them. In contrast, most of the German and Austrian internees were educated men. Some were world leaders in science, mathematics, philosophy, literature. Others were teachers, academics, craftsmen, artists, men of medicine, men of God … and one was a young bootmaker.

I soon made friends with a cabinmate called Georg Mayer, a boy from the Swabian town of Ulm, halfway between Stuttgart and Munich. His Christian name was pronounced *Gay-org*, in the German manner. On the voyage, the British guards called him *George*, which annoyed him greatly. He was exactly my age. Werner commented on how alike we were, said that we might pass for brothers. Both of us were 175 centimetres tall with fair skin, sandy hair, high forehead, and strong jawline. All the attributes of the Aryan race, the Nazi ideal. It was inevitable that we would form a bond which began on the voyage and continued for a lifetime.

On the wharf at Melbourne, all the survivors of the *Arandora Star* disembarked, while Georg and the original *Dunera* contingent remained on the ship. Rumour had it that their destination was Sydney, yet three days away.

Our Australian guards were middle-aged soldiers, dressed in drab uniforms of baggy trousers, ill-fitting shirt, slouch hat, and brown boots, attire more in keeping with farm labourers than professional soldiers. They ordered us to form two lines and marched us along the wharf. Werner and I stuck together. As I had no luggage of my own, I hoisted his duffel bag onto my shoulder. It was heavy and angular. Inside were medical books, given to him by the naval doctor on the *St Laurent*. Incredibly, the books—which were written in Latin—survived the *Dunera* luggage inspectors.

A herd of hecklers followed us, jeering in a rough dialect that didn't sound like English.

Stinkin' wogs! Nazi butchers! Shoot the bloody lot!

While the assault was not physical, it hurt to hear their loathing. Those people actually hated us! I dropped my head; my fringe flopped forward as if to hide my shame. I prayed that the timbers would open up, so I could slip quietly into the murky waters below.

'Raise your head and straighten your back,' Werner murmured in German. 'Show some pride in yourself … and in your country.'

I did as he said and felt better for it.

The march ended at a railway siding at the end of the wharf, where a locomotive hissed and snorted. We boarded the carriages. Doors slammed behind us; padlocks snapped shut. After ten minutes of freedom, there we were again under lock and key. Werner and I sat facing each other. I eased his duffel bag beneath the seat, taking care not to damage the contents. At either end of the carriage, soldiers took their posts. Rifles rested on knees, relaxed but ready. Their faces were inscrutable. I tried to appear brave, or at least nonchalant.

The train whistle blew. Slowly we rolled away from the venomous crowd. The final indignity was a barrage of missiles—eggs, mud, tomatoes—thrown at the window glass. Our last glimpse of the wharf and the hell-ship was through a foul film of slime.

'Melbourne,' said Werner with finality. He rolled a cigarette and lit up, inhaled, and released a plume of smoke. 'We should have been in Canada.'

I waited for him to say more, in particular about the scourge of humanity, our welcoming committee. Under the circumstances, I chose to keep my feelings to myself. My eyes were on the soldiers, who were older than expected. Their weather-hardened gazes moved swiftly from one internee to the next, searching for signs of insurrection, which would be nipped in the bud. The soldiers were outnumbered twenty to one, and it occurred to me that they might have been scared of us too.

'I think this is better than Canada,' Werner said at length. 'Not so cold.'

Although we were both fluent in English, we agreed to use our native tongue. Not only did conversation come more naturally, but we could also speak freely, for all the English speakers we'd encountered understood barely a word of German.

The train chugged through the business district of the city before entering the suburbs. Drab cottages with outhouses, shops with striped awnings, avenues of straggly trees, parks with swings and slippery-dips, factories with billowing smoke. Beyond the outskirts, the vista opened up to a rolling landscape of lavender hills, olive-green pastures, and caramel-coloured sheep.

The day we arrived in Melbourne was the first anniversary of Britain's declaration of war. For twelve months now I had experienced nothing but flux and uncertainty. If the war were to continue for years and years, as it seemed it might, my youth would evaporate like steam from a kettle.

The past does not predict the future, my mother used to say. You must always look forwards, not backwards.

Of course, she said this to comfort me about some little mishap or a falling-out with my friends. In hindsight, I think she was also referring to the fate of our poor country under that terrible regime. When she took me to England, she was looking forwards. There, with Aunt Berry, we were safe for a time but overnight everything changed. I knew in my heart that things would change again. Whatever happened, I had to keep looking forwards and putting the past behind me.

Gathering the cloak of reassurance around me, I settled on the hard seat and closed my eyes. Then and there I made a silent pledge to Mutti to survive one day at a time, one day at a time. No looking back, only forwards. And one of those days I would find a new beginning.

~

At the lake at Reinickendorf, Horst's voice drifted into silence. A shadow fell across his face. It wouldn't have been easy recalling those dreadful times.

'Would you like me to walk you home?' Kathy said gently.

He gave her a nod. 'Too much excitement for one day.' With a wan smile, he pushed himself up from the bench. 'Actually, I have a gift for you. I remembered just now.' He took a step towards the path and faltered. 'Bloody knee,' he said.

The Australian colloquialism sounded comical in a light German accent but she didn't smile. Instead, she offered her arm. He waved it away.

'The human body is like a machine. It needs to warm up.' He did a couple of stretches and wiggled his legs. Then, with a straight back and measured gait, he strode out like a forty-year-old. 'You see, now it works perfectly.'

At his apartment, he beckoned her into the room at the back. While the rest of the place was nicely-decorated in a cluttered sort of way, this was undoubtedly the junk room. Cardboard boxes and tea-chests, piled three and four high, ran right around the walls. Despite this, Horst seemed to know exactly where things were, for he went directly to one chest and, after a few seconds of rummaging, produced an old exercise book. Plain grey, Queensland Department of Education insignia on the cover.

'Here.' He pressed the flimsy book into her hands. 'Take it. It's yours more than mine.'

Intrigued, Kathy thanked him and let herself out of the apartment. Light drizzle had come in, a pervasive dampness that was more like mist than rain. With the exercise book tucked under a borrowed raincoat, she scurried back to her little apartment.

In the white bedroom, she sat on the bed with the book on her lap. No name was on the cover but the handwriting inside was unmistakable. The presence of her dead sister was palpable. A knot of guilt bound her hands. Private journals were not meant to be opened by anyone but the diary-keeper. Feeling like a spy, she flipped through the pages. It seemed to be a record of Alice's teenage years in far north Queensland. How it had come into Horst's possession was a mystery. Had he read it? Did it matter?

She opened at the first page and began to read.

Five

11 May 1941

Hello dear Diary, welcome to your home sweet home. School is out for the holidays so we will be together through the long boring nights of May. Nothing ever happens here at Currawong, apart from canecutters in the crushing season. Italy is at war with Australia now. We have to be careful what we say in public so we don't get into trouble with the police. Some folks around here have turned against us and would dob us in at the drop of a hat. 'You can't trust anyone anymore,' Papa said when he picked me up from boarding school.

You, dear Diary, are my secret confidante. I'll keep you under my mattress, safe from prying eyes.

These holidays, Papa has promised to take me fishing at his special spot on the Russell River. Just him and me and Pixie. Between us, we'll catch lots of barramundi, as long as Pixie doesn't bark or make a fuss. I love being out on the river, surrounded by rainforest and that wide blue sky. So quiet and peaceful. Nothing like St Bernadette's, where we squabble over who goes first in the showers, who used the last sheet of toilet paper, who gets the biggest serve of pudding.

Lately, my school friends have been taking the war more seriously. Rita Borlotti reckons we Italians are in for it. She says the Brits are at war with fascism, but the Australians are at war with themselves. She's right. At Currawong, everyone of Italian origin has to register with the police. Papa is officially an 'enemy alien', even though he's been here for thirty years and is naturalised. Mamma is too. And the Borlotti parents, who own a tobacco farm up near Mareeba. I don't know where that leaves Rita and me. We were born here, so I guess we count as British.

Today I took the initiative, as the nuns always tell us to do. I paid Gwen Morris a visit without asking Papa's permission. There's been a falling-out between our parents, you see. Papa says it's jealousy, because the Italians grow better cane and get better prices than the Aussies. As well as being our farm neighbour, Gwen is a good friend and I don't want to lose her.

I wrapped six of Mamma's biscotti in brown paper, pedalled two miles through the cane paddocks to the Morris's place and went around the back as usual.

From the kitchen, Mrs Morris yelled out to Gwen to answer the door. Out she came, in a new floral dress, her blonde hair tied in a ribbon. Without saying a word, she grabbed my hand and dragged me to the barracks. It's the slack season, so there aren't any canecutters around. Out of sight of the house, she threw her arms around me and told me how much she'd missed me.

I kissed her cheeks and gave her the brown-paper package.

'Oh, yum! I love your mum's biscuits.' She stuck one in her mouth. 'Want one?'

'No thanks. They're all for you. What's news?'

'Lots, but not what you'd want to hear. At the post office, I have to do *absolutely everything* now.' She threw a glance over her shoulder, as if checking for eavesdroppers. 'Remember the telegram boy, Bobby Fallon?'

Last holidays, the pimply creep had made a disgusting suggestion that I'd rather forget. I told him to take a running leap off a cliff and die. Maybe he did. Of course, I didn't say that to Gwen. I told her that I remembered him.

'He's joined the *army* and now *I* have to deliver all the telegrams. It's horrible. People see me coming. They know it's bad news, so they shut the door in my face. I feel like the angel of death.' She went on to list all the families who had lost sons and brothers in Europe and North Africa. Then she listed the Italians arrested in the last roundup. 'By the way, my dad is dead against you lot at the moment. I can't even mention your name.'

'But *you're* not against us. Are you, Gwen?'

'Once a friend, always a friend. Hey, tell me about your debut.'

I groaned. 'Mamma reckons the ball won't go ahead.'

What a disappointment that is! Planning takes the best part of a year. Dress materials are bought by mail order from department stores in the south and gowns take months to make. The Italian Club ball is the biggest event in the district. Hundreds of guests come from miles around. The best part is that debutantes can ask a boy to be their partner without being called a *puttana*.

I went on to talk about a boy from church who I'm keen on. If the ball is on next year, I'll definitely ask him. I'm trying to be optimistic, but I have a hunch that the war will put an end to our fun.

Without missing a beat, Gwen informed me that her debut is on 5 July at the Memorial Hall in Innisfail, right after her seventeenth birthday. 'Mum's making me the most gorgeous dress. Chiffon over satin. A big swishy skirt and appliqued roses around the neck.' She put a finger to her lips. 'Don't tell anyone. She cut up her wedding dress for the fabric. Dad doesn't know.'

I asked who her partner was and she went pink. 'Ahh ... well ... he's a soldier,' she waved her hand vaguely. 'I haven't asked him yet.'

I pressed on. 'Someone from around here?'

'Yes, but you probably don't know him. He's not Catholic.'

'Neither are you. Come on, Gwen, tell me.'

She chewed on her lip before saying that his name was Bob.

'Bob ... Bobby? You don't mean Bobby Fallon, do you? The pimply telegram boy.'

'He doesn't have pimples anymore. And he's rather nice, once you get to know him.'

I didn't have the heart to tell her about my nasty experience with a thoroughly nasty piece of work, so I chattered on about boarding school and my plans for the holidays.

A deep voice boomed from the house. 'Gwendoline! Come here and help your mother!'

'Coming, Dad!' Gwen bundled up the biscotti and slipped them into her pocket. 'See you Saturday?'

'Can't. Italian School. Next week?'

'I'm at work, don't forget. Come to the post office.'

As I mounted the pushbike, I could hear Mr Morris scolding her. 'I've told you before and I won't tell you again. This family does not associate with *Eye-ties* or Catholics. Do you understand me, girl?'

Why does a stupid war have to come between friends?

My parents were both born in Sicily. Papa works hard on the cane farm. Mamma helps him wherever she can, and runs the house, and teaches at the Italian School on weekends. As a child, Papa had to work in the sulphur mines. His family was so poor, they couldn't afford to send him to school. As a result, he values education above everything, even for me, his only daughter. Education will get me a good job and then a good partner in marriage. I'm glad he thinks that way for I enjoy school, except for the nuns.

Gwen is the opposite: she could hardly wait to leave. Straight after Scholarship, she landed a desk job in the Postmaster-General's Department. She earns good money for a girl. Now, at almost seventeen, she's the postmistress of Currawong. Her parents are battlers, working when they have to and spending every penny they earn. On Saturdays, Mr Morris and his mates meet at the Railway Hotel, where they bet on the horses and drink beer. On Sundays, Gwen and her mother go to the half-hour service at the Anglican church, while I have to sit through a whole boring hour of Latin at St Catherine's. In July, my pretty friend will be Belle of the Masonic Ball while I'll be at boarding school wearing a dowdy brown tunic, eating terrible food, and having to put up with sour nuns. The only thing for me to look forward to is the Senior public exam in November. Life is not fair!

12 May 1941

Today two policemen came to our house and took Papa away. We don't know where he's gone or when he'll be back.

All morning he'd been out in the machinery shed. Mamma was cooking and I tried to make myself useful. When *pranzo* was ready, he bounded in like an overgrown schoolkid—he's sixty-three—and planted kisses all over my head.

Those months when I'm at boarding school, he's the one I miss most. This is my final year at St Bernadette's. Next year, I'll probably go to teachers' training college in Brisbane. According to my mother, teaching is an honourable profession that will do me nicely until I marry. But I'd rather be a nurse.

Mamma brought the piping-hot dish to the table. Today we had *linguini* with tomato and basil. As usual our table talk was about the Italian Club, the war, sugar prices, friends who've been arrested and sent away. I kept quiet about Gwen's warning that her father was dead against us. For *secondo* we had home-made sausages and salad. We finished with red plums, which were half-cooked from the long journey from Stanthorpe in a freight wagon.

'*Buonissima!*' Papa pushed the chair back from the table and patted his belly. 'My wife is the best cook in the world.'

Mamma beamed. Everything felt right.

While I was clearing the table, Pixie started yapping and took off down the hall. Papa tucked in his shirt and went to see who was there.

Meanwhile, I filled the basin with water for washing up.

Raised voices echoed down the hall. Papa called out to Mamma. 'Maria, *vieni qua.*'

She wiped her hands and hurried off.

Minutes later, she was back in the kitchen. Her face was livid, her lips were pressed into a thin line. She bustled me outside, toward the machinery shed, and told me not to make a sound. Without question I obeyed. In the shed, I picked my way between tractors and farm implements and bales of hay to a spot where I couldn't be seen. For what seemed like hours, I sat on an old truck seat in the hot tin shed. Waiting. Waiting. Waiting for what?

Ages later, I saw Mamma weaving a path between the machines. Her face was a thundercloud. She threw herself onto a hay-bale and put her head in her hands. '*Bastardi!* They've taken him.'

Yesterday, Gwen had been prattling on about roundups and arrests. To be honest, I hadn't taken much notice. I thought she was talking about the canecutters' union getting back at farmers who didn't use British labour, or a crackdown on the Black Hand gang who liked to lop off people's ears. If only I'd asked sensible questions instead of daydreaming about boys and debutante balls.

'I should go to town, see our lawyer, find out how to get him back.' To my surprise, Mamma lit a cigarette and puffed furiously. I'd never seen her smoke before.

'What has he done wrong?'

'He decided to live in this wretched country for a start. We were supposed to go home to Sicily after you were born. That was the agreement. But no, he kept saying "one more season … one more season" until it got stuck in my head.' She waved the cigarette about as she spoke. If she wasn't careful, she'd set the hay alight. '*Porca miseria.* Where does this leave me now?'

I didn't know what to say. My parents had a good marriage, or so I thought. They rarely fought and, if they did, they got over it quickly. I took her hand and said we should go to town together.

As it turned out, we couldn't stop them from sending Papa away. Mamma and I rode our bicycles ten miles along the bush track to Currawong. We found him, and around fifty others, ring-fenced within a barbed-wire barricade at the showgrounds. At the centre were two rows of tents. Mamma spotted her friends from the Italian Club, whose husbands had also been arrested. At least Papa was not alone or with strangers.

Late in the afternoon, storm clouds rolled in and darkness fell early. Our bikes had no lights and the track was treacherous at night. The women decided to stay at the farm shed that was used for Italian Club gatherings. They made a simple supper of pasta with olive oil, garlic, and cheese. Later we lay on hard stretcher beds and tried to sleep. All night, rain drummed on the tin roof and mosquitoes bomb-dived my ears. Worrying about Papa also kept me awake. I couldn't imagine life without him.

In the morning, the entire population of Currawong turned out to watch a pathetic parade. In handcuffs, Papa and his comrades marched under guard to the railway station. The Italians stood proud and defiant while the Aussies yelled abuse. Amongst a drunken mob outside the Railway Hotel was a face I knew too well: Mr Morris, neighbour and father of my life-long friend. For an instant, our eyes locked. Embarrassed, he turned away, back to his mates sucking on long-necked bottles. They were singing the old song, *Bless 'em All*, but with different lyrics. Hurtful lyrics. At the end of the chorus, Mr Morris's baritone soared above the rest.

So shoot all the Eye-ties, shoot 'em all.

~

Seething with indignation, Kathy put down the diary. No wonder Alice would never talk about the war. It must have been dreadful to see her father, Bruno, suffer the abuse of the townsfolk on that march of shame. That song, how cruel!

When Kathy cleared out the family home, she'd found a book about World War II internment in Australia. Curious, she'd taken it from a box earmarked for charity and read it from cover to cover. After that, she wanted to know more about the Zanetti and Giuliano families. The half-sisters were born at opposite ends of the war that had split the world in two. They were of two different generations, the product of two different fathers. Alice Zanetti's youth ended before Kathy Giuliano was born. What happened in between was a mystery that she was determined to solve.

On her home computer, she worked her way through digitised internment records held by the National Archives of Australia and concluded that government files were as dry as old bones. Forms and reports were typed in triplicate. Interdepartmental letters began quaintly with 'I beg to request …'

Digging deeper, she learned that the Brisbane office of the Archives held the original paper files of police investigations done in the 1930s and 40s. With renewed enthusiasm, she went there in person and spoke to an archivist. Half an hour later, she was in the reading room with a pile of Manila folders containing hundreds of sheets of crumbling paper. Amongst the morass, she found photos and personal letters (thankfully translated from Italian into English), even clippings from *The Sunday Truth*, a Brisbane newspaper that specialised in scandal.

While this research revealed the policies and mechanics of internment, she had not appreciated the extent of hatred and bigotry at the time. Alice must have felt bitter and rejected, yet she'd never uttered a word. For Italians who'd lived through the war, the topic of internment was taboo.

Although she would have liked to continue reading the diary, her eyes were stinging. Overcome by remorse and sadness, she kissed the grey cover of the exercise book. 'Thank you, Alice,' she said.

The next morning, Kathy woke at 04:30, an improvement on the day before. Over breakfast she wrote a long email to Jack about what she'd been up to in Berlin. Later she acted on Horst's suggestion and took the U-Bahn to Alexanderplatz. At nine-thirty, the city's busiest transit hub was crawling with people. People from all walks of life poured off the trains, flooded the staircases and escalators, and spilt out of the exits. Not a busker or beggar was in sight; cyclists were there in their hundreds. Food vendors sold wurst on bread rolls and takeaway coffee. In every direction, people criss-crossed the concrete plaza. Everyone, it seemed, was in a rush.

Taking her bearings from the TV tower, which today soared majestically into a clear blue sky, Kathy navigated a route to the Spree, took the footpath by the river, and crossed the bridge to Museum Island. The Berliner Dom stood dark and brooding on the bank. The scale of the cathedral and the nearby palaces was colossal. In comparison, Brisbane's grandest sandstone building looked like a dollhouse.

For an hour she explored the island, took in the Humboldt University, the opera house, and a huge construction site where a Renaissance-style palace was being built to replace another that had been bulldozed after the war.

Later she visited the Altes Museum, a gracious Neoclassical building with porticos and soaring columns. Gallery after gallery displayed antiquities from Greece, Egypt, Persia, the kind of items that she'd only seen in picture books. There was too much to take in, too much to absorb. Before long she lost patience.

Outside, the warm sun beckoned. On the manicured lawn of the Lustgarten, she consulted her tourist map. It was all too confusing. In the end, she decided to go where her feet took her and explore whatever caught her fancy. With no plan and no expectations, she set out in the direction of Unter den Linden and the Brandenberg Gate.

Reminders of the war were abundant. Bullet holes on the railway bridge; brass commemorative plaques on the houses of murdered Jews; an entire city block of grey concrete pillars, a memorial to the Holocaust; the blackened shell of the Kaiser-Wilhelm Church which was bombed by the Allies in 1945. She felt grief for a city not yet recovered from its violent past.

Here the war did not end with the Battle of Berlin or Hitler's suicide or the Nazi surrender. The victors carved up the country and its former capital into sectors. In 1961, a barbed-wire barrier was erected within Berlin to stop residents of the Soviet sector from moving to sectors controlled by the Western Allies. In the one single night, family members, colleagues, friends and lovers were cut off from each other for what turned out to be twenty-eight years.

Later, a permanent impregnable barrier was built: two thick concrete walls 3.6 metres high with barbed wire, guard towers, and a 'death strip' in between. On maps of the 1960s, 70s and 80s, West Berlin was a puddle of blue within a sea of Soviet red. Within the DDR (the East), the Stasi secret service spied on its citizens, flushing out suspected subversives and would-be defectors. Many were tortured, imprisoned, shot dead. When the Wall came down in 1989, reunification was not easy. How does a population, born and raised under opposing ideologies, reconcile after such a separation?

Feeling conflicted as well as weary, Kathy caught the U-Bahn back to Franz-Neumann-Platz. She wanted to know more, to get a better understanding of Horst, of Alice, of this war-damaged city. Time was running out. The river cruise to Hamburg would depart in four days and she hadn't scratched the surface.

At the Italian café on Residenzstrasse, she ordered a takeaway pizza. At Netto, she bought a bottle of chianti to go with it. In brooding twilight, she took the dimly-lit path by the lake to her apartment. Her feet were aching; she counted every painful step. Her three-point plan for the evening was to have a meal, take a hot shower, and finish reading Alice's journal in bed.

Six

9 November 1941

Dearest Diary, sorry to have neglected you. School has been frantic, but it's almost at an end. We're in the middle of exams now. Ten of us are here to sit Matriculation, while all the other boarders have packed up and left. Lucky them! I'm good at making life hard for myself. I was hoping for a scholarship to the University of Queensland, but I don't think my grades will be good enough. The first exam was English and I mucked up the essay. Not much hope there. The Maths paper yesterday was awful but I might have scraped through. All I can do now is study like mad and pray for easy papers next week.

If I don't get that scholarship, I'm determined to go nursing. Mamma is the biggest hurdle. She thinks that nurses are glorified bottle-washers and pot-scrubbers. 'Why would you want to waste your youth wiping old men's bottoms?' she says. I know that the first two years might be like that, but then it gets interesting. Rita's cousin is a nurse and she loves it. I haven't spoken to Mamma about my decision because it will cause an argument. Applications for the Brisbane General Hospital close in six weeks. Plenty of time. I've already filled out the form; all it needs is a parent's signature. If I don't get that scholarship, she might come round to the idea.

Mamma wants me to be a teacher. Teachers are scarce because so many men have joined the army. There's talk that married female teachers might be allowed back in the schoolroom, but I don't think that will happen. According to Gwen's mother, being a wife is a full-time job as it is. There's also talk that the two- or three-year training period for primary school teachers might be reduced to six months, providing you agree to work in a small town in the bush. Perfect for me. I live in a small town in the bush.

Mother Superior has told us about an opening here at St Bernadette's. The Catholic system is easier to get through than the State's, but then you're locked in with nowhere to go unless you became a nun. I haven't told Mamma about this. I couldn't stand to work with a bunch of dreary nuns and I have no interest whatsoever in entering a convent. Wish me luck next week.

16 November 1941

School is over! I'm home now, waiting for the results that will determine my future.

Last week was stinking hot and the exam questions were horrible. I have no idea of how well or badly I've done. To make matters worse, I had my monthlies. Cramps and nausea as usual. Straight after the final paper, I packed my port, said goodbye to my favourite teacher, and took the bus down the range to Currawong. Mamma drove the truck to the bus stop to meet me.

Oh, I forgot to tell you. She's got her licence now. Before Papa was sent down south, she couldn't drive at all. But we're ten miles out of town and she has to run the farm. Without a licence that's impossible. At the ripe old age of thirty-five, she got in the driver's seat of the old truck and practised bumping around the cane paddocks. When she was confident that she could steer and stop—and this is the best part—she put on a clingy dress, stockings, and heels, and drove herself to Currawong. At the police station she asked for a licence.

'How did you get here?' said the constable.

'I drove the truck.' She thrust out her chest and put enough cash on the counter to cover the fee. Mamma's a shapely woman. Apparently, he could barely keep his eyes off her.

'I must warn you, Mrs Zanetti ...' He started scribbling on a form.

Her heart sank but she managed to maintain her demeanour.

'... as an enemy alien, you cannot take any long trips without informing us. And ... well ... take care.' Without further question or comment, he took the fee and gave her the licence.

She could have kissed him, but of course she didn't. Instead, she tucked the little card into her purse and sashayed outside, where she clambered into the rusty mud-covered truck.

With Mamma at the wheel, the drive home felt strangely adventurous. Normally Papa would pick me up. Often, he'd drive all the way up to the Atherton Tablelands so I wouldn't have to suffer the winding range road on the bus. I started to ask if he'd written from the internment camp, but she vigorously shook her head. 'Shhh! Must concentrate.'

We rounded a bend, missed one pothole, hit the second. The truck skidded sideways and stopped an inch from the drainage ditch.

'*Mamma mia!*' She crunched the gears, wrestled with the steering wheel. Her knuckles were white but she was a woman of determination. The truck reversed, waded through the mud, and then we were off again.

'Hooray!' I shouted. 'You got us through.'

'Shhh! The next patch is even worse.'

Finally, we reached the farmhouse and Pixie raced out wagging her tail like a feather duster. She jumped all over me, nearly knocked me flat. We've missed each other terribly. Covered in mud, we had to have a wash at the tank-stand before we could go inside.

After three months the place looks so different! The cane has been cut and the new crop is in the ground; the ratoon in the back paddock has sprouted like grass. The fire-break around the house has turned into a jungle. The thorny canes of the bougainvillea have taken over the veranda. Mamma refuses to go near it, but the colour—magenta—is Papa's favourite. Although pruning it is treacherous, I've promised to keep it under control until he returns.

In the kitchen, we had tea and biscuits. I asked about Papa and whether he'd written.

'Nearly every day. His letters come in batches. I got some from the post office this morning.' Mamma took a bundle from her bag and tossed it on the table. 'Here, read them.'

At St Bernadette's, I hadn't received a single letter. I picked up the envelopes and flipped through. Five were addressed to me. I could hardly believe my eyes. A spidery, nun-like hand had crossed out the school's address and written *C/- Post Office, Currawong* instead. I was furious.

All this time I thought he'd forgotten me, or was languishing in a prison cell, too sick to write. Hugging his letters to my chest, I took my port to my room and lay down on the bed. Mamma brought me a hot-water bottle for my period cramps and more letters from Papa.

I read them all, every sentence, every word. All in Italian, of course. He'd written instructions about running the farm; news that someone (name removed by the censor) had died; questions about how I was doing at school. At the start of each letter was a weather report. Papa is a farmer, so the weather is important, but to waste precious paper discussing the weather seemed a bit obsessive. Drained from the turmoil of the day, I put the letters aside and slept.

17 November 1941

Got up early, just after five. My cramps were gone and I was ravenous. After collecting the eggs, I stoked the stove and was making a cheese omelette for two when Mamma came in. I wished her *buon giorno* and told her that breakfast was ready.

'You sound bright and cheery.' She took a seat by the door, fanned herself with a folded newspaper. 'It'll be a stinker again today. Probably a storm this afternoon.'

I raised an eyebrow. Her prediction sounded like Papa's, so I asked why he always wrote about the weather.

She smiled in a conspiratorial way. 'Promise not to breathe a word?'

I nodded. 'Cross my heart.'

'No, this is serious. If anyone finds out, we're dead. I mean it.'

That's when I began to pay attention.

She said it was something they'd discussed ahead of time. All along, Papa expected to be interned. He knew that correspondence to and from the camp would be censored, so they worked out a code and disguised it as the weather. To protect me, she didn't go into detail. Suffice to say that more meaning was in the weather report than on the rest of the page.

According to a recent coded message, Papa had appealed against his internment but was unsuccessful. This was at Gaythorne in Brisbane before he was sent to South Australia.

Mamma says the appeal process is a farce. The decision is made before the case is heard. Although many have appealed, no-one from Currawong has been successful. We know because stories like this are traded like swap-cards every Sunday after Mass.

Which reminds me, I'd better stop writing and get dressed for church.

19 November 1941

Some days I think this war will never end. It's been going on for two years now and everyone is sick of it. There are almost no men left in the district. The Aussies are either fighting overseas or 'doing their bit' somewhere else in the country. Most of the Italians and Germans have been packed off to internment camps or conscripted into the Civil Aliens Corps and sent out to Woop-Woop to build roads and railway lines. The men from Currawong are farmers and workers, not fascist spies. No-one here beats his chest about Mussolini or Hitler. Most couldn't care less about politics or empires. All they want is to make enough money to live and raise a family.

Gwen's brother, who joined the RAF as a pilot, is missing in action. They've had no news in eighteen months. He could be dead or a prisoner-of-war or hiding somewhere in France. The not-knowing is almost as bad as a telegram beginning with 'I regret to inform ...'

Enough about the war; it's making me sad.

Today Mamma made a list of chores as long as the sheet of paper. 'You can count on my help until training begins in January,' I said.

'Training for what?' she said.

I launched into the speech I'd rehearsed, over and over, for weeks. 'I want to be a nurse, Mamma, and I want to train at the Brisbane General Hospital. I got the application form from school and it's all filled out. All you have to do is sign.'

For a moment she glared at me in stunned silence. 'A nurse! I thought you were going to be a teacher. Anyway, the way things are, that has gone by the board. You are needed right here on this farm until your father gets back. I can't manage on my own.'

I'd expected as much. But what she said next made me so ashamed.

'We must pull together, Alessandra. This isn't the time to chase rainbows. This is about survival. What would your father say if we lost the farm?'

Losing the farm had not occurred to me. Losing the farm meant losing our home. It's the only home I've known. Eager as I am to spread my wings, I immediately agreed to stay.

But what if the war goes on and on, like the Thirty Years' War? What if I never get another opportunity to become a nurse?

Mamma said, 'You are young. You have plenty of time. One day this will end and you can do whatever you like. For now, we must work together as partners and equals.'

She went through the chores and split them up between us. 'M' for Maria (herself) and 'A' for me. Some she marked 'T' (together) or 'H' (help required). In our community, we pull together. Favours are given and received. We don't exchange money; we exchange goods and effort. A basket of eggs for a basket of beans; a piglet for a baby goat; two days of sewing for two days of weeding the veggie patch. Thankfully the cane has been harvested and we're in the 'slack', so there's not much to do in the paddocks.

2 December 1941

Yesterday I got my driver's licence. Hooray! I've been taking lessons from the oldest man in Currawong. Signore Russo, age eighty-nine. Next week he'll show me how to drive the Fordson tractor. It'll be trickier than the truck but I'll give it my best shot.

We've made a start on the list of chores. Mamma took a scythe to the tangle of scrub around the house and I pruned that wretched bougainvillea. Now I've got scratches all over my arms. Mamma bathed them in salt water, which made them sting. Anyway, it's satisfying to cross two things off a long, long list.

Because of the heat, we do the outside work early in the morning or late in the afternoon. Never in the middle of the day. At night I sleep like the dead and at dawn we start all over again. Farm work is never-ending like housework. Our rest-day is Sunday when we go to church and trade gossip and horror stories with the other women.

This is not the life I imagined, but I must admit I'm enjoying myself. My skin is berry-brown and my body is strong. Papa is relying on us and I'm 'doing my bit' for him.

8 December 1941

Terrible news. We are at war with Japan! Just now Mamma came in from town with a copy of *The Cairns Post*. She slammed it down on the table. 'This will be the end of us!' she said.

I skimmed the front page, the Prime Minister's speech.

> *Now is our darkest hour ...*
>
> *The nation itself is in peril ...*
>
> *Our efforts in the last two years must be as nothing compared with the efforts we must now put forward.*

Mamma lit a cigarette and read over my shoulder. 'See what Mr Curtin says? Right at the end?' She poked an angry finger at the final paragraph. 'He wants everyone to sign up and fight. How many of *our* able-bodied men are rotting in internment camps? Decent patriotic Australians who were born in Italy. Will he allow *our* men to be released to protect home and country? I think not.' She snorted and the smoke streamed from her nostrils.

She's right. We have no-one to defend us except ourselves. Our soldiers are all in Africa or Europe. The Japanese threat is immediate while the war in Europe lingers on and on. Unlike her, I have no warm and fuzzy feelings for the old country, no rose-coloured memories, no familial bonds. My nightmares are not like hers. Her mother—my Nonna—lives with her sister in a hilltop town in Sicily. Two old women, alone and defenceless against enemy soldiers. That is what she worries about.

It seems to me that, if the Japanese invaded Australia, we would be two *young* women in exactly the same position. God help us!

14 December 1941

Today at church, the sole topic of conversation was the war with Japan. Everyone has an opinion and no two are alike. By accident, I found myself standing beside the boy of my dreams—Patrick Winter—and his mother. They were talking about the Japanese bombing of the Philippines. It's clear that the Japs are island-hopping south towards Australia. It's only a matter of time until they get here and then we'll be in strife.

Mrs Winter rummaged in her handbag. 'Have a look at this.' She handed me a page of *The Cairns Post*. The headline read, 'Fine British spirit in the face of adversity.'

I skimmed the article, an eyewitness account of the sinking of the *HMS Repulse* in the South China Sea and the heroic rescue of survivors. The story was as gripping as a thriller. That it was true, made it all the more compelling. As I handed the page back to Mrs Winter, my eye caught a one-line advertisement at the bottom.

The army calls for 10,000 new nurses.

What an enormous number! If all those nurses went to war, hospitals and clinics in Australia would be short of staff. There might be extra training places. An opportunity for me, perhaps.

While everyone was busy reading the article and tut-tutting about this unexpected turn in the war, Patrick brushed against my elbow. The touch was light; it could have been accidental. He was so close I could feel his breath.

'Will you come to the pictures with me on Saturday?' he whispered in my ear.

My heart skipped a beat, then my hopes sank. I would have to ask Mamma and I already knew the answer: *Not on your own, you can't.* Australians do not understand chaperones. According to Italian parents, having a brother or a male cousin tag along guarantees no hanky-panky in the back row. I have yet to experience back-row cinema firsthand, for I have never been on an actual date. The problem is, I have neither a brother nor a male cousin. In fact, the only male in the district, who might be acceptable to Mamma, is dear old Signore Russo. I can't imagine *that* suggestion would go down well with Patrick. And so, I was caught between yearning to go and not being able to accept. What could I say?

'I'd love to, but I've promised to help out on the farm. Another time?'

He smiled politely. 'I hope there *is* another time. I'm enlisting next week.'

I could have bitten off my tongue. The position was irretrievable.

'Where will you be posted?' My voice was high-pitched and thin.

'Probably Brisbane for training. After that … wherever I'm sent.' He kicked the gravel with his shiny new shoes and looked uncomfortable. Meanwhile, conversations whirled around our heads about Japs, the threat of invasion, whether Britain or America would come to our rescue.

Patrick is a few months older than me, not long out of school. Soon he'll be fighting real battles with real bullets and real blood. We're not even old enough to vote, yet we're old enough to die for our country. Welcome to the adult world. No more make-believe.

I promised to write and he seemed happy with that. I'll also pray that he stays safe.

25 December 1941

Merry Christmas, dearest Diary. Last night, Mamma and I went to Midnight Mass at St Catherine's. The church was half-empty because so many are away. Mrs Winter was there on her own, looking gorgeous as usual in a new cotton dress. Mine is old and shabby. With all the other work we have to do, Mamma hasn't had time to make clothes. I must learn how to sew. Anyway, I asked about Patrick and found out that he's already left for recruit training. He didn't waste any time! She gave me his address, so I'll write to him later.

Today we put on our happy faces and made the most of it for Christmas, just the three of us: Mamma and Pixie and me. At Mamma's suggestion, I set a place at the table for Papa, but it wasn't a good idea. The bare plate reminded us of how much we miss him, but I didn't have the heart to put it away. Mamma said a prayer of thanks for the abundant food and followed it up with a plea for Papa's release. We had *pasta con pomodoro* (tomatoes from our garden), followed by roast chicken (one of our own, which I killed, cleaned and plucked), and then a handful of beautiful red cherries (bought at great expense from Joe, the travelling greengrocer). My idea of Heaven would be an endless supply of cherries. What a pity they don't grow in the tropics.

My exam results are out. I passed every subject! Best were English and Zoology, both Bs. The rest were Cs. No university scholarship, but good enough for teachers' college or nursing. I'm waiting on an offer, but I can't take it up straight away. Hopefully I can defer until 1943, or whenever this damn war ends.

Rita Borlotti passed only two subjects, so I guess she'll be stuck stringing and grading tobacco on the farm. It's picking season in Mareeba and the women are working fourteen-hour days. Her brothers in the Australian army are fighting Italy in North Africa, while her father is locked up in South Australia because he's supposed to be a dangerous enemy. How stupid is that! He might be at the same camp as Papa. I'd write and ask, but I know that his reply will be censored so it's not worth the effort.

15 March 1942

My dearest Diary, I don't know how to tell you this. The most dreadful thing in the world has happened. This morning Gwen brought us a telegram. My darling Papa is dead!

Mamma fainted. I brought her smelling salts and Gwen got her a headache powder and some water. We both helped her into bed. Now I'm sitting in my room alone. It doesn't seem real. I don't know what to do. I'm lost, sad, angry. The telegram said he died of 'natural causes', whatever that means. He was as healthy as a bull when he left. Now he's lying in the cold hard ground someplace in South Australia. Without us and alone. What happened in such a short space of time?

Sorry, the page is wet from tears. I can't stop crying. I don't think I ever will.

6 April 1942

Today is Easter Monday, the day of Papa's memorial Mass. We left it until now because of Lent. He deserved a decent farewell with flowers and all the trimmings. At St Catherine's, we set up a table in the vestibule with photos and mementoes. Afterwards, at the Club, we put on a hearty meal to honour him.

Mamma stood up and told the story of their courtship and marriage, and I'm glad she did. I'm so proud of her for putting on a brave face and holding herself together. Her story showed Papa for the beautiful man he was. Honest and caring and loyal.

The match was made through a mutual friend. Mamma was not yet seventeen. Papa wrote to her from Australia and she replied from Sicily. For a year, they exchanged letters and photographs before marrying by proxy at Catania. At the ceremony, Papa's youngest brother, Gino, stood in for him. Later, her brother-in-law accompanied her to Messina, where she boarded the steamer to Australia. That was in March 1923.

On the voyage, she took English lessons and practiced on the British crew and any passengers who were patient enough to listen. She shared a cabin with two sisters from Naples, also proxy brides, who had not the slightest interest in learning English. Australia, they said, was a wild country full of dangerous creatures.

They'd vowed to stay two years and not one minute longer. Their husbands were plantation owners with lots of servants. In two years, they'd be back in Naples, living *la dolce vita*. No need for English.

'My husband also owns a cane farm,' Mamma said. 'He has told me all about it and I know what to expect. For me, this is an adventure, an opportunity to explore a new country and live a different life.'

You must be mad, was the response.

From then on, she was treated like a leper. She knew that no gracious homestead awaited her, nor was there any hired help, other than seasonal labourers and canecutters.

Those sisters would have been in for a rude awakening. In the sugar districts of tropical Queensland, grand lifestyles like in *Gone with the Wind* exist only on the silver screen.

Up until now, I'd never thought about what happens after a person dies. Apart from the shock and the grieving, there's an awful lot to do. Mamma asked me to help. It's good to be busy and it makes me feel closer to her … and to him.

Together we made the arrangements for the memorial Mass. Together we made our black dresses, wrote out invitations, gathered flowers and palm fronds for the church, planned the feast and did some of the cooking. All the Italian ladies pitched in with the food. Despite the shortages, there was more than enough for everyone. I made *cannoli*, the crispy custard-filled pastries that Papa loved best.

Aside from that, we've had to tackle a pile of paperwork. Legal documents, probate, transfer of assets. While Mamma speaks English fairly well, she relies on me to read important documents and write letters. Rita Borlotti used to whinge about being dragged around town to interpret for her parents in matters of business. I see it as an honour.

Now we are officially in mourning. Mamma will wear black for a whole year, and me for six months. Bright clothes are considered disrespectful, like spitting on a person's grave. Most of the Italians in Currawong wear black in memory of loved ones lost here and in the old country. Some will wear black for the rest of their lives, but I don't think I will.

Seven

Reinickendorf: October 2010

Kathy flipped the page of the journal, found nothing but blank paper. Flipped again. The next entry was dated 19 December 1943. The gap of twenty months was right in the heart of Australia's war. Those were the secret years, the years that her mother and sister would never talk about, the years she was desperate to explore.

Kathy closed her eyes and tried to imagine what it was like during the war. From the history books, she knew that the Japanese Imperial Army had Australia firmly in the crosshairs. Darwin had suffered terrible destruction; enemy bombs had been dropped near Townsville and Cairns. Despite the support of America, the country was too vast and sparsely-populated to be properly defended. Fear drove desperate measures.

Sugar towns like Currawong would have been crawling with troops. For some, being a soldier was an initiation into adult life, free of parental constraints. When it came to women and grog, Allied soldiers were not necessarily well-behaved. God forbid what enemy invaders might have done. The authorities could have taken this into account when they debated abandoning the Far North to the Japanese. Perhaps Alice and Mum were evacuated south. Or maybe they hid in caves in the jungle-clad mountains until danger passed.

Kathy skimmed the remaining pages of the exercise book. The entire period of interest was missing. The latter entries picked up where her sister and their mother returned to the farm and started over.

Her head throbbed and her feet ached from pounding the cobblestones of Mitte. She tossed the journal onto the bedside table, rearranged the pillows, snapped off the lamp.

In the dark, she puzzled over one question: what happened between April 1942 and December 1943? Tomorrow's meeting with Horst might shed some light. If not, she'd ask outright. There was no guarantee that he'd be any the wiser. Perhaps she'd never find out.

She fell asleep with the thought that, when it came to Alice, one answer was never enough. An answer always led to more questions.

~

In the morning, she met Horst at his apartment and they walked to the Swan Café. The weather had turned nasty. The clouds sagged with moisture and a freezing wind got into Kathy's eyes and made them run. Under her padded raincoat she wore an expensive woollen pullover, purchased on impulse at KaDeWe the previous day, which kept her body snug and warm.

At the café they ordered *Milchkaffee* and *Bienenstich* and sat inside. Apart from theirs, every table was vacant. Apparently, it was too early for the regulars. Horst informed her that the old men would drift in around ten.

'You said you never came here.' Kathy wrapped her hands around the hot mug.

'I lied.' He grinned. 'Remember, my dear, even elders don't always speak the truth.'

She frowned. 'What about the other things you've told me?'

His reply was a shake of the head. 'With you, I am as honest as possible. After all these years, I have holes in my memory. Just as we both have holes in our knowledge of Alice.' He paused and looked Kathy in the eye. 'Please tell me about her. Every last detail. Our correspondence was patchy. We lost contact entirely a few years ago.'

Kathy chewed on her lip. 'That was probably when she went into the nursing home.'

'And I moved into my apartment. Our letters must have gone astray.' He examined his fingernails. 'Why was she in a nursing home?'

What could she say, other than the truth? 'The last years of Alice's life were not easy,' she began. 'She had a terrible fall and broke her hip. Everything went downhill from there.'

Horst's expression was grim but he nodded encouragement for her to continue. 'I want to know every detail,' he said.

'When Alice couldn't manage on her own, she moved into residential care in Brisbane and we sold the Toowoomba cottage which, as the eldest, she'd inherited outright. By then she was in her eighties but she still had her wits about her. As you know, she never married. I was her closest blood relative and also her power of attorney. It was sad to let the cottage go, but it had to be done. My childhood home held all kinds of sentimental treasures that had to be disposed of.

'Amongst the bric-a-brac and junk were two things that caught my eye. The first was a book about internment in Australia, which I took home and read. The second was a wooden box at the back of Alice's wardrobe. Inside was a lifetime of souvenirs. An old pair of leather shoes, a train ticket, some pressed flowers, a lock of hair, bits and pieces that meant nothing to me but the world to her. I took it to her at the nursing home. Instead of thanking me, she flew into a rage. "How dare you go through my things!"

'That was typical of our relationship. When I was a kid, Alice was wonderful to me, but as adults we clashed. In her opinion, I was never smart enough or industrious enough or thoughtful enough. Meanwhile she turned into a saint. When her nursing career was over, she and her friend, Simpson, established A-Z House, a refuge for children who'd been victims of abuse or whose parents weren't able to raise them. At first, Alice and Simpson ran it together; then they employed staff and volunteers. Later it was set up as a proper charity with a board and a manager. Alice was still working there when she had the fall.

'After the operation on her hip, she couldn't remember how to walk. At rehab, she'd put one foot down then pick it up again. Concerned about a possible head injury, the therapist suggested further tests. A scan showed lesions on the brain. My dear sister, the most intelligent and determined woman I've ever known, was diagnosed with dementia.'

Kathy paused and looked up at Horst. His blue eyes were swimming in tears. She squeezed his hand and he squeezed back. For several minutes they sat in silence.

'Of course, I didn't tell her. That would have upset her even more. She went through a period of knowing she wasn't right and being frustrated with herself. Sometimes she could see the funny side. Later, reality and wild imaginings flowed into each other. Correcting her was a waste of breath. Her mind was a colander and she filled the holes with made-up stories.

'One morning I found her curled up on the bed, trembling with fear. She told me that men had kidnapped her in the night and interrogated her about our mother. Her distress was so real that I marched straight down to see the Director of Nursing.

'The DON said, "Oh no, that would have been a dream. She slept soundly all night." She showed me Alice's chart. Between the hours of ten and six, three different carers had checked on her. On each occasion, she was asleep and comfortable. "With dementia, vivid dreams are common. Dreams are their reality."

'I asked what to do. The nurse told me to sit with her until she calmed down, which I did. That's when I realised that the frail woman in the nursing-home bed was no longer my sister.

'As time passed, the things she said and the companions she invented became more fanciful. One day, while I was in her room, a little dog came and sat by her chair. "Oh, here's Pixie," she said. She babbled away and offered it chocolates that she'd won at a game of table-bowls. Only there was no dog. Just a patch of sunlight on the pale carpet. In my schoolteacher voice, I said that I couldn't see any dog and asked her where it was. Alice snapped, "Are you blind, girl? Pixie's right there in front of you!" Then she reached down and stroked the air with her hand.'

'*Gott im Himmel!*' Horst shook his head. 'I had no idea. Poor Alice.'

Kathy drained her cup. If she stopped talking now, she'd never get it all out. Those months had been heart-wrenching, not only for Alice, but also for her, the younger sister who was supposed to help but found the responsibility impossible to bear. Instead of feeling compassion, she'd become consumed by anger. She was angry with Alice for her illness; angry with the medical profession for having no cure; angry with herself for being unable to kindle the angelic flame of kindness that had burnt in Alice.

'Not long before the end, a new companion came on the scene. His name, she told me, was Horst. I took little notice. To me, he was just another imaginary visitor who turned up at night when she was frightened or alone.

'On what was to be my final visit, Alice was confined to bed. By then her body was shrivelled and her skin was transparent. Her skeletal hand pressed a piece of card into my palm. "Promise me," she said. Her voice was weak but she clung to me like a clam. "When I die, promise that you will tell Horst in person." Her eyes were moist and pleading like a puppy. But all I could feel was revulsion. My heart had turned to stone.

'To humour her, I made the vow. Then I asked if his phone number was in her little black book. Alice glared at me. Even close to the end, she could make me feel like a fool. In my family, it was always Alice and Mum against the world. That pair were like best friends or conspirators. I was on the outer, an inconvenience, the baby who knew nothing. "Horst doesn't have a telephone." Alice sniffed. "We *correspond*."

'I glanced at the card. It was an old photo of a young man. Half a photo, to be precise. Hacked with scissors, one edge was jagged and off-square. I asked if the man was Horst. "Who else would it be?" she said. "I've told you all about him."

'I raked through my memory, for I'd dismissed the tales about him as nonsense. In previous weeks, we'd had several bizarre conversations about nothing at all.

'Wondering what I'd let myself in for, I asked for his address. In her usual superior tone, she announced that her friend, Horst Schuhmacher, lived in Berlin. After that, she fell quiet and drifted off. But she was not done with me yet. A moment later, her eyes sprang open. "If that's all, you can go. My secretary will get back to you with the information. Good day."

'I kissed her forehead and said goodbye. At the doorway I turned, as I always did, for one last glimpse. She was asleep. Later, the DON phoned and broke the sad news.'

'And here you are now,' said Horst. 'You believed Alice enough to make a journey half-way around the world to find me. I am truly honoured.' His cheeks glistened with tears.

Kathy put her arms around him. 'The honour is mine. I'm so glad I came. I wish we'd met sooner.'

'Life takes us on many strange journeys, most of which we survive.'

As predicted, the café was filling up with elderly customers seeking coffee and camaraderie. Outside, the rain had stopped. She glanced at her wristwatch. Ten o'clock.

'Perfect weather for a stroll. Would you like to see my *Kleingarten*?' said Horst.

'I don't know what a *Kleingarten* is, but I'd love a walk.' She patted her paunch. 'Too much food and not enough exercise.'

'*Ach* at my age, food is what I live for. We will take with us a loaf of rye bread and some Wurst and beer.'

After leaving the café, they detoured to Netto for supplies, which Horst stowed in a khaki knapsack. They ambled past the lake and veered onto a narrow track. On either side were small fenced allotments with huts and gardens. Flower gardens, vegetable gardens, groves of fruit trees, slat benches, gnomes, miniature windmills, fairy lanterns. While no two plots were alike, they had one thing in common. Love.

Horst stopped and opened a gate. 'Welcome to my home away from home.' A flagstone path led to a painted wooden hut with a green central door and sash windows either side. Quaint and simple, like a three-year-old's drawing of a house. The garden had apple trees, rose bushes, and vegetables, all flourishing and well-kept.

He unlocked the door and they entered a single room with all the essentials for living. Table and chairs, cooker, bar fridge, sink, stretcher bed. The miniature house reminded her of the cubby that her father had built her in the backyard. She'd practically lived in that cubby, along with a menagerie of toy animals, her only playmates.

Horst said, 'This allotment has been passed down from Opa to my father, and then to me. It has fed my family and kept us amused since before the First World War.'

Such a tradition warranted a compliment in its native language. '*Dein Kleingarten ist wirklich schön*,' she said, using her best pronunciation.

'*Danke schön*.' He grinned from ear to ear. 'Glad you like it.'

A tour of the garden revealed more plants than she'd first thought. As well as vegetables, there were herbs and medicinal plants including lovage, sage, camomile, and a glossy bay tree in a pot.

Inside again, Horst produced two tumblers which he filled with beer. He cleared his throat and said, 'And so, we come to the camp. This was where I spent most of my time in Australia.'

Kathy leant on the table, wondering what would be revealed. It needled her that Alice would never talk about the war. Her mind was always on the children's refuge or matters that she'd discuss at length with Simpson, never with her.

The sisters grew further and further apart. At university, Kathy was attracted to politics while Alice cared only about saving souls. On Kathy's wedding day, Alice left early because of an emergency at the refuge. The day Stephanie was born, Alice was caught up in meetings with adoptive parents. Other people always came first.

Horst continued. 'As you've probably gathered, the camp I refer to was an internment camp. It was located deep in the countryside of Victoria, far away from towns and cities. The first day, when the truck drove us through the security gates, I was struck by the number of gardens. Except for the towering eucalypts and screeching parrots, those gardens were not so different from my *Berliner Kleingarten*. We grew cabbages, turnips, carrots, potatoes, parsley, dill. With the produce, we cooked good German meals which nourished our bodies and souls.' He paused for a swallow of beer.

'So that's it? Or is there more to your time in internment?'

'Patience, my dear. The family camp was home for five years.'

'The family camp,' echoed Kathy. 'Mum mentioned the family camp from time to time. As a youngster, I thought it was for holidays.'

'Did Alice ever speak of it?'

Kathy thought back. 'I suspected that she and Mum lived in the south for a while but Alice would never say why. I read a police report that mentioned Bruno Zanetti, her father. It made me so angry. So-called "witnesses" accused him of using a hurricane lamp to signal the enemy. Why would an Italian-Australian farmer send secret signals to Japanese fighter pilots? It didn't make sense. If he used a hurricane lamp, it would have been to work on the farm after dark. There was also a report about the Italian Club at Currawong, which named Mum. Nothing at all about Alice.'

Horst said, 'When Alice went to the camp, she was seventeen. Parents could take dependent children to the family camp if they had nobody to look after them.'

'Now I understand. Italian parents are very strict, especially with daughters.' Kathy reflected for a moment. 'According to the police report, the women of the Italian Club started a language school in 1936. They asked the Consul for suitable textbooks and funds to employ a part-time teacher. The police seemed to think that the Club was a rats-nest of fascists and enemy spies. After the husbands were interned, they suspected that the wives would cause trouble.'

'So, they locked up the women as well,' said Horst, shaking his head. 'From what I knew of Maria Zanetti, as she was then, all she wanted was to teach the children proper Italian.'

'When I was a child, she tried to teach me but I wasn't interested. In the 50s and 60s, Italian migrants swarmed into Australia and the Aussies tried to stop them. If you were Italian then, you were abused, called awful things, excluded from everything. For me, even my name was a problem. Katerina Maria Giuliano: what a mouthful. On the first day at school, I called myself *Kathy*. Later on, attitudes changed. By the time I married Jack, being Italian was considered interesting and exotic. I kept my maiden name because I liked the sound of it and I also adored my father.'

'What's in a name?' Horst paused for dramatic effect. 'A name defines and labels you. I must admit, it was a relief to shed my assumed name after the war. However, after reverting to my former name, I faced problems that were even harder to resolve.' He refilled the glasses and took a swallow of beer. For a moment his brow furrowed and he stared vacantly out the window. Suddenly he cleared his throat and turned to face Kathy. 'Now, where was I?'

'The family camp,' she said.

Eight

We arrived in September 1940. The train from Melbourne deposited us near a tiny town called Rushworth. The soldiers called the roll and sorted us by nationality: Germans at one end of the platform, Italians at the other. We climbed into the backs of army trucks, sat knee-to-knee on the luggage. Werner and I stuck to each other like glue. With hundreds of men and just three trucks, not everyone went in the first run. Some remained at the siding under guard to be picked up later.

Our little convoy barrelled along a straight dirt track through forests and pastures. As the sun dipped onto the horizon, the sky lit up in a spectacular display of red and pink and orange. The trees came alive with bright parrots; kookaburras chortled like drunken sailors. Kangaroos hopped about the sunburnt fields. I'd seen kangaroos before, at the Berlin Zoo, but this was the first time in the wild. I pointed them out to Werner, who seemed as excited as me.

The drive took about twenty minutes. The camp was completely different to expectations, which were extremely low after the rat-infested mill in England. Apart from the usual show of military security—barbed wire, guard towers, floodlights—it could have passed for a recreation camp in the countryside. Inside the enclosure, long huts nestled between lofty gum trees. In the last rays of sunlight, the roofs glittered like mirrors. Suddenly the temperature dropped and I was glad to jump down from the open truck.

On the train, I had done a headcount and ascertained that all the *Arandora Star* survivors were going to the same place. We didn't know what would become of the other *Dunera* passengers, including Georg, but I wished them the best. I also hoped our new home would live up to first impressions.

The three-metre-high gates opened, the truck rolled through, the gates were locked behind us. Some of the existing inmates gathered around to welcome us. All were native speakers of German. A stout fellow with a loud voice introduced himself as Manfred Wiesbaden, the elected leader of Camp 2 and launched into a speech.

'Make no mistake,' he said at the end, 'here we are loyal to *Der Führer* and the Third Reich.'

I glanced at Werner. His face gave nothing away, but I sensed he was seething inside. Anti-Nazis and pacifists like us would have a tough time here. Wiesbaden's words were a timely warning that I must mind my tongue.

We were given a short tour of the compound: the ablutions block; the mess hut; the cookhouse, a primitive affair with steam boilers fuelled by firewood. We stopped at a rustic café with a hand-painted sign. *Kaffeehaus*. The walls were painted red and white with black Swastikas, similar to the Nazi national flag. Wiesbaden explained that the café had been designed and built by internees. It was well patronised too. A dozen men in maroon-dyed uniforms sat at outside tables having their coffee and cake.

'Open every afternoon,' said Wiesbaden. 'A casual meeting place for patriotic Germans. In this camp, we are all members of the *Deutscher Turn-Verein*. I strongly encourage you to join.'

My mind flashed back to the *Hitlerjungend*, the youth club for the sons of good Nazis. As a boy I had been obliged to join, but I wagged more meetings than I attended. At the time, I thought it was clever to avoid all that marching and chanting, to kick a football in the Schillerpark instead. Later, I wondered if my rebellious streak had triggered my father's decision to banish me to England. The camp I was in now was indisputably run by Nazis. If I did not show respect, my life would not be worth a *Pfennig*.

The tour of the camp ended at the sleeping quarters, which were long corrugated-iron huts with timber frames, designed to accommodate twenty-four persons. Two central runs of double-decker bunks divided the space into two. Along either side was a corridor, wide enough for a small table or a desk and a few chairs. Although the hopper windows were open, the hut felt airless and stuffy. We were each issued a palliasse, a bedsheet, and five grey army blankets. Werner and I claimed two bunks not far from the second exit. I took the top one and Werner took the bottom.

Making my bed was tricky; I had to balance on the nogging and wrestle the covers into position. Meanwhile, Werner unpacked his duffel bag and arranged his medical books on a timber ledge. Later we walked to the mess hut for the evening meal, which was curiously called *tea*.

To my relief, food was plentiful and good. The basics—flour, sugar, leaf-tea, milk—were supplied by the army. Vegetables and herbs grown in the *Kleingärten* gave us the flavours of home. By luck or design, our camp was located in the Goulburn Valley, a district of orchards and vineyards.

Always we had fresh fruit on the table. Depending on the season there'd be apples, pears, oranges, peaches, plums, or grapes.

Our meal that first night was white bean soup with crusty bread, followed by *Apfelkuchen*. Warm and comforting, the sort of food Mutti would have dished up at home. I found out later that the camp cook was actually a qualified chef who'd worked at the German Club in Sydney and his assistants were fellow internees.

Afterwards, Wiesbaden gave a speech about how the camp operated. He said that we'd be paid one shilling per day for doing jobs that were approved by the army. Fruit-picking for local farmers, building huts and the like.

'However,' he warned, 'such activities help our enemies. The fruit you pick will be canned and shipped to Europe to feed the British military. The huts you build will expand the capacity of the camp. More accommodation means that more patriotic Germans will be deprived of their liberty.' He paused for this information to sink in.

Speaking slowly and with emphasis, he continued. 'In this camp, any man doing such work will be considered a traitor to the Fatherland.' The word *traitor* carried all the weight. Nobody dared ask what the punishment would be.

Wiesbaden went on to say that the compound did not run itself. All inmates were required to share the housekeeping, which included mopping floors, cleaning the latrines, chopping firewood, gardening, preparing food. 'While housekeeping is unpaid, it brings its own rewards: comradery, satisfaction, health, cleanliness. Keeping busy also helps time to pass.'

After tea, Werner beckoned to me. 'Let's walk.'

The sky was inky-black, dotted with a million stars. The night air snapped with cold. The floodlights along the perimeter fence blazed as bright as day. We strolled by the inner fence, in plain sight of the guards and other internees. The older men were out in force, taking exercise in the evening chill. Up, down, and around they marched, in pairs or alone. Waves of never-ending motion.

As a newcomer, the sounds of the night were strange and eerie. Devilish shadows glided above, shrieking and flapping leathery wings. Breathy grunts came from the trees. From a distance came ghostly screams that turned my spine to jelly. Oblivious, Werner continued walking. I swallowed my fear and kept pace.

When we were out of earshot of the others, Werner relaxed a little. 'From Wiesbaden's speech, it is clear who is running this camp. Unless we toe the Nazi line, we are in for a difficult time. Supporting a regime that I despise goes against my nature. However, for the sake of us both, I am prepared to do whatever is necessary to survive. I apologise in advance. Please do not think badly of me for being a coward or a hypocrite.'

'Don't apologise, Werner. I trust your judgement and will follow your lead.'

Werner thumped me on the back. 'That's the spirit. We must think of this as theatre; we are characters in a play. Yes, that's the answer. With practice, you and I will become magnificent pseudo-Nazis. Shhh! Promise you will *never* speak of this to anyone.'

I gave him my word and we shook hands on it, but the prospect was terrifying. For a start, I was a dreadful actor and a worse card player. My face betrayed me every time. Already I was living a lie because of my name. This would make matters worse. Werner suggested that I find a quiet spot and chant the Nazi slogans until I could do so with conviction. The kookaburras laughed at me, but after few hours of practice, I became confident.

I kept my word to Werner and, until today, I remained silent.

After breakfast the next day, Werner and I went to the camp leader's office intending to sign up for housekeeping duties. We were not alone; a queue of about twenty had already formed. All were survivors of the *Arandora Star* and the *Dunera*. Some were true Nazis who'd stood up to the British guards and terrorised the Jews on the voyage.

I am neither a Nazi nor a Jew. In Berlin, I had seen many things that made me uneasy. My observations caused conflict with my father, who was an astute businessman and a Nazi of convenience. Max saw the rise of the regime as a business opportunity and went to great lengths to cultivate friendships with the men in power. Not that he was without morals. Far from it. However, from my naïve perspective, I believed his sole motivation was to make money. After the war, when I returned to Berlin, the truth came out and I learnt about my father the hard way.

To remain safe in this camp, my performance had to be convincing. When my turn came to sign the housekeeping list, I hesitated. Even my name, Schuhmacher, was a sham. I had never written it before and had no ready signature. As I leant over the paper, the eyes of Wiesbaden's secretary bored into my skull. Panicking, I made some indecipherable scribble and told him I could repair shoes.

'Excellent,' he said. 'This will be of great use in the camp. You can start with mine.' With that, he promptly removed his boots and dumped them on the table. They were in a dreadful state. 'Have them done before dinner.'

Taking them, I asked where to find materials and a workplace.

The secretary scoffed. 'Here we improvise or perish.'

With my tail between my legs, I made the Nazi salute and retreated. How could I work with no equipment? Improvise or perish. Pah! If it weren't so serious, I might have laughed.

After leaving the tattered boots in my hut, I wandered around the compound, worrying about what would happen if I failed. Beyond the sleeping huts was a shed that was buzzing with activity. The scent of fresh-cut timber drifted through the doorway. I peeked inside. It was a workshop of sorts. Laid out on benches were projects at various stages of execution: kiddies' toys, picture frames, chess sets, jewellery boxes.

'Come in, laddie.' The fellow who spoke had a tree-root in one hand and a primitive tool in the other. 'Take a look around.'

I wandered to his bench. 'What are you making?'

'Furniture for my little girl's doll house. This will be a bathtub.'

Fascinated, I watched him remove the pulp with a curved piece of glass. Shavings curled in ringlets. The glorious aroma of fresh-cut wood took be back to the Berlin Christmas markets. I must have closed my eyes at the delightful memory.

Picking up on the sentiment, the woodcarver sighed. 'I wonder if we will ever see our dear homeland again.'

I lingered at the workshop; it felt safe just to be there. All the tools were improvised. Fret saws were made from metal strapping; scrapers from glass; chisels from fire-hardened wood; hammer heads from stone. Simple but effective. I asked if I could work there and was told to come any morning between seven and twelve. Then I told him about my impossible task.

'We can fix that, can't we comrades?' said the woodcarver. Everyone agreed without hesitation. He set down the scraping tool and turned to face me. He was fine-featured and clean-shaven all over, including the dome of his skull. 'You can borrow our tools and equipment. Everyone needs help at first.'

I thanked them all and raced to my hut to get the boots. After closer examination, my spirits sank. The upper of one was beyond repair, while the sole the other had broken apart. This was no simple glue and clamp job. At the workshop, I asked where to find leather, any variety, any condition. Try the rubbish tip, they said.

After picking through a pile of stinking refuse, I found what I needed. A single abandoned boot. It looked as if it had been run over by a truck, but most of the leather was intact. Perfect. Using borrowed tools, windfall leather, and all the tricks Opa had taught me, I set to work on the secretary's boots. When they were done, I polished them, wrapped them in cloth, and took them to the camp leader's office. Outside the mess hut, the dinner bell was clanging.

The secretary looked up from the typewriter and said, 'What do we have here?'

'Your boots, sir.' I placed the parcel on the desk.

In socks he padded across the floorboards. 'You mean you've actually fixed them?'

He peeled off the cloth and picked one up. The renovated leather glistened like coal. He picked up the other, turned it over, ran his finger along the seams. 'This work is most satisfactory.'

'Thank you, sir. I took your advice and improvised.'

The corner of his lips lifted. 'Good lad.'

'So, can I repair shoes as housekeeping? Can I put up a sign?'

'You won't need to advertise. The work will speak for itself.' The secretary wriggled his feet into the boots and gave back the cloth. 'Now, if that's all …'

Did I dare to put my big idea into words? Here was an opportunity to make use of my skills instead of frittering time away. My heart was in my mouth. I could scarcely believe it was my voice that spoke. 'There is another thing, sir. I am not a cobbler but a shoemaker. If I could get the right leather, I could make new shoes to measure.'

His eyes locked onto mine. 'You mean, run a business?'

'Not exactly. I'd make them at cost.' My courage was fading.

'Let me speak with the camp leader. I'll let you know.'

I thanked him and escaped before I crumbled. As I saw it, two major obstacles would have to be overcome: sourcing leather and purchasing it without any money. The first would take some research and the second might be possible with the help of a small loan. Sadly, my knowledge of Australian leather suppliers was zero, and I knew no-one who could help, either with information or financially. I kicked myself for being impulsive and making a proposition that was not properly thought through.

Weeks passed with no word from the secretary. Impatient, I found a quiet spot in the garden where I could think.

At our factory in Berlin, I had been Opa's understudy for as long as I could remember. While my father did the books and dealt with contracts, Opa designed the products and made patterns for our workers to cut out and assemble. It was Opa who came up with the concept of heavy-duty footwear for the military. The thick-soled boots could withstand all terrains, from marshlands to deserts, mountain tracks to city cobblestones. Worn with thick woollen socks, they were warm enough for snow. In 1938, the year I was sent to England, my father landed a contract with the Wehrmacht on one condition: that the product passed a rigorous testing regime.

The odour of leather was imprinted on my brain. One day I would inherit the family business and become a third-generation footwear manufacturer. But that was long into the future. When I made my bold proposal to the camp leader's secretary, I was a kid of eighteen, still wet behind the ears.

After giving myself a good talking-to, I decided that my ambitious plan was all too hard. I would revise my housekeeping duties and volunteer to muck out the latrines instead.

When Werner found me, I was glum. To cheer me up he invited me to the *Kaffeehaus*. 'My treat. I earned two shillings today.'

'Are you working for our enemies now?' I said sarcastically.

'Of course not! I have started a language school. For a small fee, students can receive tuition in English, Russian, or Italian from a fluent speaker.'

'That hardly counts as housekeeping.'

'Maybe not, but it beats some of the other chores on offer.' Werner gave me a nudge and a grin. 'And I also get pocket-money to take friends for coffee and cake.'

Immediately my mood lightened. I could not have asked for a better friend.

The *Kaffeehaus* was bustling. Going on four o'clock, most of the tables were taken. At the counter was a coffee urn and a selection of tempting cakes. We sat on chairs made of branches artfully bound together with twine. Rustic yet attractive, another example of quality craftsmanship within the camp.

Werner raised his water glass. 'To better days. *Prost.*'

Our glasses clinked and I downed the contents. A millisecond later I realised the liquid was not water. I spluttered and coughed and tried to catch my breath.

'Apple schnapps.' Werner buried his face in a hanky to hide his amusement.

'Where … did you get … schnapps?' I gasped.

'I know a fellow who makes it. Actually, he's a winemaker. His apple schnapps is excellent, don't you think? Have you seen the still?'

I grabbed the coffee mug and took a swallow. Scalding hot, it intensified the burning in my throat.

Werner didn't seem to notice. 'How many men are in our hut?'

'Twenty-four.'

'Incorrect. You have counted bunks, not men,' he said patiently. 'We have twenty-four bunks and twenty-two men. Two bunks are not used for sleeping.'

'What? You mean this liquor still is hidden under our noses?'

'You could say that. I think it's rather clever. If the guards found out, there'd be a dreadful fuss. But who'd suspect a sleeping hut to be also a distillery?'

Glancing around, I saw that all the other café patrons had the same 'water' glasses. 'How long has this been going on?'

'Ever since this camp has existed. Would you like another shot?'

'No thanks.' I shovelled cake into my mouth.

When Werner left the table to speak with another Austrian elder, I eased back in the chair and let my mind wander. Internment was a curse but also a salvation. Although we were confined within barbed wire, we had all the necessities of life. In fact, we were quite comfortable. One day, when the war was over, we would return to the Fatherland, untouched by the horrors of the battlefield. Here, in the most isolated continent on earth, we were quarantined from the madness that had infected all of Europe and the rest of the world.

Later, I went in search of the liquor still. Now that I knew it was there, it was not hard to find, nestled amongst timber bunk frames and covered in blankets. The device consisted of two metal drums, connected by various bits of copper pipe. The larger drum sat on a low stand with a metal fire box beneath. The smaller drum sat on the bunk above. According to Werner, most of the materials had been mined from the same rubbish tip that I'd raided myself. Ingenious.

Weeks passed. No word about my shoemaking proposal. I'd decided to pass on latrine duty. I was feeling low on account of a toothache.

Werner brought me schnapps in a tin pannikin. 'Rub this around your sore tooth. Alcohol is an antiseptic; it will clear the infection.'

I did as he said. My gums tingled and the pain eased a bit, but I feared the tooth would have to come out.

'Now, drink the evidence,' he said.

No sooner had I downed the alcohol than one of Wiesbaden's henchmen burst into the hut. 'Schuhmacher, the camp leader wants to see you immediately.'

The toothache was forgotten. What had I done wrong? As I trotted along the path, my mind whirred through the past weeks when I might have let slip some anti-Nazi sentiment. I could think of nothing, apart from a few whispered conversations with Werner.

Out of breath, I entered the camp leader's office.

'*Ach*, our young entrepreneur!' said Wiesbaden. 'My secretary says you have a business proposition. Would you kindly fill me in?'

Relief. However, I was not yet off the hook. The schnapps had stripped me of inhibitions so I gave a sketchy outline in a voice that brimmed with bravado. After talking to my woodworker friends, I'd worked out ways around the obstacles. The key was to garner the support of the Commandant, the Australian boss of the four Tatura camps. Only he could approve the purchase of the necessary materials. To do this I had to rely on Wiesbaden, for he was the only internee in our compound with direct access to the Commandant.

'What makes you think this plan will work?' said Wiesbaden when I'd finished my spiel.

'I know the business. My father is a footwear maker, and so was his father before him.' I glanced at the desk where the secretary was scribbling in a journal. On his feet were the boots I'd renovated, mercifully intact. 'As for craftsmanship, ask your secretary.'

'One thing you have, young man, is determination.' Wiesbaden signalled to one of his servants, who scurried off and reappeared with two mugs of milk coffee. 'Before we proceed, tell me your name.'

'Horst Schuhmacher.'

'A shoemaker with the name *Schuhmacher*? How very convenient.' He smirked and leant back in the chair. 'Now, tell me your real name.'

'It is true,' I said a little too earnestly.

'And your family owns a footwear business. Where is the factory? What is the brand?'

My brain was dull from the schnapps I'd skolled not ten minutes earlier. I was casting about for an answer that would not put Max or Opa in the firing line. Stalling, I took a mouthful of steaming coffee. Pain shot through my jaw. I made an involuntarily gasp; air hissed between my teeth.

'I'm waiting,' said Wiesbaden.

'The workshop is on the outskirts of Berlin. It's very small.'

'How many workers?'

'Last time I counted, two.' This was a half-truth, for my last visit to the workshop was on a Sunday.

'Hmm. And the brand?'

'We don't have a brand; we make shoes to order.' The sweat of a liar was trickling down my spine. I hoped my face had not gone red, as it usually did when I was under pressure.

After a moment that felt like an age, Wiesbaden placed his fingers together like a steeple. 'Very well, Herr Schuhmacher the Third, I shall speak with the Commandant about your idea.' He rose from the chair; the interrogation was over.

Remembering protocols, I snapped to attention, clicked my heels and raised my arm in the Nazi salute. '*Heil Hitler.*' I made a move toward the door.

'Schuhmacher,' Wiesbaden called after me.

I froze and turned.

'You should have that bad tooth seen to,' he said. 'The dentist's surgery is at Camp 1. Ask my secretary to make an appointment.'

Due to the medicinal properties of apple schnapps or the threat of the dentist's chair, my toothache disappeared the moment I left the camp leader's office. On the walk back to the hut, my mind replayed the interview over and over, and eventually I convinced myself that the venture would receive support. According to my optimistic analysis, I had little to lose and plenty to gain.

When I told Werner, he gave me a congratulatory pat on the back. 'This, my dear boy, will be your making. Experiences like this bring out the best in us.'

He poured two celebratory shots of schnapps and then I was floating on air. Yes, this was an opportunity in the midst of adversity. Our camp alone held one thousand internees. The Tatura group had three other camps, plus guards and their families. Not everyone would want to buy shoes, but I'd seen the outrageous prices in the mail-order catalogues and was certain that my products would be cheaper and better. However, before I could begin, I needed to find a reliable supply of leather. This lay in the hands of the Commandant.

While I waited for his blessing, I raided the rubbish tip and made a kit of tools, cajoled fellow inmates into parting with old leather items so that I could start on repairs. In the course of a week, I made a cutting-knife and a leather-punch, and acquired three odd boots. Word got around and I was inundated with work.

I became known as the *Bootmaker of Tatura*. Outside work, I was wary about friendships and my face was a mask when dealing with Wiesbaden and his cronies. To borrow Werner's words, I had become a *magnificent pseudo-Nazi*.

Periodically, volunteers from the Red Cross came and spoke with us about our health and the treatment we received from our captors. Mostly I had no complaints, but on this occasion, I lined up with all the old whingers. One piece of equipment was critical to my venture, and it could not be improvised from scrap metal and castoffs. I decided that asking the Red Cross was worth a shot. After all, they had supplied other items to make our lives more comfortable. Things like light summer clothing, footballs, a gramophone for the mess hall.

The volunteers spoke English and the whingers spoke German, so a soldier who had a smattering of German would normally interpret. While waiting in the queue, I heard about the terrible misunderstandings that had occurred. That day, the interpreter did not turn up; the whingers had to rely on their meagre English vocabulary.

The complaint of the day was the oversupply of some foods and the undersupply of others. At the head of the queue, one elder named Herr Fritz was bumbling through several failed attempts. Finally, his frustration exploded. '*Dieses Schaffleisch* … um … how you say … um … sheepmeat … *dieses* sheepmeat *ist Gift*!'

The Red Cross volunteer turned to his colleague. 'I don't get it. He seems upset, but then he says that mutton is a gift.'

The absurdity was driving me to distraction. I walked up the queue and stood beside Herr Fritz, who was grinding his right fist into his left palm.

I said to the volunteer, '*Gift* means poison. He says that the only meat we get is mutton and it tastes like poison. Germans like pork, not mutton.'

Herr Fritz nodded vigorously. '*Danke schön.*'

The volunteer sighed. 'Thank you. Our interpreter is sick today. Can you help us?'

I glanced down the line. Twenty of the camp's oldest and frailest inmates were standing in the hot sun. My intention was to make the request for a sewing machine and return to the workshop. I didn't have the heart to let them down.

For the next two hours, the interviews continued. During that time, I learnt more about the camp than in all the months I had been there. Buoyed that their interpreter was young and courteous, and not an Australian soldier or one of Wiesbaden's thugs, the old internees spoke frankly. Like me, most were survivors of a shipwreck and a hell-ship. On that count we were all equals.

They spoke about death threats made by their own countrymen, who'd been brainwashed by Hitler's disciples. Others said that they'd fled the Nazi reign of terror, only to be imprisoned with their tormentors. Some could not understand why they had been interned at all; their only crime was being German. They asked for the government to recognise them as refugees and release them into the community. Either that, or separate them from their enemies within the compound.

When the last of the old men had been heard and his complaints translated, the volunteers began to pack up. 'Thank you, young fella,' said one dismissively.

'Wait, you haven't heard my request.'

The other made a show of checking his wristwatch. 'We're out of time, mate. There's one train to Melbourne and we're on it.'

'Two minutes, that's all I need.'

'Very well,' said the first. 'Walk to the gate with us.'

The distance between the mess hut, where the interviews were held, and the exit gate was short. In fifty strides, I explained my shoemaking proposition and said I needed a sewing machine. 'Any brand, any condition, but I have no money to pay you.'

'We'll be in touch,' said the one in the greatest hurry.

A guard opened the inside gate and the pair scurried into no-man's land between the two fences. A moment later, they were through the second gate. With a cursory wave, they climbed into the army truck to be driven to the railway station. From there, they'd relax on a pleasant ride through the countryside, and later return to their comfortable homes in the suburbs.

Standing by the fence, I watched until the dust-cloud kicked up by the speeding truck evaporated in the distance. Not knowing what to expect, I plodded back to the mess hut for dinner. Boiled mutton with cabbage.

Nine

After a year in internment, all our shoes were wearing thin. I continued to do repairs, working long hours in the hobbies shed, the temperature of which varied from equatorial hot to arctic cold. While I had no shortage of paying customers, the lack of materials made it impossible to meet demand. I relied heavily on second-hand leather, which came mainly from old shoes and leather jackets. The coins used within the camp were tokens, which had no value in the outside world. For my efforts, I earnt lots of camp tokens. But to buy new shoe leather, I would have to exchange camp currency for pounds Sterling. Internees were not allowed to keep legal tender in the camp, so this was a significant problem.

When I discussed the matter with Werner, he suggested that I attend the Christian service held in the mess hut on Sundays. I told him I wasn't religious and that praying to the Good Lord for a financial miracle probably wasn't ethical anyway.

As usual, his response was sensible and convincing. 'Attending church won't hurt anyone and it might help you.'

I knew him well enough to get his meaning. Just as the *Kaffeehaus* attracted a certain clientele, so did the camp church. Belonging to the congregation was like belonging to a club. Werner knew all the members by name. Many were elderly and kept to themselves, but they trusted Dr Werner and consulted him for medical advice as well as language tuition.

Because I'd interpreted for the Red Cross that day, I had gained the trust of the anti-Nazis, a term loosely applied to communists, intellectuals, and Jews. While most kowtowed to Wiesbaden, the majority of inmates in our compound were neither Nazis nor anti-Nazis, but rather a cross-section of German-speaking Europeans who had differing backgrounds, loyalties, and beliefs.

The Sunday service was conducted in German by a Lutheran missionary who'd been in New Guinea. On the benches at the back of the hall sat the Red Cross regulars, the quiet antagonists of the Third Reich. Throughout the service, they remained as motionless as statues. Even during prayers, not a word left their lips. Afterwards, I asked Werner why they came if they didn't intend to participate.

'Things are not as they might seem.' Werner lit a cigarette and dismissed me with a plume of smoke. The topic was closed. He wandered away to speak with a group of language students.

I tucked his odd comment away, telling myself to be more observant, to heed nuances and loose lips. Cliques had formed, which I assumed had links to families or birthplaces or political alignments. The most vocal was the Nazi majority, which demanded loyalty and obedience. Several high-ranking Communist leaders were also in the camp, which created tensions. In my Berlin childhood, Communists and National Socialists would sometimes clash in the streets. The year I began *Gymnasium*—middle school—was the year Adolf Hitler became Chancellor. Within months, political activism ceased, replaced by military parades and 'spontaneous' demonstrations to celebrate the Third Reich. Dissidents either fled or vanished.

In February, the Red Cross volunteers returned and I was summoned to the mess hut. Expecting that I was required to interpret, I downed tools and strode through the scorching sun. The usual suspects had formed a queue outside, waiting for the doors to open. As I passed each one, I tipped my hat and received a handshake or a nod in return.

At the head of the line was Herr Fritz. '*Wir haben immer noch kein Kartoffeln*,' he said. 'How do you say this in English?'

I translated. 'We still have no potatoes.'

'*Ach, gut.* I will remember these words.' He grinned. '*Und wir haben zuviel Schaffleisch.*'

'And we have too much mutton.'

He repeated the sentence then added in accented English, 'Today you have a surprise.'

My eyebrows lifted. 'Your English is coming along nicely. Have you been practising?'

'Naturally. I learn from Dr Werner. My three friends also.' He pointed to his fellow students, who were standing further back in the queue. 'One … two … three'.

Not one would have been under the age of sixty. Each acknowledged me and smiled. The first time I met them, they were grim-faced characters without hope. Now they looked positively joyful. Perhaps Werner's lessons had helped. I tried to imagine my Austrian friend teaching English to four ageing Germans. I shook my head. The doctor certainly had a way with people.

I was supposed to be interpreting for the volunteers; the mess-hut door had just opened. Excusing myself, I hurried inside.

When I saw it, I could scarcely believe my eyes. The neat little machine had a shiny black body and *Singer* emblazoned in gold down the side. It had a shiny brass handwheel, a new leather drivebelt, and a black metal treadle. The wooden stand folded out as a work-table.

'I hope this fits the bill,' said the Red Cross volunteer. 'Tom and I went to a bit of trouble to get her into working order.'

'Too right,' said Tom. 'Stan found 'er at the dump. Dreadful condition. We fixed 'er up so she works real good.'

I ran my fingers over the smooth painted surface, gave the handwheel a turn. After all those months of waiting, I was convinced that my request had been ignored. I should have known not to expect instant results, especially during wartime.

'She's perfect! Thank you, thank you so much. This will make a big difference. I've been using a hand needle for repairs.' I unfurled my fingers to reveal callouses and scabs. 'But I still don't have the Commandant's approval to buy new leather.'

'Well, we'll soon see about that.' Stan cracked his knuckles like a boxer. 'After the interviews, we have an appointment with him. Your proposal will be top of the list.'

'Yes,' said Tom. 'It's a beauty of an idea. Everyone needs shoes. And, if it takes off, I'd imagine you'd train other blokes in the trade.'

To be honest, I hadn't thought that far ahead, but now it had been said, the idea had appeal. After seeing the difference that Werner's lessons had made to the old gents, I could see the benefits of sharing my skills. Apprentices would lighten my workload, in particular for the basic stitching and trimming. This would free me up to design and cut. Just like Opa.

Wait, I was getting ahead of myself. While Opa had shown me what to do and I had practised on offcuts, I had never actually made a single shoe from scratch. Of course I did not mention this to the volunteers, nor to anyone else. Except maybe Werner, whom I trusted with my life.

'Thank you again. Do you need me to interpret today?'

'No, we've got a soldier.' Stan took his place behind the table.

Outside, Herr Fritz slapped me on the back. 'Well, what do you think of the surprise?' He'd reverted to German. 'We helped them bring it in earlier.'

'It's exactly what I need.' And it was too. That little machine sewed like a dream.

Two days later, Wiesbaden called me in to say that leather would be purchased through the Quartermaster. I would reimburse the costs through the camp bank, which administered the money we earnt and spent. Through the bank, we could buy items such as clothing by mail order from Melbourne department stores. Through the bank, customers would pay me for shoes and I'd reimburse the Quartermaster the cost of materials.

Shortly after, the first batch of leather arrived. Even through the brown-paper wrapping, I could smell the rich bovine aroma of my childhood. At my little workbench, and under the supervision of my dear Opa, I'd make miniature boats and cars and trains from leather offcuts and a big pot of glue.

While waiting for the new Australian leather, I'd been busy taking orders, measuring feet, drafting patterns. Even guards had placed orders, which I put at the bottom of the pile. Countrymen ahead of captors. Thanks to my Singer, all the repair work was up to date.

In the hobbies workshop, I had my own bench and a spot under the window for the machine. Two woodworkers, who had asked to be 'apprentices', were learning to sew. They practised straight lines using an unthreaded needle on toilet paper. Sewing with a treadle was deceptively hard, a test of patience and dexterity. Perfect hand-eye-foot coordination was necessary, for the treadle and handwheel had minds of their own.

Tips for beginners. The handwheel always goes first, with a turn toward the operator. If the treadle starts first, the handwheel spins in the wrong direction and the thread breaks. If the treadle goes too fast, the needle judders up and down and makes a hole. If the treadle goes too slow, the feeder doesn't work and the thread tangles. Using a treadle sewing machine is like riding a bike: hard to learn and easy when you know how.

By the time the leather arrived, the apprentices had conquered the machine and could sew straight and around curves. I'm ashamed to say that I was just one step ahead of them, teaching myself at night and practising in the early morning before breakfast.

To fill all the orders, the team started work straight after rollcall and continued throughout the day, stopping only for smoko and dinner. In the evenings I'd work until lights-out at nine. Then I would creep back to my hut and fall into bed. Werner would click his tongue and say I was digging myself an early grave. But I was young and riding the wave. I got a thrill every time I saw a pair of my boots walking around the compound.

One morning, I woke to terrible pain, as if a red-hot iron was poking into my brain. Moaning, I sat up. Werner lit a cigarette; the smoke swirled up my nose. I sneezed; my head exploded. Well, that's what it felt like. I eased back onto the mattress, pulled the blanket over my eyes. At the workshop I had orders galore and customers I couldn't let down. Again, I tried to get up; the hut began to spin.

'What's the matter?' said Werner.

'I think it's my ear.'

'Roll over and I'll take a look.'

From a crevice near his bunk, Werner produced a tiny torch and a magnifying glass. He stepped up and shone the pin-light into my earholes. After a few *ah-hums*, he pronounced my ears to be perfectly clear and healthy.

'Come down and let me look in your mouth.'

With his help, I slid off the bunk and stumbled to a chair. The room whirled like a merry-go-round. I opened wide; the torch flicked from one set of molars to the other.

Hmmmm, said Werner several times.

My jaws were aching, my head was throbbing, I started to pull away.

'Hold still. Almost there.' He tapped my back teeth with the handle of the magnifying glass, starting at the top right. *Tink, tink.* On to the next. *Tink, tink.* He switched to the other side, then attacked the teeth at the bottom. *Tink, tink.* The sound vibrated like a xylophone; the pitch rose as he went up the scale.

With the heel of the handle, he touched a tooth on the lower left. To me it felt like the blow of a pick-axe.

'Ah-ha! I think we have it. You, my dear boy, are off to the dentist.'

'But I have to work,' I said feebly, cradling my jaw.

Werner shook his head. 'I'll not hear of it. Your lower second molar is badly infected; it will only get worse. You must go today. Wait here, I'll make the arrangements.'

A short time later Werner returned with Herr Fleischfresser, a man in a white coat with CDS embroidered on the pocket. The Camp Dressing Station was a first-aid clinic for cuts, strains, and sore toes. Its attendants were internees, trained by the army doctor. In a previous life, Fleischfresser had been a veterinarian in rural Baden-Württemberg, where his patients were draught horses, milk cows, and working dogs. I'd seen him before in the mess hut, but we had not spoken. Jokes used to circulate about a vet with a name that meant *carnivore* treating humans. If you got on the wrong side of him, it was said, he'd neuter you quicker than you could say his tongue-twister surname.

After a cursory examination, the vet said, 'This tooth needs urgent attention. Already I have telephoned the dentist and he will see you today. Follow me.'

I pulled on shirt and trousers and stumbled out the door. At the compound gate, we headed for the truck that transported rations and internees between camps. To my relief, I was allowed to ride in the passenger's seat and not made to sit in the tray back. Fleischfresser wished me luck and transferred my custody to a fifty-year-old army truckdriver. With every bump, pain speared through my head.

We reached Camp 1, home to the Waranga Hospital and the dental surgery. The waiting room reeked of antiseptic and primordial fear. At every squeal of the drill, my stomach did somersaults. The receptionist, a stout woman with shiny white teeth, took my details. With eyes lowered and jaws clenched, I plumped onto the nearest chair.

'Hey, Horst.' The voice was clear and familiar.

When I glanced up, I could have been looking in a mirror. Sandy hair, blue eyes, high forehead. My friend from the *Dunera*. 'Georg! I thought you were in Sydney.'

We clinched in a bear-hug.

'And I thought you were in Melbourne.' Georg was grinning from ear to ear. 'So, here we are in the Australian countryside, surrounded by birds and bushes.'

'When did you get here?'

'A few months ago. After we landed in Sydney, they sent us by train to a shit-hole in the middle of nowhere. All flies and dust and misery. Here is much better. Actually Camp 3, where I am, is rather nice.' Although we were in the waiting-room alone, his voice dropped to a whisper. 'Not so *political*, if you know what I mean.'

'I'm with Werner in Camp 2,' I whispered back. 'While we are okay so far, we have to watch what we say and do. A pack of Nazis are in charge of the camp.'

'No nasty Nazis in the family camp, thank God.'

The drill began to whine and Georg pulled a face. 'I hate dentists. I can't wait for this to be over so I can return to my nice little room.'

'What! You have your own room? Aren't you in a dormitory?'

'At Hay I was. But here, I have my own space. There are lots of activities too. Chess, theatre, art, lectures. And we have a piano. It's good to play music again.'

On the *Dunera*, Georg sometimes coaxed Beethoven out of a tuneless instrument that had survived years on the high seas. He'd confided that Beethoven was 'just for show'. The composer he admired was Mendelssohn, who'd been banned in Germany because of Jewish ancestry. I knew little about music, except for the pieces that Mutti played. Mendelssohn was also her favourite. As a child, I'd lie on the timber floor beneath the piano and feel the bass notes reverberate through my body. A beautiful memory.

The torturous drill stopped and voices through the wall indicated that the procedure was done. Georg was next. All of a rush I said, 'Do you think I could get a transfer to your camp?'

'Maybe. There's a spare bed in my room.'

'I thought you had a room to yourself.'

'For now. My room-mate was sent to another camp, but he'll be replaced for sure. If I had any choice, it would be you.' In his lap, Georg curled and uncurled his fingers. With renewed vigour, he said, 'I'll have a word with our camp leader. Camp 3 is a family camp. I'll say we are cousins. We look alike and our papers don't show otherwise.'

'I'll talk to Wiesbaden. How can we get in touch?'

'Go to the end of the corridor, the basin near the lavatories. There's a loose skirting board; behind it is "the mailbox". Make sure you're not seen.'

When I returned to my compound, I was missing two things: the pain in my head and my lower second molar. The first person I saw was Werner, who asked how it went. I showed him the cotton-wool that was packed around the wound to stop the bleeding. I was feeling a bit off from the laughing gas.

Werner made a noncommittal *ahem*. Then he put on his doctor's voice and instructed me to eat soft foods and rinse my mouth with salty water three times a day until it healed. Soft foods were no problem, as porridge and soup were always on the menu.

We were strolling toward the sleeping huts. I glanced around. Others were playing cards, smoking, reading, all out of earshot. In a low voice, I told him about Georg, the family camp, and my desire to get a transfer.

The words tumbled out without tact. Even to my own ears, it sounded as if I wished to end our friendship. He was the only person I could trust, and I'd offended him. I started to apologise, but he held his hands up to stop.

'Think nothing of it, my dear boy. I have news for you too. As you know, my medical qualifications are not recognised in Australia. However, I can practise under the supervision of a registered doctor. Medicine is what I trained for and what I love. So, next week I will transfer to Camp 1 to work under Dr Owen at the Waranga Hospital.' His eyes were sparkling. 'I am delighted at the prospect. At last, I can put my skills to good use.'

His joy gave me little comfort. How would I manage without him? I was shocked that he'd already arranged an escape … and without me! At eighteen, I was almost an adult but not quite. 'Congratulations, Werner,' I said with a wan smile. He would have seen straight through it, for he knew me better than I knew myself.

He gave me a sympathetic thump on the back. 'From the start, we knew that this camp was not for us. Thanks to Georg, you have a way out too. If things go wrong, you know where to find me.'

~

In the hut at the *Kleingarten*, Horst stretched his body and said he'd talked enough for one day. He took another bottle from the mini fridge and refilled the glasses with beer. 'Please tell me if I ramble too much. Once I get going, the words spill out and I don't know how to stop.'

Kathy shook her head. 'Your stories are like gold. You've told me so many things I didn't know. As I said before, my interest is in my family, ordinary people caught up in a war.'

In silence, they drank the beer. Outside, daylight was fading.

'We should head back,' said Horst. 'But before we go, I have brought you a gift.' From his knapsack he took a copy of *Heart of Darkness*, a novel she'd seen on his bookshelf the first day. 'You *must* read this,' he said passing it to her. 'I think you will find it most enlightening.'

Her smile was genuine, for the book was old, possibly second or third edition. 'Thank you, Horst. That's very kind of you.' She slipped the slim volume into her bag.

'Tell me what you make of it. Promise?'

'I'll start reading tonight. Tomorrow, would you like to come to my place for lunch? I'll make *spaghetti con pomodoro* and *Schinken*.'

'Italian and German, sounds like the perfect partnership.' He flashed one of those charming smiles; his blue eyes crinkled at the corners.

At her apartment, Kathy flopped onto the couch and opened the Joseph Conrad classic. Almost forty years had passed since she'd read it. Except this book was not by Joseph Conrad at all. Every page had been overlaid with rough white paper, and a whole new story had been written in pencil. There was a stiffness to the pages and a funny odour. Flour-and-water glue, if she was not mistaken. The handwriting was undeniably her sister's. The dates went right through the war, the years missing from the grey exercise book.

With trembling fingers, she turned to the first page.

Ten

Autumn 1942

Mamma and I are gaol-birds in a barbed-wire prison a long way from home. Today I managed to get paper and a pencil. Here we are not allowed to write anything but a one-page letter on army-issue notepaper once a week. I think that's a stupid rule so I will keep this a secret. I chose you, *Heart of Darkness,* from the Red Cross library. You belong to me now, never to be returned. Your title is perfect; your story has many similarities to mine. But before I go forward, I'll tell you what's happened over the past three weeks.

7 April 1942

The day after Papa's memorial Mass, I was lost and empty. Too sad to eat, too sad to read. After wandering around aimlessly all morning, I got out the hoe and set to work chipping weeds in the veggie patch. The physical activity took away my sorrow and I felt better. That is, until I heard a car coming up the track. The black paddy wagon stopped at the house and two policemen got out. Pixie was yapping like mad. I heard a sharp yelp, then fists banging at the front door.

Just like when they took Papa. A shiver ran down my spine. That was almost a year ago. I clutched my chest and sharpened my ears. Their voices were loud but I couldn't make out what they were saying. Fearing for Mamma, I put down the hoe and stole into the kitchen. The table was piled with papers, mostly bills. The pen stuck desolately out of the inkpot.

'Show me the search warrant.' Mamma's no-nonsense tone echoed down the hallway.

I hung back, not knowing what to do. The constable burst into the kitchen and began rifling through all the papers. The sergeant—the one who'd given me a drivers' licence not long before—charged into Mamma's room. I could hear him dragging out boxes and drawers and upending them onto the bed.

Meanwhile, the constable gave up on the paperwork and turned his attention to the kitchen cupboards. He peered into every cannister and container, even the crock where we kept the bread. I don't know what he was looking for, but all we kept in that room was food and cooking utensils.

I crept down the hall towards the front door. Pixie limped to me and nuzzled my leg. On the veranda I found Mamma. Her arms were behind her back; her face was as wild as a storm cloud. In Italian she spat a stream of abuse that ended with *bastardi!*

'What's going on?'

'I'm sorry, Alessandra, I have failed you.' She swivelled around so I could see the handcuffs on her wrists.

Just like when they took Papa. 'How can they do that?' I said.

'They're trying to scrounge up *evidence.*' Sarcasm sharpened her tongue. 'I could argue until my face was as purple as a *melanzana* but it wouldn't make any difference. My punishment is already set.'

From the kitchen came a loud crash and tinkle.

Her lips were pressed into a hard line. 'There goes my good—'. She fell silent and her face blanched. '*O Dio!* Where are the books?'

I knew the ones she meant. The primary readers were a gift from Mussolini's government to the Italian School. She was one of the organisers and I was one of the first pupils. Later on, I became a tutor. The covers were bright and colourful; the lessons were perfect for beginners. On the first page was *Il Duce's* message to young people.

> *Voi siete l'aurora della vita; voi siete la speranza della Patria. (You are the dawn of life; you are the hope of the Homeland.)*

Everything in those books praised Mussolini and his philosophy. There were loyalty pledges, patriotic poems, accounts of momentous events such as the 'March on Rome'. I'd read the stories so many times, I could rattle them off by heart.

After the earlier police roundup when they took Papa, the women shut down the Italian school and packed the books away. Mamma knew where they were, but not me.

No sooner had the words left her lips, than the sergeant stormed out of the house. In his hand was a book with the boot of Italy on the front. *Lettura Classe Quarta.* Fourth Class Reading.

'Mrs Zanetti, can you explain the presence of this fascist literature in your house?'

Mamma shook her head.

'Well, there is an entire box of it. Did it appear by magic? Or—don't tell me—someone who doesn't like you hid it under your bed?'

Mamma lowered her eyes, feigning interest in a column of ants marching across the floorboards.

'If you cannot provide an explanation, I have no choice but to place you under arrest.'

'What about Alessandra? If you take me, she'll be left here on her own.'

'How old is she?' said the sergeant, as if he didn't know perfectly well.

'Seventeen. A child.'

'Surely at seventeen she can look after herself.' The sergeant eyed me as he spoke. 'She seems like capable enough girl.'

'That is my point: she is a *girl*. She needs to be protected.'

'If you want her to go with you, you can lodge a formal request.'

'Rubbish! I'm her mother and legal guardian. I am *not* leaving without her!'

'Listen lady, you're not in a position to argue. Either you co-operate or we use force.'

With that, the Italian in Mamma kicked in. She spat in his face.

The sergeant wiped it off with a hanky. He grabbed her and dragged her, kicking and screaming, to the police wagon. I tried to follow but the constable held me back. I fought like a wildcat but he was too strong for me. Pixie was barking and snapping at his heels. He gave her a swift kick. She yelped and ran into the house.

Meanwhile, Mamma called them the worst Sicilian words I'd ever heard, none of which had the slightest impact on her tormentors.

'Where are you taking her?' I yelled at them. 'I don't want to be left alone.' I was terrified that I'd never see her again. *Just like poor Papa.* I howled like a wounded beast.

The skirmish was going nowhere; we all knew it.

The sergeant strode toward me. A large man, he towered over me. In a booming voice he said, 'Shut up and stop your fuss. You can come if you promise to behave.'

I glared at him, defiant.

'You have five minutes to pack. One port for yourself, one your mother. What do you say, girlie?'

After five minutes of furious packing, I returned with two cardboard ports, hoping I'd chosen the right clothes for us both. 'What about Pixie?' I said as they bundled me into the back of the wagon.

'Bloody dog can fend for itself,' growled the sergeant.

We were driven to the police station at Currawong. In the backyard was a wire pen, which we were forced to enter. Thankfully it was in the shade of a milky-pine tree, for the day had turned hot and steamy. There was a bucket of clean water and folding chairs. When Mamma's handcuffs were removed, she examined her wrists and complained about blisters. Shortly after, we were joined by four other women and two children, all of whom were involved in the Italian School. We exchanged kisses and hurled curses at the policemen.

In the early afternoon, we did the 'march of shame' to the railway station, where we boarded the south-bound train. The door was chained and padlocked behind us. Already in the carriage were several other women and children. Most wore black like us.

Mamma and I sat together like a pair of sorry crows. All the talk was about where we might be going. The optimists hoped to be reunited with their menfolk in South Australia. It made no difference to us. Dear Papa was no longer with us. The afternoon wore on. The closed-in carriage rocked like a cradle and everyone dozed.

As darkness fell, the train pulled into Townsville, 180 miles to the south. A policeman opened the padlocks and we spilled onto the platform. He shouted instructions at us as if we were deaf. I translated for the women who did not know English. We climbed into an open truck and were driven out of town, through lean country with little vegetation.

A blaze of electric light marked our destination, a place with impenetrable walls and steel bars. The truck deposited us in a barren asphalt quadrangle bounded by squat buildings. In the darkness, eyes were watching us as if we were prey. Although I could see nothing, I felt them sure enough. My skin was crawling with fear.

Three warders came out: two men, one woman. Their faces were as hard as concrete. A headcount confirmed that all sixteen women and six children were present. We marched to a small cell block, a little removed from the other buildings. The children were whining that they were tired and hungry and wanted to go home.

'The kitchen is shut. You'll have to wait until breakfast,' said a male warder.

Mamma glared at him. 'Can't you get them some bread or milk?'

Ignoring her, he opened the cell-block door. There were two compartments with bare concrete floors, each big enough for six. The stench of mould and rat pee took my breath away. Mattresses with blue-and-white ticking were piled up at the back. No-one dared to complain.

'You have ten minutes to use the latrines. Lights out at eight sharp,' said the female warder.

After a scramble to relieve ourselves, we filed into the cells and the doors were locked. Weary, I dragged a mattress across the floor and threw myself down. It was lumpy and stained. No sheets or pillows. Our mattresses covered the entire floor, not an inch of space between them. Everyone was tossing, trying to get comfortable. Children wailed and mothers sobbed.

The female warder yelled through the bars. 'Pipe down, you lot.'

I couldn't stand it any longer. Calmly and politely, I spoke to her in English. 'Please, Miss. The children are hungry. Surely you can find them a crust to eat.'

The warder looked in at the small faces. For a moment, she softened. 'I'll see what I can do.' Turning, she fired the parting shot. 'But until I get back, pipe down!'

At the stroke of eight, the lights went out. The half-moon peeped through the tiny barred window, casting striped shadows across our bodies.

Sometime later, the warder returned with two loaves of white bread, a jerrycan of water, and two tin mugs. 'For the little ones,' she said, passing the items through the bars.

The mothers grabbed the food and water. *Grazie,* they said. The children ate first, the rest was divided up between the adults. A bite-sized morsel did little to satisfy my appetite. The cell was airless. Skin touched skin; hair touched hair. Mosquitoes whined. Cockroaches scuttled. A soft voice recited the Rosary in Latin.

> *Hail Mary, full of grace ... pray for us sinners, now and at the hour of our death ...*

The click of beads.

> *Our Father, who art in Heaven ... give us this day our daily bread ...*

I must have fallen asleep.

In the morning, the cells were unlocked and we stumbled out of darkness into the dazzle of an exercise yard. Our whereabouts: Stewarts Creek Gaol, a prison for rapists and murderers. With a shiver, I remembered the creepy feeling of eyes watching. No wonder.

Breakfast was a pot of gluggy rice. After the children were served, the women set upon it like a pack of she-wolves. Black tea washed it down. No milk, not even for the babies.

At lunchtime, rice again. The same in the evening. Without proper food we felt wretched, but our complaints fell on deaf ears. During the night, some of the children got sick. The warder gave us buckets to use inside the cells. The stench was awful, enough to make me vomit as well.

On the third day, we had watery mutton broth with unidentified vegetable matter floating on top. On the fourth, we had maize porridge, which tasted like undercooked polenta.

Nothing changed until the eighth day, when we were told to pack up and assemble in the exercise yard. Spirits rose. Our prayers had been answered. The mistake would be rectified and we would be released. With hope in our hearts, we climbed onto the truck, settled the children between us, and sang all the way to the station. On the train, the guards were the same as before. Yes, we were going home!

The locomotive gave a whistle and huffed from the station. Everyone was smiling. I sat by the window, not daring to breathe in case the movement popped the vision of freedom. Eucalyptus scrublands flew past. The stench, the sickness, the despair of the past week was blown away. I rested my head against the window pane. Morning sun streamed onto my cheeks. Mamma was beside me on the aisle. The rhythmic *click-click-clack* of the wheels was a lullaby and I drifted off.

Suddenly Mumma shook me awake. 'It's the wrong way! Home is north; we're going south.'

'How do you know?' I said, half asleep.

She shot me a withering look. 'Where does the sun rise?'

The penny dropped. I didn't care if we were going north or south, east or west, as long as it wasn't back to Stewarts Creek Gaol.

16 April 1942

For two days and one night the train headed south. At the Brisbane terminus, elderly soldiers took the place of the police guards. Unlike the police, these fellows showed kindness; they carried ports for the mothers and gave us a hand as we climbed onto the back of the truck.

The camp at suburban Gaythorne was run along military lines with bugle-calls to start and end the day. Our tin hut reminded me of canecutters' barracks. We had stretcher-beds and proper bedding. It was airy and clean and we were allowed to move about within the compound, wash our clothes, and stroll along the creek. Compared to the awful food at the gaol, the mutton stew that was dished up for dinner tasted delicious.

When an official from the Swiss Consul came to ask us about our treatment as war prisoners, we didn't hold back. Our complaints about the Townsville prison rang loud and long. He told us to put it in writing and promised to investigate. Because I had the best English, I wrote the letter and the others signed. We never got a reply. Two weeks later, we were moved on.

27 April 1942

Another long train journey took us through New South Wales and across the Murray River into Victoria, two thousand miles from home. Despite the hard timber seats, meagre rations, male guards, and lack of privacy, the hope of seeing their husbands kept the women smiling. Under other circumstances, the train ride would have been fun. Pretty scenery, time to relax and make new friends. Except I was an in-betweener: too young for the mothers and too old for the kids. I drifted between both groups. My greatest joy was playing with the little ones. I made them toys out of pencils and hankies and the cardboard centres of toilet rolls.

One old digger, a veteran of Gallipoli, handed me a pack of playing cards. 'Here you go, lassie. Let the kids have some fun. I don't need 'em back.'

They were dog-eared and the British kind: clubs, spades, hearts, diamonds. After everyone had examined the odd-looking cards, we played game after game of 'snap'.

The final stretch of the journey was by army truck. The indignity of clambering on and off vehicles in a skirt was second nature to us now. We already knew about dirt under the fingernails and clothes that hadn't seen a washtub in weeks. As soon as we arrived at our camp in the middle of a paddock, we raced to the shower block.

29 April 1942

And now here we are. Right up to date. Tatura Camp 3, known as the family camp, is on a grassy knoll dotted with gum trees and wattles. A soft pastel setting, completely different from the brash colours of the tropics. The camp is divided into four compounds. Corrugated-iron huts stand in neat rows like at Gaythorne, but that's where the similarity ends. Gaythorne is a military camp. Here it feels almost like home.

Clothes lines are strung between the trees; women sit together outside, talking or knitting; children play chasey and hide-and-seek. Around the huts are gardens, shrines to the Madonna, and ornaments made of clay. Curtains cover the windows; rag mats cover the floors. If it weren't for the barbed wire and guards, the family camp could pass for a country town.

Our hut is divided into twelve bedrooms. Mamma and I have one room each, with a privacy curtain in the doorway between us. We each have an entrance, a window, a narrow bed and a chair. I think we will be comfortable here.

The camp has two schools: one for the Germans and one for us. Mamma has volunteered to work at the Italian school. She pictures herself teaching grammar and punctuation as well as the history and culture of Italy. Today is her first day.

This morning I took a stroll around the compound. There are fourteen sleeping huts, a kitchen, dining hall, first-aid clinic, and hobbies hut. On the eastern boundary is a gate—padlocked, of course—that opens onto a central laneway. Beyond is the compound for German families. On the northern boundary is another laneway, which separates us from an all-male section. As I watched, a truck went by, carrying about fifteen men in maroon uniforms. By the look of things, they were going to work outside the camp.

Hallo, Fräulein. A voice called to me through the fence.

I didn't see him at first.

'*Hallo.* Do you speak English?' His accent was German. He was handsome—blond hair, blue eyes, slim body—and dressed in shorts and a checked shirt. I might have been interested, except he looked like a Hitler Youth and I wasn't sure we should be talking.

'What's your name?' he called.

Without answering, I escaped between two rows of huts.

By the time I reached my hut, I was angry with myself. Patrick Winter is overseas and I'm in a prison camp in Victoria. It won't be easy to get another boyfriend. But what use is a boyfriend in this place? Here, we live under everyone's noses, including our mothers and the guards. Talk about restrictions! Lucky Gwen at Currawong has British parents and they let her to do whatever she likes.

Mamma was out; her pack of cigarettes was on the bed. I tiptoed in and took one, held it between my fingers, slipped it between my lips and inhaled. The taste of unlit tobacco tickled my throat. The smell reminded me of Rita Borlotti, my tobacco-growing school friend, whose yellow-stained hands always had that pungent odour.

Footsteps crunched up the path. I shoved the cigarette back in the pack and went out to meet Mamma. She was in a foul mood and had lots of complaints. The school had no curriculum, no textbooks, no paper, no blackboard, no chalk. Instead of learning grammar and numbers, she said, the pupils do nothing but play outside and collect rubbish like gumnuts and rocks and lizard eggs about the yard.

According to Mamma, all that must change. Children deserve a proper education even in an internment camp. Then she asked for my help. Although I despised boarding school, I enjoy learning and I like little kids. Being busy is better than being bored. Instantly, I agreed.

She'd made a list on the back of an envelope. Yes, my mother *loves* lists. My mission is to buy, beg, or steal nineteen exercise books, one for each pupil. 'Take the initiative,' she said. I'd heard that line before: a favourite expression of the nuns at St Bernadette's.

8 May 1942

Friday is canteen day. At the camp canteen, we can buy luxuries like soap, fruit, lollies. Hoping to find exercise books, I took my mother's camp tokens with me, but no such luck. I was told that paper was in short supply due to the war. In any case, the sale of writing materials in the camp was banned by order of the Commandant.

Disappointed but not deterred, I walked along the perimeter fence and called out to a guard who had a kind face. We spoke for a while. Shouted, more like it, with him in the tower and me on the ground. His name is Bert and he'd be about the same age as Papa. When he was younger, he had an orchard near Shepparton and employed Italian fruit pickers. 'Wonderful people. Thing I liked most was their attitude to life. *La dolce vita*. Did I say that right?'

'*Bravo!* Your pronunciation is perfect.' I thought that buttering him up wouldn't hurt.

'A beautiful philosophy and one I have adopted myself. Now, young lady, you don't want to hear an old man yabbering on.'

I told him about the school and the problem of exercise books.

His response was a shrug. 'Can't help you there, lassie.' Then he dropped the pearl. 'The only paper internees are allowed is hanging in the dunny.'

I thanked him and left. My mind was ticking over. As far as toilet paper goes, the stuff supplied by the government is the worst. Slippery on one side and like sandpaper on the other, impossible to use straight off the roll. You have to rub it together to soften it up. However, for my mission, government-issue toilet paper was perfect.

At the latrines, I tore off a couple of lengths and folded them under my waistband. Back at the hut, I cut the sheets apart and laid ten on top of each other. With a needle and thread, I stitched along the short side, finished it with pencil lines ruled across. I also had the brilliant idea of making myself a diary by pasting toilet-paper sheets onto the pages of a novel.

Mamma loved my little exercise book and so did Mr Giuliano, the schoolmaster. A few days later, I handed over nineteen of them to the school. From then on, I made a new batch every week. The army storeman must have scratched his head over the extraordinary number of toilet rolls used by the Italian women from Queensland.

18 May 1942

The school is closed for a two-week break, along with all the other primary schools in Victoria. On Friday we had a breaking-up picnic at the lake and it was more than a bit exciting.

Only women and children were allowed, no men apart from two guards, one of whom was Bert. The walk to the lake took us through forests of wattles and blue-grey eucalypts. The guards carried the food and drinking water. The mothers took blankets, plates, towels. I had two tennis racquets and balls, which Bert lent us for the occasion.

At the lake, we arranged the blankets on the grass overlooking a beach of yellow sand. The children kicked off their shoes and raced to the water. Splashes and squeals mingled with the cackle of kookaburras and the sigh of the wind through the she-oaks.

We laid the food out like a buffet. Bread, cheese, *polpetti*, tomatoes, *biscotti*, apples. Hungry kids galloped in for a snack and took off again. After lunch, the mothers chatted or dozed on a blanket; the guards sat on rocks and smoked.

I rounded up a few children for a game of French cricket with tennis racquets. Young Livia burst through the scrub, screeching and waving her arms. 'Help, Miss! Tino's dead!'

I dropped the equipment. 'Whereabouts?'

'In there!' The little girl pointed to the scrub.

'Get his mother!' I yelled as I thrashed into long grass. I found a goat-track and followed it to the distant sound of wailing. At least he wasn't actually dead.

I found him in a clearing, sitting on a rock, sobbing and holding his ankle. Bundling him into my arms, I asked him what happened.

'S-s-snake,' he sniffled.

'What kind?' I tried to remove his hands and take a look at the wound, but he shook his head and howled in pain.

'It was brown,' piped a small voice behind me.

I spun around. 'Livia, I told you to get Tino's mother.'

'She was sleeping.' The girl hung her head, about to cry.

'Never mind. What I want you to do is very important. Run back and get the guard called Bert. Can you can manage that?'

'Yes, Miss.' She sprinted off the way she had come.

I returned my attention to the boy. While I'm no expert in reptiles, I know that brown is not a good colour for a snake. More often than not, brown snakes are venomous. I had to stop the poison from spreading. In a split second, I thought to immobilise the leg in a splint. I found two sturdy sticks and tore my black petticoat into strips.

I'd just finished tying the splint on when Bert charged into the clearing. 'Hang on to me, sonny.' He scooped Tino into his arms and thundered down the track away from the picnic ground. 'Come on!' he yelled to me. 'Time is of the essence.'

I caught up to them on the side of a dirt road. Miraculously, Bert had flagged down a car and asked the driver, a travelling salesman, to take us to the Waranga Hospital. We all piled in. Bert sat in front, while Tino and I squeezed in the back between boxes of brushes and feather dusters. The boy rested his head in my lap. His skin was clammy and his breathing rapid. With every bump he whimpered. My heart went out to him.

What if my amateur first-aid was wrong? The idea to make a splint came from intuition. The old-timers' remedy was to cut the puncture marks and suck out the venom. On the farm, I'd watched Mamma attend three stomach-churning accidents. One fellow was burnt when a fuel drum exploded. Another severed his fingers with a cane knife. A third broke a leg when he fell off a horse. Every time she immobilised the injury and kept the victim calm until the ambulance arrived.

In the brush salesman's car, I stroked Tino's arm and told him he'd be all right. At the hospital, Dr Owen rushed him into the examination room, shot questions at Bert and me. We didn't have much to say, except that the snake was brown.

I held the boy tight while the splint was removed. Beneath it, the ankle was swollen and red. The doctor cracked a glass ampoule and drew the fluid into a syringe.

At the sight of the needle, Tino's eyes popped. With a yelp, he tried to squirm away but I managed to hold him. After the injection, he fell asleep.

'To be sure, we'll keep him in overnight,' said Dr Owen.

Bert lifted him, as gentle as a baby, and lay him on the bed. After tucking him in, he said that we should be getting back to the camp.

As we turned to leave, the doctor said to me, 'Thank you, young lady. Your quick thinking saved this little fellow's life. The splint was a stroke of genius. Stirling effort.'

'I'm glad he'll be all right.' Heat rushed to my face; the splint was no more than a lucky guess.

Without noticing my embarrassment, the doctor pressed on. 'We always have openings for bright girls like you at the Camp Dressing Stations. In fact, I'm running a first-aid course for CDS volunteers next week. Let me know if you're interested.'

I couldn't believe what I was hearing. A foot in the door to the job of my dreams. Without hesitation I said, 'Thank you, Doctor. I'd love to.'

'Excellent. I'll make the necessary arrangements.'

19 May 1942

I've been mulling over my knee-jerk response to that first-aid course. Normally I'm not impulsive, but without Papa around I've changed. The first-aid clinic in our compound is run by internees. The person in charge is a maternity nurse from Sicily. I don't know why I want to be a nurse, but saving a life yesterday gave me a boost like no other.

However, I'm not brave like Mamma, and I don't know if I have the stomach for the work. The reason I didn't suck out the venom was weakness. And that's the truth. The thought of taking another person's blood into my mouth makes me want to vomit. Yesterday, fortune had shone on us. The splint worked and the boy was saved. What if I'd found an uglier scene? Would I have been so calm or would I have run away?

I suppose there's one way to find out. I'll do the course. If I pass, I'll work at the CDS clinic.

When I told Mamma, she gave me a hug. 'You were the hero of the day. Tino's mother was beside herself when she found out what happened. We packed up and rushed back to the compound. Opportunities like this don't come along every day. Go ahead, Alessandra. See if you like it. If not, you can always come back to the school.' With that, she picked up her cigarettes and went to bed.

8 June 1942

I am a CDS officer now, as well as a part-time helper at the school, and I've made a new friend. Teresa Moro is the same age as me, the third child of four. Ivan, her fifteen-year-old brother, is also here. Her two older brothers are soldiers in the AIF. Her father is Dan Moro, our camp leader. According to Teresa, he owns a newspaper and is a distant cousin of the king of Italy. Viktoriya Moro, her mother, teaches Russian, Romanian, Hungarian, and Italian. Her pedigree goes back to the Romanovs. If it weren't for the Russian Revolution, she'd have lived like a princess, and so would Teresa.

Mind, I wouldn't put money on any of this being true. Teresa is fun but she's also prone to exaggeration. When I told Mamma about the Moro family history, she laughed and shook her head.

'What utter nonsense!' she said. 'A classic tale of riches to rags.'

She went on to explain that it was easy for astute migrants to crow about their ancestry. The Moros, being astute migrants, took the opportunity and became the darlings of Sydney society. Their appeal was undeniable: good looks and an aristocratic manner. Dan Moro, whose English was impeccable, became a reporter with *The Sydney Morning Herald*. He fell from grace after writing an article that praised Mussolini for his *autostrada* projects. The reaction of the editor-in-chief was swift: Dan Moro was sacked. Undeterred, he moved to Parramatta and founded *La Posta*.

Mamma said that *La Posta* was the newspaper she'd turned in the early days of the Italian School. In 1936, Dan Moro published her open letter to the Italian mothers of Australia. As a result, the school received dozens of enrolment requests and donations. The interest convinced Mussolini's government to fund a part-time teacher and send her three cartons of primary school readers from Italy.

10 June 1942

Today at the clinic, Teresa and I cut up old hospital sheets for bandages. Each strip had to be exactly three inches wide and as long as the fabric allowed. She measured and marked and I wielded the scissors. When each strip was done, Teresa rolled it up and put it into the bandages box. It was a good chance for us to talk and get to know each other.

'My parents suffocate me,' she said. 'I'd do anything to get away.'

'Including this?' I was joking. For me the CDS job was a dream. I'd loved the course and was looking forward to seeing real patients.

'It's better than nothing.' She wound a bandage around her head and tied a giant bow. 'Hey, how do I look?' She stuck out her tongue.

'Like a crazy rag-doll.'

She danced a silly jig that made me laugh.

The Sicilian nurse, who'd gone out to see a patient, stomped up the steps. The moment she spotted us, she put her hands on her hips and said to Teresa, 'Take that stupid thing off and get back to work.'

The first patient arrived after lunch: one of the boys had come a cropper off a billy-kart. I picked bits of gravel from his knee and cleaned up the blood while Teresa manicured her nails.

15 June 1942

To pass the time, Teresa and I practise first aid on each other.

Mondays: splints and slings. Always a giggle.

Wednesdays: observations. At half-hourly intervals we take our temperature, pulse rate, blood pressure and plot the readings on charts.

Fridays: twenty questions. We quiz each other about bites, belly aches, heat rash, sprains, burns, etc and how to treat them.

From time to time, Ivan wanders in to check up on his sister and she talks him into being our guinea pig. Although it's a blessing that the compound is practically accident free, shifts can be long and boring. All that training, gone to waste. Some days I wish for an accident to happen. I made the mistake of telling Mamma. Be careful what you wish for, was the reply.

Eleven

Reinickendorf: October 2010

Kathy spent the morning preparing lunch for two. Italian pasta with tomatoes and German ham. The only cooking vessel in the kitchenette was a miniature saucepan suitable for boiling an egg. She wrote a shopping list and went to Netto to purchase ingredients for the meal, a bottle of red Italian wine, and a proper cooking pot.

At the appointed time precisely, Horst knocked on the door. In her K-mart jeans and the new KaDeWe pullover, she ran down the stairs and let him in. He was dressed for a business luncheon at a restaurant. Grey sports jacket, white button-down shirt, pressed trousers, and black lace-up brogues, probably his own brand. He presented her with a bottle of white German wine. After some small-talk about the weather and the sights of Berlin, they sat at the table.

Horst poured the wine while Kathy dished up the food.

'This is delicious,' he said tucking in. His spaghetti-twirling technique was seriously lacking. She gave him a soup spoon, and a tea-towel to cover his nice clean shirt.

'*Buonissima!*' he said when the plate was empty. 'Where did you learn to cook?'

She smiled. 'Mum. She was the best. Dad loved pasta. She made it for him most days.'

'I never knew Maria could cook,' he said. 'I thought she was the intellectual type. In all the years I knew Alice, she never once mentioned her mother's cooking. Or her own, for that matter. Of course, circumstances went against that in the camp, and then later.'

'Oh? What happened later?'

'All in good time, my dear. Now, did you read *Heart of Darkness*?'

'Some. I'll finish it tonight.'

'What are your thoughts?'

'About the arrest and the journey to Tatura? Appalling!'

'The gaol at Townsville was horrible,' he said. 'And their complaints went unheard like whispers in the wind.'

Kathy smiled and shook her head. 'Not quite. I found the letter on a digitised file but I didn't know that Alice had written it. That letter was a catalyst for change. Weeks after it was sent, it triggered an official inquiry. A magistrate was appointed to investigate the women's complaints. His findings, which were damning, resulted in a war of words between the army, the prisons department, and the superintendent of Stewarts Creek Gaol. All the accusations were denied or downplayed, and excuses were made for things that were hard to deny, all to cover the backs of the men in charge. But, despite that, the government listened and made changes. Never again were internees held in State prisons.'

Horst's eyes shimmered with tears. 'Good on her. What an inspirational young woman she was.'

Kathy's heart swelled. Yes, he was right. Alice was an inspiration, right up until the last years of her life. But her energy was for others—orphans, rejects, lost souls—not for her family. In the days and months after Alice's death, Kathy swallowed her feelings and got on with arranging the funeral, tidying up affairs, and organising an international pilgrimage to fulfil her promise.

To get through all that took enormous self control. At the service she'd read the eulogy, which she'd written herself. More than a hundred people attended, some flying in from other parts of Australia. All went off without a hitch. Everyone commented on the meticulous attention to detail, the choice of music and readings, the floral arrangements, the delicious food, most of which she'd made herself. Then there was the casting of the ashes at Coolangatta Beach, the exact spot specified by Alice before her mind turned into honeycomb. Weeks later, Kathy boarded a flight to the other side of the world.

Her grief was still raw. She'd allowed herself no space to mourn. Pressure had been building and building. Horst's praise blew the safety valve and she began to sob. Once the tears started, they streamed down her cheeks. She searched her pockets for tissues, found a paper serviette and buried her face.

Horst remained silent, as if giving her permission to let her emotions out. When she looked up through stinging watery eyes, he was pouring water from the kettle for tea.

'Sorry for blubbering,' she said.

He waved his hand at the apology. 'Grief is a personal thing; we all react differently. Remembering helps. Talking about it helps. The two of us together, this helps us both.'

'I loved my sister but I don't think she cared much for me. We always had … I don't know … an emotional barrier between us. I should have had it out with her years ago, and now it's too late.'

Horst brought the teacups to the table. 'Believe me, my dear, I know what you mean.'

A good strong brew did wonders to restore the equilibrium. At Horst's insistence, she remained seated while he cleared and washed the dishes.

'I feel as if I've known you forever,' she said. 'We seem to be on the same wavelength. Jack and I could never have spoken like this, and we've been married twenty-four years. Earlier you said that a person must look forward and not backwards. But, for me, the past is as important as the future.'

'That was Mutti's philosophy, not mine,' he said. 'I have spent a lifetime wishing to forget, but I cannot. What happened in the past affects who we are now. Without the past, I would be a shell of a man with no substance.' He pressed his hand to the left side of his chest. 'Your heart, that is what counts.'

'Tell me, Horst, do you believe in life after death?'

He returned to his chair. 'My dear, I gave up on religion long ago. However, I feel a kinship with souls who have left us. Sometimes I talk aloud to Opa, or I dream about Mutti. Perhaps these are the mental meanderings of an old man, yet the memories comfort me.'

Kathy gave his forearm a squeeze. 'Perhaps Alice is guiding us both. Perhaps her spirit is here with us now.'

'Ha! Alice in Berlin? Never!' He laughed. 'She is where she wants to be. Amongst the gum trees and magpies and kangaroos. In her beloved homeland, Australia.'

'Tell me more about the camp,' said Kathy. 'How did you and Alice meet?'

'A stroke of luck is the short answer. But it was far more complicated than that.'

~

A week after my toothache ordeal, I was due back at the surgery for a check-up. I'd followed Werner's advice to the letter and my gum had healed nicely. I was determined to make the most of my brief respite from Camp 2. I would find the secret hidey-hole where letters were 'posted' and send a note to Georg. My appointment was at nine-fifteen. When the army truck picked me up from the camp, two other internees were in the back. We were told to be outside the surgery at ten o'clock sharp for the return journey. I would have thirty precious minutes between my consultation and our departure.

As expected, the dentist gave me the all-clear. Afterwards, I ambled along the corridor towards the lavatory and loitered nearby until I was certain no-one was around. As an added precaution, I turned out my pocket and 'accidentally' dropped a camp coin, the perfect alibi for being on all fours beneath a washbasin.

The loose panel of skirting board was easy to find. It was about thirty centimetres in length and had an upside-down U cut in the middle to accommodate the drainage pipe. After double-checking that the corridor was deserted, I reached in and lifted the panel out. Behind it was a small empty space and a piece of folded-up toilet paper.

The paper was addressed to *Herr Erik Flesser, Camp 2*. The writing was neat, the hand of a woman, probably from the family camp. Although tempted, I did not read it. Instead, I slipped it into my pocket, placed my note to Georg in the space, and refitted the panel.

Back at the camp, I went in search of Herr Flesser, whom I did not know. I was directed to his hut, which was several rows removed from mine. He was sitting at a small table by the window, surrounded by a collection of leaves, seedpods, and blossoms. His attention was on a sprig of gumnuts. Pencil in hand, he was scribbling on a rough sheet of paper. As I moved closer, I saw that he was not writing but sketching. The drawing was as perfect as a photograph. Mid-stroke he paused the pencil and looked up.

'Herr Flesser?'

'That is correct.' Flyaway white hair gave the impression of an absent-minded professor. The odour of eucalyptus, earthy and astringent, hung about the room.

'I have a message for you.' I removed the note from my pocket.

He took it with a simple *danke schön* and put it down beside the gumnuts.

I couldn't help gazing at other sketches on the desk. 'These are beautiful.'

He shrugged. 'I do my best to portray the subjects accurately.'

'Are you a scientist or an artist?' I asked.

'A botanist. I am making use of this enforced sabbatical to record the native flora of northern Victoria. Already I have identified several new species.' Proudly he spread his drawings across the desk. 'It keeps me busy. My wife, Lotte, is in the family camp with our four children. The note is from her; we write most days. For eighteen months I have been asking for a transfer, without success. I will keep trying.'

I wished him well. This exchange made me think twice about my own transfer. If a married man was not allowed to be with his wife and children, what right did I have to ask? As comfortable and easy as it sounded in the family camp, my conscience did not allow me to seek a place ahead of someone more deserving.

Sunday morning came. In two short days, Werner would be working at the Waranga Hospital. When we would meet next was anyone's guess. Possibly for the last time, we sat together at the Protestant service in the mess hut. Herr Flesser was on the other side of the aisle near the wall. His eyes were closed, his head was bowed, his cheeks glistened with tears. Already I had delayed asking Camp Leader Wiesbaden for a transfer to the family camp. Now I wondered if I should proceed at all. The image of the old man praying made the choice easy. I was nineteen, almost a man. A man would grit his teeth and endure whatever was dished out. We had food, a roof over our heads, activities to keep us amused. My little problems could wait.

In the end, decisions were made for me. A month after Werner's departure, I was summoned to the camp leader's office.

'I hear you wish to transfer to Camp 3 to be with your cousin,' Wiesbaden began. Leaning over the desk, he offered me a cigarette from a wooden box with the Nazi eagle on its lid.

'No thanks, I don't smoke.'

He lit a cigarette, tipped his head back and blew a stream of smoke at the ceiling. 'Why have you not spoken to me about this transfer?'

'I didn't think it would be allowed.'

His eyebrows lifted. 'Why not?'

'I know a man whose wife and kids are there and he can't get a transfer.'

'Is that so?'

'I … I understand that is the case.' I was floundering like a small boat on a stormy ocean.

'Tell me why you wish to leave this camp.'

Rocks reared up and my courage deserted me. I recounted what Georg had said about the family camp: private rooms, greater freedom, classes and activities.

The more I spoke, the redder Wiesbaden's face became. 'What!' he spat. 'Do you mean to say that the filthy *Dunera* Jews live in a holiday resort while we patriotic Germans squeeze into overcrowded barracks and work like slaves?'

'That's only what I've heard,' I said unconvincingly. At that point, I wished for the boards to crack open and for me to slip through.

'Well, we'll soon see about this!' He crushed the cigarette butt in the lid of a jar. 'Is your cousin a Jew?'

'N … no.' My somewhat unstable voice had gone squeaky.

His steel-blue eyes bored into me. 'Are you?'

'No!' I said emphatically. A sick feeling flooded my stomach. 'We are both pure German and of the Lutheran faith.' I hated speaking for Georg, for I was unclear about his ancestry and beliefs. On the *Dunera*, I recalled, he had mentioned Pope Pius XII but that did not mean he was Catholic. In fact, he might not have been Christian. What if he were a Jew? Would that change our friendship? Of course not.

Wiesbaden remained silent; I felt compelled to keep talking.

'I would not have thought about a transfer, except that my good friend, Doctor Werner, is working at the hospital in Camp 1. Georg is my only relative in Australia so I thought …'

'… that you should be together,' he finished for me.

'Well … yes.'

'Hmm. Perhaps he should come here instead.'

I had to get out of there before he had any other bright ideas. It seemed that whatever I said would be misconstrued. My efforts to set things straight were making matters worse.

He muttered beneath his breath, 'It seems we have a rotten deal while the Jews lead a life of luxury in their ghetto. We shall speak on this again, Schuhmacher.'

After my meeting with Wiesbaden, which had brought the matter of the *Tatura Ghetto* to a head, the mood in our camp slipped from 'on the nose' to downright putrid. Fights broke out between supporters of the fascist right and the communist left. Those in the middle—the moderates, the anti-Nazis, the *Jew-lovers*—bore the wrath of both sides. While there were no Jews in Camp 2 that I knew of, there were plenty who hated them. Anyone who defied the Nazi majority didn't dare visit the latrines after dark for fear of their life. I kept a low profile, buried myself in work, spoke to no-one other than customers, and did not stray from safe topics such as the weather and shoes.

The responsibility for this dismal turn of events was mine. If only I'd kept my mouth shut about what was essentially hearsay. I had not one political bone in my body, yet I'd unintentionally detonated a war. Early on, at Werner's suggestion, I'd feigned support for the Nazis and had made the one-arm salute more times than I could count. Earlier still, when I was a boy in the Hitler Youth, I'd parroted the oath of allegiance to *Der Führer* with my fingers crossed behind my back. The ghosts of all my poor decisions had come back to haunt me.

The atmosphere was thick with distrust. Everything that was said was picked apart, analysed for hidden meaning. Accusations and reprisals went hand in hand. Whenever my back was turned, eyes stabbed me like daggers. I did not know whether others felt the same; I had no friends or confidantes. Perhaps I was going crazy.

In the mess hut, men sat with their respective factions. The place in the room announced the allegiance. At the right of the servery sat the Nazis; at the left were the Bolsheviks. Those at back of the room were stupid or senile or Jew-lovers. Lacking in nerve, I sat in my regular spot at the centre, far away from Wiesbaden's crew and the Commies, and not close enough to the back to be the target of everyone's wrath.

Most of all I missed Werner. For the first time since Warth Mills we were in separate compounds. Without him, I had no-one to talk to, no-one to trust. My mood did not improve when his vacated bunk was allocated to a man everyone knew as 'The Gorilla' on account of his enormous size and strength. The former *Dunera* passenger had caused trouble in Camp 2, had been banished to an internment camp in South Australia, and then promptly sent back.

One morning while I was out, he brought in his duffel bag and set out his stuff where Werner's had been. In pride of place were three items made at the Loveday camp: a truncheon with Nazi symbols, knuckledusters made from a metal pipe, a handgun carved from mulga wood. All three looked genuine enough to kill.

At night he snored like a demon. He slept flat on his back, which sent the noise straight up, into my eardrums. Lack of sleep added to my distress. I was a timebomb, ticking down to self-destruction.

The explosion, when it came, was real. In the middle of the night, our hut was rocked off its stumps by a blast. The force was so fierce that half the roof flew off. We never knew the exact cause, but it was probably someone smoking near the liquor still. My straw mattress burst into flames. Shouting, I leapt to the floor. Smoke filled the hut. I held my shirt over my nose and mouth and crouched low, as we'd been shown in air-raid drills in England.

Everyone was scrambling to get out. The nearest exit was to my left, but it was blocked by two large drums. I crawled to a window and pushed against the frame. It was jammed shut. I sank down close to the floor, gasped for air. The hut was completely alight; flames spilled across the floorboards. We were trapped like rats in a cellar.

From somewhere behind me came the scream of a madman and a whoosh like birds' wings. The window glass cracked and crumbled. Strong arms picked me up and threw me out.

Smack! I hit the hard ground. My ribs were crushed; my skin was fried. Someone grabbed me by the armpits and dragged me away.

For hours, or days, or maybe weeks I drifted in and out of consciousness. Dreams were my constant companion. Awful dreams. Dreams about suffocating, drowning, being burnt alive. In between the nightmares, I floated on clouds in a rainbow sky and thought I'd gone to Heaven.

When I came down to earth, my throat was burning and my body felt like it had been stung by a swarm of bees. My legs, arms, and torso were wrapped in white bandages. Alongside me was another bed, and then another, and another. Right along the corridor. Ten in all. Like me, my neighbours looked like Egyptian mummies. Some had their limbs suspended from a web of cords and weights.

Then I saw the angel. Rosy cheeks, hazel eyes, dark wavy hair.

'Would you like some water?' To my ears, her voice was a song.

She held a straw to my lips and I managed a sip. The effort was too great and I dropped back onto the hard bed. I must have slept. When I woke, the room was dim. The angel had gone and Werner in a white doctor's coat stood in her place.

'My dear boy, what *have* you done to yourself?' he said to me in German.

I managed a half-smile. He touched my arm, which proved he was not a ghost. My memory was disjointed and fuzzy. Of one thing, I was sure. 'There was a fire,' I said weakly.

Werner chuckled. 'I never would have guessed.'

'Where am I?'

'Waranga Hospital. I am your physician, under supervision of course.'

'What's wrong with me?' I lifted a bandaged arm.

'Burns, cuts, cracked ribs. You're on morphine, which explains the odd dreams.'

'Did someone throw me out a window or was that a dream too?'

'Yes, someone saved you.'

I pursed my lips to form the word *who*, but Werner cut me off. 'His name is Yuri Vostok and he was on the *Dunera*. Big fellow, very quiet. Sombre, in fact. You never knew what he was thinking. They nicknamed him "The Gorilla", I recall. To tell you the truth, I was rather scared of him. But now …'

'He was in the bunk where you used to be. We never exchanged a word,' I said.

'Fearless and heroic would also describe him. He saved your life and two others before the smoke got him. For his bravery, he's paid a high price. He's in the base hospital at Shepparton. Third degree burns. It's not looking good.'

'I want to thank him.'

'Get some rest first and heal. Now, please excuse me. I have to continue my rounds.'

As if seeing him for the first time, I watched the ageing doctor move along the row of beds. In our compound, *Herr Doktor* Werner was just plain Werner. Here in the hospital, he was a demigod. He stopped and spoke with every patient, sometimes touching a forehead or grasping a wrist. His bedside manner was calm and direct, demonstrating his experience and professional confidence.

A younger doctor—an Australian by the looks—came in and spoke with him. Werner finished attending the patient, jotted notes on the chart, and rushed out.

Later, the angel returned. She was pushing a trolley that rattled with crockery and metal containers of food. She was young, maybe a year or two my junior.

She worked her way along the corridor, making pleasant small-talk as if she had known the patients for years. Whether they understood English or not, she was able to communicate through a flick of a hand or the lift of an eyebrow. The choices were hot tea or cordial; sweet or salt biscuits; sandwiches with egg or tomato. She had a lightness about her and an easy smile that was contagious.

At last, she reached my bed. 'Hello. You're looking better. Would you like afternoon tea?' In the golden light, her eyes sparkled like gemstones.

I made my choice from the trolley and asked her name.

'Alice Zanetti.'

'Where are you from, Nurse Zanetti?'

'Oh, I'm not actually a nurse,' she said with a blush. 'But I hope to be one day. I'm from a town up north that nobody's heard of.'

'You have a lovely voice.'

She seemed taken aback, as if nobody ever paid her compliments. For a moment she busied herself, pouring tea and putting biscuits onto a plate.

'Your name is Italian, *nicht wahr?*'

'My parents are from Italy, but I was born here.' She helped me sit up, and placed the tray on a pillow on my lap. 'Where are you from?'

'Before this … um … *vacation* … I was a student in England. But I was born and raised in Berlin.'

Her eyes flashed with interest. 'Berlin,' she breathed. 'An exciting city, I am told. I would love to visit … after the war, of course. After the war, I want to see the whole world.'

A patient down the corridor was calling her.

'I can come back later, if you like.'

'Yes, I'd like that a lot.' I sipped the tea and devoured the biscuits, discovering in the process that I was ravenous. This shouldn't have been a surprise since I hadn't eaten for … well, I had no idea how long, but it had to be a few days. Beneath the bandages and dressings and ointment, my legs were crawling with imaginary ants. It was hard to stop myself from scratching, but I didn't want to make the itch worse.

Shortly after, Alice returned and removed the tray. Seeing my discomfort, she massaged my legs through the bandages. A soothing touch. 'Tell me about Berlin,' she said.

I didn't know where to start, so I described my childhood before the war. Schillerpark, the hectares of lawns and trees and rose gardens, where we went after school to kick footballs or practise calisthenics. Excursions to the lakes in summer, where we'd hike or sail or swim. And winter trips with Opa to Mitte, where we'd visit the Pergamon or the Altes Museum. And afterwards, a treat of hot chocolate in a café on Unter den Linden. We'd sit by the windows and watch the passing parade. Ladies in fox furs, gentlemen in overcoats and felt hats, soldiers in smart uniforms with shiny black boots.

'Is there snow in winter?' she said.

I laughed. It felt good to laugh; I hadn't done it in ages. 'Some years we get a lot; other years just a sprinkling. If the temperature stays below freezing, we can skate on the lake near my home.'

A cross-looking nurse strode into the ward. Tea trays weren't collected, bedcovers weren't straight, an empty tumbler rolled in the corridor. Hands on hips, she scanned the room, searching for someone to blame.

Alice groaned. 'Gotta go.' She took my tray and my neighbour's and slid them into the trolley, then busied herself tidying the ward.

I sank into the pillows, hoping I had not caused any trouble. Without female company for two years now, I had almost forgotten the art of conversation. When my mother was alive, we would talk for hours about … about anything. The difference between men and women is that women discuss relationships and feelings, while men talk about problems and solutions. In Camp 2, they discussed politics and war, traded technical knowledge, worked out how to fix things. They never reminisced about life or love.

When I lost Mutti, I lost all that. Even her photo was the bottom of the ocean. The only picture I had was the one in my memory. Alas, over time it had faded.

That evening, the cranky nurse gave me two white pills to swallow.

'What are these for?' I said, half asleep.

'Doctor's orders.' She took my blood pressure, pulse and temperature, and jotted notes on the chart. What she lacked in bedside manner, she exceeded in efficiency. Before I'd swallowed the second pill, her examination was complete.

'How am I doing?'

'That's for Doctor to say.'

Before I could ask when Doctor would visit, she was off to the next patient.

Afterwards, I lay on my side and contemplated the ward in the glow of a dimmed electric light. The patients, bandaged and fitted with tubes, cables, and medical devices, had an otherworldly appearance. Clinical and mechanised, the place reminded me of the futuristic film, *Metropolis,* that Opa had taken me to see at the *Ufa-Palast* near the Berlin Zoo. Dearest Opa. I wondered how he was faring. At this rate it seemed I would not return to Germany anytime soon. Maybe not at all.

Although I was tired beyond measure, sleep would not come. My legs were stinging and making me irritable. A white-coated man came into the ward. His gait and the way his body listed to the right was unmistakable. As he worked his way along the corridor, he paused to check each patient, before materialising at the foot of my bed.

'*Hallo*, Werner. What's news?' I said softly, careful not to wake those around me.

'Inside this camp: not much. Everywhere else: war, war, war.'

'I meant with *me*. How much longer do I have to stay here?'

'You are lucky, my dear boy. Your burns will heal quickly. Providing you get no infections, of course. If all goes well, you should be back in the compound in a week.'

'But the fire destroyed our hut.'

'Your hut-mates are being temporarily accommodated in tents.'

I beckoned for him to come closer, lowered my voice. 'You know who runs that place. It's worse than ever. I have to get out. Is there any chance of going to the family camp?'

'For convalescence, you would certainly be better off in a hut. It's freezing out there. No snow, but the wind ...' He shivered involuntarily and trailed off into his own thoughts.

'Can these injuries be used to argue my case?'

Werner stroked his chin. 'A single room and the help of a friend? That would be perfect.'

'A *cousin*.' I corrected him. 'Camp 3 is for families. Georg and I are *cousins*, remember?'

'Of course, I won't forget. Let me see what can be done.'

With that, he departed. My fate was in his hands.

A week in hospital would quickly pass. Mid-morning, I was dozing when a shadow crossed my face. I opened my eyes and my heart leapt for joy. My angel was there.

Soundlessly, Alice set down the tea tray, plumped my pillow, and drew up a chair by my bed. 'I thought you'd enjoy some company,' she said in whisper. 'I can't stay long. Warn me if you see Sister Kelly. Yesterday she gave me a terrible dressing-down.' She poured me a cup of tea and another for herself.

'It's your turn today,' I said. 'I want to hear about Australia.'

'Gosh, it's an enormous country.'

'Then tell me about where you live.'

She described the farmhouse and Currawong, the town named after a bird, and the cane fields of tropical north Queensland. The humidity, the bucketing rain, the vibrant colours, the wildlife. The stories she told hooked me from the start. As she spoke, my eyes stroked her dark wavy hair, slid down her lustrous arms, and returned to her beautiful face.

I asked about platypus, echidnas, cassowaries. She seemed surprised that I knew of such creatures. I told her about the kangaroos at the Berlin Zoo, and that I used to read an animal encyclopaedia with black-and-white pictures.

'If we ever get out of this place, I could show them to you in the wild.'

'Yes, please,' I said without a thought. Already, I was in love.

The other patients began to stir. She told me she should get back to work. Her list of tasks was already long and Sister Kelly would invent dozens more to keep her busy. Polishing doorknobs, ironing pillowcases, darning moth-holes in the blankets.

'Will you visit me again?'

'Depends on Dr Owen. I could be sent back to the CDS clinic at any time,' she said.

'Can we write then?'

'How is that possible? We're in different camps.'

I explained the secret mailbox. 'I'll go first. There's plenty of paper in the lavatory.'

She laughed, for she understood my joke. Suddenly her face paled.

In the doorway stood Sister Kelly, arms crossed. 'Miss Zanetti, I have said time and time again *fraternising with patients is forbidden*. Did I not make myself clear?'

'I understand, Sister.' She grimaced and slunk to the door.

The exchange between nurse and assistant took place within earshot. I kicked myself for allowing her to take the blame. On the other hand, I knew that an explanation would not help matters, so I held my tongue and hoped that Alice would not be sent back to the compound.

Alice was not at work the next day. Without her, the ward was cold and dismal. I spent long hours worrying about Opa and Max. That they lived far from the city centre, in a borough where housing was interspersed between lakes and forests, might give some protection from bombing. If the British propaganda was to be believed, the RAF was targeting munitions factories, railways, airports, bridges, places of military importance where minimum effort would make maximum impact. This gave me some comfort.

I had already lost one parent. Although not caused by a military attack, Mutti's death was definitely war-related. Her decision to leave Berlin and all that she loved, followed by my arrest in England, would have contributed to her untimely death at the age of forty-five. Opa was still spritely, but how many more years did he have? And Max, my father. On many things we disagreed, but without him I was alone in the world.

Once or twice a day, Werner stopped by my bed. However, he was too busy to talk the way we used to. Time expanded, as endless as the ocean. As endless as the voyage to Australia. Locked below decks, inside cramped compartments with too many men. Swill, unfit for human consumption. Beatings, sickness, despair.

Whenever a trolley rattled along the corridor, I would lift my head, hoping to see Alice. But no. Now our food was distributed by a wiry woman whose bedside manner was like a machine. Sister Kelly would have been pleased.

Assuming that Alice was back in her compound, I wrote her a message on toilet paper, saying that I missed her company. Of course, I didn't reveal my plan to transfer to the family camp. While I waited for a chance to sneak to the 'mail box', I hid the note in my pillowcase.

Night fell, painkillers emboldened me. The lights under blackout shades emitted a soft electric glow. I slipped out of bed and tiptoed to the lavatories, which were shared by the hospital and the dental surgery next door. In a snap, I went in one entrance and out the other. Ahead was the washbasin. Thanks to morphine, my arms and legs moved painlessly. After removing the skirting board, I slid in the note. Then I heard someone cough.

I stood up and tried to run, but the atmosphere was as thick as syrup. My feet were sticking to the floor. The harder I pushed, the slower I went. My heart was pounding in terror.

When my eyes opened, I was not near the lavatories as I'd thought, but in the ward, tucked up in bed. How could this be? I put my hand in the pillowcase … and found the note. Damn.

In the morning, Dr Owen removed the dressings and examined the burns. 'You're healing well. You can go home after lunch.'

Although I was glad to be recovering, I was also taken aback. Home? Camp 2 was not home. I would not be able to return to my real home in ages. Every day, newspaper clippings were pinned to the notice board. In Europe, Hitler had turned his attention to Stalingrad, but the Red Army was better-equipped to fight through the perishing winter. America was developing high-speed bombers that could turn the cities of Europe to rubble. If America entered the war now, Germany would not stand a chance.

The Nazis of Camp 2 would have ignored these reports. For them, only the shortwave broadcasts from Berlin told the truth. It seemed to me that two wars were in progress: a physical war of blood and destruction, and a psychological war fuelled by propaganda. The hospital gave me respite from all that. In Camp 2, I was no longer safe.

All this flashed through my mind as Dr Owen concluded the consultation.

'Twice a day for the next week you must go to the CDS clinic in your compound and have the dressings changed. Until your skin is completely healed, keep out of the sun.'

A simple *thank you* was all that I could manage. In an hour or two, my home would be a tent in the Nazi camp.

After lunch, a guard collected me from the ward. Outside was the army truck, its khaki paintwork gleaming darkly in the sunlight. I was invited to sit with the driver.

Out on the road, the truck bounced in the direction of Camp 2. Through the gum trees I could make out the perimeter fence and guard towers. I spotted the German café, its customers outside, smoking. There stood the blackened skeleton of my hut at the end of a row of corrugated-iron barracks that a duplicating machine could have spat out.

I was doomed.

Twelve

Instead of turning into Camp 2, the truck driver bypassed the gate and continued south along the sealed road. About ten kilometres on, he veered onto a dirt track that zig-zagged between paddocks. There on the rise was another barbed-wire enclosure and, within it, were dozens more corrugated-iron huts.

I held my breath, not trusting myself to speak. We stopped at the guard house, where a bored-looking soldier let us in. The truck trundled along a path between compounds, crossed an intersection, and halted.

'Here you are mate. Safe and sound.' The driver unlocked the gate of the northernmost compound and accompanied me on foot to the camp leader's office. With the delivery complete, he made a half-hearted salute and departed.

The camp leader was a short stout man of about fifty. Wire-rimmed *pince-nez* balanced precariously on his impressively large snout. 'Permit me to introduce myself,' he said. 'I am Professor Franz Klein. I hope you have recovered from your terrible ordeal. Your cousin is expecting you. Please follow me to your hut.'

My heart fluttered like a sparrow in dust bath. I would not permit myself to feel joy or relief, for fear that this too was a morphine-induced dream. In silence, I fell in behind him.

Slap, slap, slap went his feet on the concrete. His gait was as flat-footed as a duck's. I glanced at the soles of his shoes; they were tied to the uppers with bits of string. What luck for me and an easy path into the good books. All I needed were my tools from the other camp.

I trotted to catch up. We meandered between huts that were similar to Camp 2 but with six doors along each side. The furthermost hut, where we stopped, was shaded by trellises of flowering creepers. Surrounding it were several neat *Kleingärten*, bristling with maize, cabbages, and beans.

Georg dashed out, grinning from ear to ear. 'My dear *Cousin* Horst.'

'My dear Cousin Georg,' I responded in an even tone. The wary self-restraint practised in Camp 2 overcame my urge to hug him.

With unbridled enthusiasm, he pumped my hand and welcomed me to my new home. Although I was delighted to be there, I felt awkward in the presence of Professor Klein. I wondered if he was in on our little charade. I could not risk relaxing my guard, for fear that we'd both be punished.

For a moment the professor stood a little removed, then he wished us good day and walked off.

On our own now, Georg whooped with delight and ushered me inside. The room was like a rectangular wooden box. It contained two narrow beds, a desk with two folding chairs, side-tables made from packing cases. On one of the beds was a pile of clothing—my clothing—magically transported from Camp 2.

'I can't believe I'm here,' I said.

While I was delighted to be free of the Nazi camp, I was more delighted to be with my friend. At last, I could be myself again. Well, almost. I had switched from being a pseudo-Nazi to a pseudo-cousin. We would both have to watch what we said.

Georg insisted on taking me on a tour of the compound which ended at the hobbies workshop. To my amazement, my shoemaking tools and materials and the precious Singer machine had already found their new home. Beneath a window my bench was set up ready for me to start work.

'I've been fielding enquiries ever since Klein announced you were coming,' Georg said.

'How do they know about me?'

Knowingly, he tapped the side of his nose. 'We might be holed up in a chicken coop but that doesn't stop us from talking. You, my dear *cousin*, have quite a reputation. It seems our friend Werner and Klein are like this.' He crossed his index and middle fingers. 'That's how you got here.'

My gaze wandered around the busy workshop. It seemed that the specialty in this camp was silver jewellery made from melted-down coins. The pieces on display—brooches, rings, pendants—were intricate and beautifully-crafted. Some were masterpieces of Teutonic design while others were modern and original.

'Step outside and I'll tell you what happened,' said Georg. Turning my back on the workshop, I followed him to a secluded spot where we could talk.

Georg began. 'Klein convinced the Commandant to make a prisoner swap. Nazis in this camp for anti-Nazis in Camp 2.'

'But Australians think we are all Nazis, don't they?'

'At first that was so, but attitudes have changed. Here, most inmates are German-Jews. On the *Dunera,* you and I experienced mistreatment, but these fellows have survived the unimaginable. Klein has cultivated a relationship of trust with the Commandant. Let's just say that a little education goes a long way. Have you heard of Sachsenhausen?'

Slowly I nodded.

In fact, I had visited Sachsenhausen when I was fourteen. The concentration camp was a short train ride north of Berlin. Once, on school vacation, Max had taken me to see Herr Koch, his friend who was the Commandant. As I recall, it was mid-summer and terribly hot. From the station, we walked along a blistering asphalt road. The high prison walls were built of stone and the gate was made of steel bars. Three words were welded into metal: *Arbeit macht frei.* Work sets you free. A nice sentiment, I thought. My father was always badgering me to work harder at school. In my adolescent world, freedom meant playing soccer in the park. Much later, I learned that the words on the gate had a more sinister connotation.

Herr Koch's office on the first floor overlooked the entire complex of low buildings and yards which were enclosed within the electrified fences and coils of barbed wire. Herr Koch took me to the observation tower in the administration block, said I should wait there while he and my father talked business. From the broad bank of windows, I could see every detail of the camp.

That day, the grounds shimmered in a soup of radiated heat. Prisoners in blue-and-white striped pyjamas were taking exercise on a semicircular track below me. From my eagle's nest, I watched them trudge around and back, around and back, time and time again.

I squinted into the glare. The prisoners, all skin and bone, seemed to be in poor condition. Some were barely capable of a shuffle.

After a while it occurred me that this was not an exercise session. Guards, armed with whips and batons, were posted at regular intervals along the track. If a prisoner stumbled or fell, he received a lick of the whip. The track itself was a patchwork of uneven surfaces. Cobblestone, gravel, asphalt, slate, mud, sand. There could have been others, but I was too far away to see properly. On and on, under the blazing sun, the prisoners trudged. Around and back, around and back. Not a whisper of shade, not a breath of wind. Just watching made my eyeballs feel sunburnt. I thought they must be dangerous men to be disciplined so severely. Later, my father explained that they were more dangerous than common criminals.

'They are enemies of the Third Reich,' he said. 'What you saw was punishment for crimes against the State. The circuit makes or breaks them, and it can also bring salvation.'

'*Arbeit macht frei*,' I said.

He slapped me playfully on the back. 'That's the spirit, son.'

Georg said, 'Some former Sachsenhausen prisoners are right here in this camp. Academics, politicians, writers, imprisoned because they spoke out against Hitler. If they were lucky enough to be released, they fled Germany. But in Britain they were interned, along with all other Germans. Professor Klein is seeking justice on their behalf. He has written to the Prime Minister, Mr Curtin, asking for political prisoners to be classed as refugees.'

These revelations were news to me; it was a lot to take in. What did my father know about this? At the time, he was in thick with Herr Koch. He must have known what was going on.

Wherever I went amongst my countrymen, politics and religion were touchy subjects. Even here, in the family camp, I would need to keep my opinions to myself. Thankfully this lot seemed less brutal than the ones in Camp 2. One thing was certain: without the intervention of Professor Klein, I'd still be languishing in the Nazi camp. I would show my appreciation by making him a pair of shoes and said as much to Georg.

'Did you see what he's wearing?'

'Held together by a string and a prayer,' I said.

Georg laughed. 'My dearest *cousin*, I'm so glad you're here.'

The shoes were meant to be a surprise, so I enlisted Georg to get Klein's measurements. This proved simpler than expected. Within half an hour, my accomplice returned with the dilapidated pair I'd seen earlier.

'Apparently this is the *new* pair,' Georg said. '*Christus*, I would hate to see the *old* ones. I said you'd glue them up.'

I examined the shoes. The leather was of fair quality but the stitching was completely rotten. 'These are handmade and not by a professional. I wonder where he got them.'

'Do you want me to ask?'

'No, just curious.' I set to work, positioning the presser foot of the Singer in line with the existing needle-holes to preserve the integrity of the leather. I painted glue between the inner and outer soles and clamped them together. When they were dry, I traced around them and recorded the dimensions.

The real work began the following day. The style I chose was a lace-up with a rounded toe. Classic, smart, unpretentious. Although I barely knew the professor, from what I'd observed, the shoes would suit his personality. This was an important aspect of bespoke shoemaking. According to Opa, men who wore incompatible shoes paid dearly for their choice. Incompatible shoes were not only uncomfortable, but they also showed up the wearer as an ignoramus pretending to be someone he was not.

For several days I worked on Klein's new shoes, building up the layers of the soles, scraping and sanding the edges until they were as smooth as glass. While the glue was drying, I tackled the uppers and linings. It never ceased to amaze me how many pieces of leather went into a single pair of shoes.

At last, they were finished. After giving the repaired shoes and the lace-ups a good polish, I put them in a drawstring bag and took them to the camp leader's office.

Klein was writing at his desk. At the sound of my footsteps, he put down the pen and stood up. '*Hallo*, Herr Schuhmacher. How's it going?' He rose and shook my hand. 'Are you settling in?'

'I am delighted to be here. Thank you also for bringing my sewing machine and equipment.' I bowed slightly and gave him the cloth package. 'This is for you.'

He seemed taken aback, but accepted the package nevertheless. Toying with the drawstring, he said, 'Should I open it?'

'Yes, of course.' I clasped my hands behind my back.

He opened the bag and removed the shoes I'd repaired. 'Look at these!' he said with astonishment. 'I thought they were beyond redemption but you've given them new life.' He turned one over and stroked the age-soft leather. 'My thanks to *you*, Herr Schuhmacher.' He pushed the drawstring bag containing the other pair back across the desk.

I held up my hands. 'These are yours too. If they don't fit, I can make adjustments.'

Klein took off his shoes—the *old* pair—which were actually in better shape than the ones I'd mended. The lace-ups slipped easily onto his feet. He smiled and ran a fingertip over the shiny leather.

'The fit is perfect! But how did you know?'

'Trade secret. I'm glad you like them.'

'You're a bright young man with great potential.'

Lavish compliments like that always made my face burn. 'I am, and will always be, a bootmaker.'

'Nonsense! Don't limit yourself. You could do anything.'

'But I have an obligation ...' I said weakly.

'Don't waste your talents. Further your education; learn about the world.'

'Our business in Berlin spans three generations. After the war, my father expects me to return and take it over.'

'Do you know what the Nazis are doing to our Fatherland? Do you think this shoe business of yours will even exist after the war?'

I had never considered this scenario. The family business had always existed. It was my legacy, something I would pass onto my own son when the time came. Although that was decades into the future, I could not imagine my life playing out any other way. But what if Berlin was flattened like London and our footwear factory was a pile of rubble? Klein had planted a seed of doubt, and also a seed of possibility. I had much to think about.

Four years had passed since my escape from Germany. A lot would have happened; a lot would have changed without my knowledge. Since our transportation to Tatura, none of us had received letters from loved ones back home.

Opa was in his eighties now; my father was in his sixties. In his last letter to me in England, Max had crowed about a government contract to supply ten thousand boots to the Wehrmacht. Two designs—one for hot climates, one for cold—and five standard sizes. Extreme durability was the brief. The army did its own testing. Manufacturers who did not meet strict standards would see their contracts torn up. Max had written:

> *Our boots must be the best. Soldiers rely on their boots; armies rely on their soldiers; countries rely on their armies. Never forget that. Our factory is part of a chain that determines the future of Germany and the world.*

Klein interrupted my reverie. 'Come to one of our *Collegium* classes. Plenty to choose from. History, art, natural science, astronomy, botany. You name it. Some of the best brains in the world are in this camp. Our little university, our *Collegium Taturense,* has professors from Germany, Austria, Poland, Palestine. Just last month we negotiated an agreement with our colleagues at the University of Melbourne to collaborate on teaching and research.'

My secret wish was to attend university. Even in the family business, a degree in economics or accounting would be useful. The war had put an end to my ambitions. Although I'd studied hard in England, I'd missed taking the final exams. The key to a higher education had been snatched away. Somewhere between putrid Warth Mills and the Nazi camp at Tatura, I'd resigned myself to the life mapped out for me by my father.

'I was interned before I matriculated,' I said lamely.

Klein raised his hands in a generous gesture. 'No problem. Pick a subject, give it a try. If you like it, we can work out the details later.'

'What if I'm not good enough—?'

'Stop. No more arguments. On good authority, I know that you are capable.'

I took a breath, not quite believing what I was about to say. 'You mentioned natural science. Could I do that? I'd love to learn more about Australia and its animals.'

'Excellent choice! Science teaches a man to observe and understand the world. You can start straight away. Classes have been running for two weeks already, but you'll soon catch up. See you in the mess hut, tomorrow morning at ten.'

'Thank you, *Herr Professor*.' I shook his hand and turned to leave. At the door, curiosity got the better of me. 'Can I ask one more question?'

'Of course.'

'Who told you about me?'

'Let's just say a mutual friend.'

In our hut that evening, I told Georg about my surprising conversation with the camp leader. Except for the ting of a brown-spotted moth batting against the naked lightbulb, the hut was silent. We were at the end of a long summer. Both of us had stripped down to boxer shorts, donated by the good Lutherans of Melbourne. We were lying on our beds, our arms folded beneath our heads. The moth circling above might have thought it was seeing double.

'I think I'll give it a shot,' I said.

Georg shrugged. 'What's the point if you're stuck in here? One day the war will end and you'll be back in Berlin. Your old home, your old neighbourhood, your old job. The effort you put into study will be wasted.'

We spoke in a whisper. Georg had warned me that the partitions between rooms were paper-thin and our neighbour could hear every breath.

'I feel as if my brain is rotting,' I said.

'What about the shoes? People rely on you.'

'I can still make them; I like being busy. *Gott im Himmel!*' I sat bolt upright in bed. 'Her birthday is in two weeks. I wanted to give her a surprise.'

'Who is she?' Georg rolled onto his side and propped himself up on his elbow.

Without meeting his gaze, I reached for pencil and paper—toilet paper, that is—and began sketching. 'We met at the Waranga Hospital. She's in the Italian compound.'

'What does she look like? I might know her.'

Instead of asking how Georg knew an Italian girl, like a lovesick fool I went on to describe my angel, ending with 'skin as soft as silk.'

His eyebrows shot up. 'Sounds like you know her *rather* well. How far did you get?'

I put down the pencil and glared at him. 'It's not like that at all. She nursed me in the hospital. Her skin had this sheen … like silk … or velvet … a golden lustre.' I sighed and hastily added, 'We've been exchanging letters.'

That seemed to satisfy him. He flopped onto the mattress, which released a puff of dust. Hay fever was my constant companion. I sneezed six times in quick succession, wiped my eyes, and gave my nose a good blow.

Georg roared with laughter. 'You sound like a fart trumpet.'

Our neighbour banged on the wall. 'Shut up and go to sleep!'

Turning my back to Georg, I resumed sketching. Alice's shoes would have to be stylish and practical. I sketched a few ideas before 'lights out'. The trickiest part would be getting her foot measurements. Our only contact was through the secret mailbox. It would be downright strange to ask about her shoe size. The lights snapped off and I closed my eyes, trusting my mind to work on a solution while I slept.

The answer came not the next day but the day after. At breakfast, Klein announced that an Easter picnic would be held at the Waranga Basin for the children of the camp schools. It had been arranged with the Commandant as a reward for Camp 3 internees, who were industrious and compliant and never caused much trouble. He called for volunteers to carry the equipment and to keep the teenage boys in check. I knew which ones he meant: some of the German youths were running wild without a father's discipline.

One thing was certain: the CDS girls would be there. I put my name down immediately.

Not everyone was as enthusiastic about the picnic as me. Many in our compound did not celebrate the holy days of Easter. Georg said he had no intentions of 'herding snotty-nosed brats all day'. By then it was after lights out and we were in our room. Georg, who had taken up smoking, was visible by the glowing tip of a cigarette, which darted about in the darkness like a firefly.

'What have you got against kids?' I said, shocked at his strong reaction.

'I'm the eldest of three. All boys. I've seen enough ruffians to last a lifetime.'

Although we'd shared accommodation on-and-off for months, Georg had never mentioned his family. I talked about mine all the time, especially my dear Mutti—bless her soul—and Opa, who had practically raised me.

I'd never asked Georg about his loved ones either. Not that I was indifferent, but I respected his wish to keep his private life to himself.

That night he opened a door, so I pressed on. 'Where are your brothers now?'

The cigarette end crackled and glowed. 'Hard to know for sure.'

I lay there, wondering about the only two blood relatives I had left in the world: the bootmakers of Berlin. I pictured my home in Reinickendorf. The neat white house with green trim, ivy creeping on the walls, rose blossoms in the garden. Two streets away, the red-brick factory, the rich scent of leather ingrained in the woodwork. I knew and respected all our loyal employees. Herr Goldstein, Frau Goldstein, Frau Fränkel, Herr Zimmerman, Frau Zimmerman, Herr Meier. As their names popped into my head, I counted on my fingers. Twenty-two. I remembered them all, the men and women who'd been part of my life since birth.

My family was small: just Opa, my parents, and me. No siblings, no aunts, no uncles. The factory workers were my surrogate family. When I turned thirteen, they threw me a party to celebrate my becoming a man. *Bar mitzvah* they called it. After school that day, they presented me with a cake made by Frau Goldstein, the best cook in Berlin. Cherries on top glistened like baubles. Beneath was a layer of nut crumble and a rich chocolate base. So delicious, so good.

Not long after, the workers began to disappear. Sour-faced Poles were hired as replacements. When I asked Max where my friends were, he said 'on vacation'. No-one returned. The one I missed most was dear Frau Goldstein, my second mother. It was not like her to leave without saying goodbye. Every day I checked the mail. No letters. Then Mutti and I went on our own 'vacation' to England.

The chain-wire base of Georg's bed creaked as he shifted his weight and stubbed out the cigarette. The room was in complete darkness now, save for a shaft of light beneath the door. Perimeter lights: the constant of the night, so brilliant that our camp would have been visible from space.

Georg cleared his throat. 'My family is probably …' His voice cracked and he drew a sharp breath.

I didn't know what to say so I made a sympathetic grunt. How distant we all were, separated by oceans and a treacherous war. No contact, no information, and no end in sight.

In a husky voice, Georg said, 'I was on a *Kindertransport*. We left Germany months before the war began. My family was dirt poor; our neighbours in Ulm arranged our escape. They were Quakers, pacifists. They knew what was coming and did what they could to get us all out. But with only two places left, our parents chose to send Hermann and me. I felt awful leaving them behind, especially Josef, the baby. Lots of other children were on the boat-train that night. Some, like me, were in their teens; some were much younger. The smallest one was six.'

A match flared; smoke drifted into my nostrils.

'We disembarked in London. They sent us to Pakefield, a holiday camp at the seaside. In the dead of winter, it was deserted. Polar winds and bleak skies. The little huts for six had no heating and not enough blankets to go around. It was so cold that we put our mattresses on the floor and huddled together for warmth. That was when Hermann got sick. He died of pneumonia. He was seven.' Georg dragged hard on the cigarette. 'I was my job to look after him and I failed.'

I felt dreadful then for having asked. 'Oh Georg, I had no idea.'

'It's all right. Professor Klein has been helping me. It wasn't my fault, not completely. As for the rest of my family …' He stubbed out the cigarette and rolled over to face the wall.

On the morning of the picnic, I went to the assembly point, along with five other volunteers who'd been handpicked by Klein. The compound gate was open, so we walked along the central roadway towards an excited mob. There were dozens of children and almost as many women. The German kids were standing quietly in line like soldiers. The Italian kids ran about squealing while their mothers gossiped and gestured and juggled bundles and baskets.

A guard blew a whistle; we prepared to set off. The volunteers shouldered crates of food and equipment and stood at the rear. Up ahead was Alice. Today she wore the drab uniform of the CDS and carried a Red Cross satchel. Her mother, who was younger than I'd imagined, looked stunning in a red cotton dress. The pair could have passed for sisters.

The inner perimeter gate opened. In lots of ten, we filed into no-man's land. For a moment, we were locked in a long narrow cage like a chicken-run right around the camp. The outer gate opened and through we went to freedom. Well, almost. Outside the barbed wire prison, the sun seemed brighter, the air seemed clearer, and the colours of the landscape seemed more vivid. Two abreast, we crossed the drainage ditch, skirted the firefighters' shed and the motor vehicle workshop, and entered a bush track that meandered through paddocks and scrublands.

After a brisk half-hour walk, my shoulders ached from the load. To my right a break in the tree-cover gave glimpses of a vast blue lake. The older children took off. Throwing hats, shoes, and clothes to the ground, they careered into the water.

The women chose a picnic spot and the volunteers set to work clearing debris, collecting firewood, digging a fire pit, unpacking the contents of the crates onto blankets.

Alice patrolled the shoreline, a strip of yellow sand that melted into mud at the water's edge. Three small boys were dog-paddling offshore. Alice blew a pea-whistle and waved. Two swam in, but the third was lagging. I padded down to the sand. Alice and I exchanged a brief smile, but our attention was on the boy. He was clearly having difficulty.

Stripping down to my undershorts, I sprinted into the water. It was ice-cold and the bottom was slimy. The boy was thrashing about like a fish on a hook. After a dozen or so strokes, I was out of breath. Adrenaline propelled me forward. By the time I reached him, he was face-down and limp. I turned him over, held his head, prepared to give the 'kiss of life'. At that moment he spluttered and drew a breath. Panicking, he grabbed my neck and fought me with all his might. We both went under.

Resurfacing, I yelled at him to float. After a final struggle, his eyes locked onto mine and he surrendered. I brought him to shore.

Dozens of spectators lined the beach. After carrying him from the water, I lay him on his side on a towel. His mother rushed in and sat beside him.

Alice checked his breathing and pulse, looked in his eyes, took his temperature. Satisfied, she covered him in a blanket and spoke to the mother in rapid Italian. Now that the excitement was over, everyone drifted back to the picnic ground.

Dripping wet, I sat on the grass in the sun. I was shaking, partly due to the cold, partly due to the memories that flooded in. I was back in the North Atlantic Ocean, where each breath might have been my last. I'd given up all hope. Just like the boy, my body went limp.

In that moment, I hadn't thought about rescue. In truth, I'd willed the end to come quickly. But strong arms had plucked me from certain death. That day I became a survivor.

Alice came and sat on the grass beside me. She'd brought my clothes up from the beach. 'I'm convinced that boy is part cat.'

'Cats hate water.' I pulled my shirt on over my head. Even in the hot sun, I was shivering.

'Nine lives,' she quipped. 'It's not his first brush with death.' She snapped off a stalk of grass and nibbled on the sweet end before turning to look me in the face. 'Gosh, you're pale. Are you all right? I've got smelling salts in my satchel.'

'Stay with me and I'll be okay.' I hugged my knees and gazed across the lake. 'Perhaps I'm part cat too.'

'Do you want to tell me? Dr Owen says it's good to talk about our problems and our fears.'

'I thought I was over it, but then something happens and the memories come back.' I made an involuntary shudder.

She touched my arm, a gesture of kindness and sympathy. 'We all have nightmares. Mine was the day my father was taken away. I'll never forget my anger and the fear that we'd lose him.' She looked down at her hands, folded in her lap.

A short distance away, the picnic continued. Bread topped with melted cheese and tomato was passed around. Alice called it *pizza*, said that the Italians made it in the camp. The children stuffed their mouths as if they hadn't eaten in a month. The rescued boy, wrapped in a blanket, was asleep in his mother's lap. Alice's mother, Maria, and the Italian schoolmaster were in deep conversation on a shared picnic blanket. The guards smoked and looked bored.

In a voice no louder than a whisper, I told Alice about the torpedoing and sinking our ship. The nightmare of the *Arandora Star* would never leave me.

'Oh my goodness, it's a miracle you survived.'

'Out on the lake today, I relived the whole thing. I've never spoken about this, not even to Georg, my roommate.'

'I'm glad you're here and I'm glad you told me.'

I gazed into her sultry eyes. 'So am I.'

She put her arm around my shoulders. 'We are safe here. Teresa always complains about lost freedom. But what use is freedom during a war? In a war we are all prisoners. One day this will end and life will return to normal.'

'What is normal? Our countries are changed forever.'

Alice considered this. 'I'm lucky. I have a home and a mother I adore.'

'What about your father?'

Her eyes filled with tears. 'He died.'

I squeezed her hand. 'I'm sorry. I had no right to pry and no right to burden you with my misery.' I stood and pulled her to her feet. 'Let's get some food and talk about happier things.'

We each took two slices of pizza down to the sand, made a game of stepping in each other's footprints. Squatting, I traced my finger around one of hers.

'What on earth are you doing?'

'Committing your dainty feet to memory.' I pressed my large foot into the sand next to her print and stood back to compare. 'Yours belong to a princess … and I am the Beast.' I roared like a demon and chased her up the beach. She ran to the picnic spot where the women were packing up, turned and stuck out her tongue. Laughing, I pretended to stumble and fall to the ground.

With closed eyes, I lay silent in the ankle-deep grass.

Her shadow fell across my face. 'Are you okay?'

I grabbed her ankle. 'Better now, thanks.'

'Cheeky thing!' She kicked my side and offered a hand up.

We collected our shoes from the beach. While we were putting them on, I asked for her hut number.

'Twenty-three. Why?'

'I might be able to contact you directly. Would you like to see me again?'

'Of course. What's yours?'

'Fifteen. I share with my … um … cousin.'

'Oh? I thought all your family were in Germany.'

She'd caught me out. I scolded myself for being careless. When it came to fabricating stories, Georg was the master. Me? I was the opposite. Every time I strayed from the truth an imaginary alarm went off, screaming *Liar! Liar!*

'My immediate family is in Germany. My extended family includes a cousin, who is here, and an aunt in England.' That was not completely true either, but it was close enough.

'Was that the aunt you stayed with in Kent?'

I couldn't recall having said anything about my time in England, but then I'd probably said lots of things while I was in hospital and under the spell of morphine.

'Yes, before I was interned. When Mutti was alive.'

'Oh!' Alice put her hand to her mouth. 'I didn't know that your mother—'

'Don't apologise. She died and I couldn't go to the funeral.'

'Just like my papa. He was in Loveday and we were at home, two thousand miles away,' she said sadly.

I wanted to wrap her in my arms and give her comfort but we were in plain sight of everyone. I caught her gaze and said, 'The most precious thing now is friendship.'

~

In the all-white living room of the holiday apartment, daylight was beginning to fade. Horst's animated expression wilted and he rubbed his eyes. Recalling the difficult aspects of the past must have been exhausting.

Kathy offered him another coffee. He declined, said it would interfere with his sleep. She boiled the jug for herself. Today she was determined to beat the jet lag and stay awake until nine. More importantly, she wanted to finish *Heart of Darkness* and learn more about her sister.

'Before you leave Berlin, there's one place you must see,' said Horst. 'It is not pretty, but if you want to understand what the Nazis did to this country and our people, you must go to Sachsenhausen.'

Kathy swallowed, unsure she could stomach visiting a Nazi death camp. 'How far is it?'

'A train ride and a short walk.'

'Will you come with me?'

He shook his head. 'I do not wish to go. Too much shame and sorrow. The complex is vast. Allow several hours to look around.'

'I have two days left. But, if it's important, I'll do it tomorrow.'

'Good. Go in the morning and we'll have lunch at my place. I'll cook you *Spätzle*.'

'*Spätzle?*'

'German pasta.'

'Okay, it's a deal.'

'You will not enjoy Sachsenhausen, but once you've been, the knowledge will stay with you for a lifetime. Be sure to see the gold display in the museum.'

Later, Kathy curled up on the couch with *Heart of Darkness*. Some of the pasted-on sheets had come loose. She fingered a piece, smooth on one side and rough on the other. Rolls of the same awful stuff hung in the toilets at her primary school decades ago. At lunchtime, the girls would make paper chains, much to the janitor's annoyance.

Smiling at the memory, she opened the journal and returned to Alice and the family camp at Tatura during the last world war.

Thirteen

26 April 1943

Dearest Diary, I've met the nicest boy in the world. He's funny and kind and makes me feel happy. We met at the hospital after a terrible fire at his camp.

Teresa and I, and all the other CDS officers, were called out in the middle of the night. Twelve men were seriously injured; two were so bad that they were taken directly to the base hospital at Shepparton. My first time as a hospital assistant and I was excited, as well as a bit nervous. We were kept hopping. Cutting off clothes, bandaging burns, making beds, boiling linen, cleaning up mess.

Once the crisis was over, we were asked to stay on. There were too many patients and not enough nurses. Days flowed into weeks.

When there was time, Sister Kelly showed us the proper way to do things in a hospital. She taught us how to sluice bedpans, disinfect floors, prepare and serve food for invalids. But most of the lessons were about bed-making. How to mitre and tuck in the corners so the edges were as sharp as knives; how to change the sheets with a patient lying in the bed. We practised until our knuckles bled. At every lesson, Sister Kelly would repeat her cardinal rule. Over and over, she said it, until it became a standing joke. 'Do not fraternise with patients. You are not here to find yourself a husband.'

Behind her back, we'd tease each other about whether this or that patient was 'husband material'. It was fun to have a laugh with the other girls, but I don't think I'll ever marry.

For a whole week, Horst was one of my patients. At the end of each shift, I'd sit on his bed and we'd have the most fascinating conversations. Eventually, we were sprung. As punishment, Sister Kelly sent me home to Mamma.

Horst has recovered now and has been transferred to the German compound in my camp. At the Easter picnic, we snatched some time together. He promised to write, but I don't know how that can happen. I'd really like to see him again.

6 May 1943

When I came back from the clinic today, I found a message from Horst under my door. How it got there is a mystery. Luckily Mamma was out, so I read it straight away.

His writing in English is beautiful, better than most native speakers. I don't know much about him, other than he was born in Berlin and went to school in Kent. The letter is bright and newsy, written as a penfriend, not a boyfriend.

The routine in his compound sounds as boring as ours. Rollcall, work, eat, sleep. Currently he's studying at the *Collegium Taturense*, which I've never heard of. Perhaps Mamma knows, but to wheedle information out of her without raising her suspicions will be tricky. Her scandal detector is super-sensitive. For now, I want our friendship to remain a secret.

17 May 1943

My birthday today. Mamma gave me a pair of pink woollen socks that she'd made herself. I've never seen her knit; I don't know how she found the time. Where we live in the tropics, there's no need for warm socks, but I need them here. In Currawong, my entire winter wardrobe consists of two long-sleeved blouses, a pair of dungarees, and a green cardigan. Thanks to the Red Cross, I now have enough warm woollies to see me through a freezing winter to come.

Breakfast was special: pancakes with pears. Cook made enough for our table of eight. There's Mamma and me; Teresa Moro and her brother, Ivan; the Moro parents; Mr Giuliano and his little boy, Maurice. Everyone sang 'Happy Birthday' and I even got presents. A packet of caramel toffees from the Moro family and an almost-new copy of *Little Women* from Mr Giuliano.

When I took the gifts back to my hut, I found a drawstring bag on the step. I could hardly believe what was inside. Shoes. Gorgeous shoes. Natural leather, hand stitched, laces at the front. They're as soft as kid gloves and a perfect fit.

Inside was a square of cardboard. On one side was a drawing of a cake and nineteen candles. On the other was a greeting. *May your birthday be as dazzling as your smile.*

I hugged the shoes to my chest. Such an amazing gift from a boy I barely know. Each time we've met—which I could count on two hands—I float on air. Maybe he feels the same about me. Yet there is a hitch. The nuns always warned us that boys can't be trusted. A girl can't be too careful.

I slid the shoes back into the bag, changed into my CDS uniform. *What you do on your birthday, you do the whole year round.* That's what Papa used to say. I didn't want to be late for work so I grabbed the shoe-bag and raced out the door.

Teresa had already opened the clinic. She tossed me a bundle of bandages and said, 'What's up?'

I dumped the bandages on the examination table. Whoever had washed them had taken no care; they were as tangled as a bowl of spaghetti. She hovered about, waiting for a reply.

In a low voice, I told her about the gift from Horst.

Teresa knows all about him and of course she approves. She approves of boys in general. In fact, she's seeing someone herself, another boy from the German compound. The pair meet regularly, which is quite a feat considering how protective her parents are.

I passed her the drawstring bag.

'Oh my Lord!' she gushed. 'They're so ... *chic*! He must *really* like you. How do you feel about him?'

'I don't know. That's why I wanted to talk to you. Promise not to breathe a word.'

'Cross my heart and hope to die.' She drew an invisible cross on her chest.

'The truth is, I am attracted to him—'

'And he is to you ... obviously,' she interrupted. 'So, what's the problem?'

'We don't know the first thing about each other.'

'Then have fun finding out! What are you waiting for?'

'In case you haven't noticed, we're surrounded by barbed wire and nosey parents.'

'No need to be sarcastic. There are ways around obstacles.'

'Such as ...?'

Although no-one was around, she lowered her voice. 'Swear never to tell.'

I crossed my heart. There, we were even.

She perched on the table. 'Near the boundary between the two compounds there's a grove of wattle trees. You've seen them, right?'

I nodded. The wretched things burst into bloom every winter. The yellow pom-poms smelt like rancid honey and made me sneeze.

'At night it's as dark as a cave and the fence-wires have been cut. All you have to do is squeeze between the wattle trees, unhook the wires, and you're in. Simple. The best time is at change of guard around midnight.'

I was truly impressed and asked if she'd take me there. Her response was to draw me a diagram on a piece of bandage. Getting there seemed easy enough. 'Do you think your … um … friend could get a message to Horst?'

'I'm seeing him on Saturday night. He'll pass it on for sure.'

I wrote the message on another bit of bandage.

> *Thank you for your lovely gift. Meet me near the wattle grove at midnight on Sunday 30th May.*
>
> *Yours affectionately, Alice.*

There, I'd set things in motion. Sneaking out at night to meet a boy is the most daring thing I've ever done. 'Wish me luck,' I said.

'What could possibly go wrong?' said Teresa.

31 May 1943

Last night, I took extra care to behave normally. After tea and evening rollcall, Mamma and I went to our rooms. As usual Mamma sat at the little table to write lesson plans and make notes about the pupils' progress. That's been her ritual ever since the Italian School at Currawong, which seems like a century ago.

To pass the time until midnight, I sucked on a birthday toffee and opened *Little Women*. The novel was about four sisters planning Christmas without their father, who was away at war. The book was written in 1869 and their war was different from this one. But the absence of a father struck a raw nerve and filled me with sadness. Never again would I have Christmas with Papa.

Brushing away tears, I put the book down and lay on the bed. Butterflies flitted inside the cage of my ribs. What if we were caught? What if Horst didn't show up? What would happen if he did?

I had an inkling of what a night-time liaison might bring. Teresa's stories about the world of love are risqué and exciting. I know nothing about such things. My parents and the nuns made sure of that.

Lights out. From Mamma's room came the whisper of prayers, the creak of the chain-wire bed base. Silence. Then the deep, even breath of sleep. I yawned. Fully-clothed, I lay on that narrow bed, wondering how long I could stay awake. When the temperature dropped, I pulled up the blankets, warm and cosy. My body became as light as feathers and I drifted out of the hut, out of the camp, up to our farmhouse in the tropics.

Papa came in from cutting the cane and sat beside me in the kitchen. His clothes, his face, his hands were black with soot and he reeked of burnt sugar. Normally he didn't come in without having a wash. He prided himself on looking respectable, even at home, even when he cut cane.

'Why do you want to go out tonight, Alessandra?' He took my hands and drew me close, so close that the sugary smell rubbed off on me. 'What are you trying to prove?'

I told him that I only wanted to see my friend.

His eyes flashed a warning; his grip tightened. 'I don't want to lose you.' The odour of caramelised sugar was intense, intoxicating, suffocating. I tried to pull away. Then, to my horror, he opened his mouth and released a bloodcurdling scream.

In a cold sweat I woke; my legs were entangled in the blankets. Goosebumps galloped up and down my spine. A foreign object was stuck to my left cheek. My terrified fingers reached up to explore. They found a wad of stickiness which smelt like caramel toffee. The wrapper was stuck to my pillow.

When the awful scream came again, I knew what it was. Curlews. Earlier I'd spotted a pair down by the wattle grove. All legs and knees, they'd stared me down with eyes that were almost human.

According to my watch, the time was a quarter to one. I'd slept right through our appointed meeting time. How stupid and rude of me!

Then my thoughts returned to Papa. I've never felt so close to him. After death, he has become my guardian angel.

I must send Horst a note of apology. I hope he forgives me.

18 July 1943

Sunday. My favourite day of the week. On Sundays, we dress in our best clothes and pretend everything is normal. Father Ryan, the Irish priest, says Mass at eleven in the mess hut. Latin spoken with an Irish accent is hard to follow. Not that it matters. I let my mind wander and only join in the hymns.

Mamma is disappointed in me. 'Disappointed' is her new favourite word. You see, I've stopped going to Confession. In this place, there's not much to confess. Besides, Sunday is my day off. Every other day I go to work. After Mass, we stay in the mess hut for *pranzo*. Today we had pasta with peas, stewed rabbit and fried cauliflower. For *frutta,* fresh oranges. Good food and good company always brings out the best in us.

I couldn't help thinking of our Sunday gatherings at the Italian Club before the war. Even in the rainy season, Papa would wear a suit and tie.

Every month, Mamma would make a new dress, which she'd wear with stockings and a hat. After the meal, Papa would join the farmers' debates about cane varieties, sugar prices, Mussolini, the canecutters' union, taxes. And he'd emphasise each point with a thump of his fist on the table. He was an excitable man but a loving man. How I miss him!

After the meal, Camp Leader Moro stood and raised his hands. We all knew what would come next. Every week he reports on the progress of the war. He gets his information from the Melbourne newspaper, *The Age*, and also from Rome by means of a shortwave radio receiver hidden in his hut.

Once the hubbub quietened, he told us that the Allies had landed in Sicily and were pushing north through the centre of the island toward the Straits of Messina and the mainland. His audience gave a collective gasp. Lots of animated chatter followed, some of the women wept for relatives still in the old country.

Mamma clutched her blouse. '*O Dio!* My poor mother.' I squeezed her hand. Nonna's hilltop town in central Sicily would be right in the thick of it.

Dan Moro held up the newspaper. Normally, papers weren't allowed inside the camp. *Sicily to fall* was the headline. Beneath was a picture of a burnt-out German panzer surrounded by American soldiers. He went on to say that the Nazis were on the run and the battle would likely be over in days.

A commotion erupted. The elation of being liberated from German occupation was counterbalanced by fear that Americans were also invaders. Were the Yanks any better than the Nazis? The women fretted. More lives lost, more homes destroyed.

In closing, Dan Moro said that *The Age* would come every day now and he would pin it on the notice board for everyone to see.

20 July 1943

The promised newspaper has appeared. Alas, like letters from outside, the censor has snipped bits out, which renders both sides of the page useless. Not that I have tried to read it, for there's always a crowd, squabbling over the meanings of English words. I don't want to stir the wasps' nest, so I keep walking and let them enjoy their little arguments. In my opinion, we will hear the important news when it comes.

26 July 1943

Now *this* is important news. Mussolini has been ousted from office and is under arrest in northern Italy. As soon as we heard, Mamma and I gave a big cheer. Others, including Dan Moro, are not so happy. *Il Duce* has been the leader for twenty years. Change is not easy, but I think this is for the best. In charge now is Marshal Badoglio, a military leader, not a politician. I hope he can end this damn war.

Closer to home, the threat from Japan continues. Everyone is talking about a 'Brisbane Line', which abandons north Queensland in the event of an invasion. As many of us here are from the north, we are very nervous. Our lives are in the hands of God and America.

While I was listening to Dan Moro, I glanced around the mess hut, at the hundreds of attentive faces. The children are rosy-cheeked; families are together. Yes, we are captives. But we are also housed, fed, clothed. While no-one can leave, no-one can get in either. It could be that this camp is the safest place on earth.

8 September 1943

Italy has surrendered to the Allies! We are no longer enemies. Does that mean we can go home?

9 September 1943

Dan Moro has spoken to the Commandant. The government has not yet agreed to our release. The biggest barrier, he says, is the war with the Japanese. North of Townsville is a military zone now. A special permit is needed to go there. Many of the residents have been evacuated or have left of their own accord. Mamma and I have nowhere to go, apart from the farm at Currawong, which is 180 miles north of Townsville. I think it would be better to stay here, but some of our friends have already packed and are agitating for a quick release.

According to Teresa, her father is being bombarded with questions that have no answers. It's so bad that he's locked himself in his office and she has to take him meals. She doesn't want to leave the camp without her lover, says she'd sell her soul to stay. He's German, so he isn't going anywhere. Only Italy has made her peace.

16 October 1943

Today I sent an application to the Brisbane General Hospital for a position as a trainee nurse. I gave them my Currawong address, for we are expecting to be released any day now. As I stuck on the stamps, an awful thought flashed through my mind. I pictured the camp censor steaming the stamps off the envelopes. Tuppence halfpenny multiplied by the number of prisoners in this camp would make him a nice bonus.

No, I must believe that my letter is on its way, complete with the red stamp of King George. Over the years, I've sent letters to all my friends in

Queensland and received replies every time. Perhaps I am going stir crazy like everyone else. Soon enough the gates will open, and life will return to normal.

25 October 1943

It has been six weeks since Italy's surrender. Mamma is getting impatient, but I am torn. I'm used to the camp, to the feeling of safety, to the routine. My job at the CDS clinic is a dream and I have friends here.

All the talk is about our release. Waiting is hard and emotions are running high. Mamma has thrown herself into work, devoting all the daylight hours and half the night to the Italian school. She and the other teachers want to tidy things up and give the pupils proper end-of-year assessments that will be recognised in the outside world.

Teresa is mooning over her German boy, who might have to stay here for years. She's full of schemes about how she can stay too. In my opinion, he isn't that interested. The Moro parents have no idea that their daughter is in love, even though it's right under their noses.

The other day Teresa said, 'If I go home to Parramatta, he'll forget me and I'll end up an old maid.'

I tried to talk sense into her about opportunities and freedom, but she didn't want to listen.

'Freedom. Pah! Obviously, you're not in love.' She lit a cigarette and stormed off.

There's no point arguing, but I worry it will end in tears.

And then there's Horst. Our friendship seems to have fizzled out. In the last message, he said he was too busy to write. The reason was flimsy and unconvincing. He's studying for exams in November but I think that's an excuse. Next year he wants to do science at the Melbourne University by correspondence. According to him, he can do this through the *Collegium Taturense.*

I screwed up the letter and threw it in the bin. A real university would never allow its courses to be taken in an internment camp. Does he think I'm stupid? My conclusion: he wants to shake me off.

I should forget about him and move on. Yet I can't get him out of my mind. How utterly confusing is war and love!

26 October 1943

Would you believe it? Teresa is getting married! She's asked me to be her bridesmaid. Should I be excited or scared? I hope she's doing this for the right reasons.

8 November 1943

Finally, our fate is decided. We are to go home. Instead of releasing us all at once, we must leave in dribs and drabs. This applies only to the women and children. The men are required to join the Civil Aliens Corps and work in the outback, building railroads and bridges. From what I've heard, it's a hard slog and the living conditions are rough. Although they're no longer behind barbed wire, the CAC workers are prisoners of the landscape.

The first lot went today, a group of ten women and children. Everyone turned out to wave goodbye. Ten happy faces and tears all round. In a matter of days or weeks, we too will walk out those gates forever.

In the meantime, Mamma and I are busy with the school and the CDS and making dresses for Teresa's big day. Well, it's mostly Mamma doing the sewing. I can manage a straight seam on the treadle machine but no curves or fancy stuff. We went through all the Red Cross donations and chose dresses that could be altered easily. Mamma's is pink, mine is blue. She's also remodelling a white gown for Teresa. It seems that Viktoriya Moro, for all her sophistication, never learnt how to sew.

13 November 1943

The wedding was glorious. The bride looked radiant, the groom was handsome, the food was better than any feast I have been to. That this could be achieved at short notice in an internment camp is amazing. Horst, who was best man, sat the bridal table at the opposite end to me. After the meal, we grabbed some time together and patched up our little misunderstanding. I'm glad we're friends again. I told him that we'd soon be released and promised to write.

16 November 1943

After my shift at the CDS clinic, I went to my room for toiletries before heading to the showers. Mamma was smoking on the step. When I said *hello,* she didn't seem to hear me.

I sat beside her and asked if something was wrong.

She took a drag of the cigarette. 'Darling, I meant to tell you this sooner. I've been seeing someone. Until now, we've kept it under wraps. It isn't right to find love in a prison camp.'

I know what she means. My love life is also causing me concern. But unlike Teresa, I'm realistic. I don't want to rush into marriage with someone I barely know.

'Who's the lucky fellow?' I said brightly. Inside I was squirming. The thought of my mother in a romantic relationship was uncomfortable to say the least.

When she said his name—Luca Giuliano—I could scarcely believe my ears. He's an ageing schoolmaster with meaty hands and a bulbous nose. Most unattractive. But, beyond that, he has this *attitude*. He thinks he's a peg above everyone else. And he shows off by quoting Homer in Ancient Greek, which nobody can understand. He has never swung an axe nor had dirt on his hands, but he's fluent in five languages and writes books about European culture in his spare time. The complete opposite of my practical, down-to-earth Papa.

'We began as colleagues, then became friends. Six months ago—'

'But he's married with a kid,' I snapped.

'His wife ran off with a Yank. You're fond of little Maurice, aren't you? We'll find a way to make it work.'

Never did I expect my mother to find another man. Holy moly! If this plays out, I stand to get a new father and a ten-year-old brother. That needs more than a few minutes to digest.

'I wanted to tell you sooner, but you're always preoccupied with that German boy of yours,' she said.

My mouth opened in surprise. It was impossible for her to know about Horst. The only other one who knew was Teresa, and she had plenty to hide.

'Everyone has their secrets.' Mamma stubbed out the cigarette and took another, offered the pack to me. 'Take one, Alessandra. I know you sometimes smoke.'

With a sense of disbelief, I accepted the cigarette.

'At the wedding I saw you slip out together. When you came back, all flushed and doe-eyed, you could barely keep your hands off each other.'

'Horst is really nice. But we haven't done anything … you know … not like Teresa.'

'What about Teresa?'

Me and my big mouth. That's when I realised that Mamma didn't know the real reason for the hasty wedding. The imminent release of the Italians was a good alibi. To avoid interrogation, I turned her question around. 'What about you, Mamma? What are your plans?' I sucked the smoke into my mouth and let it out again without inhaling. My head was spinning, and it was not all due to nicotine.

'Tomorrow Luca is being released to the CAC and he isn't thrilled about it. He's 42 and an intellectual. Physical fitness, nil. I don't know how he'll survive in the outback and I'm worried. Anyway, I've agreed to look after Maurice while he's away.'

'Oops.' She put a hand to her lips. 'There's another thing I need to tell you. Maurice is too young to be on his own. You don't mind sharing your room, do you darling?'

25 November 1943

Today, the gates of the camp opened for Luca Giuliano and a dozen other Italian men, destined for hard labour. Mamma, Maurice and I joined the farewell party and waved as the army truck rumbled off in a cloud of dust. Back at the hut, Mamma tried to amuse the boy with children's books borrowed from the Red Cross library. I left them alone to get acquainted. Although I wasn't on the roster, I went to the CDS clinic.

It isn't the same without Teresa. I miss her terribly and wonder if she's enjoying the role of wife and soon-to-be mother in the camp for German families. While the other girls at the clinic are nice, we aren't close friends. The wedding sparked a lot of interest. Their chatter about boys, and Germans, and German boys was a good diversion. Despite the temptation, I was careful to not let slip about Horst, or my mother's crush on the schoolmaster.

30 November 1943

At last, we are free of our barbed-wire prison! The three of us. Mamma had to get special permission to take Maurice, but that's all organised now. One year, seven months, and twenty-four days have passed since our arrest.

We are waiting at the little station at Rushworth for a train that will take us north. The weather is hot and a dry westerly is blowing. My hair is crackling with static. Maurice is down at the mouth. I think he misses his papa and is worried about living in the tropics. The other kids have been teasing him about crocodiles and snakes. Like his father, he's not the outdoors type.

Five other women and their children are taking the train with us to Queensland. The journey will be the same as coming here, only in reverse. This time, I hope, there will be no putrid gaols or staging camps or padlocks on the carriages. This time we are free! Well, almost. On parole would be a better description. We must report to the local police station once a fortnight, and not go anywhere without their permission.

I don't care. I just want to go home!

14 December 1943

I should have known it: the railway network is in chaos due to troop movements, which take priority over civilian trains. It took two weeks to reach Townsville, which is where we are stuck now. We had to apply for a permit to travel north into the 'military zone' where we live. It could take some time to come through.

Townsville is overrun with Australian and American troops and women's auxiliary services. Uniforms are everywhere. All day and half the night, military vehicles whizz up and down Sturt Street and along The Strand to the fort. Local businesses are pandering to soldiers, especially cashed-up Yanks. As well as the usual sandwiches and tea, cafés serve hot dogs, hamburgers, and coffee. Dancehalls and picture theatres are open every night and have queues out the door.

Decent accommodation is impossible to get. We are sharing a cockroach-infested room in a mildewy pub that overlooks the sandflats at low tide. Through the day the place is quiet enough, but that changes in the late afternoon, when the public bar beneath us overflows with men. Like pigs at a trough, they swill beer as fast as they can before six o'clock closing time. After dark, the soldiers and their girls take grog down to the beach and get up to all kinds of mischief. Through the open window, we hear them laughing and squealing until the small hours of the morning.

17 December 1943

Our travel permit came through and Mamma got train tickets this morning. Now we are rattling north to Currawong. In another six hours or so, we'll be home.

These past few days, Maurice has been a real pain in the backside. To keep him amused, Mamma bought him a Biggles novel from the book exchange but he's barely looked at it. Says that reading is boring and he'd rather be in the camp with his father. I know he's only ten, but his whinging is getting on my nerves. I hope he improves once we reach the farm. Then there'll be plenty of work to do and he won't have time to be bored.

Fourteen

Reinickendorf: October 2010

Kathy turned the page of the book, only to find that the overlay of toilet paper had run out. Flipping through the remaining pages, she refreshed her memory of Marlow's voyage up the Congo to retrieve a crazed ivory trader. While Joseph Conrad's story had a beginning and an end, the narrative she'd been following so keenly—Alice's—simply stopped.

In frustration she shut the diary-within-a-novel and slammed it down on the table, strode to the kitchenette and snapped on the kettle. Twilight had dissolved into darkness and the lights of the garden had come on. The silhouette of a rat skittered along the wall. A few stars twinkled feebly. In the distance, the glow of city lights tinged the low-hanging clouds a bilious shade of yellow.

Sipping tea from a mug, she stood at the open window, ruminating over what she'd just read. Although Alice and her mother had been forcibly taken from their home, the experience of internment was not as bad as she'd imagined. For that, she was thankful. She'd expected the Tatura camp to be grim and cruel like the gaol at Stewarts Creek. But, at the family camp, the guards had been friendly and helpful and the female internees had been treated with respect.

Even behind barbed wire, love had flourished. In fact, Kathy reflected, if it weren't for the camp, her own parents—Maria and Luca—would never have met. All along, she'd believed that they'd connected at an Italian *fiera* at Currawong. She'd believed that Luca was a widower, when in fact his wife was very much alive.

In the Catholic religion, marriage was forever. Divorce, while recognised by the State, was not recognised by the Church. But Luca was not divorced either; he was separated. If the wife had indeed 'run off with a Yank', then he could not have married Maria in any case.

Putting all this information together, Kathy almost choked on her tea. There were no other words for it: she was an illegitimate child. In 1955, the year of her birth, she would have been referred to as a 'bastard'. In the seventies, the slur softened to 'love child'. Nowadays, people didn't bat an eyelid if a child was born out of wedlock.

She didn't care that her parents were never married. What infuriated her were the lies that they'd told her. Her scheming mother had an answer for everything. On one occasion, a young Kathy had asked why there were no wedding photos. Her mother had explained that a tropical cyclone had destroyed all their possessions. Even Alice, who was visiting, chimed in.

'Oh yes, I remember that well. We tried to rescue a few photos but they were sodden and stained with mud.'

Kathy snorted. How could she have been so naïve? What other lies had she swallowed without question?

Fidgety and furious, she grabbed her jacket and keys, thundered down the steps, marched through the cold courtyard, out into the dimly-lit street. Oblivious to her surroundings, she followed her feet along the pavement. Her breath was a fuming jet of steam.

Much later and still seething, Kathy returned to the apartment. It was clear that her sister was in on the entire charade, which made Alice as much of a liar as their mother.

On the table lay *Heart of Darkness*, the only reliable witness. She opened it at the last entry and checked the date. 17 December 1943. What happened next was critical. Then she remembered the inexplicable gap in the earlier journal.

Before condemning the two women she loved, she should first read all the evidence. She dashed to the bedside table and retrieved the grey diary. It fell open near the middle, at the precise place where she'd left off. The transition was seamless; the timeline flowed from the grey exercise book, to *Heart of Darkness*, and back to the grey book. With dubious hope, Kathy devoured the remaining pages.

~

18 December 1943

Home sweet home. The first thing I did was call Pixie but she didn't come. Hopefully one of the neighbours has taken her in. I'll ask around later. The second was to find you, my dear old Diary. And there you were, right where I'd left you under the mattress.

How wonderful it is to touch your soft cover, to smell the earthy sweetness of cane land, to hear tropical rain on the tin roof. Memories of the family camp are fading. I never want to think of that place again. I will hide *Heart of Darkness* at the back of my wardrobe: out of sight, out of mind.

When we stepped off the train at Currawong, I could have kissed the platform. At last, I am back where I belong.

Keen to see Gwen Morris, I volunteered to collect the mail while Mamma scrounged a lift to the farm.

As usual on a Friday afternoon, the post office queue was out the door. Gwen, looking smart in her PMG uniform, was busy selling stamps, weighing packages, filling in forms. I stood in line, hoping we could speak for a moment.

When she saw me, her mouth dropped open. 'I thought you were down south.' Her eyes looked everywhere else but at me. After what her father did to us, no wonder she felt ashamed.

I asked if there was any mail. She rummaged through boxes and put several bundles of envelopes on the counter.

'Are you okay?' she said. 'I mean, you've lost a lot of weight since ...' Her voice petered out.

'I'm fine. You?'

She flashed a gold ring. 'I'm Mrs Peter Thomas now. We got married three months ago. He's an officer, very good-looking.' Her chest puffed out with pride. 'Right at this moment, he's on a ship off New Guinea, defending our country from the Japs.'

'Peter Thomas. Is he new around here?'

'New to Australia,' she said. 'He's from Oklahoma. Soon I'll be living a grand life in the U.S. of A.' She leant in. 'I can't wait to get out of this dump.'

I gasped at the intensity of her response. 'Maybe we could talk on your day off.'

'Sure,' she purred like an American.

I picked up the letters and left.

Outside, Mamma announced that the police sergeant would drive us home. 'He's the one who took us, so he can bring us back. Anyway, I had to report our whereabouts. My duty here is done.'

I'm sad to report that our farm is in a dreadful state. With no one to look after it, the paddocks are overgrown with weeds. The shed is bare of machinery and implements. The garden is an overgrown jungle, and the chooks have probably become someone's dinner. Inside the house is worse: an utter mess. The day we were taken, I didn't think to lock the doors. Apparently, this was seen as an invitation for burglars and light-fingered neighbours to come in and take whatever they fancied. A mammoth effort will be needed to put things right.

Mamma is wandering from room to room, crying out at each new discovery of destruction. Her precious dinner set is in a thousand pieces. 'Look at this! Our wedding present from my mother. Hand-painted in Sicily. Irreplaceable.' She kicked the fragments across the floor.

Maurice shoved his hands in his pockets and went outside.

'Watch out for snakes!' I called after him like a big sister.

That stopped him. He sat on the step, his feet safely off the ground. 'I *hate* snakes!'

I couldn't help myself. 'They probably hate you back.'

He scowled at me, picked up a stone and threw it across the yard. 'When's Papa coming to get me? I *hate* it here and I *hate* you too.'

I walked over to him, put my hand on his shoulder. He was sobbing softly. I bit my lip and sighed. I'm not overly keen on him either, but he's just a kid and he's with strangers when he wants to be with his father.

In a gentler voice I said, 'He'll come as soon as he can. In the meantime, we must be civil to each other. Do you think we can manage that, Maurice?'

He glared at me for a moment. 'Stop calling me Maurice. I *hate* my name.'

'What should I call you then?'

'Mick.'

'All right, Mick. Deal?'

He wiped his nose on his sleeve. 'Deal.'

Back in the kitchen, Mamma was picking up shards of her destroyed dinner set and putting them down again. She lit a cigarette and tossed the pack to me. 'Where on earth should we begin?'

I didn't feel like smoking; my fingers were itching to set things straight. Even if we tidied one room, the place would not seem so bad. Mamma was more inclined to wallow in misery and touch all the things that were broken.

I suggested that we look at the mail. She sniffed as if she didn't care. Undeterred, I untied the string and flipped through the letters. Most were bills, which I put aside. One, marked *Confidential,* was addressed to me. The envelope was mustard yellow and stamped with the Queensland Government coat of arms. I tore it open.

I am pleased to inform you that your application for the position of trainee nurse at the Brisbane General Hospital has been successful. The next intake commences on 10 January 1944.

Please confirm your acceptance in writing before 30 November. If you do not respond by that date, the offer will be withdrawn.

I whooped for joy and rushed to show Mamma. Then I noticed the dates and my spirits fell. It was too late. The offer had lapsed. I'd have to wait a whole year to apply again.

'Phone them. Explain what's happened. I'm sure they'll still want you,' she said.

I raced out to the shed, found my pushbike beneath some fallen sheets of iron. Despite lying in the dirt for two years, it was still in working order. I cleaned it and pumped up the tyres.

But now it's after five and the post office is closed. That phone call will have to wait until Monday.

20 December 1943

First thing in the morning, I pedalled into town. Half way, my legs cramped up and I had to stop and stretch. After so little physical activity in the camp, I'm out of condition.

At the post office, Gwen was alone at the counter. I told her about the nursing offer and she wished me luck. We talked for a while and I'm glad to say that we are still friends.

Half an hour later I was on the phone, speaking to the matron-in-charge at the Brisbane hospital.

'If it weren't for such a glowing reference, my answer might have been different,' she said. 'I contacted Dr Owen myself. He was a surgeon here before the war. Lovely man.'

I was jumping out of my skin. Who'd have known that a lowly first-aid position would have led to this? Silently I thanked the camp doctor who had written my reference and also the little boy whose encounter with a venomous snake had steered me onto this path.

Matron continued. 'As you know, training commences on the tenth of January. Can you promise to be here, ready to start?

'Absolutely,' I said without hesitation.

'Excellent,' said Matron. 'I'll post you the necessary papers. As you are under-age, a parent must sign. Return them immediately.'

With renewed vigour I sped home. In three weeks, I would begin training and my dream to be a nurse would come true. Mamma's mood improved, as if my imminent departure was a blessing.

31 December 1943

I'm on my way to Brisbane, super excited about the next part of my life. If not for Gwen, I would have missed the train. She's a good friend and I'll never forget her.

Last night a storm blew, bringing enough rain for the rivers to rise. All night I lay awake, worrying that the railway line would be cut and my nursing career would end before it started. At dawn, I poked my head out the window. The rain had eased and patches of blue peeped through the grey.

After breakfast, the Morris's farm truck pulled up at the back door. I kissed Mamma, ruffled Mick's hair, and climbed into the passenger's seat. Gwen shifted gears, tooted the horn, and drove off. The truck is old but reliable. Gwen inherited it from her father. He drowned in a 'fishing accident', which involved a small boat, a bottle of rum, and a large crocodile. That was in 1942, a few months after we were interned.

Poetic justice, I thought when I heard. The incident certainly set tongues wagging. According to the rumour mill, the true cause of death was murder by Italians as retribution for dobbing them in. Despite that and all the other bad things he'd done—the drinking, the lying, the bigotry—the coroner concluded that his death was accidental. What really happened will never be known, for the crocodile disposed of the evidence.

As Gwen's truck bumped along the boggy track, we reminisced about the wet seasons when we were girls. We'd ride our bikes flat out through the puddles and skid in the mud. What fun we used to have!

In too short a time, the curved-iron roof of the station came into view and Gwen tramped on the brakes. She offered to wait with me, but I told her not to bother and that she'd be late for work.

Opening her arms, she said, 'Friends forever.' We embraced.

'I suppose this really is goodbye,' I said through tears.

'Promise you'll remember me when you get old?' she said.

We spat on our palms and pressed them together to seal the promise. Then we laughed at our silliness.

'Dearest Gwen, you will always be with me.' I pressed my hand to my heart. 'In here, where it counts.'

With that, I picked up my suitcase, walked through the gate and onto the platform. The truck turned across the tracks. I raised my hand in a wave.

She was at the intersection, glancing each way for a break in the traffic. The truck revved, backfired once, and was gone.

~

Kathy removed her reading glasses and rubbed her eyes. It was sad that, as an adult, she had not known her sister at all. Perhaps the age difference had held them apart, or the gulf between generations. Her memories were tainted by Alice's later years, when a cruel disease destroyed her mind, leaving nothing but a prickly shell.

With a sigh Kathy put away the diaries. The list of questions for Horst was getting longer by the day. But she would not ask until he reached the end of his narrative. Patience was critical, for he didn't like to be rushed. In good time, all would be revealed.

Tomorrow she would visit Sachsenhausen to learn more about the evil dictatorship that had ruled Nazi Germany. In preparation, she consulted the vintage Berlin guide book in her apartment. The single paragraph about the concentration camp was heavy on figures and light on sentiment.

> *Around 200,000 people were incarcerated at Sachsenhausen over a nine-year period, including after the war when it was a Soviet prison. Estimated deaths were 30,000, most of whom were civilians. Prisoners perished from hunger, disease, and mass extermination.*

These days, all those horrible deaths would be classed as murder. She knew that visiting the camp would be hard going. The Pergamon antiquities museum would be a more pleasant option. But then she would never understand this country. And that was important. Even after she returned to Australia, she knew that her ties to Germany would remain.

Fifteen

Oranienburg: October 2010

Sachsenhausen was surprisingly easy to locate: take the U-Bahn three stops to Gesundbrunnen; change platforms and take the S-Bahn to Oranienburg; follow the signs to the camp.

On a day that promised to reveal a litany of evils, the sun beamed bright and warm from an innocent blue sky. The road to the camp ran beside a high stone wall overhung with naked branches. After a stroll of about a kilometre, the wall curved inwards to a driveway of old cobblestones. There were no signs or plaques to announce the arrival. The gates were open, an unwritten invitation to enter. Others, whom Kathy recognised from the train, were standing quietly in the shadows. Setting her jaw, she marched in.

Beyond the entrance was a long white two-storey building, symmetrical, with a clocktower at the centre. She recognised it immediately from Horst's description. The main administration building was where Max and Herr Koch met to discuss business.

She climbed the staircase to the Commandant's office on the first floor. Framed black-and-white photos showed what it looked like during the war. The restoration was perfect. When she closed her eyes, she could almost hear the roar of guards' voices, the cracks of their whips, smell the smoke released by the ovens.

Up a second flight of stairs was the observation room and an uninterrupted view over the entire complex. Directly below her was the semicircular walkway that Horst had spoken about. Today a tour group was following the footsteps of those wretched prisoners. Even in sun hats and with water-bottles, the tourists wilted in the heat.

At ground level again, Kathy paused at the metal gates that led to the prison proper. Incorporated into the bars were the three words that had captivated a young Horst. *Arbeit macht frei.* Although he didn't know at the time, the slogan was written on most of the Nazi death camps across Europe. With bated breath, she passed beneath the ominous sentence. *Work sets you free.*

The open-air space was vast, mostly bare, and pancake flat. Many of the original buildings had been destroyed while some had been rebuilt. In 1945, the Soviets repurposed the prison camp for criminals and opponents of Stalin. After the reunification of Germany, the WWII version of the camp was restored as a memorial to those who had perished at the hands of the Nazis.

Using a tourist map as a guide, Kathy located the women's section, the Jewish section, the section for political prisoners, the multi-pan latrines and communal bathrooms, the concrete basement where food was prepared. Inside the huts, items made or used by the inmates were displayed. Triple-decker bunks, rough palliasses filled with straw, threadbare blankets, chipped enamel bowls, fragile blue-and-white-striped pyjama uniforms.

At one side of the compound was the 'clinic', defined by a high screening wall and a deep trench. The explanatory notice was written in German and English. At the clinic, prisoners were forced to have health checks. There, 'doctors' examined their bodies, looked in their mouths, sorted the 'patients' into categories. Some were sent directly to the shower block where they undressed in preparation for cleansing. Others were sent to another office to be measured and for further testing. All were reunited later in the trench.

Overcome, Kathy stood silent and breathless at the space where the clinic used to be. The souls of those prisoners lingered; their anguish rang in her ears. Her stomach was churning, her heart was pounding, yet she couldn't drag herself away.

The spell was broken by a group of young tourists, laughing and chattering in a language she didn't understand. How could anyone make jokes in a place like this? She felt like telling them to show some respect. But what was the use? Respect would not bring back the lives that were brutally taken, nor would it punish the murderers. She swallowed the bile that had risen up her throat and walked on.

At the pathology building, she forced herself to enter. The white-tiled operating theatre contained concrete slabs with drainage holes. Just from its appearance, it was apparent that 'operations' were not performed on the living, but on the dead. Beneath was an immense mortuary. Again, Kathy pushed through her revulsion. The dimly-lit cellar writhed with lost souls. Feeling faint, she escaped to the brilliant midday inferno only to encounter another section called the 'infirmary', where prisoners became guinea-pigs in medical and psychological experiments and those classed as 'homosexual' were forcibly sterilised or castrated. Many died or were maimed for life.

Feeling sick, Kathy wandered past a series of concrete slabs. 'Mass graves' said the guide map. Visitors had placed hundreds of rounded stones on the slabs in remembrance. She'd witnessed enough horror and brutality and was about to leave when she remembered the museum that Horst had recommended.

The modern building was located just outside the main complex. Glass separated visitors from the artefacts, which somehow softened the emotional blows that she had felt so strongly inside the camp. On display were items made by the inmates, as well as uniforms, flags and banners, excluding Nazi symbols, which were banned. There were even samples of a special currency called *Lagergeld* that was used to trade within the camp.

On another day, the museum would have been interesting, but Kathy was spent. In a vacuous state, she did a lap of the exhibits. The one that Horst was so insistent about was nowhere to be seen. She was preparing to leave when she spotted a nondescript mound of rubble in a glass box. The exhibit was so underwhelming that she'd almost walked past it. A small sign described it as 'dental gold'. The gold was not in shiny ingots or even yellow, as gold was supposed to be. Instead, it was dull and brown. Hopeful that Horst would provide an explanation, she snapped a photo and left.

Late in the afternoon Kathy went to his apartment. Her mood was gloomy, her mind preoccupied with the death camp. Intellectually she knew about the Holocaust, and the unimaginable things done in the name of patriotism and science. Out there she had felt the suffering in every cell of her body, a visceral response. Her visit to the camp was not educational; it was life-changing.

The *Spätzle* that Horst made were delicious but she had little appetite. He seemed to understand her mood and made no attempt at conversation. They ate in comfortable silence, broken by the popping of a wine cork and the clink of cutlery. When they were done, Kathy cleared the table. Questions eddied about her mind, but the experience was too raw. She needed time to process her thoughts and make sense of her reaction.

'Would you like to call it a day? Sachsenhausen is confronting.' His eyes were liquid blue.

'Thank goodness you and Alice weren't prisoners *there*. I'm glad I went, but I won't go back. No, the pain went straight through my heart.' Involuntary tears seeped from her eyes. She took a long swallow of water before continuing. 'If you don't mind, I'd like to hear more about the family camp. I find your stories light and uplifting. And that's what I need at the moment.'

'Then I shall continue. And nothing morose, I promise you.'

She smiled. Listening to him was a tonic.

~

Near the end of 1943, I sat the Victorian matriculation exams in four subjects: English, Mathematics, Geography, Zoology. I'd put in a lot of study and was well prepared. Professors from the *Collegium* had gone out of their way to help me, answering my questions about *King Lear*, quadratic equations, the formation of rocks, and the reproductive systems of monotremes. The German community in the district had come to my rescue and provided me with the necessary textbooks, stationery, and equipment that I couldn't have bought myself. Shoemaking was on hold. In fact, the last pair had been made for Alice's birthday in May.

I had little to do but wait for the exam results, and I was quietly confident that my grades would be good enough for a scholarship. But, while I'd been focussed on study, I'd neglected my friends: Werner, the woodworkers of Camp 2, and of course Alice. Even Georg, whose room I shared. At last, I had time to write letters again.

The day after the final exam, I sat at the little desk in my hut, sharpening pencils and tearing blank pages from the backs of exercise books. Where to start? Alice was probably the one I'd offended most. Some months earlier she'd sent me a note that read like an apology. Apology for what? I was puzzled. Afterwards, I'd written to say I was going into self-imposed isolation. I didn't ask about her curious note, didn't even mention it. When she hadn't responded, I thought she was angry with me. Georg was always warning me that women were unpredictable. If only we could have spoken face-to-face instead of exchanging squares of toilet paper on occasion.

I chewed the end of the pencil. No, I'd start with Werner, my dear old friend. I'd just begun when Georg burst in. His face was the colour of a beetroot.

'Oh,' he said in surprise. 'I didn't think you'd be here.'

'Where else would I be?'

'I … I thought … now that the exams are over … you might be … at the workshop.'

'You seem upset.'

He glanced around the room. His eyes skimmed the carvings and paintings that he'd made while I was preoccupied. He looked everywhere but me.

'Do you want to talk about it?'

He threw himself onto the bed. The wire base twanged; dust puffed out of the mattress. I sneezed. He lay on his back and folded his arms under his head. He stared up at the corrugated iron roof and sighed. 'I'm in big trouble.'

I swivelled to face him. 'I won't breathe a word, I promise.'

'I'd trust you with my life, but I don't trust these walls.' Georg knocked on the divider and our neighbour replied with a thump.

It was mid-morning and already the hut was like a bread oven, a taste of the torrid summer to come.

Georg lowered his voice to a whisper. 'I've told you about Teresa Moro, haven't I.'

I'd moved to the edge of his bed. Our heads were almost touching. 'The Italian girl you're keen on?' I murmured.

'Yes. We've been seeing a lot of each other. That's why I haven't been around much.'

Actually, I hadn't noticed, further proof that I'd been obsessed with my studies.

He lit a cigarette and continued speaking. 'We have a standing arrangement. Saturday nights we meet near the perimeter fence. She's a nice girl. Good looking too. Silky-soft hair and the biggest smile in the world. And … well … one thing kind of led to another.'

'Go on.' Frankly, I was mystified.

'Anyway …' He blew a plume of smoke at the roof.

I waited for him to finish.

'Now she's in the family way and all hell is about to break loose.' The last part came out in a rush.

My jaw dropped. Recovering I said, 'Are you sure it's yours?'

'Of course it is! I know for a fact. She was a virgin, for Christ's sake.'

'What will you do?'

He sat up and massaged his forehead.

'Do you love her?'

Slowly he turned his head in the negative. 'Don't get me wrong. I like her. Really, I do. But I don't want to be saddled with a wife and child. I'm only twenty. I've been locked up for four *bloody* years.' Although we spoke in German, English had the best swear words. 'Anyway, who in his right mind gets married in an internment camp in the *arse-end* of the world?'

I was completely out of my depth, for I'd never been with a girl. Although I was strongly attracted to Alice, I wouldn't have risked doing *that* for fear of the consequences. My life was mapped out, thanks to the *Collegium* professors. A degree, a well-paid job, a place of my own. In ten or fifteen years, I might find a girl and settle down. At my age then, time was plentiful.

'Do you need any help?' I offered. Mutti would have said that, except the problems I'd dumped on her were trivial. Not like this.

'Just let me be alone.'

Without another word, I took my hat and satchel and departed.

I had not been to the hobbies workshop in months and everything was different. On my former workbench was a lathe, a vice, and an array of woodworking equipment. Clamps, chisels, and the like. An elderly internee was in the process of carving a lump of mulga wood into a kangaroo.

My first thought: where was the sewing machine? The familiar clack and rattle gave me the answer. Working the treadle was a balding tailor called Herr Auerbach, one of the Jewish contingent on the *Dunera*. At Tatura he was remaking shirts, trousers, and coats using donated clothing and blankets. The little Singer was roaring up a length of grey cloth. The seamlines of the jacket were marked in chalk. Curved here, straight there. Punctuated by dots and crosses, the Morse code of the rag trade.

The sound took me back to the Berlin of my youth. The rows of workbenches. The hum of busy-ness, the shambolic symphony of machinery. The jovial factory workers: my surrogate family. How I missed those carefree days! I wondered what happened to Frau Goldstein and the others who'd simply vanished. Since being in Camp 3 with Jewish refugees, I had learned that in Nazi Germany there were no vacations. That was another of the many lies that Max had told me.

In the workshop I searched for my things. While the place was generally tidy, storage was limited. Every spot was packed with bags and boxes containing glass, wire, canvas, wood, clay.

On one crate, hidden beneath three others, someone had kindly marked my name in chalk. In the camp, we worked to the rule of 'finder's keepers'. While I was thankful to be reunited with my things, I also hoped that Herr Auerbach was a reasonable man, for I needed the machine for making shoes.

I carried the crate to a bench at the end of the hut. It was vacant for a reason: little light and no ventilation. A ratty odour tickled my nostrils and I began to sneeze. For now, it would have to do. My previous work space was taken and I had no right to ask for it back. I blew my nose and unpacked the crate. Found several boots, green with mildew, tied in pairs by the laces.

Repair jobs were my least favourite occupation. Cardboard tags identified the owners and the work to be done. All were neglected; all were overdue.

In self-pity I sighed. The promise of an education had lifted me out of this prison. During the months of study, I'd been released from working for no reward. Now I must return to using my hands, not my brain. Mending old boots smelt like failure.

Then I remembered Georg's predicament and tried to pull myself together. Mending boots was easy compared to the prospect of a loveless marriage. Two lives sacrificed for fleeting pleasures. I dared not think of the punishment that an Italian father might dole out to his fallen angel and the devil who'd taken her.

The very thought made my brain hurt. I needed to calm down. Perhaps I should take up smoking like Georg, except I hated the smell. Then I remembered that, in my satchel, was a chocolate bar bought from the canteen as consolation for a difficult exam. Emergencies like these demanded chocolate. I rummaged amongst gumnuts, bootlaces, pencils, bits of leather, but couldn't find it. Instead, my fingers touched a wad of soft cloth. Curious, I took it out.

The edges were stitched together like an envelope and my name and hut number were on the outside. The handwriting was Alice's. But how did it get there?

I pulled out the thread; the cloth fell open. Her message began, 'Meet me near the wattle grove at midnight ...'

The date that she'd written was long past. Perhaps that explained her out-of-the-blue apology. A change of plan? A change of mind?

If I'd received the invitation in time, would I have gone? Of course I would! But then, when she failed to show, I would have been angry or disappointed. What if we'd met that night? To borrow Georg's expression, would one thing have led to another? I swallowed the lump in my throat and tucked the message into my pocket.

In the evening, I returned to our hut to find Georg at the desk. His hair was a mess, as if he'd just woken up. He was scribbling in pen-and-ink on proper notepaper. The floor was littered with screwed-up balls of failed attempts. So immersed was he that he didn't look up, not even when my shadow fell across the desk. Quietly, I made my way across the room and sat on my bed.

At length, he put down the pen and lit a cigarette. 'I spoke to Professor Klein today.' He paused to draw in smoke.

'And?' I prompted.

'*Gott im Himmel!* What a *bloody* nightmare!' He put his elbows on the desk and dropped his head into his hands. Cigarette smoke curled up to the roof.

'Mind if I join you?' I reached for the pack.

He glared at me. 'You don't smoke.'

'Now is a good time to start.' I placed the cigarette between my lips and struck a match. The sharp odour of burning phosphorous hit me like smelling salts. Eyes smarting, I touched the flame to the tobacco and sucked until it caught. Smoke shot up my nose and down my throat. I coughed and spluttered. Our neighbour thumped three times on the wall.

Georg roared with laughter. I was glad that my antics had broken his misery.

'Here, let me show you.' He assumed the stance of a *Collegium* professor. 'You hold it like so.' He placed the durry between his index and middle fingers. 'Inhale. Breathe into your lungs now; not into your mouth. Now, exhale.' Showing off, he blew a few smoke rings.

Like a good pupil, I followed his instructions. All went well until the third drag, when the room began to turn and I felt woozy. I stubbed it out in the jam-tin ashtray. By then he'd lost interest and was picking at a scab on his forearm; his mind was obviously back on the problem.

'Klein says I should meet her father and live up to my responsibilities like a man. In the Italian compound, Dan Moro is held in high regard. He's the camp leader and the owner of a newspaper in Sydney.'

'Impressive.'

'Daunting, more like it. I didn't know any of this until today. Teresa never talks about her family. Under the circumstances, we didn't much time for conversation.' He smirked.

'What will you say to her father?'

Georg took another cigarette and offered me the pack. I declined; my experiment was over, never to be replicated.

'That's the hard part. I've been trying to write it down. A letter would be easier than a confrontation, don't you think?' he said.

'I think you should go. Have you spoken to Teresa?'

'Not since Saturday. She dropped the bombshell in a note this morning.'

'Shouldn't you ask what she wants first?'

Georg shook his head. 'Klein says I should do the right thing. In the old days, lots of marriages were arranged. Sometimes the couple met for the first time at their wedding. Imagine! He said that when a man and a woman commit to a life together, love grows over time.'

'What would Klein know about love?' I sniffed. 'He isn't married.'

'Actually, he's a widower. Before the First World War, his parents pressed him into an arranged marriage. A good match, he said. His wife died in childbirth.'

I shook my head in disbelief. 'All the time he tutored me, he never said a word.'

'Today the poor fellow was in tears.'

Klein was one of the strongest men I knew. Intelligent, resilient, persuasive. Never had he shown weakness or regret. In those turbulent times, his was the voice of calm and reason. He'd just cajoled me through a difficult year when it would have been easier to let me fail.

'It wasn't his intention to tell me. He tried to make me feel better and it slipped out,' added Georg.

We fell silent. What a day! Although it was not yet lights-out, we could barely keep our eyes open. I'd intended to quiz him about the note in my satchel, but it could wait.

'There's something I'd like to ask you,' Georg said from his bed.

I swallowed a yawn. 'What?'

'If Teresa accepts, will you be my best man?'

'I'd be delighted.' Sometime in the night, it dawned on me that Alice would probably be at the wedding. My sprits rose; I might have a chance to retrieve our friendship.

Two weeks later, on the day of the wedding, I entered the Italian family camp for the first time. It was the mirror image of ours. On the opposite side of the central road were Compounds C and D, which were for 'anti-fascists' and German families respectively. Upon marriage, Teresa would become not only a wife but also a German national. Compound D would become the couple's new home. At the end of the war, all three—Teresa, Georg, and their baby—would probably be deported to Germany.

Walking along the path through the Italian compound, Georg and I looked sharp, or so we thought. Our woollen suits were made by our resident tailor, Herr Auerbach, and our shoes were made by yours truly. In a show of solidarity and friendship, we walked shoulder to shoulder like warriors. Dressed in their Sunday best, the Italian internees stood outside their huts and watched us pass. The sky was cloudless; the sun was merciless. Even through the soles of my shoes, the red-hot gravel singed my feet. Sweat trickled down my back; beneath the jacket, my shirt was soaked. I glanced sideways at Georg. He stood as straight and tall as a soldier. His jaw was set, his gaze steady. Coming into view directly ahead was the camp leader's hut, the venue for the ceremony.

Earlier, Georg had told me that the meeting with Dan Moro had gone surprisingly well. Instead of throwing a tantrum and flinging his arms about, which was how he'd expected an Italian to react, the man had been polite and reasonable. He'd quizzed Georg about his intentions and prospects, his financial position, and whether the marriage proposal was motivated by love or obligation. Georg had responded as truthfully as he could. At the end of the hour-long meeting, Georg returned to our compound and announced that he felt lighter than air. He'd taken a shine to Dan Moro, and it seemed the feeling was mutual. Teresa had not made an appearance, which her father explained with a wave of his hand. 'A little sickness this morning. She'll get used to it.'

I trailed Georg into the camp leader's hut. It had been cleared of the usual furniture and set up like a chapel, with rows of folding chairs off a central aisle. At the far end was the altar: a table with a white cloth cover, a gold crucifix, two fat candles, and a colourful arrangement of flowers. Close by stood an elderly priest and a well-dressed middle-aged man.

Georg strode ahead and shook hands with them both. 'Father Ryan and Signore Moro, I'd like you to meet Horst, my friend and best man.'

I stepped forward and we all shook hands. Moro seemed taken aback. His gaze flicked between me and Georg a couple of times. '*Mamma Mia*! You two could pass as brothers.'

Quicker than a snap, Georg cut in. 'Actually, we're cousins.'

'You didn't tell me that the other day,' said Moro. 'Not that it matters.' Turning to me, he said, 'Welcome to our family, Cousin Horst. Please, take your places at the front and I'll round up all the guests.'

We sat on our allocated chairs. As the congregation filled the chapel, the noise level rose from a murmur to a roar. The scuffle of shoes on floorboards, the rustle of skirts, the swish of paper fans, the high-pitched babble of children. The cadence of the language was unfamiliar to me; everyone seemed to be talking at once.

'Are you ready?' I whispered to Georg, whose eyes were fixed on the altar.

He made the sign of the cross and nodded.

Father Ryan took his position at the front. 'All rise.'

The opening chords of the *Bridal Chorus*, played on a piano accordion, reverberated through the tin hut. With her arm linked to her father's, the bride glided down the aisle. Her tulle dress was as light and fluffy as a summer cloud. Then the heavens parted to reveal a vision in sky-blue. My angel, Alice. My heart skipped a beat; my knees trembled so much that I thought I'd drop to the floor.

With the bridal party in place, the service began. To my dismay, it was in Latin—which I didn't understand—and it went on for an eternity. Father Ryan obviously enjoyed the pomp of the performance. I imagined him on stage at the Berlin Opera, hamming it up to an enthralled audience. Not being Catholic myself, I copied all the standings-up, sittings-down, and kneelings-on-the-floor of the congregation. Finally, the priest asked me to hand over the ring, which I'd kept in my fob pocket. The plain gold band, I'd been told, was on loan from Viktoriya Moro until Georg was able to purchase one of his own. To my relief, it fitted Teresa perfectly.

With the formalities over, the four of us signed the register. I shot a half-smile at Alice as she stepped back from the table. Momentarily our eyes met, then she looked away. Was she embarrassed? Angry? Disappointed? Certainly, there was a strong reaction on her part, and it didn't look like love. I was sure that the misplaced letter had something to do with it. Somehow, I needed to speak with her alone and clear up the misunderstanding.

Arm in arm, the bride and groom made their way up the aisle to the door, followed by the two attendants, and the guests. Outside, Dan Moro led us to a small garden, which must have burst into bloom for the occasion. A guard with an army-issue camera shot two spools of film featuring the happy couple with various combinations of significant others.

Afterwards, we trooped to the mess hut for a feast. The head table was set for eight. The bride and groom were at the centre. I was next to Georg, then came Ivan Moro—Teresa's young brother—and Father Ryan at the end. On Teresa's side, was Alice followed by the Moro parents. Waiters, who were fellow internees, served us from large oval platters. There were three courses: pasta with mushrooms, meat in spicy tomato sauce, peaches with honey syrup. All were delicious and unlike anything I'd tasted. Ivan, who turned out to be good company for a fifteen-year-old, told me that Cook had prepared the entire meal using standard rations and produce grown in the camp gardens.

Speeches followed. When they were over, the mess hut filled with chatter that grew louder and louder until my ears shut down. The waiters moved the furniture, the accordionist struck up the *Bridal Waltz*. The newlyweds danced, then everyone else joined in.

At the table, Alice and I were alone. I shuffled across the vacated chairs to sit beside her. As I opened my mouth to speak, she cut across me. 'Well? Shall we dance?'

Although I could make a pair of shoes from scratch, quote Shakespeare's *King Lear* from memory, and solve quadratic equations in my head, I had never learnt to dance.

To find space on the floor, we navigated between swirling couples. After tripping over my own feet and treading on her toes at least four times, she suggested that we go somewhere quiet and talk.

In withering heat, she led me to a shady spot beneath a gum tree. We sat on a log, a body-width apart. Sweating profusely, I loosened my tie and popped open the top button of my shirt.

Her silky skin was pearled with sweat. She lifted the edge of her long blue skirt and kicked off her shoes. I stared in amazement: the shoes were the ones I'd made for her birthday back in May.

She caught me looking. 'They don't really match the dress but they're so lovely I had to wear them. Thank you.'

For the first time in ages, our eyes locked and I saw, in hers, something more than friendship.

'Oh Alice—' I began.

She held up her hands. 'Me first. I'm sorry about that night. Please forgive me for standing you up.'

'I didn't get your invitation. I found it my satchel two weeks ago.'

She began to laugh.

'What?'

'Teresa put me up to it but I chickened out. I wasn't ready to take the next step.'

'And I was slaving over the textbooks. I owe you an apology for not writing.'

She grinned. 'I thought you didn't want to see me again.'

'And I thought the same of you.'

'We are a pair of sillies,' she chuckled.

I grasped her hands and drew her to me. 'My angel.'

Her eyes glistened. She was so close that I could smell the peaches on her breath. A tingling sensation like an electrical current zinged through my body. My heart was pounding; my pulse was racing.

We fell into each other's arms. I covered her face with kisses, ran my fingers through her lustrous hair. Our lips met; I almost fainted with joy. Surely this was Heaven.

She pushed me away. 'We must stop before—'

'I've loved you the moment I saw you at the camp hospital.'

In her eyes was not love, but sadness.

'Don't you feel the same?' I said a little too earnestly.

Her face was a mask. She stood up and smoothed down her dress. 'I don't know how much longer I'll be here. We could be released any day.'

'Then we should make the most of what we have.' I jumped to my feet and kissed her again with renewed passion. She held onto me as if she'd never let go. When at last we drew away, my shirt was moist with her tears.

'Whatever happens, will you wait for me?' I said.

After a moment's silence she replied, 'That is an unfair question.'

Smarting as if I'd been slapped, I turned and plodded back to the mess hut. Inside, the raucous party was in full swing. Everyone was dancing, everyone was singing. Smiles of delight on every face. Our absence, it seemed, had not been noticed.

A respectable time later, Alice slipped in and motioned that I should join her on the dance floor. A reprieve, of sorts. We shuffled into a corner, where my two left feet could do minimal damage. In my ear, she whispered an apology, said we must take each day as it comes. We agreed to correspond, an arm's-length friendship. I wasn't ecstatic but there were no other options.

Late in the afternoon, the bride tossed her bouquet to the crowd. As if by magic or pre-arrangement, it landed squarely in Alice's hands. Everyone clapped and cheered. Her cheeks turned a deep shade of pink. Accompanied by guards, the young couple was escorted from the Italian compound to the neighbouring one for German families.

I returned to my compound, my hut, my room. A short while ago, I would have loved having a room of my own. Now the prospect depressed me.

I shed my wedding clothes, dumped them on the spare bed that was formerly Georg's, collapsed onto my own. The dying sun cast eerie shadows on the wall. Possums grunted; unseen birds wailed like murderous demons. My emotions were a turmoil of love and grief, hope and desolation. Sleep finally found me.

While I willed myself to dream of my angel, dreams have minds of their own. For the thousandth time, I was back on the *Arandora Star*. The blast, the smoke, the horror of being adrift on a wide empty ocean. I prayed it was not an omen.

Sixteen

Without Georg, I could not settle into work or study. Even daily activities were done mechanically and without interest. Bugle calls morning and night bookended a monotonous hollow routine. News of the war in Europe painted a worsening picture. The Wehrmacht was thinly spread across multiple fronts and ill-prepared for a freezing winter. Clearly the Allies had the upper hand. Two of our greatest cities, Berlin and Hamburg, were bombed. Judging from the press photos, the number of casualties must have been enormous. Not only airfields and bridges and ports were destroyed but also homes and schools and hospitals. Whether through incompetence or by design, the air strikes were indiscriminate. Of two bustling cities, little was left but smoking rubble.

For me, this was devastating. Remember, I hadn't heard from Max or Opa in five years. Were they alive or buried beneath the dusty remains of our factory in Reinickendorf?

With heavy hearts, we Germans awaited the finale. But, for the Jewish members of our *Collegium*, things took a turn for the better. Recognised as refugees at last, they were being progressively released to live as free men in Australia. One, a former teacher of mine and a doctor of psychology, introduced me to the phenomenon of the 'phantom limb': the ability of the brain to 'feel' sensations after an arm or leg has been amputated.

In a similar way, my brain responded to a 'phantom friend'. After lights out, I would catch myself talking aloud to Georg. Sometimes I'd wake to his snoring, which would stop the moment I opened my eyes. In the mornings, as I shaved or combed my hair, I'd see his face in the mirror. Absence made me value our friendship more than when we had been together. Sometimes, fellow inmates would call me Georg. Even Alice had remarked on our similarity. Perhaps the story we'd invented about being cousins was true. In our household, family relationships were never discussed. I had no idea where my roots actually lay.

A year passed. Correspondence with Alice was patchy. I received two letters from the nurses' quarters at Brisbane General Hospital. She said that she was enjoying the training. My reply was woeful. You see, the Army had invented a new form of communication to eliminate the need for censors and translators. The lettergram was a two-sided sheet of printed paper. On one side were lists of statements and tick boxes; on the other was space to write the receiver's address. Once completed, it was examined for unauthorised scribbles, then folded and glued to become its own envelope. It read like a military checklist.

The one I sent to Alice went something like this:

Health	*- satisfactory*
Activities	*- work, study*
General	*- in fair spirits*
Salutation	*- missing you.*

No wonder I didn't hear back.

An electrical storm tipped a bone-dry Victorian autumn into a frosty winter. Caught between the workshop and my hut, my clothes were soaked to the skin. The next day, I came down with the sniffles, which became a fever, which became a lung infection. Even the tarlike concoction that the CDS gave me did not ease the cough that kept me and my hut neighbours awake all night. Drained and breathless and sore in the chest, I was given an injection and woke up in the Waranga Hospital.

I had not been in hospital since the fire, which was when I met Alice. The ward had not changed. Same depressing colours, same uncomfortable beds. Mine was two beds along from where I was before. In my hazy state, I confused the two admissions. Any minute I expected my angel to sweep in with a dazzling smile. Of course, that didn't happen, for she was far away in Queensland.

My mind drifted between delirium and dreams. I didn't know if it was day or night, Sunday or Thursday. One morning, I woke to the sound of my name. Through the brain-fog I saw an old man in a white coat.

'My dear boy, what have you done to yourself this time?' said Werner.

I turned to face him. The bed squeaked like a rusty gate. My teeth were chattering from cold or fever or sheer exhaustion.

Werner stuck a thermometer under my tongue and pressed a stethoscope to my chest. Stepping away, he murmured instructions to a nurse. To me, he spoke in German. 'We'll have you better in no time. We're trialling a new drug that cures everything, even syphilis.'

'Do I have *syphilis*?' I said, incredulous. Men in my camp had spoken of the disease, said it was transmitted by women who hung about dancehalls and bars. I didn't know about such matters, except that the cure was worse than the illness.

'Of course not.' Werner laughed. 'You have pneumonia.'

The nurse returned with a kidney dish containing a syringe and a phial of clear liquid.

Werner filled the syringe, told me to roll over and pull down my pyjama pants. In an eyeblink, the injection was over. 'See you tomorrow,' he said and departed.

The next day, I was well enough to sit up in bed. Again, Werner pressed the cold metal disc to my chest. 'Breathe in. Out. In again.' Each instruction was punctuated by a noncommittal *hmm* that made me wonder if my lungs were better or worse.

'Now, cough.'

I did not need to be told to cough; I'd been doing that all morning. The intake of air tickled my windpipe and set off another spasm. From somewhere deep within, I coughed up a lump of brown muck, which pleased Werner enormously.

'Excellent, my dear boy.' He thumped me on the back. 'Now for your injection.'

On the third day, I felt like myself again. After the inevitable stab in the rump, I asked Werner if he'd stay and keep me company.

'Of course, my dear boy. My rounds are done. I always leave the best patient until last.'

'Thank you for curing me. Three days ago, I thought I'd die.'

'I have a great deal of faith in this new drug. And, for you, it has worked. Remarkably well, in fact.' He pulled up a chair and sat by the bed. 'Actually, I have something to tell you.'

I turned and suddenly we were eye-to-eye. His sharp blue irises were ringed with fuzzy grey, just like Opa's. I had no idea of Werner's age, but as I gazed into those old-man eyes, I realised that he would not be around forever.

As if reading my thoughts, he said, 'Yes, my time is coming to an end.'

'Werner! No! How long—' Tears of shock and sorrow blurred my vision.

'I don't mean *that*. I'm as strong as an ox. This is *good* news. I have been offered a position as a medical researcher at the Melbourne University. Next week I'll be released to live on campus.'

'Oh, what an opportunity!' I tried to sound happy, but I was a bad actor. It had been comforting to know he was just down the road. Melbourne was a half-day by train and impossible to visit for an internee like me.

He rummaged in his coat pocket for a scrap of paper. 'Here's my address. The lab is developing drugs which need to be clinically tested. We have government approval to use internee and prisoner-of-war volunteers as subjects. I will be responsible for the drug trials at Tatura, which means I will come here often.'

'Those injections you gave me ... am I one of your guineapigs?'

'Technically, no. I administered penicillin because I had some and you needed it. Given the extensive damage to your lungs from the fire, you might not have recovered so well without it.'

I pulled at a thread on my pyjamas. It hadn't occurred to me that my life had actually been at risk.

'Chin up,' he said. 'Soon you'll be back with your friends at Camp 3.'

'Most of them have gone. Georg is in another compound with his wife and baby. The Italians have been released, and so have the Jewish refugees.'

'Have you heard from Alice?' he said.

'How do you know about Alice?'

'You've been talking in your sleep. I understand our CDS girl is training to be a nurse.'

'But—'

'Dr Owen gave her a glowing reference. She's a remarkable girl. Someone to hang on to, if you get my meaning.'

'She's stopped writing. I think it's because I can't write back. Have you seen the stupid lettergrams?'

'Perhaps I can help.' Without elaboration, he pushed back the chair, patted my arm, and wandered off.

Later, Werner returned and gave me a brown-paper packet. 'Write her a nice long letter and I'll post it in Melbourne. Give her my address at the university, and I'll bring her letters when I visit. Internees should be able to correspond with their loved ones. To prevent it is inhumane. That's my belief. Now, I must attend to some paperwork. I'll see you tomorrow.'

Before I could thank him, he was out the door. I slid my hand into the packet. Inside were envelopes, a writing pad and pencil. Immediately I set to work. Instead of the usual tick-box charade, I could write whatever I wished, confident that my words would not be censored or analysed for coded meanings. I wrote that I missed her; that I longed for the end of the war; about my loneliness amongst hundreds of others; my dashed hopes for a university education. At the end, I asked her to write and signed off with 'warmest wishes, from your loyal friend'. I wondered if it would be too cheeky to finish with xx. Instead, I wrote: 'P.S. Remember the wedding? I think of you every day.' I folded the pages and addressed the envelope. Later, I gave it to Werner, who promised to mail it on Monday.

The end of the war in Europe was announced on a Tuesday afternoon by our new camp leader, Pastor Holtz. Professor Klein had snared a position at a Sydney university and had been released from Tatura. Holtz, along with a hundred or so other German-Australians, had come in from Loveday, which had been a camp for 'internal' internees, meaning those captured within Australia.

Holtz was a Lutheran pastor, originally from Düsseldorf, whose ministry was on the southern Darling Downs. His crime had been to deliver Sunday services in German, which was seen as 'preaching insurgency from the pulpit'. On that September day in 1939 when war was declared, he was captured and interned. Tatura was the third permanent camp where he'd been held. Despite the injustice, his optimism prevailed. He was respected as a man of wisdom as well as a man of God. I warmed to him immediately.

The reshuffle of internees also gave me a new room-mate. The fellow who moved in was one of the Nazi thugs from Camp 2. His presence expanded until he took up the entire room, leaving no breathing space for me. Not only was he short tempered, but he also had no idea of hygiene. Muddy boots were dumped on the floor; discarded clothes lay where they fell; taking a shower seemed to be against his beliefs. At night, he took schnapps for his nerves, enough to knock him out.

Hoping to learn more about Australia, I befriended some of the internal internees. Most were farmers, market gardeners, orchardists, wine growers. They told me that life on the land was similar to the old Germany before the disastrous First World War and the volatile Weimar Republic and the insanity of the Third Reich. They had been sponsored by Germans who'd migrated: a streamer ticket in return for two years' labour. In Australia, they said, arable land was plentiful and cheap. With a good water supply and hard work, a man could grow almost anything and make a living. Of course, there were droughts, bushfires and floods, but communities pulled together and nobody went hungry.

I tried to imagine myself as a farmer. Much could be said for a rural life in a big sun-drenched country. Peace, contentment, friendship. Until my capture I'd been a city lad, using my hands, not my muscles. Although I was grateful to Opa for teaching me the shoemaking trade, I was more attracted to the professions. My talent for raising crops or caring for animals was nil.

While at Aunt Berry's country house in Kent, I'd once attempted growing French beans. Caught up with a school assignment, I'd forgotten to water the seedlings. The poor little plants curled up and died. She roused on me for wasting the precious seeds, declared that if my heart wasn't in it, my thumbs would be forever brown. I was banished from the garden. No, farming was not for me.

On a May afternoon in 1945, Camp Leader Holtz called us to assemble at the mess hut. We were on the cusp of winter. A perishing wind blustered in, bringing drizzle that chilled us to the bone. Inside the hut, optimistic banter lightened the bleakness of the day. The howl of the elements without and the press of bodies within made the tin building seem warmer and cosier than it was.

When everyone was settled, Holtz addressed us in German. 'This morning I was informed that the Fatherland has surrendered to Allied Forces. A ceasefire is now in place. The war in Europe has ended.'

The reaction of the crowd was mixed. Applause, curses, whoops of delight, growls of derision. One voice rose above them all.

'To Hell with their bloody lies!' My room-mate, his face livid, punched the air. '*Der Führer* would *never* surrender! Never!'

The mob fell into argument and disarray. Pastor Holtz stood his ground, waiting for the fires to burn out. 'I will read in English from today's edition of the Melbourne newspaper.'

> *The German high command has agreed to unconditional surrender, effective from 12.05 pm today. The surrender was signed by General Jodl for Germany, and for the Allies by General Eisenhower's chief of staff, General Susloparov for Russia, and General Sevez for France.*

My room-mate swore again and stormed out.

Holtz switched back to German. 'I believe this news to be genuine, and I urge you, regardless of your allegiance or faith, to do likewise. Earlier today, the Commandant called all the camp leaders together for a briefing. He read out a bulletin from army headquarters and also gave us copies of this newspaper. Today is being called *VE Day*. Victory in Europe. For us, it is not a victory but a defeat. However, we must accept what has happened.

In Germany, the task ahead is enormous. It will take the power of God to see it through. Pray for our families, our friends, our compatriots who have suffered or perished. Give us strength to recover, repair, rebuild.'

A chorus of *Amen* echoed around the hall. Some of the older men bowed their heads, closed their eyes, let the tears flow as they prayed.

'If we are no longer at war, when can we go home?' A shout from the floor.

'If the release of the Italians is any guide, it could take many months. Remember, this is not the end of Australia's war, for they continue to fight the Japanese. Defence of this country is their first priority. As for returning to Germany, we have no ships to take us. And, if the reports are true, our largest cities—Hamburg, Berlin, München, Dresden—have been severely damaged by Allied bombs.'

I struggled to take this in, to comprehend my position and that of my family. While I was aware that the Wehrmacht was in trouble, I did not believe that the Nazis would ever surrender. A week ago, Berlin radio had announced that that *Der Führer* had gone to his bunker to plan the next attack. At the same time, the BBC reported that the Red Army had stormed the centre of Berlin and destroyed all the buildings, including the New Chancellery, which I'd seen under construction just a few years before.

As if it were yesterday, I pictured the steel cranes, turning and dipping over the site on the corner of Wilhelmstrasse and Voss-strasse. Through a gap in the fence, I'd watched the Meccano-set skeleton of poles, girders, and concrete blocks emerge from the earth. That was the day Opa had taken me out for my fifteenth birthday. The date was 1 April 1938. We'd gone to a good German restaurant on Unter den Linden. Before the meal, he bought me a glass of beer and said I made him proud. At the building site, he'd whispered in my ear. '*Der Führer's* new house will be grander than the Palace of Versailles. He has ordered it to be ready in one year. A waste of money, if you ask me.'

The building was barely begun. Although I knew little about the construction of palaces, it seemed impossible that in ten months all the work would be complete.

'*Genau.* In January next year, Herr Hitler will move in.' As an afterthought he added, 'I would not wish to be that builder, not for all the *Reichsmark* in the Treasury.'

In the mess hut, I silently thanked God that Reinickendorf was a long way from the centre of Berlin. For the Allies, the borough had little of military or political interest. Residences, factories, shops, schools lined the streets. I prayed that Opa and my father were safe.

In five long years we'd had no contact. Even when we were in London there'd been just a few letters and phone calls before war was declared. After that, communications between the two countries were curtailed.

~

'It's getting late,' said Kathy yawning. 'It's been a long day. I should get back to my apartment.'

Horst placed a small leather book on the table. 'This is the last of her diaries, the one she kept, on and off, when she was a young nurse. Ten years ago, she posted the three of them to me. Said she didn't want them anymore and thought I might find them amusing.'

Until a few days ago, Kathy didn't know the diaries existed. She wondered why Alice hadn't given them to her instead. Another example of her sister's perversity. How frustrating to be angry with someone who was dead. Instead of having an argument to clear the air, nothing. Perhaps she should follow Alice's example and vent her feelings on paper.

Horst added, 'I felt honoured to receive them. She and I lived through difficult times; we understood each other. In reading them, I hope you discover the real Alice.'

In her apartment, Kathy put the nurses' diary on the table. She was tired. Too tired and frazzled to concentrate. Tomorrow, she'd take a peek into the next phase of Alice's life and then visit Horst in the afternoon.

Time was ticking and she was not through with Berlin, hadn't even scratched the surface. Horst treated her like family and she was genuinely fond of him. She wanted to listen to his stories and spend time in his company. Her promise to Alice had come with plenty of strings attached. But first, she must stop the clock.

In the morning, she phoned Jack in Australia. In Brisbane, it was evening and he'd just arrived home from work.

Briefly she sketched out her plan.

'Considering Horst's advanced age, you might not have another opportunity,' he said. 'Cruises can be cancelled; flights can be changed. Make a few phone calls and send me an email.'

Her heart swelled. What a lucky woman she was to have a husband like Jack. Of course she could rearrange her itinerary and she could do it now with his blessing. The urgency had gone and she could relax. Without her realising, the purpose of her visit had shifted from obligation to love. Thanks to the diaries, young Alice was emerging as entirely different from the aloof elderly woman that Kathy remembered.

If only they'd been closer. Was it possible to patch up a relationship after death? With this thought in mind, she opened the leather diary and began to read.

Seventeen

10 January 1944

A new beginning warrants a new journal. I bought this gorgeous leather notebook from the McWhirters department store in Brisbane. Dearest Diary, I hope you like your new home. By the way, I have kept my previous scribblings and have brought both the grey exercise book and *Heart of Darkness* with me. I couldn't bear for Mamma—or anyone else—to read them.

My accommodation here is the People's Palace, a lovely old brick building with wide verandas and iron lace. It's a temperance hotel (a pub without beer) run by the Salvos. Very affordable. So far, I've browsed the shops, strolled through the botanical gardens, gone to the pictures, and had lunch at Coles cafeteria.

Today is my first day at the hospital and I arrived half an hour early. The place is enormous and the layout is like a maze. I asked for directions to the lecture hall but they were impossible to follow. Through the blue door, turn left, turn right, up the stairs, down the corridor, etc, etc. Everyone else seems to know their way around, but they're all too busy to help me. By pure luck, I stumbled upon it.

The lecture hall is cavernous with chocolate-coloured walls, a caramel-cream ceiling, shiny green lino, and a big bank of windows that lets in the light. The desks are set out like at school: ten rows across and four deep.

A dozen or more trainees were already inside, talking and joking as if they'd been friends for years. I added my suitcase to the collection at the rear of the room and joined a group of newcomers who looked as bewildered as me. Three were from small towns in the country; two were Brisbane girls. All of us will live-in during the training period and later too, when we become registered nurses.

On the stroke of nine, a matronly nurse stepped up to the lectern. I've nicknamed her Soursop, on account of her sour face and prickly demeanour. One icy stare that took in the entire room brought us to silence. We scrambled into our seats. A humourless two-hour lecture followed, in which the duties of a trainee nurse were outlined in graphic and gory detail. At the end, Soursop threw us lifeline. 'If you have any doubts about your commitment to this vocation, raise your hand now.'

No-one moved a muscle.

We collected our belongings, followed her out and along a bitumen path to a tall red-brick building with arched colonnades and open verandas. We were told to choose a partner before being allocated rooms to be shared by two.

My home for the next three years is a rectangular box with a double-hung window and a view over the railway line. It contains two narrow beds, two sets of drawers, and one wardrobe. My roommate is June Simpson. She is slim, freckled, and homely, mainly due to wire-rimmed glasses and a frumpy home-sewn frock. She looks far too bookish to be any good with people. I hope we get on. Three years is a long time to share with someone you don't like.

Also on our floor are the common facilities: bathrooms, a laundry, and a recreation room where we can go to write letters, listen to the wireless, or play cards. There's a piano too, and Simpson plays jazz like a demon.

The second-year trainees have warned us that Matron runs the nurses' home like an army camp. Bedtime is 22:30; breakfast is 06:30; lectures start at 07:50 sharp. The following is a verbatim quote from the Sergeant Major herself.

Woe betide any nurse who disobeys the rules.

I fear that this will be boarding school all over again.

11 January 1944

My second day as a nurse. After a boring lecture about hygiene, we were issued uniforms and taken to the wards. When we are not at lectures, we do whatever work is needed under the supervision of a qualified nurse. I've been allocated Ward 8-9, ENT (short for ear, nose, and throat). It's a busy place. Every bed is occupied; mostly by old men with awful hacking coughs. While I've patched up grazes and burns before, I've never seen serious or chronic afflictions like throat cancer.

As a trainee, my duties are rather different from expectations. Within ten minutes of entering the ward, I was handed a bucket and mop and told to clean the lino until it glistened. I filled the bucket, added disinfectant, and mopped my way carefully along the corridor. My supervisor nodded her approval. Hooray, I'm already a floor-cleaning expert. I remembered my former nemesis, Sister Kelly. She would have been delighted with my progress.

As I mopped around the beds, an elderly gent called out to me. 'Nurse, get me a bottle.' The effort of speaking set off a paroxysm of coughing.

A bottle of what? I had no idea. He was choking on his tonsils so I didn't want to ask. Dropping the mop, I scurried off to find someone with more than one day's experience in the ENT ward.

With a sigh of exasperation, the duty nurse handed me an enamel vessel with a handle and a long neck. My cheeks burned with embarrassment, for now it was clear what he wanted.

'Can you manage it yourself or do you want me to demonstrate?'

'I'll be right, thanks.'

'When he's finished, empty and disinfect the urinal in the sluice room.'

Mortified, I carried the bottle back to the patient, who thanked me with a wheeze and a fart.

30 January 1944

This evening after work, I went to the rec room to start on my list of letters. The urgent ones are Mamma, Gwen, Rita, Dr Owen, Teresa, Horst. Six letters and two hours until lights out. My intention is to send everyone my address and give a summary of my adventures in the big smoke. I tackled the easy ones first and saved the hardest until last.

I haven't written to Horst since I left Tatura and, to be honest, I've been putting it off. Although I think about him all the time, it's impossible to express my feelings on paper. Unless he's telepathic, he doesn't know how much I miss him. Should I write a love letter? I've never written one of those, nor have I received one. I don't know how to begin.

Horst is still at the family camp and will probably stay there until the end of the war. Of course, my letter will go through the censor, so I have to be careful. We both do. Even if I pour out my heart, his reply will be bland and brief. Perhaps I should wait until restrictions are lifted. No, that could take years. Better to write something puerile than nothing at all.

P.S. In the end, I scribbled a few sentences about my job and the hospital. Due to all my dithering, my two hours are almost up. Now I must run to the shower before the lights go out.

14 April 1944

If I can survive this training, I might actually enjoy being a nurse. I have been here for three months now. The pace is exhausting. As first-year trainees, we are given the worst and filthiest tasks you could imagine. Scrubbing out bedpans, mopping up vomit, washing blood-soaked sheets on operation day. It's an initiation of sweat, tears, and intestinal fortitude. If I can overcome my aversion to bodily fluids, I will fly through the course.

Nurses are the backbone of a hospital; they make the difference between a patient's quick recovery and lingering ill health. A good nurse encourages and cajoles her patients as much as she keeps them clean and fed. If a patient *believes* he will recover, he often does. The converse is also true. A bad nurse ignores her patients and disobeys instructions. In my experience, the General has no bad nurses. Anyone who fails or is lax about her work is dismissed. I know what is expected and I've thrown myself into it. Within three years, I am determined to earn the white veil of a fully-fledged nurse.

Our theoretical training covers a lot of ground. We have regular exams and rotations through the various wards of the hospital. My third rotation is to *Wattlebrae*, the isolation ward for infectious diseases. My colleagues tease me that *Wattlebrae* is where all the naughty nurses go. Many of their jokes and jibes are lost on me but I laugh anyway. I don't want to be labelled naïve, which I am. But I don't want them to know.

Wattlebrae is separate from the rest of the hospital. One section is for children with terrible childhood diseases such as whooping cough, diphtheria, polio. There are few vaccines and no magic cures. In the children's wards, patients with the same ailment are clustered together, which minimises cross-infection and makes our job easier. Caring for children who are desperately ill is both heartbreaking and rewarding. The smallest thing can give such joy. Each day, I bring my young patients something to amuse them—a cicada's shell, a butterfly wing, a bright flower—and their faces light up delight. Sadly, not all the little ones pull through. Losing a child is the hardest thing ever.

The adult section is divided into male and female wards. The spread of disease is prevented by handwashing, disinfectant, and masks. However, the prevalent malaise is not really contagious in a hospital environment. With the troops in town, venereal disease is out of control. According to Soursop, the cause of the epidemic is too many Yanks and too many loose women. She has warned us not to get friendly with the patients.

According to her, the female patients at *Wattlebrae* are 'the worst of the worst'. Statement of fact, no explanation necessary. It seems that we are expected to be bastions of virtue as well as streetwise enough to deal with the ailments of our promiscuous patients.

In my second week at *Wattlebrae*, I nursed a woman a little younger than myself. While I was doing the trays, we struck up an easy conversation. According to her chart, her name was Mrs Smith. Our innocent chat ended with an invitation to a party at Spring Hill on Saturday night. After months of study and drudgery, a night out sounded like fun. The venue was a nearby boarding house, a grey stucco building that I'd seen on my rambles into town.

'Could I bring a friend?' I said, thinking I might ask Simpson along for moral support.

'The more, the merrier. We're expecting a good turnout and lots of lovely soldier boys. Even if you come alone, you won't be lonely. We have a piano; there'll be dancing and sandwiches. Bring a few shillings to cover the booze.'

'Thanks, Mrs Smith. I'll let you know.'

'Mrs Smith indeed! Call me Gabby. Doctor says I'm out of here tomorrow. Thank God I've done my penance.' She laughed and plumped her bottle-blonde hair. 'I can't wait to be free again. Look, you don't need a printed invitation. Just turn up on Saturday sometime after eight. You and your pal are both welcome.'

Just then, the ward sister bustled in. I turned away to attend another patient.

'Zanetti, a word please. Finish the trays, then see me at the nurses' station.'

From the tone of her voice, I was in the doghouse. Hastily I completed the task. With head held high—for I was confident that I'd done no wrong— I marched to the nurses' station, which was separated from the ward by a screen.

'Zanetti, what did I just witness?' hissed the ward sister.

I chewed my lip. There I was, a schoolgirl again about to get a lick of the cane.

'I was being pleasant to a patient,' I said.

She frowned. 'I was not aware that your responsibilities toward patients included attending their parties on a Saturday night. Please, forgive my ignorance.'

'The party is outside work hours. I'd be back before curfew.'

'Do you have any idea who that young woman is?'

I was about to answer with shrug, but then thought better of it. I was in enough trouble as it was. 'No, Sister,' I said politely.

The ward sister lowered her voice until it was little louder than a breath. 'She is Gabrielle Smith, if *Smith* is indeed her surname. Her police record is as long as your left arm. As you are no doubt aware, she is a *gonny* patient. You don't get gonorrhoea from knitting socks and listening to the wireless, do you?'

'I suppose not.'

'Dear girl, I am trying to protect you. That woman is a *professional*. Do you understand what I'm saying?'

'Yes, Sister.' I took a step back and turned to leave. 'Thank you, Sister.' Despite a slightly bruised ego, my gratitude was genuine. The warning was a timely reminder to be cool and reserved around patients. Smoothing down my uniform, I stepped back onto the ward with renewed determination not to become one of the naughty nurses.

On our precious days off, we trainees try to do something fun and active. In summer we play tennis at the hospital courts or swim at the Spring Hill Baths. Sometimes Simpson and I walk down the hill to the Valley to spend our meagre wages on dress fabric or a new hat, followed by lunch at Coles cafeteria. My all-time favourite lunchtime treat is hot waffles with ice cream and caramel sauce.

The Valley is always buzzing with servicemen on leave, which the Americans call 'R and R'. Rest and Recreation. Even off duty, their uniform is smart and neat, and they carry themselves with pride. Always, someone offers to pay for our lunch or invites us to a tea-dance or the pictures. Unlike our brash Aussie boys, they are polite and confident in conversation. No wonder my friend Gwen Morris fell for a Yank.

Sometimes I think of Mamma's warning: *Don't trust a man with a silver tongue.* Although she meant door-to-door salesmen who talk housewives into buying rubbish at exorbitant prices, the term could equally apply to GIs and Marines. I must always be alert.

After nursing so many 'fallen women', Simpson and I have made a pact to stick together when we go out. Henceforth, an invitation from a soldier means both of us or none. As an added precaution, we will no longer go on dates after dark. Simpson has turned out to be a good friend and she's also rather fun.

30 May 1944

I've been nursing for five months now and have settled into the routine: work, eat, study, sleep … and sometimes a soothing breath of recreation. Every week I write half a dozen letters, and receive about the same number in return. Everyone I know and love lives far away. For me, letters are our only means of communication. As wartime postal delivery can be unreliable, I have learnt to have patience.

Today, after returning from a waffle-and-ice-cream feast at Coles with Simpson, I went to the pigeon-holes to collect my mail. Three were for me: one from Mamma, one from Rita. The third was a mustard-yellow envelope with a return address in Melbourne.

I started with Rita's. Bright and newsy as usual. An airfield has been built near Mareeba. All hours of the day and night, fighter planes take off and land. Apparently, the Tablelands are crawling with handsome pilots, but she's stuck on the farm, picking and stringing tobacco instead of having fun.

I eyed the mustard-yellow envelope. It looked awfully official with an insignia and all, but no clue as to the person who'd sent it. Inside was a second white envelope, addressed to me. My heart skipped a beat as I recognised the writing. I tore it open and devoured the words. Somehow, he had found a way around the censor.

Overjoyed and saddened, I wept from start to finish. Horst hasn't forgotten me at all. He explained what happened and how Dr Werner is to be the go-between. However, my heart almost broke in two when I read that he will be deported when the war ends. He had hoped to stay here and study. We might have married and had a life together. Now it will be a miracle if we ever see each other again.

Perhaps this is a sign. Already I am twenty; I need to think of the future. Nursing is not a job but a vocation. To be a nurse, I can never marry. I must choose between a family and a career. A nurse cannot have both; that is the law.

I stuffed the pages back into their envelope and opened the letter from Mamma. Her news also took my breath away.

Shock number one: she's sold the farm! My jaw dropped in disbelief; I re-read the sentence three times before its meaning sank in. Without a peep to me about her plans, she has sold the only place I can think of as home. I'm furious.

Shock number two: she's moved to Brisbane! She and Mick came down on the train and decided to stay. Of course, Mick was over the moon to be with his father again. The CAC was a disaster for Luca. He was working with a roadbuilding gang in western Queensland when he was stuck down with heat stroke. He fainted, fell into a ditch, and fractured his ankle. In Brisbane with his foot in plaster, he wrote dozens of applications for teaching positions. Nudgee Boys College snapped him up. He starts after the school holidays.

Shock number three (and this one rattled me to the core): she and the schoolmaster are living in sin! Although he's legally separated from his wife, divorce is out of the question due to our religion. Mick needs a mother and mine seems happy to oblige. To cover it up, she has changed her name to Maria Giuliano.

I hurled the letter onto the bed, wondering what had happened to the conservative God-faring woman who'd borne and raised me. Since Papa died, she's a different person. Impulsive, decisive, outrageous. While this will take some getting used to, I have nothing against Luca Giuliano or his son. Luca seems a decent man and Mick can be rather sweet.

I suppose everyone, including my mother, deserves happiness.

13 August 1945

More than a year has passed since my last diary entry. Suffice to say that nursing has kept me hopping. I'm in 'Cas' now. The Casualty Department is not for the fainthearted, and certainly not for novices. Eighteen months into my training, I've seen more gore and muck and pain than most have seen in a lifetime. Thankfully I am desensitised to all that now and can work without my emotions getting in the way.

Cas is where ambulances drop off human catastrophes: the result of bashings, accidents, rapes, dog bites, stabbings, heart attacks, poisonings. The list goes on. The department operates around the clock and we nurses have to be ever vigilant and ready for anything. The worst cases come in late at night. Working here is exhilarating, rewarding, and terrifying. And I love it!

I'm so engrossed in my work that I've almost forgotten we're at war. Straight after my shift, I go to my room and hit the books before crashing into bed. Meanwhile, Simpson and her friends gather around the wireless in the rec room, clutching onto news about bloody battles in the Pacific and the sad state of affairs in Europe. When they turn up the volume, the plummy voice of the ABC announcer reverberates down the hallway and into my room. With no soft furnishings to dull the sound, I can hear every word loud and clear.

Although I haven't consciously listened to the progress of the war, I seem to have absorbed every turning point through osmosis. I know about Mussolini's blood-thirsty execution by his own people; the Red Army's storming of Berlin; Hitler's death by his own hand; the German surrender. In the Pacific, I know about the New Guinea campaigns; the American bombing raids on Japanese soil, the atomic bombs—the weapons called the 'Little Boy' and the 'Fat Man'—that obliterated two major cities. Putting all that information together, I know that the war is about to end.

15 August 1945

It has happened! We are at PEACE!

I was on duty in Cas at the time. It was the busy hour, mid-morning Wednesday, when all the pensioners come in for free treatment. I was dressing an ulcer on an old codger's leg when the PA system crackled to life.

> *Your attention, please. The following news has just come in. The Japanese Government has agreed to an unconditional surrender. Hostilities will cease immediately. Ladies and gentlemen, the war is over!*

An enormous cheer erupted in the waiting room. All the nurses, even the cranky old biddies, squealed and whooped for joy.

My mind immediately flashed to my friends 'down south': Horst, Teresa, Georg. The war in Europe ended three months ago, yet they are still in the camp awaiting deportation. I would dearly love to see them, especially Horst, but travelling to Victoria is impossible while I am here in training.

Momentarily, I stopped wrapping the bandage and glanced at my patient, expecting to see jubilation. Instead, his leathery cheeks were streaming with tears.

'Four boys I lost in that bloody war,' he croaked. 'One son, three grandsons. God bless 'em, wherever they might be. I got nothin' to shout about. Nothin' to celebrate at all.'

I gave his hand a brief squeeze and continued my task, cool and calm as if nothing had happened. However, my mind was a whirlwind; everything in our world was about to change.

Yes, the war is over but now comes the fallout. The homecoming of the sick and injured. Operations, amputations, shellshock, malaria. Oh yes, and babies. Lots of babies. As trainee nurses, we have learnt about the aftermath of the First World War. According to Soursop, it will all play out again. Generations may change, but human nature stays the same. Better to prepare than be caught unaware.

When our shifts were over, Simpson and I walked down to the Valley to see what was going on. People in their thousands were out in the streets. Soldiers, shop girls, school kids, Council workers, factory hands. Flags flew from the rooftops announcing *PEACE!* and *VICTORY!* The marvellous words were repeated in three-inch capitals on the front page of *The Telegraph*.

A lone trumpeter played songs of the war years. Everyone was singing about bluebirds over Dover, kissing the Sergeant Major, and promises to meet again. A conga line of jubilation snaked along Brunswick Street. Tickertape confetti fluttered down; the street was ankle-deep in paper snow. Church bells, clock bells, school bells rang out across the city. The crowd moved as one, laughing and weeping and dancing.

Caught up in emotion, I burst into tears. Victory for us meant defeat for others. My family had made it through almost unscathed. But what will Horst find when he returns to Berlin? Will Teresa be able to live in Germany? Will Georg stand by her and their infant son?

Simpson grabbed my hand and dragged me into the swirling morass. The exhilaration was contagious and as unstoppable as the maniacal trumpeter and stomp of feet in the victory dance.

As darkness fell, Simpson and I strolled up the hill to the hospital. All the off-duty nurses were in the rec room. The wireless blared the speeches of politicians and reports about celebrations across the world. One of the girls popped a cork, splashed sparkling wine into our teacups. We made toasts to peace, to the return of our menfolk, and to the American heroes who'd saved us from the Japanese.

22 August 1945

The victory parties continue; spontaneous demonstrations of joy are the new way of life. My workmates can talk of nothing but when the men will come home: fathers, brothers, cousins, sweethearts. Six years is a long time apart.

The early recruits were sent to North Africa and Europe. Later, they were redeployed to Singapore and New Guinea. They had to acclimatise to desert, snow, and tropical jungles. They had to learn about weapons and tactics employed by three different enemies. Adapt, adapt, adapt. Over those six years, they'd survived landmines, tanks, U-boats, snipers, hand grenades, booby traps, death marches, and kamikaze pilots, knowing that any moment could be their last.

Some of my friends are waiting for news about soldiers 'missing in action', a terrible label that leaves families in limbo. Their loved ones have become war zombies: neither living nor dead.

Simpson's sister, an army nurse, is missing in Singapore. If she's alive, she might be in a Japanese prisoner of war camp. Little comfort in that. Prisoners who've been liberated from Burma are walking skeletons. I pray that nurses are treated better than soldiers.

Tonight I wrote to Horst, care of Dr Werner at the Melbourne University, and wished him a safe voyage home. As I don't know his Berlin address, I've asked him to write as soon as possible. I hope he hasn't already left Australia.

20 January 1946

Four months ago, I posted the letter to Horst and still there is no reply. I don't know the name of his ship or where it will dock. Frankly, I'm worried. Danger is everywhere, even in the shipping lanes. Reports have come in of troop carriers and hospital ships striking sea mines and sinking. After the near-death experience on that first ship from England, he must be terrified. In my heart, I know he will write as soon as he can.

We are told there is terrible destruction in Europe. London is in ruins. In Germany, entire cities have been destroyed. Houses, schools, office buildings, railway stations, churches. Blasted and burnt to the ground. Ordinary people in their thousands were killed or maimed.

What will he find when he reaches Berlin?

Horst once told me that he'd happily live in Australia. If nothing is left for him over there, he might return. I hope he does. Not that I wish anything bad for him. It's just that I really, really want to see him again.

15 August 1946

The war has been over for exactly one year. On my way upstairs, I picked up the mail from the pigeon-holes and there was Horst's letter. My letter to him, that is. The one I'd posted a year ago, care of Dr Werner in Melbourne.

On the front was a purple *Return to Sender* stamp and several forwarding addresses scratched out. Internment Camp Tatura; Defence Department Melbourne; C/- Currawong Post Office. Finally, Brisbane General Hospital, the address I'd written on the reverse side of the envelope. Now what do I do?

Eighteen

Reinickendorf: October 2010

By the time Kathy made her way to Horst's apartment it was early afternoon. With the time limitations on her stay lifted, she felt as light as air. On the way, she bought a kilo of fresh plums and a six-pack of Berliner Kindl.

He greeted her with a hug.

She put the beer in the fridge, washed the plums and arranged them in a bowl. All the while he looked on with amusement.

'What?' she said.

'Mutti used to arrange fruit, just like you did now.'

'Must be a girl thing,' she quipped.

'It makes this place feel like home. I don't know what I'll do when you're gone.'

'Speaking of which, I have a surprise.' She told him about her changed itinerary.

'How long can you stay?' he said.

'As long as it takes.'

'Marvellous! Stay with me if you like. Under all the boxes in the spare room is a bed you can use.'

'Thank you, I accept.' She opened two beers and they went to the living room, where she settled in her usual spot on the settee. *Prost*, they said in unison. In a week, or two, or maybe three, she'd miss this little ritual. And she'd miss him too.

'And now for the next chapter,' he said by way of introduction.

~

Shortly after VE Day, and with the encouragement of Camp Leader Holtz, I wrote a letter to the government requesting Australian residency. I attached two references: one from Dr Werner and another from Professor Klein, both of whom praised my abilities and commitment and argued that I would be an asset to the country.

Within a week, the response came. One terse sentence, like a slap in the face.

> *As an internee of Great Britain, you will be returned to that country on the earliest available vessel.*

That night, under the blankets of my narrow bed, I cried myself to sleep like a child.

Two months after the war in Europe ended, thirty-nine of us were driven from Camp 3 to the rail siding near Rushworth. In locked carriages, we travelled six hours south to the Port of Melbourne. Soldiers armed with rifles patrolled the docks to keep us deportees—and the furious mob that was out to kill us—under control. This was a stark reminder that, although we were no longer captives, neither were we free. A troopship would take us to England, that much we were told. We were given no other details of the voyage or what would happen when we landed.

Of all the war prisoners awaiting embarkation, one person stood out: my 'cousin' Georg. I was enormously relieved to see him, but disappointed to find that he was there without his wife and baby. He looked older than I remembered. His shoulders were hunched; his stance was one of a broken man. My impulse was to run to him, to give him comfort. The menace of the guards' rifles held me at bay.

In single file, we shuffled toward the gangplank. Our ship was the *Dominion Monarch*, a sleek grey vessel with artillery bristling from her flanks. Once on board, I stowed my suitcase in a cabin with two sets of triple-decker bunks. The space was small but adequate, nothing like the sardine-tin crush of the *Dunera*.

Until the ship cleared port, we were locked down below. Later we were allowed to roam the decks at will. I found Georg leaning on the rail, a cigarette smouldering in his lips. He didn't acknowledge me; his mind was in another world. I stood beside him, gazed out across the water to the city that was sinking into Port Philip Bay.

'*Hallo*, stranger,' I said at length. 'Remember me?'

He gave a slight nod but did not speak. My heart went out to him. It must have been hard to be leaving Australia alone, but he probably had no choice in the matter. Teresa's circumstances were not straightforward.

While she was German by marriage, she was an 'internal' internee and a natural-born British subject. The *Dominion Monarch* was returning 'external' internees to their countries of capture, in this case England. It could be many years until Georg and his family were reunited. In the interim, the baby would grow into a boy, and that boy would not know a father's love.

The voyage was uneventful, pleasant in fact. The ship docked at Liverpool in August 1945. On disembarkation, we were told that our papers would be processed at the wharf, and we'd be released to travel to the British address on our landing form. I'd stated that I'd stay at Aunt Berry's farmhouse in Kent. Any deviations or changes were to be reported to the police. How we would return to our homeland was not mentioned; I assumed we'd need to make our own arrangements before our visas ran out.

Our release should have brought me joy, but instead I fell into a pit of despair. I was about to re-enter the country that had killed my mother and stolen my youth, a country that indiscriminately hated all Germans, no matter who they were or what they believed in.

Wars may end, but hatred lingers. Camp Leader Holtz had said this in his parting sermon. By now, Holtz would be on the Darling Downs, working on his farm during the week and for the Lord on Sundays. The final line of the homily was: *In order to heal, we must be kind to one another.* In the pandemonium of the Liverpool docks, it was hard to imagine that kindness would be found in England.

Dozens of ships were arriving and departing and even more waited offshore for their turn to dock. Troop carriers, hospital ships, merchant vessels. Hundreds of civilians—mainly women and children—braved the summer sun to welcome the men home. Lines of war-worn soldiers snaked along the wharves.

A hospital ship disgorged a sorry lot dressed in the various uniforms of the British forces. Boys in their teens, men in their twenties, elders who would have seen action in the First World War. Faces were disfigured by burns or shrapnel. Empty sleeves were where arms used to be. Torsos had no limbs attached. Crutches, bandages, wheelchairs, stretchers. Few were able to walk without assistance. Along the uneven timbers they hobbled, a parade of human tragedy.

Any one of them could have been me. When this war began, I'd cursed the British for sending me away. I'd been in the wrong place at the wrong time, I'd thought. But what had I actually lost? A few years of personal freedom. I have never been a soldier. I could not imagine the horrors that these men had seen. I've never been shot at or tortured. Nor have I bloodied my hands in the name of victory. My scars are insignificant: a few patches of withered skin from an accidental fire which, by the grace of God, I survived.

In silence, we stood and let the line pass.

We entered a vast shed and joined a queue of thousands waiting for entry documents to be stamped. Suddenly it hit me that the name I'd adopted five years earlier might allow re-entry to Britain but not to my own country. German recordkeepers are meticulous. Even under foreign administration, as the country was then, it would be difficult to explain the mismatch between my British documents and the name under which I'd departed Germany. As the queue shortened, my palms grew sweaty and the papers wilted in my hand.

Two men stood between me and the official.

Then there was one.

Gott im Himmel, I was next.

'Papers,' said the official in a bored tone.

I put my documents on the desk but did not push them across. Instead, I cleared my throat and said in my best English, 'There is an error here. I didn't notice until now.'

'What do you mean, an error?'

'My occupation and surname are written the same.'

'Show me.'

I spun the papers around and pointed to the relevant sections. 'It says here that my surname is Schuhmacher, and here that my occupation is shoemaker. *Schuhmacher* is German for shoemaker. I am indeed a shoemaker by trade, but my surname is not Schuhmacher.'

'This is most irregular,' said the official, examining the papers. 'How could this happen?'

'The originals were lost at sea. These are replacements.'

'When was this? What was the name of the ship?'

'July 1940. I was on the *Arandora Star*, which sank after being torpedoed.'

The official's steely eyes locked onto mine. He held my gaze as if to evaluate the veracity of my story. 'I have heard of this incident. You are one of the survivors?'

'Yes. I was rescued and brought back here. Soon after, I was transferred to the *Dunera* and sent to Australia.'

'Wait here.' The official pushed back his chair. Taking my papers, he withdrew to an office at the other side of the building.

My temples were throbbing. I licked my lips and tried to swallow. My mouth was as dry as dust. Although I was telling the truth—well, sort of—doom hung over me like an executioner's axe.

After what seemed like an age, he returned. 'Is this address in Kent correct?'

'Yes, I'll be staying with my aunt.'

'You must go there directly and not leave until you hear from us. Do you understand? Severe penalties apply if you don't.'

'I understand.'

He stamped my papers and shoved them back at me. 'Next,' he called to the queue.

Abruptly dismissed, I grabbed my things and walked into England a free man. I glanced down at the stamped papers. My surname had been crossed out. Written above it in red ink was the name I'd received at birth. With the stroke of a pen, I was myself again. Horst Vogel, first and only child of Max and Elsa Vogel of Berlin.

Outside, Georg was waiting for me. 'What took so long?'

'A misunderstanding. Come on, we'll catch the train.'

'Does your aunt know about me?' he said.

'Don't worry. She'll welcome you like family.'

The station, which was adjacent to the wharf, was jam-packed with people and luggage. It seemed that half of England had assembled to welcome their heroes. Everyone was beaming as if they'd found the pot of gold at the end of the rainbow. Ugliness and disfigurement were brushed aside. Mothers whispered, *Look into Daddy's eyes; don't stare at his scars.* Later the colours would fade and darkness would prevail.

I stood in the queue for an hour, bought two one-way tickets to Kent. We waited in a spot by the wall and discussed our next move. If the ticket seller was to be believed, the journey could take up to a week, for the railway network was not fully operational. In some sections, rail bridges had been bombed out. Train schedules were unpredictable and subject to last-minute change. Georg smoked while I counted our pooled cash. After purchasing the tickets, we had barely enough money for food, let alone accommodation for up to a week.

He was gazing at a wounded soldier, a man our age who would never need boots again. 'I have a suggestion. If your aunt isn't expecting us, it doesn't matter how long it takes to get there. Let's make this journey an adventure.'

For the first time since landing at Liverpool, my mood lifted. We were indeed the lucky ones. We pushed our way onto next train, destination Birmingham. Standing room only. Midsummer. Though the windows were open, the carriage was stuffy and hot. As the carriages groaned away from the platform, stowaways leapt onto the running boards and clung to the side of the train. Inside, the crush of bodies held us upright like a full crate of bottles, even as we swerved around bends.

For a while we travelled in silence; then Georg put his lips to my ear and spoke in German. 'Here's the plan. We'll avoid cities and towns. The weather is warm, so we'll sleep where we can and live off the land.'

A nuggety man standing nearby must have caught the foreign words. 'Bleedin' Kraut-talk. Speak the King's English or get orf the bleedin' train.' He clenched his fists.

Georg spoke to me in English, loud enough for the brute to hear. 'Our station's next.'

'Where are we?' I whispered back in German.

'It's green and I can see cottages. Let's go.'

In between tramping through the English countryside, we hitched rides on various conveyances including tractors, horse-drawn carts, 'borrowed' bicycles, and goods trains that were going in our general direction. On the way, we ate raspberries and blackberries straight off the bush; burgled eggs from chicken runs; drank milk straight from the cow; gathered mushrooms in forests; caught fish in streams with our bare hands. We slept under bridges, in barns, amongst ancient ruins, in bomb shelters, and in two comfy beds, thanks to an elderly couple who'd lost both sons in the war and took pity on us.

Eventually we found Aunt Berry's country cottage, encircled by a dry-stone wall and rose gardens. While Georg waited by the gate, I went up the path to the door, which was open. I peered into the dark tunnel of the entrance hall. 'Hel-looo!' I sang. 'It's Horst. I'm back.'

Slippers shuffled across the floor. 'My dear Horst, is it really you?' Her voice wavered. Bent over a walking stick, she came into view. She was older and frailer than I recalled. I stepped into the hall and met her half way. She dropped the stick, flung her arms around me. 'My dearest boy! My dearest boy!' She could say no more as she choked back tears.

Once the initial shock was over, I beckoned to Georg at the gate. 'Aunt Berry, I'd like you to meet a good friend of mine, Georg.'

On cue, he came forward, made a slight bow and extended his hand.

Aunty's mouth opened. 'Oh my Lord! After all these years!'

I looked at Georg, who looked back at me. Simultaneously, we shrugged.

My aunt went so pale that I thought she might faint. I grabbed her elbow and guided her inside to an armchair. Georg brought in the walking stick.

'Can I get you a glass of water, Aunt Berry?'

'Ugh! Not water! There's brandy in the kitchen. Bring the bottle and three glasses.' She straightened her skirt and refastened a clip in her silvery hair.

I tucked the bottle beneath my arm and brought three sherry glasses, which I half-filled and handed around. Aunty took a swallow and colour instantly returned to her cheeks. Whatever had caused her little turn seemed to have resolved itself.

'Oh, my dears,' she said. 'I must apologise. It's just that you look so alike.'

I grinned. 'At the internment camp in Australia, we pretended to be cousins so that we could share a hut.'

'Nobody guessed that we aren't related. Not even my wife,' added Georg.

'You are married? Is she here too?' she said, looking around.

'Teresa and the baby are with her parents in Australia. It's complicated.'

'Life isn't easy. Never was, never will be.' Aunt Berry held out her glass for a refill. 'A shot or two of brandy helps.' She took a sip. 'Ahh, that's better. Brandy stimulates the brain … and lubricates the tongue.' She settled back in the chair and sighed. 'So, my dears, what are your plans?'

I jumped in first, answering for us both. 'We want to return to Germany, but travelling is a problem. Can we stay here? Georg wants to go back as soon as he can. His family is in Ulm.'

'Stay as long as you like. Ahh, Ulm,' she said wistfully. 'My brother, Jakob, lived in Ulm. I spent a lot of time there. Lovely town. Jakob was a teacher.' Like an eagle watching its prey, she fixed her gaze on Georg.

'What a coincidence!' he said. 'My grandfather's name was Jakob and he was also a teacher. He died when I was very young.'

Aunty leant forward, her hands on her knees. The skin was translucent, showing a scribble of blue beneath. She made the sign of the cross. 'Bless his soul. He didn't suffer.'

Georg raised an eyebrow. 'Yes, it was quick. A motoring accident, I understand.'

She made a tutting noise. 'And how is his daughter, Gertrude? If I'm not mistaken, her surname is Braun, or it was until she married.'

His face turned bright red. 'How … how … do you know my mother?'

I shook my head in disbelief. There must be some trick to it, or maybe Aunty was psychic. Although we'd shared accommodation and swapped stories for six years, I knew little about Georg's family.

'Are you a friend of hers?' he said.

'Actually, I am her aunt.'

His eyes popped. 'But,' he spluttered, 'the aunt who moved away was Bertha.' He said *Bear-ta,* as it was pronounced in German.

I gazed in astonishment at the tiny silver-haired woman, whose name, as far as I knew, was Berry Brown. The surnames sounded the same but the spelling was different.

'*Braun* in English is Brown. But Berry?' I said.

'My first name is Bertha, but nobody in England is called Bertha. When I moved here, I anglicised my name to Beryl and got a British passport. I used Berry for short. Berry Brown had an amusing ring to it. It suited me then.' Aunty topped up the glasses with brandy.

For the first time, I noticed the slight accent that belied her origin. Until then I'd believed her to be British born and bred. She had fine features, a peaches-and-cream complexion, and fitted into the English landscape as if her family had been there forever.

Georg skolled his brandy and grasped her hands. '*Es ist mir eine Ehre, Sie endlich kennenzulernen.*'

'The pleasure is all mine,' she said.

'Should I call you Great-aunt Berry?' he added in English.

'Stick with Aunty; it makes me feel younger. I never thought I'd see you again, my dear.' She took another gulp of brandy and mopped her tears with a hanky.

Georg glanced at me. 'So, we really are second cousins. No wonder we look alike.'

I shook my head. 'Aunt Berry and I are not related by blood. She cared for my mother when she was a girl.'

'Our families have secrets that neither of you understand,' she said, turning from me to Georg and back. 'And it is not my place to enlighten you.'

'Then who ...?' we said in unison. We glanced at each other and laughed. The brandy had indeed loosened tongues and inhibitions.

'Enough chitter-chat,' she said, rising. 'You must be half-starved after your long journey. What would you rather have for lunch: sandwiches or *Spätzle*?'

'*Spätzle bitte,*' we chorused.

On 15 August 1945, the Second World War officially ended after two atomic bombs convinced Japan's Emperor Hirohito to surrender. The London newspapers seized on the event, filling their pages with pictures of celebration: women kissing soldiers, people dancing through clouds of tickertape, that sort of thing.

Meanwhile, in rural England, Georg and I stuck close to Aunt Berry's house. Our whereabouts had been duly registered with the local constabulary and we had been warned to stay put. That didn't stop us from going on rambles and picnicking beside streams that meandered through the checkerboard landscape. Sometimes Aunty accompanied us, but only if we promised not to walk too far. 'My poor knees,' she would say by means of excuse. With so many farms and so few men to work them, we easily found employment, which put cash in our pockets. Aunty refused to accept payment for board, insisting that we were family and, anyway, she had more than enough money to see her out.

At the end of summer, Georg announced his intention to return to southern Germany via France. As the oak trees turned from green to yellow, he thanked Aunt Berry, slapped me on the back, and set off on the train for Dover.

After he left, the cottage felt barren, as if the winter drapes had been drawn and the shutters had come down and I was left there as the caretaker. For all her chirpiness, Aunty was old and of a different generation. Physical activity tired her now, even the daily stroll to the village for the newspaper and bread. As the hours of daylight shortened, I chopped and carried wood and set a fire in the open hearth so that she could sit, warm and snug, in her favourite chair and read or knit or doze as she pleased. At last, my government-approved identity papers came through, which meant I was cleared to travel. However, I promised her that I'd stay until spring.

Most evenings, she and I would take a glass or two of 'medicinal' brandy to grease the throat and let the memories flow. I opened up about my experiences in the camps—the dreadful Warth Mills and the not-so-dreadful Tatura—focussing on light incidents and omitting the dark times when I wondered how I'd survive.

'My dear, Tatura sounds like a lovely place,' she said, her eyes twinkling with relief that I was neither tortured nor starved like prisoners of the Nazis, whose troubled accounts were being published in the British newspapers. 'Better there than here. I never want to live through another Blitz. Every night, searchlights, air-raid sirens, and a dash downstairs to the bomb shelter. Then the *thud, thud, thud* of the bombs. We never knew if we'd live to see the morning.'

I patted her knobbly hand. 'Thank God it's over.'

'Oh, it's not over yet,' she said. 'We have years—no, decades—of rebuilding ahead.'

Although I yearned to find out what happened to Mutti after my internment, I didn't want to upset Aunty. Sometimes I would steer the conversation in that direction, but she'd swerve into a side story. She was old and had been through a lot. I did not press her. Then, by the fireside one bleak winter's evening, she took an extra shot of brandy and launched into a monologue that she must have been mulling over for weeks.

'Three days after your arrest, the policemen returned. Your poor mother had fallen ill with a fever and a terrible cough. So many wild stories were going round. Germans are all Nazi spies, and rubbish like that. Mr Churchill gave the order, so the police rounded up every German in the country. We were worried sick about you. Elsa was convinced you'd be executed.

'Right here in this room, she confronted the policemen. Demanded to know where you'd been sent. She gave them a right tongue-lashing. But they'd come to arrest *her*. Good Lord, then I was in trouble for harbouring an enemy of Britain but I managed to talk my way out of it. I told them I was nursing my niece, who was delirious with fever. The last part was not a lie. But they pushed me aside and took her regardless.

'She died of pneumonia. I never knew where she was taken or exactly what happened. The funeral was small, but nice all the same. Just the minister and me, and a couple of my close friends. Dreadful shame you couldn't come.'

'It wasn't for the lack of trying,' I said. 'With the help of a friend, I got a leave pass but the trains had stopped running. Some big military exercise, apparently.'

'The evacuation of Dunkirk. What that war has to answer for!'

For several minutes we sat in silence, Aunty clicking her false teeth and me gazing at the flickering flames, remembering my mother. Her gentle smile, her quick wit, her dark silky hair plaited around her head like a halo. Wherever she was in the realm of souls, I hoped she'd found peace.

Aunty interrupted my reverie. 'I was nearly arrested in London too, not long after you arrived. Everyone hated Germans then. Just as well they didn't know my ancestry.'

'Is that why you brought us down to Kent?'

'I thought it would be safe, but I was wrong.' She worked her jaws as if chewing gristle. 'Neighbours are such busybodies! In London, one of my neighbours—a nasty piece of work—found out about you and Elsa. "Bleedin' Nazis," she called you. Probably put a glass to the wall to eavesdrop on our conversations. Anyway, it was she who dobbed us in, I'm convinced of it. The police went to my terrace house in London but we had already gone. They doorknocked the street and Mrs Busybody kindly gave them my address here.'

'After Elsa …' she made a shuddering sigh. 'After … it was lonely here on my own so I returned to London. The air attacks we expected never came. We called it "the fake war". The bombers arrived months later. And then, how those bombs rained down! Every night it went on, and for weeks and weeks. I managed to hire a man with a van to take whatever he could carry. And lucky I did too. The London house took a hit. Everything lost. Books, furniture, the lot. Those bombing raids went on and on, even here in Kent. I spent more nights in the backyard trench than in my own bed. The police came after me again! As you know, I was born in Germany but my husband was English, so I thought I was in the clear. How naïve of me!'

'I didn't know you were married.'

'It didn't last. After two years we went our separate ways. Divorces are expensive and hard to get, so we never bothered. Henry is dead now, so technically I'm a widow. For all intents and purposes, I was single so I used my maiden name and tried to put a bad marriage behind me.'

'How did you meet Mutti?'

'Her father—your grandfather—was an engineer. Her parents were always moving around. Poland, Prussia, Britain, France. So disruptive for a young girl. As soon as she was old enough, Elsa became a boarder at St Mary's Girl's School in London, which was where I worked as the house mistress. She was a sweet little thing. Full of energy and cheek, she stole my heart. In the summer holidays, I suggested that she might stay here in the countryside. Her parents agreed. Elsa loved the horses. I had two then, a mare and a filly. She rode that filly bareback, clung on like a little monkey.'

This was news to me. No matter how hard I tried, I could not picture my mother, so proper and correct, hurtling bareback through fields of gorse and bracken.

'After Elsa passed away, I wrote a long letter to your father. Max never replied. To this day, I don't know if he received it. Or if he is still …' She paused to wipe her eyes. 'We were right in the thick of it then. I don't think the mail would have gone through.'

'When I was in Australia, I wrote a few times through the Red Cross. No answer either. In my case there was a complication: I was using an assumed name. For five years I was Horst Schuhmacher.' I smiled. 'Not very original, I'm afraid.'

'Why would you do that?'

'The Nazi government was paranoid about dissidents and informers. My father had friends high up in the Party. I worried that my arrest in

England might be construed as desertion and they'd come after Max and Opa. I wanted to protect them. When my identity papers were lost at sea, I grabbed the opportunity and changed my name.'

'*Ach*, we are more alike than I imagined,' said Aunt Berry. 'Tomorrow we will go through the boxes in the end room. Remind me or I'll forget.' She yawned and stretched her body like an old tabby cat. 'Help me up, my dear. It's way past my bedtime.'

In the morning, Aunty led me to a room at the back of the house. She unlocked the door, flicked the light switch. The tiny space was like a pirate's cave: musty and claustrophobic, lit by a dim glow, packed with a variety of chests and boxes.

'No need for that ugly thing.' With the walking stick she pointed to the lampshade fixed to the ceiling. The melamine brownout cover was shaped like a chamber pot.

I unclipped it and the room filled with electric light.

'Now, help me shift all this stuff.' She settled herself on a tea chest and directed where I should move the boxes. Somewhere beneath the pile was a wooden trunk with *Braun* and *Southampton* painted on the side.

'That one. Bring it here.'

I slid the trunk across the floor, attempted to raise the lid. It was locked. At the front was a metal plate with a large keyhole.

Aunty dipped into her pocket and produced an equally large key, an old-fashioned thing with a long shaft and an oval bow. The lock clicked. I lifted the heavy lid and propped it against the wall. Inside were dozens of stuffed pillowcases.

'Your mother's things,' she said sadly. 'I kept it all. Take whatever you want. Some of this would be rather valuable.' She picked up a pillowcase and untied the knot. 'Here, look at this.' She pulled out what seemed to be a giant rabbit.

'Ugh!' I said. The smell of dust and fur made me sneeze.

She held the disgusting thing against her cheek and stroked it like a pet. 'I bought this coat for Elsa when she was seventeen. It was almost new, kept her as warm as toast.'

I sneezed again. 'Can we please put it away?'

Together we opened the other pillowcases, unearthing knitted cardigans, woollen skirts, felt hats, platform shoes, leather handbags. At the bottom was Mutti's writing set, a trinket box, and a manila envelope containing her German identity papers and her death certificate. Aunty passed me the envelope, saying I should give it to my father so that he could finalise her affairs.

I lifted out the writing set, held the silver pen in my fingers. It was slim and delicate, suited to the hand of a woman. A woman like my mother who wrote letters. In the trinket box was the dragonfly brooch that she wore on her coat lapel.

Aunty took it out and held it to the light. 'Elsa loved this piece. She called it her "lucky dragon".'

Reverently she placed it on my palm. The gemstones glistened. I remembered the morning we escaped Berlin. My father's rough hands, the masked panic, the taxi ride to the station, Mutti nervously fingering her good-luck charm.

'Can I keep the writing set and the brooch?'

'They're yours. Anything else?'

I surveyed the pile of female accoutrements and scratched my head. 'If you don't want these things, Aunt Berry, we could sell them or give them to charity. Maybe the Red Cross? They were good to us in the camp.'

'I'll think about it later. Let's pack up and have a nice cup of tea.' Aunty heaved herself up and shuffled toward the kitchen. I stayed behind to tidy the room.

'I expect you'll be leaving soon,' she said, pouring the tea. 'Spring is almost upon us.'

'Yes, I should go home and face the music. I'll book a steamer for April. Will you stay here or return to London?'

'There's nothing left for me in London. I'd have to rebuild the terrace house and that would be a nightmare. Besides, I'm too old for hateful neighbours. I'll miss you, my dear. Do write and tell me about Berlin.'

I embraced her birdlike frame and kissed her forehead. I knew that I'd miss her too.

Nineteen

The week before Easter 1946, I stepped down from the train at Friedrichstrasse in the centre of Berlin. My brown cardboard suitcase bumped awkwardly against my knee as I bumbled through the crowd. The once-grand station was like the skeleton of a long-dead animal, incomplete and caved-in at the centre with millions of ants scurrying about. The platforms, which used to be roofed in glass, were open to the elements now. Blasts of icy wind skittered dust and leaves across the flagstones and penetrated my heavy woollen overcoat as if it were cotton gauze. The press of bodies swept me through the exit, carried me down the stairs, spilled me into the street below. Outside, the human ants scattered in all directions, leaving me there on my own.

I had been warned to expect damage, but what I saw was utter devastation. Burnt-out ruins, twisted metal, piles and piles of brick and stone. Not an untouched building in sight. No cars and few bicycles. No well-heeled ladies promenading with fluffy pet dogs. The city I had landed in was nothing like the one I had left.

Ragged survivors laboured amongst the debris. In their thousands they toiled—men, women, children—each with a part to play. Men attacked the heavy objects with poles and pipes and shovels. Women in bucket-lines cleared rubble to the street. Children picked and carried whatever they could. There was no machinery, only muscle power and determination.

Surely this wasteland was not my beloved Berlin.

The stench of scorched earth and death made me sick to the stomach. With a sense of unreality, I drifted along Friedrichstrasse, not knowing what to do. The further I walked, the more disoriented I became. All the old landmarks were gone. Churches, hotels, offices, cafés. Reduced to charcoal and dust.

Then I saw it. Amidst the chaos, one structure remained. The icon of the city: the Brandenburger Tor. Two hundred years ago it was erected as a symbol of peace. The elegant columns stood proud and tall. At the top, damaged but not destroyed, was the quadriga—the four-horsed chariot—and the winged goddess clutching the reins.

Dropping my suitcase, I gazed at the wondrous sight. I could have wept but I'd already shed so many tears that my eyes had run dry. Instead, I thought of Opa and our afternoon strolls through the Gate into the leafy forest of the Tiergarten beyond. I wanted to freeze that memory or turn it into bronze, a memorial to a happy childhood. Today the Tiergarten was a refugee camp with no trees, bare earth, and makeshift shelters for people with nowhere to go.

From behind me came the tramp of boots. A squad of soldiers wearing Red Army uniforms and arrogant sneers was patrolling the street. Rifles were at the ready. One growled at me in Russian. I didn't need to understand the words; the threat was in the tone of voice. I picked up my suitcase and moved on.

This was my first encounter with the post-war reality of my poor country and it was hard to stomach. After our defeat, the victors had carved Germany into four occupation zones. My train from Hamburg had traversed the British zone and entered the Russian zone at Brandenburg. Berlin, a city within a sea of communist red, was similarly divided into quadrants. I had no idea where each one started or ended, but the presence of those soldiers suggested that I was in the Soviet sector. I stumbled from one burnt-out block of ruins to the next, searching for a route that would take me north to the borough of Reinickendorf and my home.

For several hours I wandered through unrecognisable parts of my city. From time to time, I asked passers-by for directions but, without landmarks or signs, I became lost. With little to guide me apart from the angle of the sun, I could have been walking in circles. In my estimation, two hours of daylight remained. After dark, my path would be lit not by street lights but the moon and the stars. As far as I could tell, even the lamp posts had been destroyed.

Eventually I arrived at Leopoldplatz. Thankfully all the buildings were intact, including the red-brick church, which was exactly as I remembered except for the spire, which was missing. The large open square where weekly markets were held before the war was deserted. No shops were open and there were no food stalls. Hungry and footsore, I limped along the avenue of chestnut trees. From there, I knew the way home. So well, in fact, that I could have walked there blindfolded.

Half an hour later, I was at Hermann-Göring-Strasse. The plane trees, glistening with spring leaves, cast deep shadows across the cobblestones. Ahead was the house. Compared to my childhood memory, it looked tiny. The hedges were neatly clipped and ivy crept over the white stucco wall. Relief: someone was living there. I prayed for it to be Max and Opa. With my heart in my mouth, I strode up the path and knocked.

Soft-soled shoes flip-flopped across floorboards. The door opened slowly to reveal a pair of shabby *Pantoffeln*. I swear they were the same slippers that Max had on when we left seven years earlier.

I'd steeled myself for this moment, this reunion with my formidable father. Despite my efforts to show that I was now a grown man, when I glanced into his sunken eyes, my lips began to quiver. For the first time ever, he threw his arms around me and we embraced like father and son.

We entered the house. Max mumbled something and went into the kitchen. I hung my overcoat in the vestibule and pulled off my boots. In my socks, I padded to the sitting room and dropped into one of two armchairs. Nothing had changed. Same woollen rug, same framed pictures, same flecked wallpaper. It was as if I'd just woken from a long and confusing dream.

I caught my reflection in the mirror. My hair was matted, my face was grimy, my clothes stank of sweat. I hadn't had a proper wash in two weeks. But I'd made it! I was home.

Max returned with a tray of food and two steaming cups. We sat at the round table that overlooked the street. Night had fallen. The garden was dappled in moonlight. Mutti's rosebushes were gone; vegetables grew there instead.

Don't grow what you can't eat: Opa's advice. Those rosebushes had always been a bone of contention. *Roses add sweetness to our lives*: Mutti's counter. So far, no mention had been made of either Mutti or Opa and I had no desire to open Pandora's box.

My father and I had a lot to catch up on, yet neither of us seemed to know how to start. I wolfed down slices of rye bread and cheese from the tray and sipped *ersatz* coffee, which tasted like sawdust and hot water. All the while we prattled on like strangers about topics as safe as the weather. After we'd eaten, my father brought out a bottle of schnapps and poured two good-sized shots.

We clinked glasses and downed the liquor in one gulp. It was herbal and bitter, stronger than Aunt Berry's tonsil-tingling brandy. He set his empty glass down and refilled it, waggled the bottle to ask if I wanted more. I declined. My head was throbbing but I wanted to clear the air before I turned in for the night.

Taking a determined breath, I launched onto thin ice. 'Did you get my letters?'

'I got three. All from England, years ago.'

'Then you don't know what happened?'

'I know about Elsa, if that's what you mean.' His voice was thin and tight. Our escape to England had been his idea. Perhaps, if we'd stayed here instead, she'd still be alive.

'How did you find out?' I asked.

'*Das Deutsche Rote Kreuz* sent a female volunteer to tell me that my dear wife had died in an English prison. That was the message. No details, no explanations, no way of finding out more. To make matters worse, I received a letter from Elsa shortly after. For a while I wondered if it was a cruel joke. I wanted to believe that she was alive, but months later I received official advice that she was dead.' He downed the schnapps and refilled his glass. 'Your Aunt Berry filled me in. She also told me that you'd been taken prisoner.'

'I wrote to you from the internment camp in Australia but got no reply. They wanted us to believe that Hitler was on the run. My fellow inmates made a shortwave receiver that could pick up the Berlin news. Hitler was in control, the announcer said. Germany was undefeatable. Nobody in the camp knew what to believe.'

My father reached across the table and gripped my arm. 'I'm glad to see you, son. You can't imagine how awful it was.'

'When I got off the train this morning, I thought the world had ended. Never have I seen such destruction. It's a miracle our house was spared.'

'In Reinickendorf we were fortunate, not so in the city centre. The bombs fell thick and fast. *Poom. Poom. Poom.* Not a noise so much as a feeling. Shockwaves reverberated right through your body. On the nights of the full moon, you'd wake with a pounding in your chest and know that the bombers had arrived. The clouds glowed orange from all the fires. I have not visited Mitte; I have not witnessed the damage. I can't imagine …' He dropped his head into his hands.

But I had been there. I had seen the ruins. Thousands of Berliners would have perished or been trapped beneath wreckage, injured and frightened, waiting for rescue or death.

I poured myself a shot of schnapps, skolled it, examined the empty glass. 'Where is Opa?'

Max shook his head. 'Taken by a stroke in 1942. Quick and painless. He was lucky. He loved Berlin. To have witnessed its fall would have crushed him.'

I moistened my forefinger and ran it around the rim of the glass. The lead crystal released a haunting ring. My heart ached for my dear Opa, but the news was not unexpected. He had lived a long and productive life. I recalled the lazy afternoons after school when I visited him at the factory. The smell of the leather, the clatter of machines, the jovial banter of the workers. And Opa, always wanting to show me something new.

'What happened to the factory?'

'I shut it down. The building, the machinery, the materials are still there. We had a lucrative contract with the Wehrmacht, but in 1944 it was cancelled. With no income, I had no choice.'

'I remember us visiting a prison camp to see your army friend.'

'SS Major Koch, Commandant of Sachsenhausen. The contract for army boots was signed soon after. For a while the business was more successful than I'd ever dreamed. To keep up, I leased extra space and took on a hundred more workers. But then the tide of war turned and the government payments stopped. Fortunately, I put away some of the profits. Knowing what happened after the First World War, I converted paper money into gold.'

'How did you manage that in the middle of a war?'

'You'd be surprised how much gold was traded in this country. Gold is portable wealth and universally accepted when currency fails. Desperate people hide it in their bodies and in their teeth.'

Involuntarily, my eyes flicked to his mouth but I saw no flashes of gold. 'So, what now?'

'We wait and see what happens under foreign occupation.'

How long that would take was anyone's guess. I yawned. It had been a long day. The schnapps had dulled my mind. My eyes stung; I could barely keep them open.

'Go to bed.' He lit his pipe. 'Your room is as you left it.'

For once, I was happy to obey. Taking my suitcase, I climbed the creaky staircase.

'*Gute Nacht*,' he called after me.

'*Gute Nacht*,' I replied. Some things never changed. It was good to be back.

A year slipped by with surprising ease. I remained at home with my father. Slowly a new Berlin emerged from the ashes. In Mitte, which had suffered the worst, workmen were demolishing buildings beyond repair and patching up others. The bomb-damaged apartment blocks looked like soft-drink crates turned on their side. Without windows and balconies, roofs and staircases, they formed a grid of squares within squares. Inside, people in overcoats and mittens moved about their open-air apartments, which had no privacy from the street and no protection from looters. Still, people had to live somewhere and a half-there apartment was better than sleeping under canvas in the Tiergarten.

I had just turned twenty-four. Like most young men, I was full of energy, ambition, and big ideas. Seeking opportunities in that bizarre post-war period, I badgered my father to reopen the factory and manufacture city shoes instead of army boots. Workers in droves were flowing out of Berlin to work in cities such as München, Bonn, and Hamburg in the Western zones. Operating under a Stalinist regime would be financial suicide for business owners. Already, cracks were appearing in the agreement between Russia and the three western Allies. Rumours circulated that Germany would be split in two.

Luckily Reinickendorf was in the French sector. Our streets were patrolled by amiable Gallic soldiers, who smoked brown cigarettes that stank like horse manure. Most knew no German at all. We managed to communicate using hand signs and a pidgin version of the two languages. Generally, they didn't seem to mind what we did, so we continued our everyday affairs without interference.

After much debate, Max agreed to my suggestion and offered to raid his stash of gold to fund it. He kept the ingots in a locked safe at the factory. Nobody knew the combination but him. I asked how much gold there was. He said he didn't know exactly and suggested we go there together and weigh it. Gold ingots were of little practical use. We needed cash. I assumed that he knew of some way of converting them into legal currency.

We left our visit to the shut-down factory until Sunday, when not many people were in the streets. Although we owned the place, entering via the alleyway and the back door made us look like robbers. Upstairs in my father's office, we stood before the large portrait of *Der Führer* and the red Nazi flag.

'A sad end for our gallant leader,' he said with admiration.

I said he should cut the picture up into tiny pieces. When he reached up and grasped the gilt frame, I thought he would destroy it then and there. Instead, he lifted the painting off the wall, which revealed a metal safe behind it. Turning his back to me, he fiddled with the combination lock.

From where I was standing, I could see over his shoulder. Eighty-two left. Twenty-one right. Thirty-nine left. I committed the combination to memory, for I knew he'd never tell me of his own accord. He turned the dial to the right and the door swung open.

The inside was surprisingly spacious, large enough for a treasure-chest as well as two document boxes. I wondered what sort of paperwork could be so precious. I didn't ask. In the realm of business, he was king and I was a lowly servant.

He removed a metal container the size of a shoebox and relocked the safe. Its weight must have been considerable, for it made a solid thump as it landed on the desk. With a key hidden in the top drawer, he unlocked it. Inside were scores of ingots. They were not shimmering bars as I'd imagined, but irregular shapes as if made by melting down scrap. He produced a set of balancing scales, weighed the gold in batches, totted up the numbers as he went. The smile on his face increased in direct proportion to the pile of precious metal on his desk.

'I'll sell this on the black market. It should bring a good price.' It was obvious to me now that the black market was where he'd acquired it in the first place. His plan was to trickle it out in dribs and drabs in order to not raise suspicion. He promised that, when he'd accumulated enough cash, he'd reopen the factory.

My role would be to manage the workshop and he'd attend the books, an arrangement that suited us both. To speed things up, we decided to clean out Opa's room and offer it to prospective employees to rent. Accommodation was scarce; a room in a private house would be an attractive incentive. I suggested that we start by contacting former workers who were familiar with our workshop methods.

To that end, I asked Max for the pay books from 1939 to 1944. He retrieved them from the bookshelf behind his desk. Running down the list, I expected to see dozens of familiar names but there were none. By the middle of 1944, when the journal entries ceased, the number of people on the payroll had dropped to five.

'If the business was thriving, why were there so few employees?'

'The others were paid by the piece,' he said.

'Then where are those payments recorded?'

'The workers were paid directly by the government.'

I scratched my head, wondering how that would have worked.

He continued. 'The government supplied the labour and we provided materials, machinery, know-how. It was a lucrative deal.'

'What happened to the workers we had before? The Goldsteins, Frau Fränkel, the Zimmermans, Herr Meier ...' I counted them on my fingers.

The more names I said, the more attention he gave to his pipe. He refilled the bulb, tamped it down, held a flame to the tobacco. I thought he hadn't heard, but the deepening furrows in his brow suggested otherwise. I wondered why a simple question demanded such concentration.

Abruptly, he stood up and exited the office.

I shrugged. His reaction was odd, as if I'd offended him. I decided to contact the five people on the 1944 payroll. Three lived in Reinickendorf, one in neighbouring Wedding, and one in Pankow. I composed a letter outlining the offer and typed it out five times on the portable Olympia in his office. The letters were posted on a Monday afternoon. On Tuesday afternoon I received the first response.

It was addressed to me personally, not *The Manager* as on the address block. Puzzled, I tore the envelope open and slid out two thin pages. The signature at the bottom made me smile, for I had not heard from my 'cousin' since we parted company in Kent. He announced that he was moving to Berlin and asked if he could stay with me. 'I'll sleep on the floor, if necessary,' he wrote.

Would this alter my plans? I thought for a moment. If the two of us had amicably shared a tiny room in an internment camp, we could do it again. The offer I'd made to the former workers would stand. Besides, Georg had what the British call 'the gift of the gab'. His easy-going manner would make others believe that they'd snared the deal of a lifetime. He was more affable and outgoing than I'd ever be. If he agreed to my suggestion, he could help us rebuild the business by expanding our clientele. Most importantly, he was a man we could trust. I put the proposal to my father and he agreed. Straight away I wrote back.

Georg, our new company sales representative, landed on the doorstep ten days later.

~

It was a good time to take a break from the past.

Kathy offered to tidy Horst's spare room, for she was obliged to vacate her holiday accommodation by ten the next morning. He led her to the rear of the apartment, to the room piled with boxes and bags.

'This came from the old house,' he explained with a shrug. 'I don't know what to do with it all.'

'Perhaps I can help. But first, let's make some space.'

They shifted half the boxes into Horst's bedroom and restacked the rest along the wall out of the way. Underneath all that stuff was a single bed and a chest of drawers. When the job was done, they celebrated with beer and plums.

Later, Kathy returned to the white apartment for the final time, intending to enjoy a quiet evening with Alice.

Twenty

10 January 1947

Excellent news! I've passed my exams and with distinctions I might add. Today, for the first time, I donned the hard-earned butterfly veil of a qualified nurse. One more step to get registration, then I'll be able to work at any hospital in Queensland. I've been offered a permanent position at the Brisbane General—live-in, of course—and a nice pay rise. I'm happy here, so I've accepted.

My first placement is at Children's, my favourite. I love caring for the little ones who are so desperately sick. Although they are impulsive and sometimes naughty, they cause little trouble and generally do as they are told. Kids are easy compared to adults, who tend to treat us like servants.

1 February 1947

Alas, my joy was short-lived. The Repatriation hospitals at Windsor and Greenslopes are overflowing with returned servicemen. Ex-diggers who can't get into Repat are flocking here and we're struggling to find enough beds. After just three weeks at Children's, I've been reassigned to Male Medical, which is every nurse's nightmare. As a trainee, I endured eight dreadful weeks of night shift in the 'bear pit', an ordeal that continues to haunt me.

When I found out about the transfer, I stormed to my room.

Simpson came in, lit two cigarettes and passed one to me. 'What's up?'

We moved to the window to blow out the smoke. Smoking is not permitted anywhere in the nurses' quarters; there'd be trouble if we were caught. I told her about my new placement.

'Of all the stinking rotten luck!' she said sympathetically. 'Hey, remember Tommy?'

'I'd rather not,' I shot back.

Tommy was nineteen, going on thirty-five. When I was a first-year trainee, he was admitted to Male Medical after his motorbike crashed into a lamp post and he broke a few bones. Until then, he'd dodged conscription and led an unfettered lifestyle. To earn a crust, he'd turned his hand to SP bookmaking and selling sly grog and fast women to the Yanks. With one leg in traction and an abundance of spare time, he amused himself by tormenting the nurses. Me in particular.

Every night when I was on duty, he'd try to charm me into bed. In an open ward, this was the source of much hilarity and teasing by the other patients. Even my colleagues would have a giggle. Night after night, I'd politely refuse to 'have a bit of fun'. At the time, my main duties were to deliver bedpans and change the bedding if necessary. Throughout the shift, I had to do regular checks on all the patients and make them comfortable, but my chief challenge was to get them all to sleep.

Every time I came near Tommy's bed, he'd grab me and tell me he was in love. Extracting myself, I'd tell him to pull his head in, which was the only sort of language he understood. His dirty fingernails and slimy leer made me feel sick to the stomach. After weeks of fending him off, I heard that he was cleared for discharge. Hurray! Soon I'd be free of him forever.

On the last night, I did the usual rounds of the ward, checking the bedding, fluffing pillows, bringing urinals and glasses of water. I worked my way along the line of beds. Tommy, at the end, was the last. His injured leg had been liberated from its rigging of cords and weights. He was sitting up in bed, grinning and as perky as a peacock. Through clenched teeth, I asked if he was comfortable.

'Could be better, darlin'. Me sheet's all scrunched up. Right here, under me bum.'

'Why should I believe you, Tommy?' A dozen male eyes were watching in anticipation of another hilarious performance.

To prove the point, Tommy flipped back the covers, revealing a messy bed that could have been made by a three-year-old. 'I'd fix it meself, only I still got me anchor.' He rapped on the heavy plaster-of-Paris cast that encased his entire left leg.

Realising that the bottom sheet would have to be refitted, I took a step towards him. 'If I move your leg, can you wriggle down the bed and roll to the left?'

'Whatever you say, sweetheart.'

The first manoeuvre went off without a hitch. I straightened the sheet and tucked it in securely. 'Now the other side.'

All went well until he rolled to the middle of the mattress and I reached across him for the pillow. In a snap, he grabbed me and pulled me down onto his chest. In the next second, his lips were on mine and his tongue was halfway down my throat.

Gagging, I pushed myself off and bolted down the corridor.

He called out after me. 'Marry me, darlin'. I can't live without you.'

The audience erupted into laughter.

Humiliated and seething, I ran to the staff bathroom, washed out my mouth, lit the emergency cigarette that I carried in my pocket. Sitting on the closed toilet lid, I made a vow. Never again would I let a patient get the better of me. The next morning, Tommy was discharged and thankfully I haven't seen him since.

Now I face the prospect of spending days and nights in the bear pit again. In my favour are three extra years of experience and maturity, little consolation when I march into the ward for the first shift. While few patients are as infuriating as Tommy, I dread what lies ahead.

6 February 1947

As it turns out, my charges in Male Medical are mostly ex-militia, who are generally polite and grateful to be out of the army. They enjoy a chat while I take their observations or give injections of penicillin, the miracle drug that cures everything. A few try to treat me like a lackey, but I don't let them get away with it. Sometimes I'm the butt of crude jokes, but I've learnt to give as good as I get. I also employ a military tactic: attack is the best form of defence. It works.

Today I was on the graveyard shift which finished at dawn. A new patient called Bob Watson was brought in with a relapse of malaria. As with all new patients, I began by reading his file. A former soldier in New Guinea, he'd received treatment for tinea, pneumonia, and sunstroke in addition to malaria, which was the disease that sent him home.

His first night was rough. Several times he woke in a delirium, yelling and cursing like the devil, then he sweated so profusely that I had to change the bedding twice.

At four in the morning, I gave him a sedative and he finally went to sleep. At the end of my shift, I went back to check on him. For a full minute, I stood at the end of his bed. His eyes were closed; his breathing was even and deep. His dark wavy hair had fallen forward over a suntanned forehead. His fleshy lips were slightly parted. Something about him touched my heart.

I'll have to watch myself with this one, I thought. A nurse can't become involved with a patient if she wants to keep her job.

10 February 1947

Bob has been here four days now and we've become friendly. He is charming and outgoing and lends me a hand if I need to shift heavy equipment. His nights are generally sleepless. While those around us slumber on, he talks to me about his experiences in New Guinea. He is quite the storyteller. I find him fascinating. Here's what he told me last night.

'My platoon was on patrol in the jungle near Buna. Monsoon season. Stinking hot, bucketing rain. Mosquitoes as big as blowflies. We were drenched to the bone and our boots were heavy with mud. Visibility nil. In single file, we tramped through dense vegetation, following trails made by wild boar. All of a sudden, *rat-ta-tat-tat*. Japs of course. I dived for cover in a ditch, lay motionless in the ooze. Daylight faded but I dared not move. God, what I would've given for a smoke! When night fell, as black as coal, the rain stopped and I slept.

'In the morning, I crawled out and looked for the others but they must have moved on. My entire body was covered in mud, even my face. Perhaps, in the darkness, they hadn't seen me in the ditch. Easy to do when you're under enemy fire in a downpour. Bad luck it was me who was left behind.'

'What did you do?' I was at the edge of my seat.

'Walked. Ate grubs and insects and berries that I hoped weren't poisonous. One thing was certain, I didn't go thirsty. There was plenty of rainwater; I just had to pick out the leeches. On the second day, I stumbled upon a Jap. Literally, I fell over him. He was hiding in long kunai grass. Horrible stuff that, rips your skin like hacksaw blades. The Jap was alone and as lost as me. Before I could say "sorry mate", he jumped up and yabbered a stream of abuse. Of course, I couldn't understand a word. When I didn't respond, he raised his rifle and shot me. The bullet hit my chest, right here, near my heart. The force threw me backwards, my head hit the ground.

'When I came to, the Jap was gone. Probably thought I was dead. My head was bleeding and my chest was awfully sore. In need of a smoke, I took the cigarette case from my top pocket. It wouldn't open because of the dent made by the bullet. Later, a scout found me and took me back to the camp. By then I was shaky with malaria and they packed me off home. I'm still no bloody good. But you could say that smoking saved my life.'

He chuckled and reached under his pillow, brought out a battered metal case. 'Cigarette?' he said, cracking it open. Inside were two tailor-mades, which was all that would fit in the tight space.

'Is that …?' I took the case and turned it over.

'Yep. My good-luck charm.'

I took a cigarette and handed back the case, suggested we go outside where we could smoke without getting into trouble. He slid out of bed, put on his sandshoes. The covered veranda overlooked Bowen Park and the showgrounds. A north-easterly over the mangroves brought with it a hint of the sea, a sweet perfume in comparison to the phenol stench of the ward. Moreton Bay fig trees and Bunya pines formed a living wall around the park; a pale quarter-moon cast moving shadows across the footpath.

In a comfortable silence we smoked. No need for idle chatter; we were content to sit and absorb the serenity of the night. I checked my watch. Twenty past four. In an hour it would be dawn and the city would wake.

'After I'm discharged, will you come to the pictures with me?' he said.

'As a rule, I don't date patients.' It was meant as a tease. I wondered how he'd react and was about to follow up with 'but I could make an exception' when he cut in.

'But I won't be a patient then. So, the answer is yes?'

I laughed. In my pocket was my emergency cigarette. 'Would you like to share another before we go in?'

'Thought you'd never ask.'

The match flared. I took a drag and passed him the cigarette.

'Perhaps, before I decide whether to accept your kind offer, you should tell me more about yourself. All I know is your blood type, medical history, and stories about New Guinea.'

'I'd be delighted.' He inhaled and released a gush of smoke. 'Name: Robert James Watson. Age: 33. Occupation: motor mechanic. Father: dead. Mother: lives in Cairns. Brothers and sisters: nil. Accommodation: a one-bedroom flatette at Windsor shared with Felix.'

'And who, might I ask, is Felix?'

'Full name: *Felis Catus.*'

'Oh, I get it. Your cat.' I hadn't enjoyed a playful conversation like this in ages. 'You haven't mentioned marital status. A girl can't be too careful.'

A moment passed. 'You got me there. I am, in fact, married. However, my dear Adeline threw me out as soon as I returned from New Guinea. It seemed that, in my absence, she'd amused herself by having an affair with a dentist. Not that I care.'

Without a second thought, I agreed to a matinee on Saturday next week. We've arranged to meet at 'the clocks' at ten. A real date. I haven't done this in a very long time.

22 February 1947

Before catching the tram to the city, I scanned *The Courier-Mail* to find a film suitable for a first date. A film that would be light and enjoyable. Nothing scary, and no war movies, tear-jerkers, or hot romances. I settled for *Two Sisters from Boston*, a musical comedy with Kathryn Grayson and June Allyson.

At ten, we met beneath the clocks at Central Station. Bob looked dapper in grey trousers, sports jacket, and tie. He greeted me with a smile and a handshake, which took me by surprise.

Most Aussie men have no idea about welcomes. Italians like me kiss everyone: family, friends, acquaintances. Men kiss men, women kiss women, and both sexes kiss each other. Australians shuffle self-consciously from foot to foot and mumble *g'day*. The correct response to *g'day* is another *g'day*. In a group, the *g'days* bounce from person to person like ping-pong balls.

'You look gorgeous this morning,' he said.

The pastel-blue fabric of my new cotton frock made me feel like Doris Day. 'Why thank you, kind sir.'

'Where are we off to?' He folded my arm through his.

'The Metro, Albert Street. It starts in half an hour.'

'Plenty of time then,' he said. 'It's too hot to be rushing around.'

We crossed the road and began the steep descent down Edward Street. We walked in step, his hip gently brushing against mine. It felt right, as if we were meant to be a couple.

Already, the temperature was pushing ninety Fahrenheit. Later there'd be a storm. After an overnight drenching, steam curled up from the asphalt. Despite the sticky heat, I'd brought a cardigan, for the air-conditioning at the Metro was always freezing.

In the foyer, I waited by the staircase while Bob bought tickets, two cups of cordial, and a fruit-and-nut chocolate bar. We found our seats and settled in.

The story was predictable, the songs were catchy, the chocolate bar was weevil-free, and Bob kept his hands to himself. In all, a pleasant morning's entertainment. Afterwards, we had sandwiches at the Shingle Inn. He asked for a second date and I accepted.

After a peck on the cheek, we went our separate ways. On the tram ride to the hospital, I concluded that I liked him more than anyone else I'd dated.

I can hardly wait to see him again.

18 October 1947

How the months have flown! Romance has blossomed. But I have to keep it secret. I'll be in the doghouse if Matron finds out. Despite my variable shifts, we see each other several times a week. As a garage mechanic, Bob's schedule is regular and predictable. He works from eight to five, Monday to Saturday. Friday evenings, he has a few beers at the Crown Hotel with his mates, before walking home to his flat at Windsor.

The other reason this must remain secret is that estranged wives can go to extraordinary lengths to prove their husband's infidelity in order to get a divorce. Hiring a private detective is not uncommon. Incriminating photographs, recorded conversations, and eyewitness statements are tabled in court. Ugly divorce cases are fodder for the press. Headlines such as *Caught with his pants down*, along with blurred-out photos of faces and unmentionable body parts, litter the pages of *The Sunday Truth*. As I have no wish to become famous one Sunday, I've invented a story to explain my overnight absences.

My alibi is Mamma, who now lives in the suburb of Northgate with her 'husband' Luca and young Mick. 'Women's problems' is a delicate condition that is never questioned and to which other women are sympathetic. I've told my colleagues, including Matron, that Mamma has been having 'women's problems' and often needs my help at short notice.

And so, I lead a double life. At work, I am Sister Zanetti, single, dedicated nurse. Outside work, I am Mrs Bob Watson, loving wife and homemaker. The same story is used to explain my absences from the Windsor flat to the neighbours.

The person who is completely in the dark is Mamma. I haven't actually seen her in months.

I have no choice but to continue the pretence. I've known about Adeline from the outset. Bob has not kept his marriage secret. Nor has he made promises that he hasn't kept. He is attentive and caring and, when he has the money, he showers me with gifts. Flowers, chocolates, silk scanties. Just like the Americans. Perhaps he learnt a thing or two from our 'friendly invaders'. Sometimes his boss delays paying the wages and he runs short of cash, so I lend him a few quid, which he always pays back. He doesn't ask often, and I'm happy to help out.

Although my wages are barely enough to live on, I save all my pennies and have a nice nest egg put away. Who knows? One day we might buy a cosy weatherboard cottage in the suburbs. Hundreds of new timber houses are popping up all over Brisbane to cater for our returned soldiers and their brides. Soon I'll have enough money for a deposit.

19 August 1951

For four years now, Bob and I have lived like a married couple and still the charade goes on. All along, I've sat on the fence, unable to make a decision about my future. I'm twenty-seven now and the biological clock is ticking. Although I've let him call the shots, I've also suggested that he should bury his dead marriage. I'm tired of being second best. The truth is, he's so comfortable with the way things are that he can't be bothered to take action. It's time to bring this matter to a head.

Yesterday my shift was swapped at short notice, so I thought to surprise him with a home-cooked meal. It was Saturday. I knew he was at work and wouldn't be home until early evening, which gave me plenty of time to prepare.

We'd arranged to see each other as usual on Sunday. After six straight days of work, Saturday evenings were for rest, he said. I understood perfectly. Malaria had a habit of recurring whenever he had insufficient sleep. As a nurse, I knew this was in his best interests. But I also wanted to give him a surprise, one that he'd enjoy. Mamma always said that the way to a man's heart is through his stomach. I hadn't tested the accuracy of this theorem, but my eye was on a cosy weatherboard cottage within walking distance of Bob's flat. I hoped that my surprise would soften him up for an Important Discussion.

What I had in mind was the sort of hearty food that Mamma used to make. I haven't cooked in ages. Mostly, when we eat at the flat, we have bangers and mash or baked beans on toast. In Bob's world, the purpose of eating is sustenance. A necessity, not a pleasure. His culinary skills are non-existent and he discourages me from 'making a mess'. The tiny kitchenette is woefully underequipped.

In the morning I went to the Valley to get ingredients and a cooking pot. With my purchases in string bags, I boarded the tram for Windsor and walked from the stop to Cox Road on the western side of the hill. The rambling house had been divided into ten flatettes. As I climbed the front staircase, laden with groceries, I nodded to Mrs Worland from Number 2. Across the central hallway, I let myself into Number 3. The living image of a good housewife, I congratulated myself on my performance.

All afternoon I chopped and fried and stirred the concoction in the shiny new pot. By five-thirty it was ready. The meat was as soft as butter and the sauce was glistening red. Any minute he'd walk up the steps, open the door, and be seduced by the most delicious aroma in the world. I boiled the water ready for the pasta and uncorked a bottle of red. At the table, I flicked through the Saturday newspaper which he'd left open at the races, drank a cup of tea, smoked a few cigarettes. Six o'clock came and went. He should have been home. It was dark and I was starting to worry. Common sense told me that it was not his fault he was late. It was a surprise, for goodness sake. He was blissfully unaware of my intentions. Perhaps he was caught up with an urgent job or he'd met a friend after work. I wasn't legally his wife. We were both free to do as we pleased. Except I had gone to so much effort. Through food, I'd show him my love.

Just before seven, heavy footsteps stumbled along the hall. A key jiggled in the keyhole, but the door was not locked. He swore and kicked it open, possibly expecting a break-in. When he spied me at the table, his face turned to steel and he stormed toward me.

'What are *you* doing here?' he snarled.

'Surprise,' I said weakly. 'I had the day off and cooked dinner.'

'We had no arrangements for today.' His jacket was askew, his shirt-tails hung out. His breath stank of beer.

'I thought you'd be pleased.'

'Well, I'm not! I don't like surprises, especially not ones contrived by women.'

Tears stung my eyes. I could not believe the overreaction. In the years we'd been together, we had barely exchanged an angry word. Ours had been an extended honeymoon, more passionate than our married friends boasted about. They could keep their guesthouses and deserted beaches. What we had in the flat at Windsor was perfect.

Now, it seemed, the honeymoon was over. I'd overstepped the mark and encroached on the life he led when we were apart. What *was* that life? The question remained unasked. Bob had another side that I had not seen before. A secret side, from which I was excluded.

Like a spoilt brat, he threw himself petulantly onto the sofa. After fumbling in his pockets, he found and lit a cigarette. The smoke hovered about his head like a storm cloud. Tentatively, I moved towards him. His face was dark, his thoughts unreadable.

'I won't do it again,' I said.

Through the smoke haze, he glared at me as if I were to blame for his filthy mood. 'I've got a lot on my mind. You should go.'

I was trembling, unsure if our relationship was over or if he simply wanted time alone. 'Will I see you again?'

'What makes you think you won't?' he snapped. 'Look, I apologise for tonight but I can't help it. Bloody boss can't pay me until next Friday and I'm cold stony broke. Could you spare me a couple of quid, luv?' His voice was softer now, the tone of an adolescent asking his mum for spare change.

I opened my purse. After the morning's shopping excursion, I had ten shillings and a few pennies to last the weekend. I offered him the tan-coloured note.

He took it and sighed. 'I don't suppose there's any cash in your room at the hospital.'

'That's all I have until the bank opens on Monday.'

Wearily he closed his eyes. He looked so distraught that I almost pitied him. 'You should go before it gets late. Can you take yourself to the tram stop?'

Dismissed, I picked up my handbag. Half way out the door, I said, 'There's food on the stove. If you don't want to eat it now, put it in the ice-chest. It'll last a few days.'

Brushing away tears, I made my way to Bowen Bridge Road, the main thoroughfare to the hospital. The street was well-lit so I decided to walk and save the threepenny fare. My heart was breaking; I couldn't bear to lose him. All the way to the nurses' home, my mind replayed the awful scene. Try as I might to blame myself, his harshness was inexcusable.

9 September 1951

I haven't seen Bob in three weeks now and I'm determined not to go crawling back. He caused the argument, so he needs to patch it up. I wonder if he wants to. I expected to have heard by now. But no, not a word. A cold war is brewing. Who will be the first to crack?

30 October 1951

Bob seems to have disappeared off the face of the earth. Still no word. My anger has passed now and I'm wondering if he's all right. What he did and said were completely out of character. He was so desperate for money that night. I hope he hasn't done something stupid.

Curiosity got the better of me. This afternoon after work, I went around to his flat at Windsor. It's Tuesday, so he should have been at the workshop. To be sure, I knocked on the door first. No answer. I've still got the key, so I let myself in to look around.

Felix met me at the door, meowing as if he hadn't been fed in a month. The place was messier than usual, which was not surprising since I'm the one who cleans it. The cat followed me from room to room. As my visit was for surveillance purposes, I was loath to touch anything, but the pathetic sound of feline pleading touched a soft spot.

'Poor little fellow,' I said scratching Felix under the chin. He began purring, then abandoned me to stand beside the ice-chest.

'Okay, okay. I know what you want.'

When I opened the ice-chest, I had to step back due to a foul odour. I took out some scraps for the cat, which he gobbled as fast as I put them on the saucer. Guess what else I found inside. The pot of pasta sauce I'd made weeks ago. Untouched. The surface was coated in blue-green mould, which was the source of the nasty smell.

My first reaction was to remove it and dump the lot in the bin. But then he'd know I'd been there. Was this some kind of trap or a set-up? Who in his right mind would store meat sauce in an ice-chest for six weeks? I looked at Felix licking his chops, at the tongue-cleaned saucer on the floor, at the pile-up of dirty dishes in the sink, the newspapers scattered across the table, the unmade bed whose sheets, no doubt, had not seen a wash tub in a long time. The decision was made then and there. I wanted no part of this world.

I shut the door of the ice-chest, leaving the fermented sauce to bubble. Took the saucer from the floor and returned it to the stack of clean plates on the shelf. Scratched Felix under the chin one last time and departed.

Back in my room at the nurses' home, my anger has faded. It is clear to me now that Bob is not coping. Should I try to make amends or walk away?

3 March 1953

Well, here I am in Male Medical again after a reprieve of four years. The last time I worked here was as a newly-qualified nurse and, before that, as a fresh-faced trainee. Now I am the nurse supervisor. My pledge is to prevent patients from belittling the staff, in particular the young nurses. What happened to me as a trainee will not happen again, not on my watch any rate. The scars made by Tommy have faded but not disappeared. When it was announced that my promotion was to the 'bear pit', my blood ran cold. I accepted the position, of course. I am no longer timid. After nine years of nursing, my hide is thick and my tongue is sharp.

But the other reason for my hesitation was Bob. The bear pit was where we met, and what a disaster that turned out to be. He has never bothered to contact me. Eighteen months and not a peep. Fury has been replaced by pity. That he still carries around that bashed up cigarette case—his good-luck charm—tells me he will never put the New Guinea incident behind him. Now I think of him as a man damaged by a war that he wanted no part of. That is the only way I can rationalise what happened between us.

30 August 1953

Mamma used to say that if you don't deal with your problems, they come back to bite you. She was right. Who turned up in the ward today? Not

Tommy, thank God. With the sort of lifestyle he led, it wouldn't surprise me if he was pushing up daisies.

Yes, the other bane of my life. Bob Watson. Another relapse of malaria. You should have seen the look on his face when he saw who was in charge. A cross between shock and horror, followed by a sort of cringing expression that might have looked cute on Felix. On a man it came across as the hallmark of a coward.

All afternoon I gave him the cold shoulder and he pretended not to see me. When evening came in, his condition worsened. His temperature shot up and he fell into a delirium. His pyjamas were wringing wet with sweat. I gave him some medication, then got a trainee to help change the bed. After all, he is a patient. My job is to make patients comfortable and take care of their needs.

When my shift ended at six, I raced up to my room, threw myself onto the bed and wept. After all this time, I am still hurting. Stupid, stupid, stupid, I know.

I must speak to him in private. Ask him what went wrong. I need to know what the problem was in order to deal with it.

2 September 1953

Bob and I had our little chat today. Out on the veranda where we first got to know each other. I don't smoke anymore but he smokes like a chimney. And yes, he still carries around that battered cigarette case like a security blanket.

He started with an apology that seemed genuine enough. I also apologised for storming off, but my remorse is considerably less than his. In my mind, I have done no wrong. He went on to explain that his boss had been 'a real bastard', not paying him or his workmates on time. His rent had been overdue, the landlady threatened eviction, and he owed his drinking buddy fifty quid. That was why he'd asked me for a loan.

'You know me. I always pay off my debts.' He drew back on the cigarette and blew out a stream of smoke.

Although he still owed me ten shillings, I decided to let it slide. I explained that I didn't have much cash that day because the dinner had cost rather a lot, and that my entire day off had been spent trying to please him, which was why I was so upset. I bit my tongue about the other clandestine visit, when I'd checked up on him, fed the cat, and discovered the putrid mess in the ice-chest. Let him think what he likes; I'll never admit I was there.

'Why didn't you contact me?' I said.

He leant on the railing and stared into the distance, across the thousands of rooftops and treetops that went all the way out to Moreton Bay. 'I thought you hated me,' he said in a quiet voice. 'I was hurt and you couldn't see it.'

'Dear Lord, I can't read your mind. If you were having problems, you should have told me. I'm a nurse; I just might understand.'

He smoked in silence for a minute or two. Then he asked if I'd give him another go. 'I miss you so much. My heart aches for you.' He took my hand. Until then I'd been the cool, calm senior nurse. But the warmth of his touch melted the ice inside me and I agreed.

Now we are back to the way we were. Except I'm a little wiser and warier. As they say, *once bitten …*

4 April 1954

Our second honeymoon lasted exactly six months: from the day Bob was discharged from the hospital until the big spat today. A drunken rant over money and infidelity. Ha, he can talk! Honestly, that man is a different person with a skinful of beer.

Apparently, he dived into my handbag seeking to 'borrow' a few pounds behind my back. As if I wouldn't notice that amount of money missing. As well as two crisp green banknotes, he found a letter from Horst. As if I were the thieving one, he accused me of having a secret lover. Horst and I have been corresponding, on and off, these past few years. Ours is a friendship, not a romance, and I value it dearly.

Thankfully Bob and I have retained our separate living arrangements, him at the Windsor flat and me at the nurses' home, and to the best of my knowledge our affair remains a secret. So, when I lost my temper, I simply walked out of the flat and kept walking all the way back to the hospital.

This time, I know it's the grog talking. He's only like that when he's drunk. I'll give him a few days to dry out and mull over his bad behaviour. Then I'll pay him a visit.

10 April 1954

Apparently when Bob gets mad, he needs more than a week to cool off. My attempt at reconciliation today went horribly awry. To add to my woes, I had a run-in with Matron. She'd caught me sneaking in late after I'd genuinely gone to visit Mamma. She accused me of being a floosy and making up stories in order to go out with men. I wonder who has been spying.

Normally, we nurses have a pact of solidarity when it comes to personal matters. If I wanted to, I could dob in every one of my colleagues for infringements of hospital rules. Even Simpson, who leads the life of a nun, has been known to sneak in late through the ground-floor window, which is never locked for that reason. Sometimes she tells me where she's been—usually some underground jazz dive in the Valley—but more often than not, she keeps things to herself. Sometimes I wonder if she's a communist, or an agent for the secret service. She took a course in Russian last year and is very knowledgeable about world politics. Probably neither. My imagination is running wild at the moment.

I've hit a brick wall and need to make a change. I've been in Brisbane too long, at the hospital too long, and in a stale relationship with Bob too long. Teresa wrote to me recently from Sydney, inviting me to visit. She has found a nice man—of Italian origin, much to her parents' delight—and they've bought a cottage at Leichhardt. I have a good mind to go. If I like Sydney, I might even move there.

I've written to Horst. Of late, our correspondence has become more frequent. He seems to be doing well in Germany. What a joy it is to express ourselves openly and honestly, without having to worry about the camp censor.

2 June 1954

Today I received a letter from Horst, full of concern about my welfare. I had to think back to what I'd written almost two months ago. It must have been after the last blow-up with Bob when I wanted to throw the towel in.

Since then, we've made amends but our relationship will never be the same. Relationships are built on honesty, a quality in short supply when it comes to Bob and grog and money. So now we go through the motions of being together, still with secrecy I might add. Never would I give up my job for him. When he's sober and reasonable, we go out and have a few laughs. At least I know where I stand.

I wrote straight back to Horst, telling him not to worry.

29 October 1954

Today is the day! I'm so excited. Everything is arranged. My holiday leave has been approved and I've booked a nice little getaway place at the seaside.

Best of all, Bob is safely packed away and completely oblivious. How sweet and how perfect!

Twenty-one

Reinickendorf: October 2010

In the morning Kathy packed her wheelie bag and checked out of her accommodation. So far, she'd cancelled the river cruise and the flight from Hamburg to London. If necessary, she'd make other changes later. The extra week in Berlin filled her with the kind of excitement she couldn't explain.

Horst gave her a key to his apartment so she could come and go as she wished. For that she was thankful, for he was over eighty and became tired quickly. On the other hand, she'd finally conquered jet lag and was itching to explore the city.

After settling in, he suggested a short stroll to the old footwear factory. They came into Herbststrasse from the other end, but she immediately recognised it as the picturesque avenue she'd stumbled upon that first day. Outside the boarded-up building with the bird-and-shoe painting over the door, Horst stopped.

'This is it. *Vogel Schuhwerk*,' he said.

Kathy recalled what the old woman had said. *Vogel, famous all over Germany.* Her heart leapt as she realised the significance of the logo. *Vogel* meant bird and it was also Horst's family name.

He led her down a forsaken laneway, unlocked the rear door. The musty fug of abandonment flowed out. Mildew, rising damp, a chemical undertone of turpentine and glue.

'I should go first; there might be vermin. I haven't been here in a long time.' Horst took a few steps inside and disappeared into darkness. A beam of torchlight swept around the walls. Moments later, the room lit up as bright as day. Returning, he invited her in. 'We're in luck. The electricity is still connected.'

She followed him through a despatch room lined with criss-cross shelves the size of milk crates. Once they would have held shoeboxes and order forms for customers. The workshop was voluminous: high ceilings, florescent tubes hanging from chains, rows of workbenches fitted with industrial cutters, mechanical presses, and sewing machines. Here the dominant smells were machine oil and leather. The combination was rich and earthy: the odour of quality. Vogel shoes were made to last. These days, footwear was cheap and shoddy. No-one cared that they wore shoes made from melted-down plastic bottles. Heels snapped off, soles fell apart, uppers split after a few wears.

Horst opened his arms as if to embrace the workshop. Beaming with pride, he said, 'Opa started this factory one hundred years ago. Of course, it was quite small at the beginning. When I was a boy, my father took over the business and expanded operations. On my return from Australia, I was given more and more responsibility. When Max died, I ran the place on my own. Five years ago, I shut it down for good. Imports killed us. How can you compete with shiny new shoes that retail for under twenty Euros? People won't pay for quality any more. It's all about *fickle fashion*.' He shook his head. 'I could not prostitute the business by using low-grade materials and underpaying workers. Call me proud or stubborn, but I could not put my name on inferior shoes.'

'*Bravo!*' she said. Her old-world upbringing had taught her the value of craftsmanship and pride in a job well done. She understood now why Horst had made a lasting impression on her sister.

He rolled out a chair and sat at a sewing machine that was older than all the rest. Its slim black body was decorated with gold swirls. *Dürkopp* was scrawled across it in gold lettering.

'This was Opa's first treadle. It was built especially for shoe-making. One century old and it still sews beautifully.' He ran his hand across the metal body as if it were a sleek cat.

'It's a beautiful piece.' Kathy sat down opposite. 'When I was little, Mum had a treadle. Alice didn't have a machine of her own, so she'd come over and use ours. Actually, she was the one who taught me to sew. Mum was too busy, always out socialising or organising fund-raisers. She took the role of Principal's wife very seriously. My sister had the patience of a saint. If I snapped the needle or made holes in the fabric, she never got angry.'

'Where did you live as a child?'

'Toowoomba, two hours west of Brisbane. Do you know it?'

'Alice's mother—I mean, *your* mother—moved there after she re-married. I recall that Alice grew up on a cane farm in the north.'

'Yes. When I was eighteen, she took me to Currawong during the university break. Mum refused to go. Too many ghosts and bad memories, she said.

'Alice showed me around as if nothing had changed in the thirty years she'd been gone. But everything *had* changed. From what I knew, Currawong had once been a bustling town with canecutters and contractors and mill workers. In the early sixties, mechanical harvesters arrived, the seasonal workers left and the town died. When we visited, half the shops along the main street were empty.

'We hired a tinnie and found the spot on the Russell River where she and her father used to fish. The glare was so brutal that I got a headache, but I was glad we did it. By then, Alice and I had grown apart. That road trip had been a reprieve, a rare occasion when we were able to connect and enjoy each other's company as if we were friends.'

'You have to leave home to discover yourself,' said Horst.

It was true. In just one week, Kathy's mind had expanded with insights about herself and where she fitted in the world. The brain-shift was sudden and enlightening, like a burst of fireworks. When she eventually returned to Brisbane, she'd be a changed woman. A thrilling thought but also a little frightening. Would her new and different self still be attractive to Jack, whose main aim in life was to keep everything exactly the same?

'Come, I'll show you my office upstairs.' Horst led the way to the reception foyer at the front of the building. The entrance was impressive. Tiles, brass fittings, timber reception desk. On the wall was a hand-tinted photo of two men in suits and top hats. One looked about thirty, the other was at least two decades older.

'Max and Opa,' he said.

'Looks like an important event.'

'It was taken at a State function in 1933. Opa used to say that he shook Hitler's hand before it was stained with the blood of innocents. If only we knew ...'

'With the benefit of hindsight, we'd all do things differently,' she said.

They climbed the staircase to the first floor where three offices were linked by a hallway. Horst's was the first on the left. The room was untidy: open folders on the desk, mail in the tray, an unwashed coffee cup on the shelf. A snapshot in time, as if he went out to lunch one day and forgot to come back.

In the office, he opened a wooden press and sorted through a stack of shoeboxes. 'Here they are.' He removed the tissue paper and placed a pair of sturdy black boots on the desk.

'This was our specialty,' he said with a touch of sarcasm. 'The product that kept our business alive during the war.'

She picked one up and weighed it in her hand. 'Wow! They certainly feel durable. These would last a lifetime.'

'Yes, endurance was our forte.' He replaced the boots in the box and frowned. 'There's not much else to see up here.'

They breezed along the hall past another open office. At the end was a third door, which was shut and seemed to be out of bounds.

'That's enough for one day.' Abruptly he turned, thundered along the hall, down the stairs, and through the factory to the rear exit. Kathy trailed behind him, wondering why the sudden change of mood.

'Are you hungry?' He averted his face as he turned the key in the lock. 'There's a *Biergarten* nearby.'

'Okay. My treat.'

'No, no, no. You are my guest. Let me spoil you.'

Away from the factory, his spirits brightened. 'Thank you for indulging an old man.'

But the pleasure was hers. The one she wanted to thank, but couldn't, was Alice.

The *Biergarten* was behind a block of solid pre-war apartments and completely concealed from the street. If you didn't know it was there, you'd walk straight past without a second glance. Picnic tables were set out in a rustic courtyard surrounded by four-storey buildings and towering trees. The place was packed with workmen in safety-yellow jackets, office workers in suits, mothers with prams and children capering about. All locals. The atmosphere was relaxed and convivial, like a backyard barbeque. Horst ordered the food: *Schnitzel* and *Kartoffelsalat* and a good German beer. They shared a long table with three others.

'Are you bored with my story?' he said.

'How could you even think it? I want to hear everything, right to the very end.'

~

By 1954, seven years after our factory reopened, *Vogel Schuhwerk* was one of the most successful footwear manufacturers in West Germany. Our focus had shifted back to fashion shoes for women and children. The collapse of Nazi Germany meant the military market was *kaput*. Soon after the war, came a boom in weddings and babies. After years of shortages, austerity and making-do, everyone wanted smart new shoes made by first-rate German artisans.

Borrowing an expression from the Americans, Georg suggested that we *jazz-up* the business. We would have a logo and packaging that appealed to a new generation. Because our brand name was *Vogel* and most of our customers were young mothers, he suggested a sweet little bird. We chose the red-breasted robin and hired an artist to draw the design. The logo was embossed on the sole of each shoe and printed on the lids of the boxes. Our bestseller was the children's range, which flew off shelves as fast as we could make them. When I strolled down the Kurfürstendamm, the busiest shopping street in West Berlin, I'd count the number of Vogel shoes that walked by.

In the summer, we reached a new high point. The famous department store, KaDeWe, added our shoes to their inventory. I scheduled a few hours to see the display on the second floor. The day was hot; the woollen suit I wore was a poor choice. With my shirt clinging to my back, I entered Berlin's bastion of style. The building had been badly damaged in bombing raids and was partially repaired. At the time, just the lower storeys were open. Inside, the temperature was almost as hot as it was outside. There was no cooling system, only heating for the winter. I mopped my face with a hanky and wove through masses of female shoppers.

On the second floor, five of our new styles were on display. My heart swelled with pride. An enormous amount of effort had gone into this client. Georg's persistence had pulled off the coup. But it was wrong to gloat over our success or to puff ourselves up with self-importance. The sudden upswing in our profits was probably due to the *Wirtschaftswunder,* the economic boom in West Germany, rather than our business acumen. Manufacturing in general had mushroomed and there were more jobs than workers. Rationing had ended and everyone had money to spend. Stores stocked a startling array of labour-saving appliances—fridges, vacuum cleaners, food mixers—designed for the modern *Hausfrau.* The rising middle class snapped up German-made cars. Volkswagen, Mercedes-Benz, BMW. Shows of newfound affluence were everywhere.

In the KaDeWe shoe department, I introduced myself to the sales staff and gave them business cards. I hoped that the personal approach would inspire them to promote our products. As the place was teeming with customers, my pitch was short by necessity. Two pairs of Vogel shoes sold even as I watched. That was a good sign indeed.

Afterwards, I had coffee and cake at the Café Kranzler, followed by a stroll around the Zoologischer Garten. To my delight, my favourite childhood haunt was being rebuilt. Some of the new animal enclosures were already open.

I'd heard that, during the war, the Nazis tried to protect the animals by transporting them to other zoos in Europe. However, the plan was not a complete success. When the Allied bombers flew over Berlin, the zoo was right in the target zone. Some of the smaller animals were rescued by their handlers, who smuggled them into their homes. Basements and bathrooms became temporary cages. Floors were covered in straw and newspapers; handbasins became water troughs. Meanwhile, air strikes reduced the beautiful zoo pavilions to rubble and killed hundreds of beasts. Rhinoceros, antelope, giraffes, bison. After each bombing raid, the workers would pick through the carcasses. My father used to joke that zoo workers had the best-fed children in Berlin.

According to Georg, on the eastern side of the Brandenburger Tor, buildings were springing up like mushrooms. Massive Soviet-designed apartment complexes covered entire city blocks. He described the transformation from razed earth to metropolis with great enthusiasm. 'Come for dinner on Sunday and I'll show you around,' he'd say.

He and Isabell were renting a two-room apartment in one of those huge brutalist blocks. They lived in the East because it was cheap. Isabell worked for a State-run *Kita* in a sparkling new neighbourhood. The job suited her, for she loved little children and was expecting a baby herself. As an employee of the DDR government, she already had a *Kita* place reserved. Eight weeks after giving birth, she was required to return to work. I didn't know whether Isobell knew about Georg's other child, but I was not one to disclose secrets. I also suspected that his first marriage had not been annulled. Did it matter? All that happened long ago and far away.

When I returned to Reinickendorf, the sun was low in the west and a light breeze brought relief from the heat. In the kitchen, my father was preparing the evening meal. Rye bread, cheese, gherkins. He wore a loose cotton shirt and short pants, which revealed his skinny white legs that were usually encased in trousers.

The table was set for two. Klaus, the workshop foreman who'd moved into Opa's room, was absent. An easy-going man, he knew when to keep out of our way. Tonight, he must have sensed a change in the air. He'd left a message that he'd have his supper at the *Kneipchen*, the little pub on the corner of our street.

I opened a beer and poured two glasses. Max brought the food to the table. An idea had been playing on my mind for weeks now, ever since Alice's last letter.

When the war-time restrictions on mail were lifted, we'd resumed our correspondence. We wrote about what we'd done and how we felt, and I confessed to changing my surname. Through Mutti's silver pen, I poured out my heart. What a joy it was to dip a proper nib into good ink and write on thick quality paper. Letters are precious, like snapshots with words. I kept every one of Alice's.

Her last letter made me sick with worry. Instead of her usual warmth and optimism, she seemed downright gloomy. She said she'd 'hit a brick wall' and might resign and move to Sydney.

I'd written straight back, asking what had happened and reassuring her that I'd be there if she needed me. Her reply was probably in a mailbag on a ship somewhere between Colombo and Aden. I wanted to do something more.

As far as I knew, Max was not aware of our relationship. Sometimes he'd comment on the frequency of her letters, or teasingly call her my girlfriend. My counter was that collecting pen-friends was her hobby, like others collect stamps.

Time for the truth. I began with the family camp and told him everything. He listened without interruption. By the time I'd finished, the supper plates were bare and six empty beer bottles were lined up by the wall.

'When do you intend to leave?' he said.

My mouth opened in surprise. 'Do you think I should go?'

'*Should* is not a reason. From what you've said, you have strong feelings for each other. *Love*, now *that* is a reason. If she needs you, then of course you must go.' With that, he rose and shuffled, a little unsteadily, up the stairs to bed.

Our discussion was over. Permission was granted. I would leave as soon as I could get a visa and a steamer ticket.

~

At the Petrie Bight wharves in Brisbane, I sweltered on the deck of the *Stratheden* and waited to disembark. The morning sky was the deepest of blues, streaked with gossamer white. My shirt, fresh from the laundry, was already limp with sweat and humidity. I surveyed the crowd on the rough-hewn timbers below, searching for one person amongst hundreds.

Straight after booking the voyage, I'd written to Alice with dates and details and asked if she'd meet me at the wharves. In late September, I travelled by train from Berlin to Hamburg, then by ship to Southampton.

On the marathon voyage to Australia—my third across the vast ocean—we called into Marseilles, Port Said, Aden, Colombo, Fremantle,

Melbourne, Sydney. Unlike previous voyages, I was free to go ashore and see the sights of those exotic ports. At sea, I lazed in deckchairs, read books from the ship's library, played deck quoits, and kept my body in shape with callisthenics.

My cabin was shared with three other men, all Britishers. After sharing a few beers on the first night, they'd slapped me on the back and declared Germany forgiven for starting the war. As if I'd had any say in it. Anyway, with the air cleared, the war was not mentioned again and we got along famously.

In Brisbane, the mooring ropes were tied, the gangplank was lowered and the first-class passengers began their descent. As I stood ready with my suitcase and overcoat, I worried that Alice might not come.

My passport was stamped without a hitch. My cabinmates shook my hand and made me promise to visit them in England before a taxi swept them away. I ambled up a steep laneway that rose from the wharf to the city centre.

At the top, I put down my suitcase and took one last look at the *Stratheden*. She was a handsome vessel, sleek and modern and white, built for passengers and pleasure. Beyond her was the twin-peaked bridge of steel that we'd passed under earlier. It was the sole link between the spectacular orange cliffs on the one side and marshlands on the other. Beneath, snaked the lazy brown river.

I turned my back to the water. Across the way was a three-story hotel with a red telephone booth outside. Perhaps Alice had forgotten or had been held up at work. Thinking to phone her at the hospital, I glanced to the left and marched onto the street. Brakes squealed, a horn blared, a stream of verbal abuse followed. The vehicle was close; one more step and I might have been killed. Then I remembered that I was in the land of upside-down, where winter was summer and people drove on the wrong side of the road.

Safely inside the phone booth, I was about to dial when a woman in a sky-blue dress ran along the footpath near the wharf. Without a thought, I grabbed my suitcase and dashed through the traffic, risking life and limb for the second time in as many minutes.

At the sound of multiple car horns, she spun around. 'Horst! I'm so sorry to be late. I was on night shift and—'

I threw my arms around her. 'Thank God you're here.' I smothered her face with kisses. Her skin was salty with tears. For a long while we stood there, clutching each other in joy and disbelief. Even after all those years, the feelings of affection were still there.

Suddenly she stepped back; her cheeks were flushed. 'We should go. The place where you're staying is tiny, but there's a comfortable bed and everything you'd need. It's yours on two provisos: that you feed the cat and leave the place clean.'

Hand-in-hand we boarded a tram marked *Chermside*. Alice insisted that I sit by the window. There wasn't much to see, apart from a row of painted buildings and an overgrown park. After two stops, she became animated. 'Here's the Valley, our commercial hub.'

I wasn't sure if the comment was meant to be serious or sarcastic. It wasn't much of a hub: a couple of banks, several pubs, shops with displays of furniture or clothing in the windows. Hardly anyone about. Mothers pushed prams along the pavement; sparrows fought over crumbs.

'Is it always this quiet?'

'It's Friday: payday. By lunchtime, the place will be crawling.'

The tram made a crackling noise as the overhead trolley-arm switched lines. We turned and crawled up a gradual slope. At the top was a mass of large buildings.

'That's where I work. The Brisbane General Hospital.' Proudly she pointed out the nurses' quarters high on the hill. Twin towers, eight storeys, Spanish arches.

'There must be a lot of nurses,' I said.

'Hundreds. And we're all single.' She smirked. 'Actually, we have to be. If a nurse marries, she has to resign. Matron is a stickler for rules. No male visitors, curfew at ten-thirty, beds made before breakfast. Not that different from … well, you know …' Her voice trailed off as if she didn't want to mention the family camp in public.

Tatura seemed a lifetime ago.

She continued. 'As a trainee, nursing was fun. The Americans were in town and we were always going to the pictures or parties and sneaking in late. When you're young, rules are meant to be broken.' She sighed. 'That was ten years ago and I'm tired of juvenile antics. It's time for a different life. That's why I thought of going to Sydney.'

The tram glided past the hospital. A few stops on, she tugged the bell-cord and we got out. Under a scorching sun, we walked alongside the railway line and turned left into Cox Road. Timber cottages peeped over the edge of an embankment retained by high concrete walls. We turned through an archway and climbed the stairs. At the top was a rambling weatherboard homestead with sweeping views of the distant mountains.

'Yours is Flat 3.' Alice pressed a key into my hand and made me promise not to lose it.

The central hallway ran from the front to the back of the house. Doors were numbered on either side. I unlocked number 3 and went in. On one side of the room was a kitchenette with a blue painted table and chairs. On the other side was a sofa, some bookshelves, and a curled-up grey cat. Through a doorway was a bed and a wardrobe.

'Are you sure your friend is happy for me to stay?'

'Yes, yes, yes.' Alice flopped onto the sofa. The cat jumped onto her lap and touched its pink nose to her hand. 'By the way, this is your flatmate, Felix.' She tickled it under the chin. 'Now, here's the plan. You're here until Saturday morning. Saturday afternoon we're off to the South Coast for a week. I've taken the liberty of booking us into a guest house. Did you bring your swimming togs?'

I shook my head. Bathers were optional in Berlin.

'No matter. I'll take you shopping.' She got up and opened the ice-chest. Inside was a bottle of milk, two bottles of beer, and pat of butter. 'Hungry?'

'Starving.'

'Spam and eggs?'

'What's Spam?'

A wicked grin crept over her face. 'Never mind.' Without explanation, she opened a yellow can and turned out a loaf of unidentifiable pink matter, which she cut into slices, fried in a pan, and served with an egg—sunny side up—on top.

The aroma was a bit like *Leberkäse*. The flavour was salty and not unpleasant.

'What's it made of?'

She shrugged. 'Yank food. It's supposed to be meat.' She cut off a sliver, placed it in her mouth, pulled a face. 'Could be anything. I think it's best we don't know.'

While we ate, we chatted about what we'd been doing, what we planned for the future, and the people we knew from 'down south'. The conversation flowed easily, as if weeks—not years—had passed since we were last together.

At length, she began to yawn. 'Must sleep. I'm on night duty for the rest of the week. Help yourself to any food about the place. If you want to see a movie, there's a cinema nearby. The Crystal Palace. Sounds grander than it is, but it's cheap and they have good films.'

'Will I see you tomorrow?'

'Of course! Is eight in the morning too early?'

'Perfect. I'll cook you Spam and eggs,' I said.

Alice laughed. 'Once a year is enough.' She picked up the cat and gave him a rub. 'Feed him twice a day, morning and night, and he'll love you forever.' Felix purred and licked her fingers, savouring the flavour of the Spam.

I locked him inside and we walked up the hallway.

'The ice-man comes Mondays and Thursdays at nine. Put a shilling in the jam jar and he'll leave you a block.' The sun blazed from a white-hot sky. Alice fanned herself with her hand. 'Welcome to the sub-tropics. See that haze over the mountains? We're in for a storm later.'

We retraced our steps to the main road. A tram was trundling up the hill. With a look of urgency, she turned to me. 'If anyone asks, you're my cousin.'

My mind flashed back to Georg and the deception we'd pulled off at Tatura. How many other pseudo-cousins were there in the world? Smiling, I gave her a peck on the cheek. She leapt onto the tram and waved from the window.

Crossing the road, I stood outside the arched portico of the Crystal Palace. The feature film at seven o'clock was *Niagara*, a thriller with Marilyn Monroe and Joseph Cotten. My wristwatch told me it had just gone three. With nothing better to do, I decided to explore the 'commercial hub' that I'd seen earlier.

A tram marked *Ashgrove* arrived. I climbed aboard and rode past the hospital and down the hill to the Valley. Alice was right: the place had come alive. The footpaths were bursting with shoppers with bags of groceries for the weekend. I wandered through the three department stores—McWhirters, Waltons, TC Beirne—which were tiny in comparison to KeDeWe. In one of the even smaller variety stores, I purchased swimming trunks, a pair of shorts, two cotton shirts, and some sandals. At a continental deli, I bought a square of cheese, a loaf of brown bread, chocolates for Alice, and some *Wurst*, which the assistant called 'Windsor sausage'.

At five o'clock the shops shut their doors. Men with felt hats and Gladstone bags swarmed onto the footpaths. Some veered into beer halls that stood on the corners of the main intersections. Thirsty and hot, I ventured into one called the *Royal George*. The bar was packed. Men jostled and shouted for service. By the windows, rowdy drinkers joked and swore and guzzled beer. Dozens of glasses, full and empty, were lined up along the sills. The rabble was deafening, the atmosphere brutal. My thirst disappeared.

Standing room only on the tram. I clutched my purchases, wrapped in brown paper and string, to my chest. Bodies lurched this way and that as we rounded the bends. The air was thick with the odour of armpits and hair oil. Steel-grey clouds loomed over the western mountains. As the hospital slipped past, the sky cracked and the ground beneath us trembled.

At Windsor, I stepped down from the tram. The storm was approaching fast. Fat raindrops clanged onto corrugated-iron roofs like dropped pennies. Although it was not yet six, the street was as dark as midnight. As I turned into Cox Road, hailstones pinged off my hat. A flash lit up the archway; an ear-splitting crash shook the staircase. Inside the flat, I dumped the packages on the table and dried off. The electricity was out, so I made a meal of Windsor sausage, bread and cheese, and climbed into bed. Felix didn't make an appearance.

At dawn, I woke with a weight on my chest. Gingerly I opened an eye, which sparked a small motor. A moist triangle touched my nose. Felix. I wasn't used to cats, but I fancied that he was checking that I was alive. I swept him off and rolled over. He yowled and padded to the door. In my undershorts, I let him out. The storm had passed; the air smelt new and as fresh as laundered linen. A cold wind skirled up the hallway. I shut the door. Shivering, I pulled on trousers and a sweater.

In the kitchenette, I boiled the kettle and made tea. Bare branches scritch-scratched against the windowpane, a disconcerting sound that reminded me of fingernails on a blackboard. Teacup in hand. I was drawn to the bookshelf. All the titles were in English. Classics by British authors: Dickens, Conrad, Tolkien. Novels by Americans: Orwell, Steinbeck, Hemmingway. I selected *The Old Man and the Sea* and read a few lines at random. The language was simple. Deceptively so, I suspected. I turned to the beginning and had reached page forty when someone knocked.

'Hurry up. It's freezing out here.'

I opened the door and Alice blew in with a flurry of leaves. It was after eight and I hadn't made breakfast. While she scoured the flat for Felix, I sliced the bread, boiled the eggs, and cut up the cheese. Then I remembered.

'He went out,' I said.

She shot me an exasperated expression and stomped down the hallway, calling *puss, puss, puss.*

Minutes later, a streak of grey darted in. 'That damn feline has a mind of his own,' she muttered. 'Like someone else I know.'

'Not me, surely,' I said lightly.

'No, just … someone.' She put some chopped meat on a saucer for the cat, then sat at the table and poured tea for herself.

While we ate, Felix attended to his ablutions, legs stretched into impossible positions, tongue combing the fur of his belly and the nether regions. Momentarily I closed my eyes and imagined that married life might be like this. A pretty woman, a home-cooked meal, a comfy flat, a furry pet. What more could a man wish for?

We made plans for the day, which was Saturday. We'd walk the city streets until the shops closed at noon. In the afternoon we'd visit the zoo in the Botanical Gardens, catch a ferry across the river, and wander back across the twin-peaked bridge that I'd seen from the ship.

Thus ran the week. Alice worked nights and we had the mornings together. We visited every attraction in Brisbane: the clocktower at City Hall, the red-brick museum and art gallery, the Regent picture palace, the Spring Hill Baths, where I tried out my new bathers and lost them diving in. Wherever we went, I floated on air, for my angel was with me at last.

The following Saturday, we cleaned the flat from top to bottom, took a tram to South Brisbane and a train to Coolangatta at the seaside. We arrived in the late afternoon.

Standing high on the hill, our guesthouse was an attractive structure with verandas and timber balustrades. A turret promised views of the wide curve of beach and the glistening Pacific Ocean. We humped our suitcases up a steep track to the crest of the headland. Below us, beach umbrellas clustered like multi-coloured mushrooms. Children splashed in the shallows; youths bodysurfed the waves; young women sun-baked on the sand. The crash and sigh of the surf was a tonic for jaded minds.

Beside me, Alice was fidgeting. 'Before we go in, I need to tell you something.' She seemed so anxious that I feared she might call the whole thing off. My heart sank. Where would that leave me? I might as well take the next ship home. My life was over.

The sound of her sweet voice brought me back from the brink. 'This guesthouse is very popular. The only room available was a double, so I took it. I don't know what it's like in Germany, but here you have to be married to get a double.' She produced a plain gold band and slipped it onto her finger. 'It cost a shilling at Coles but it looks convincing enough, don't you think? The names I gave were Mr and Mrs Horst Schuhmacher.'

'You're full of surprises, Frau Schuhmacher.' Relief. I laughed a little louder than necessary.

'Let's do this before my courage deserts me.' She looped her arm through mine and we marched to the reception desk. Our performance was so convincing that we exited with the key to the honeymoon suite, courtesy of a last-minute cancellation. The room was not as opulent as the name suggested, but it was quiet and comfortable. The sole window gave a glimpse of distant mountains. The shared bathrooms were along a covered veranda. An external staircase led down to a goat-track which wound around the sandhills to the shore.

As evening fell, a blustery wind blew in, sending beachgoers indoors. In the dining room we ate early, for Alice was already yawning, exhausted from continuous night duty at the hospital. At eight o'clock she curled up on the double bed and promptly fell asleep. I sat in a wooden chair, reading a brochure about things to do at Coolangatta. The moans and bumps that filtered through the cardboard-thin walls suggested that our neighbours were genuine honeymooners, not fakes like us.

Leaving Alice to sleep, I tiptoed out and down the back stairs. By the light of a near-full moon and a galaxy of stars, I strolled along the headland. Across the water was a path of shimmering light. The next patch of dry land, thousands of kilometres away, was South America. All that water, all that sky. The isolation overwhelmed me. Out there at night, I could have been the only person alive on earth. While Germany is practically surrounded by other countries—not all of whom are friendly, I might add—Australia is separated from the rest of the world by immense oceans.

At Tatura I had not felt like that. There, I was with countrymen who spoke my language, who shared my culture. Despite all our differences, the German compound was a scaled-down replica of the Fatherland. My thoughts turned to Werner, who'd moved to Queensland after the war. To Georg and Teresa, whose loveless marriage was doomed from the start.

What of our relationship? Was it doomed or would it succeed? Certainly, we were not without love, at least on my part. Alice played her cards close to her chest. What if I asked and she accepted? Where would we live? Australia is remote and full of adventure, but Berlin is where I belong. I could not see myself settling down anywhere else. Would Alice give up her job, her mother, and her friends to live in my world? Those ties were strong, but ours were stronger. Language was another issue. While she spoke English and Italian, she had not one word of German. In Berlin she'd struggle to communicate as much as I would in Rome.

My thoughts returned to Georg, whose natural charm everyone admired. His philosophy was simple: *If you don't ask, you don't get*. At Tatura, he'd ask the unthinkable and get his way. That was how I'd been rescued from the Nazi camp, how we two 'cousins' had come to share a room. That was how he'd seduced Teresa. That was how he'd landed free accommodation at Aunt Berry's, and later a good job at Vogel Schuhwerk, and then an attractive German wife (though I doubted they were married). As our sales representative, he asked customers for orders every day and got as many as he wanted. Asking was a talent that he'd honed into an art-form. If only he could help me with the most important question of my life.

After midnight I returned to the room and the sleeping woman I adored. After stripping down to my underwear, I slid between the sheets. The well-used springs of the honeymoon-suite bed groaned under the extra weight. Alice stirred and rolled towards me. Wide awake, I lay on my back, willing myself into slumber that would not come. The ceiling was dappled with reflected moonlight and the shadows of trees. Alice's breath against my cheek smelt like honey; her warmth radiated across the narrow gap between us. So agonisingly close, yet untouchable. I sighed, a long shuddering breath of yearning.

'Horst?' She sounded half asleep.

'I'm here.'

'Hold me?'

I rolled towards her and wrapped my arms around her. Our lips met and our bodies entwined like ivy. Passions ignited and, at last, we surrendered to love.

Afterwards, I held her close. This was the moment for me to ask the impossible question. *If you don't ask, you don't get.* I drew a breath but could not squeeze the words from my throat. Her breathing slowed; her body grew heavy. Another opportunity lost.

Trouble was, I didn't know what I truly wanted. More pressing questions had gone without asking. When I was alone in the flat at Windsor, I'd come across clues that Alice's absent friend was not female. A black sock was hiding under the bed; a razorblade was on the ledge beneath the basin. Even the books on the living-room shelf were unusual choices for a woman. In addition to the classics, there were dozens of crime novels and war stories. One was *The Colditz Story* by Major Patrick Reid. According to the blurb, it was written by a British army officer, based on first-hand experiences of being held prisoner-of-war at the 'impregnable fortress' near Leipzig. Inside the front cover was an inscription, hand-written in blue ink.

> *To Bob, partner in crime and jolly good chap.*
>
> *Living proof that miracles really happen.*
>
> *Best wishes always, Patrick.*

Who on earth was Bob? Tomorrow, I would ask her. In the meantime, I leant across and kissed her forehead. Sleep did not find me until dawn.

Twenty-two

Reinickendorf: October 2010

Kathy had been so engrossed in Horst's story that she'd not noticed the lunchtime crowd at the Biergarten dwindling. She glanced at her watch, surprised that it was after three.

'We should be going,' said Horst. 'I have some personal matters to attend to this afternoon. Can you amuse yourself?'

'Of course. I'll spend the afternoon with Alice.'

'Do you know how to get back to the apartment?'

She had no idea. He'd led and she'd followed. 'I'll find it.'

Out on the street, she walked in the direction from which they'd come, hopeful that she'd spot a landmark—a building or a street sign or a garden— that would show her the way. All the chunky post-war apartment blocks looked exactly the same. She should have paid more attention. What had they passed earlier? Yes, there was the ice-cream shop, the playground with swings, the cemetery amongst the trees, the overgrown expanse called Schillerpark, where Horst said he'd played as a kid.

At last, she came to Residenzstrasse, the shopping street near the lake. Finally, she was on familiar ground. It took twice as long as it should have, but she'd managed on her own. Inside his apartment she settled on the sofa with a cup of tea and Alice's leather diary.

16 November 1954

I've had my chance and I've blown it. My life is a mess. Two days ago, Horst and I quarrelled and I haven't seen him since.

At Coolangatta before the tiff, he'd said he would visit Dr Werner at his Marburg farm on Tuesday. That's today. With no other information to hand, I put two-and-two together and came up with the nine-thirty train to Helidon. Just after nine I was at the Roma Street Station, hoping to put things right. Apart from a dozen pigeons, the platform was empty.

I sat on a bench and lit a cigarette. These days, I rarely smoke but this morning I bought a pack at the kiosk. As I handed over the coins, my ears rang with Matron's disparaging words: *so unbecoming for a woman*. Feeling defiant, I took a drag and released a plume of smoke. The pigeons cooed and pecked around my feet. The hands of the station clock barely moved. I consulted the little makeup mirror that I keep in my purse. Fixed my hair, retouched my lipstick, silently practised what I'd say.

At nine-thirty precisely, the Helidon train slid into the platform. A few passengers got out; a few latecomers boarded. My hunch was wrong. Horst was not there. Maybe he caught a bus instead.

I stubbed out my second cigarette and stood to leave. Footsteps reverberated up the stairs; shouts rang across the platform. A grey blur of a man almost collided with me as he raced toward the train.

My stomach lurched.

As the stationmaster blew the whistle, he yanked open the door of the nearest carriage and threw himself in.

I called out and waved my arms.

Inside the carriage, he dropped the window.

The locomotive hissed and the carriage groaned into motion. I said I was sorry for everything. As it moved faster, I yelled that I loved him. I don't think he heard through the chug and clatter of the train.

As it disappeared around the bend, I waved my white nurse's hanky, my flag of surrender. Long after he had gone, I stood on the platform. Half of me was glad, half of me was shattered.

Outside the station, the Roma Street markets were in full swing. Fruit and vegetable vendors whistled tunes as they stacked crates of produce for sale. The carnival atmosphere lifted my mood.

When we left for our holiday at Greenmount, I had an inkling that Horst might propose. All along, he'd been dropping little hints. The week at the guesthouse was a honeymoon in every sense and it came as no surprise when he said, 'There's something I want to ask you.'

However, the question was not what I'd expected.

'Who is Bob?' he'd said.

I'd planned to keep my two lovers apart and had done a lot of planning and preparation. First, I'd convinced Bob to visit his mother in Cairns. To that end, I'd booked and paid for—from my own savings, I might add—a return trip on the new diesel train, the *Sunlander*. With Bob away, I was able to spend time with Horst with no questions asked.

Straight after Bob's departure, I let myself into his flat and cleaned the place from top to bottom. All traces of him were removed. Clothing, shoes, toiletries were locked in the wardrobe. I stripped down the bed and remade it. The sheets were stretched tight and mitred like knives at the corners. Sister Kelly would have been proud. Before I went to the wharves, I visited the corner store for provisions and missed the tram as a result. That was why I was late, the reason we got off to a bumpy start from which we never quite recovered.

When Horst asked about Bob, I told him the truth. He didn't take it well. He said that, if he'd have known I was already in a relationship with a married man, he wouldn't have come halfway around the world to see me. We sparred for a short while, then made up over a bottle of champagne that he'd smuggled into our room. I'd never been with anyone but Bob, so it was a revelation to discover how tender and passionate lovemaking could be.

On the last day of our 'honeymoon', Horst took my hands and asked me the question I'd been dreading. 'Will you marry me?'

'I can't.' My destructive words came out loud and harsh, and he stepped back as if he'd been physically slapped.

On the train ride back from the coast, we barely spoke. In silence, we walked from the station, across the bridge to the People's Palace, where I'd stayed when I first came to Brisbane. Outside the hotel, I wished him good night. Without so much as a peck on the cheek, he said *goodbye* and left me standing on the footpath.

His coldness shocked me. If the boot were on the other foot, would I have reacted differently? Of course, I would. I'm Italian for heaven's sake. I would have demanded explanations, argued, flung my hands about. His apparent lack of emotion—his *iciness*—was foreign to me. I didn't know how to react.

I took the tram from Roma Street to the hospital. Simpson was reading a book in the garden outside the nurses' quarters. I said hello and she gave me a smug grin that reminded me of Felix with a dead rat in his mouth. We chatted for a moment, then she handed me the photograph that changed everything.

An unsuspecting Bob had been snapped by a camera at a place where he shouldn't have been. Undeniable evidence that he could never be trusted.

Too furious to speak or ask any questions, I shoved the photo into my pocket. On the way to my room, I picked up my mail. Two items: a letter from Mamma and a postcard from Bob. The postcard pictured a beach that looked suspiciously like Redcliffe, a short drive north of Brisbane. On the reverse side he'd written:

Greetings from Cairns. Miss you, darling. Love Bob.

My blood shot to boiling point. I stuffed the mail into my bag, thundered to my room, threw myself onto the bed. I've made that bed and now I'll have to lie in it.

In less than two weeks, Horst will be on the ship to Germany. After what happened, he'll probably never contact me again. The path ahead without him will be long and lonely. Because of selfish ambition, I've rejected the most decent and respectable man I've ever known. How could I be so stupid?

Tomorrow, I will confront Bob about the postcard and that photo. As far as I'm concerned, our affair is dead and buried. Tomorrow, I will pay him a visit and put an end to it. No ifs, no buts, no maybes.

17 November 1954

It is done. Bob didn't argue or try to talk me out of leaving him. Now I have what I wished for. Freedom. Why do I feel so wretched?

21 January 1955

I've taken a week's leave to visit Mamma at her new home in Toowoomba. The train journey to Helidon was pleasant but the bus ride up the Range was winding and torturous and made me feel sick. At the terminus, I was met by this glamorous woman in a sundress. Mamma is well into her forties now, but she looks my age.

We rushed into each other's arms.

'Missed you,' we chorused. Laughing and holding hands, we walked to the car, a new dove-grey Ford Consul. A gift from Luca, she told me. 'Such a generous man. I wish you knew him better.'

'I will after a week under the same roof,' I quipped. In truth I was terrified at the prospect. In my experience, he was dour, surly, and completely lacking in humour.

We got into the car. In one elegant motion, she pressed the ignition button, wound down the window, and lit a cigarette. 'Want one?' She tossed the red-and-gold tin onto the bench seat between us.

'Only the best.' I fingered the expensive tin. 'Maybe later. That road up the Range has made my head spin.'

'Well, it's a straight run all the way home.' She crunched the gears, stepped on the accelerator. The car took off like a stallion. We cruised along an avenue of stately homes with neat hedges, pulled into the drive of a bungalow with flower gardens and a white picket fence. Of course, Mamma had described the house in her letters, but it's even nicer than I expected.

Inside is a far cry from the musty old farmhouse at Currawong. Stained-glass windows, polished wood floors, Persian rugs. The dining suite is antique mahogany. The sideboard sparkles with silverware. There are three big bedrooms, a kitchen with all the latest appliances, and an informal eating area with a long table to seat ten.

'Well, what do you think?' Her chest puffed out with pride.

'It's fabulous. But how …?' I didn't mean to sound sceptical, but she picked up on it.

'How could we afford such a place? Is that what you want to know?' she snapped.

'You're so well set up. It looks like you've lived here for generations.'

'We bought it at auction. Deceased estate. The chattels were included in the sale. Of course, we added a few touches of our own. As for money, I sold the farm, don't forget. And Luca contributed as well. Did I tell you he's been promoted to Principal?' She had, several times in her letters.

It was well past lunchtime and breakfast for me was a distant memory. My stomach, recovered now from dozens of hairpin bends, was complaining of hunger. Mamma told me to settle in and freshen up while she rustled up some food.

I put my travel bag in the third bedroom, which opens out to an enormous camphor laurel tree in a neat yard. For several minutes, I stood at the window, elbows on the sill, soaking up the tranquillity. Unlike the nurses' home, which is always bustling with activity and the noise of road traffic, Mamma's house has an air of peace and permanence. These past few months have been difficult. I am thirty now, unsettled and in need of a change.

The day I broke up with Bob, he'd been at the racetrack and lost his entire week's wages. I told him that it was time to move on, that I was tired of coming last to a mob of thoroughbreds, that I wanted a man I could trust.

'But you can trust me.' His eyes were brimming with tears. He always got emotional after losing money and drowning his sorrows in beer. 'I'll make it up to you, I promise.'

I opened my purse and handed him the photo, snapped by a street photographer two weeks before. Accompanied by an unknown male, Bob was standing outside the front gates of the Eagle Farm racetrack. The image was undeniably him; the date stamped on the back was irrefutable. He was at the Brisbane races on a day he should have been with his mother in faraway Cairns.

He held the black-and-white print as if it would bite him. 'Where did you get this?'

I didn't answer. With my arms folded, I stood my ground. This time he wouldn't get away with it. He looked to the left and the right, but his eyes wouldn't meet mine. His lower lip trembled like a child caught with his hand in the lolly jar.

'You were supposed to be a thousand miles away. I bought you that train ticket, remember? How could you be in two places at once?'

Guilt was written all over his deceitful face.

'Did you cash in the ticket and lose it on the nags?' I snarled.

Silence.

Impatient now, I tapped my shoe on the lino. 'Yes or no?'

To my astonishment, he nodded. That was a first. Never before had he admitted to wrongdoing. As far as I was concerned, it would be the last.

'Thank you and goodbye.' I stalked out the door, making a conscious effort to not look back. It was over. I was glad. Too much of my life had been wasted on his lies.

When I returned to the kitchen, Mamma had set the table for three with a platter of sandwiches at the centre.

'Luca will be home any minute.' She straightened her apron and plumped her hair. 'If you're hungry, you can start.' She offered the sandwiches and I grabbed two with salami and cheese.

'You can stay with us as long as you like.' She frowned. 'In your last letter, you sounded dispirited, as if something was wrong.'

My eyes prickled, but I fought the tears back. My voice wavered as I told her about the breakup with Bob.

Her response was short and sharp. 'That lazy good-for-nothing! I'm surprised you didn't wake up to him sooner.'

I took a bite of sandwich and debated whether I should mention Horst. Good heavens, here I was, a grown woman, hesitating to discuss my love life. I asked if she remembered 'the German boy'.

'Of course. How could I forget Teresa's wedding? It gave us all a boost. Georg looked exceptionally handsome that day.' She poured two cups of tea from a large china pot.

'I meant Horst, the best man.'

'The one you drooled over all afternoon? Yes, I remember.' She sipped the tea, which she took black with three teaspoons of sugar. *To support the canegrowers*, she used to say. Despite her sweet tooth, she never put on an ounce of weight.

'About two months ago, Horst came to Australia and asked me to marry him.'

Mamma jumped off the chair and threw her arms around me. 'I'm so happy for you, darling. Maybe I'll have grandchildren after all.'

'No! Stop! You don't understand. I turned him down.'

'Why would you do that? He seemed such a nice chap. And you're not getting any younger, Alessandra. Surely you don't want to be left on the shelf.'

'Mamma, that's enough! I turned him down because I don't want to live in Germany and he can't leave because of the family business. The situation is impossible.' I wanted to say more, but Luca walked in and the moment was lost.

He gave me the customary Italian greeting: a kiss on each cheek. 'Welcome to our home, Alessandra. I'm glad you could come.' He sat down at the table and helped himself to four sandwiches. 'School holidays and still a teacher has to work.'

I congratulated him on his promotion and thanked him for letting me stay.

He squeezed my hand briefly. 'My pleasure. I know you'll never think of me as a father, but I hope we can be good friends.'

Perhaps I've been worrying needlessly about the future. A plan has formed: a way of escaping the city and the past, of continuing my career as a nurse, of keeping my head above water through a difficult time ahead. If Mamma and Luca agree to this crazy proposition, I just might pull it off.

Twenty-three

Reinickendorf: October 2010

Kathy flipped through the rest of the journal but there were no more entries. She'd sought answers, but the unsatisfactory ending raised even more questions. What was the meaning of that last paragraph? The careful wording suggested there was more to this, but Alice had left no other clues. Although Kathy had gone through piles of files and papers when she'd cleared out the Toowoomba residence for sale, she'd found nothing of interest. No letters or cards or photos. Nothing but a box of worthless souvenirs at the back of Alice's wardrobe.

For as long as she could remember, her sister had been a nurse at Toowoomba. At first, she'd worked at the Base Hospital, and later at a centre for disadvantaged children that she'd founded with her friend, Simpson. Although she could simply ask Horst, he seemed intent on revealing Alice's story in his own methodical way. No, she wouldn't ask; she'd trust him to tell her. With an extension of her stay in Berlin, she had time to take it all in.

In the evening Horst returned, carrying a bunch of flowers, a loaf of ryebread, and a package from a German delicatessen.

'Did you finish the diary?' he said.

'Yes. It made me feel closer to Alice than we were in real life.'

'I'm glad. I don't have to tell you that she turned me down.'

'What a pity. You would have made a nice couple.'

'I don't know. I loved her, but we were too different for marriage to have worked.'

Kathy asked if there any more diaries or letters.

'No other diaries that I know of. I kept her early letters for a while but, after the disastrous trip to Australia, I burnt them in the fireplace.'

Kathy felt a pang of disappointment, for she was itching to know what happened next. The narrative had simply stopped without an end.

What did she expect anyway? She'd found what she was looking for. In particular, confirmation that her mother and sister were interned during the war and a glimpse inside the family camp where they'd been held. She'd come to know and love Alice as a young woman. And, thanks to Horst's contribution, she knew more about WWII and internment now than most other people in Australia.

After a snack of pastrami on rye, they repaired to the living room with a bottle of apple schnapps. Horst introduced the next segment by announcing that, after he returned to Berlin in 1955, everything changed. Not only his hopes and ambitions, but also the relationship with his father and his country.

'I cannot take these secrets to my grave.' His voice cracked with emotion. He skolled a glass of schnapps, then took a juddering breath and launched himself into the past.

~

February is the worst month in Berlin. February 1955 was the coldest I could remember. Carrying my heavy suitcase, I trudged through ankle-deep snow from the U-Bahn. The temperature was well below zero. The midday sun was hidden behind a thick blanket of cloud. The eerie half-light made it difficult to see. Slowly, I picked my way along a path coated with treacherous black ice. Chestnut trees stretched skeleton branches into the gunmetal sky. I pulled down the brim of my hat, tucked in my scarf, and silently thanked Max for insisting that I take my heavy overcoat. While it wasn't needed in Australia, on the return journey I would have perished without it.

I took the track that ran by the lake. Through the fog, I could barely make out the buildings along the shoreline. Before leaving Hamburg, I'd sent Max a telegram advising my arrival time. He would be home, expecting me for lunch.

As I reached the corner of Frühlingstrasse, my pace quickened. The dear gabled roof, crusted with snow, bobbed into view. I imagined the warmth of the open fire, the hearty aroma of soup simmering on the stove. As I didn't have a key, I rang the doorbell. On the porch, I slapped my half-frozen body with half-frozen hands and waited for the shuffle of slippers in the hall. A feeling of *déjà vu* crept over me: this was a replay of my prodigal-son return nine years earlier.

I rapped the brass knocker. Minutes passed. No answer. Peeking through the glass was impossible, for the windows were shuttered and the winter drapes had been drawn. Had the telegram not arrived?

I decided to take a short walk to the factory. The wind had picked up. Sleet was coming in sideways, frosting my uncovered face. Ill-equipped for a blizzard, I moved as fast as I could. My leather-soled shoes skated across the treacherous cobblestones. My feet were like two blocks of ice, completely without feeling. Frostbite was the least of my concerns.

At last, a light in the wilderness. I wrestled with the wind to open the door and was blown inside. In the warmth of the foyer, I stamped moisture off my shoes and shrugged off my sodden coat. The workshop was deathly quiet. At this time of day, the workers had their lunch break; Max usually ate in his office.

I climbed the staircase and bypassed the two front offices. As I strode along the corridor, a head poked out of Max's office at the end. We both started in surprise.

'Oh, you're back,' Georg observed with trepidation.

'Yes, just now. I thought my father would be here.'

His eyes skipped about the place, looking at everything but me.

'He's not at home either,' I added.

Georg's behaviour was odd and out of character. It was as if he wished I wasn't there. 'Look,' he began and then stopped. He patted his pockets for cigarettes but found none. I knew him as well as I knew myself. Clearly something was amiss.

'I don't know how to say this, so I'll say it straight,' he said.

Panic stabbed my heart. In that split second before he spoke again, I knew what he would say. Unconsciously I pressed my hands to my ears as if to block it out, but I could do nothing to avoid the inevitable truth.

He cleared his throat and the words came tumbling out. 'Your father passed away suddenly three weeks ago. I sent a telegram to Alice. She telegrammed back to say that you'd already departed.'

I felt my face sag then break apart. In September, when I'd left Berlin, Max had been as healthy and active as ever. Dizzily, I stumbled into a visitor's chair. I was numb, cold, exhausted. My mind went blank and refused to function.

'Can I get you a glass of water? Or some schnapps?'

I opted for water. By the time he returned with a tumbler and a pack of cigarettes, I'd recovered enough to ask for details.

'Your father was right here in this office. I came in to ask him about a customer order. His forehead was on the desk as if he were asleep. I tried to wake him, shook him by the shoulder. His body was limp and unresponsive. The post mortem showed that he'd had a massive stroke. No pain. A good death, according to the doctor.'

'But he was alone,' I said. 'What sort of son am I? My mother died while I was interned in England. Opa died while I was interned at Tatura. Now my father has died while I'm on a ship half-way across the Indian Ocean. The three most important people in my life, and I was missing in action when they needed me most.'

Georg held up his hands to stop me. 'Don't beat yourself up. No-one knows when they'll leave this world. That's for a power greater than us. You did your best under the circumstances.'

I felt as if one of those sturdy all-purpose boots we'd made for the Nazi army had kicked me in the guts. Of course, he was right. I covered my face and wept.

Georg reached into his breast pocket and produced a small flask. He half-filled my empty tumbler, made a toast to Max, and took a deep swallow. He pulled up a chair beside me. 'I know what it's like to lose the people you love.'

Our eyes met. His were blue and liquid, just like mine. 'Your mother?' I said with hesitation.

'Not only my mother. My father, my brother, my uncle, my cousins. Gone. Murdered. Innocent victims of the war. I have not been able to speak of it. I had to leave Ulm; it was too awful to stay. My home was flattened; half the town was blown to smithereens. That's why I came to Berlin.'

'*Gott im Himmel!* You went through all that and didn't tell me?'

'I couldn't. I can't explain why. I just couldn't.'

Between us, we finished the flask of schnapps. It was four in the afternoon. Georg had a long distance to travel home and darkness came early in February. Before he left, I asked where my father was buried. It was too cold and bleak to go straight away. I would visit him in a day or two, when the weather improved.

I knew that a set of house keys would be in his desk drawer, hidden amongst pencils and paper clips, bottles of antacids and headache tablets, tubes of his pick-me-up pills, Pervitin. To search for the keys, I sat at his desk on the swivel chair, the one in which he'd drawn his last breath. The sheet of blotting paper that covered the desk's surface had an oily patch where his forehead had rested. Hair oil, if I was not mistaken. I covered it with my hands, closed my eyes. That was the closest I'd ever felt to him. He had not been an easy man to love. But, despite everything, I believed he was an honourable man.

For the best part of a week, I wandered about in a daze, aware of my obligations to finalise my father's affairs, to obtain and lodge certain government documents, to run the business. Luckily, I could rely on Georg and Klaus to manage the day-to-day operations, leaving me to puzzle over the ledgers and financial matters.

While at Tatura, I had taken a short course in bookkeeping, so I had some idea of what to do. But my father's books were not set up the same as in the *Collegium* textbooks. He had a unique system that must have suited the business and himself. Understanding how it worked was like trying to solve a puzzle. The figures in his account books gave me no confidence that the business was financially viable. According to his records, we'd been making losses for years.

On Saturday, I bought a bunch of white flowers and took it to the cemetery in Wedding. His grave looked freshly dug and was lacking a headstone. Another thing to arrange. I squatted beside him, placed the flowers on the mound of earth covering his body. Said a few words to the good Lord about eternal peace. Then I asked my father about the set of books. To other cemetery visitors, I must have sounded insane, discussing financial matters with a dead man. But voicing my concerns helped me organise my thoughts and, believe me, I also gave him a piece of my mind about the woeful state of the business. With the troubles off my chest, I slept soundly that night. In the morning, I had an answer.

In my father's office, I removed the oil painting from the wall. The picture was of Plötzensee, the lake where we swam when I was young. I'd bought it from a local artist soon after the war to replace that horrid portrait of Hitler. The dial of the safe glared at me like a one-eyed monster, daring me to touch it.

I'd seen my father open it once, years before. The combination was etched in my memory. I placed my fingers on the dial and turned. Eighty-two left. Twenty-one right. Thirty-nine left. Then around to the right until it stopped. A tug on the handle and the steel door swung open. Inside was the grey metal strongbox and stacks of paper files. I removed the box. It was heavy, too heavy to be empty.

Opening it, I was astonished to find that it contained as many gold ingots as before. I could only scratch my head in surprise. He said he would sell them to restart the factory but he must have changed his mind. That amount of gold was worth a fortune. I should have been overjoyed, but I couldn't quash the suspicion that he was not the rightful owner. After relocking the box, I slid it back into the safe. My attention turned to the mountain of documents, which I removed and spread across the desk. There were accounting journals, schedules, envelopes stamped with the *Hakenkreuz*, the Nazi emblem. Amongst it all I hoped to find answers.

The accounting books dated back to 1901. The early ones were written in pen-and-ink in Opa's *altdeutsche Schrift*. Elaborate lettering, neat and perfect. Then, in 1935, the writing switched to my father's minimalist style. The dates rolled on, one after another after another, right up to the present. The only gap in the records was two years around the end of the war when operations ceased.

I opened the current ledger, studied the entries that he'd made. My hands trembled as I reached across the desk for the ledger that I'd been trying to decipher all week. Opening both books to November 1954, the last complete month, I scrolled down the page, comparing entries, one to the other. It was like reading two novels—one fantasy, one true crime—set at the same time in the same location.

Two sets of accounts. One was a watered-down version for the government; the other was presumably an accurate record for himself. The business was doing very well indeed, despite the figures provided for taxation purposes.

'The old scoundrel!' I said out loud.

The discovery solved one problem but created another. What should I do now? Coming clean would mean a hefty fine—maybe worse—and payment of decades of back taxes. Keeping up the charade would probably land me in prison ... eventually ... if this was ever found out.

No, I would *definitely* be found out. Dishonesty went against my grain. 'Guilty' would be written all over my face. I could never keep such a secret. The gold in the safe was more than enough to pay any penalties that might be imposed.

Ah yes, the gold. Another matter to consider. I didn't know how Max had come by so much 'portable wealth' and whether it was legally his.

Hoping I'd not find further incriminating evidence, I turned my attention to the thickest of the Nazi envelopes. The document inside was a ten-year contract for the supply of boots to the military. Dated July 1937, it was signed by Major Karl-Otto Koch and Max Vogel. I read it with interest. Clause 15.2 stated:

> *The product shall undergo regular and rigorous testing to*
> *be performed under strict military conditions. If the product*
> *fails to meet the highest standards of performance and*
> *durability, this contract may be terminated forthwith.*

My mind flashed back to the day I'd accompanied my father to Sachsenhausen. The frail pyjama-clad prisoners; the tramp, tramp, tramp of boots around the semicircular path. The differing surfaces: gravel, cobblestones, asphalt, sand, rubble. The crack of the whip when a prisoner stumbled or fell.

A wave of nausea passed over me. *Max knew.*

As a fifteen-year-old schoolboy, I had witnessed the boot-testing process myself. At the time, I was too young and naïve to comprehend what I had seen.

Then it hit me.

All that gold, all that 'portable wealth'. Ordinary Germans like me did not know about the Nazi extermination camps until thousands of walking skeletons in rags were liberated at the end of the war. After my return from Australia, I'd seen photos taken by American soldiers of the naked cadavers piled up in pits. I'd read about the process used in Sachsenhausen. How, on the pretext of a dental examination, inmates with gold teeth were identified and separated from the rest. That occurred just before they were taken, one by one, to another 'clinic' for their height to be measured. There, the prisoner was ordered to stand with his back to a measuring device. The 'doctor' behind him took the reading. *Click!* Execution by gunshot was quick and easy. The gold teeth were removed, the bodies were sent to the incinerators. The people of nearby Oranienburg knew not to do their laundry on incinerator days. Too much damn soot.

I rushed to the bathroom and heaved into the bowl. Then I washed my hands over and over, in the hope of eradicating the guilt of touching that gold. I did not know how he came by it, but it had to have been some under-the-table deal done with the Nazis.

Later, in soft-falling snow, I went for a long walk around the lake, along the streets, through Schillerpark, bypassing the cemetery where he lay. Knowing what I did, I could not bring myself to see that grave.

Eventually, I found myself back at the house. My house now. I switched on the lights, made a cup of sage tea, sat in my usual spot in the living room. That room had not changed for as long as I could remember, yet my entire world had turned upside down. My father was probably a war criminal. If not, an accessory or an associate. What a dreadful proposition! Every cell of my body wanted to scream, yet I was forced to remain silent. My life stretched out before me, for I was still a young man with hopes and ambitions. This was none of my doing. The next steps were critical. I would have to plan carefully.

Of one thing I was sure: I was glad he was dead.

My eyes rested on a framed photograph on the mantlepiece. Black and white. My parents—Elsa and Max—before I came along. Their hair was dark against a pale background. My hair was fair. Their faces were round.

Mine was long. Their bodies were stout. Mine was wiry. Was there any family resemblance at all?

My mind was a whirlpool. Other documents still lay on the desk in his office. So far, I'd read half the story. Before I leapt to conclusions, I should know all the facts. However painful those facts might be, I needed to ascertain the full extent of the damage.

With renewed determination, I grabbed an umbrella and strode through falling sleet to the factory. The temperature dropped again; I was thankful that my winter boots were wool-lined and waterproof. The familiar hum of activity floated from the workshop. The scent of leather was the stimulant that drove me on.

The upstairs offices were unoccupied. The door of the end office was open, for I had escaped in haste. I locked it behind me. Such was my disgust, that I wheeled his swivel chair into a corner and replaced it with one for visitors. The blotting paper I ripped to shreds and burnt in the bin.

The other Nazi envelopes contained mementos. A photo of Hitler, signed by himself. A medal inscribed: *To Max Vogel, for services to the Third Reich.* In one I found engineering plans for a substantial factory to be constructed at Oranienburg.

I unfolded the plans and perused them. The place was double the size of our existing workshop. My father had told me about a factory that he'd leased, how all the workers were paid directly by the government. All he supplied were materials, machinery, training. In my mind, I returned to the vast concentration camp of 1938. Within those high concrete walls was ample space to build a workshop. Sachsenhausen was in East Germany and we were in the West. It was not possible to go there and confirm my hunch.

Much later, after reunification, I had no stomach for it.

I refolded the Nazi documents and returned them to the safe, along with the secret accounting books. A nebulous plan was forming, one that would take all my courage to execute. The idea needed to mature, for I had learnt that quick solutions were seldom effective. Actions always have consequences.

All that remained on the desk were three plain white envelopes, spotted with age. Although my head ached, I was compelled to push on until it was finished.

The first envelope contained a letter from Aunt Berry to Mutti. Short and sweet and undated. The phrase of interest was 'an opportunity in Ulm'. Were they seeking to expand the manufacturing empire in the south?

The second contained two return train tickets—Berlin to Ulm—stamped 12 May 1923. A calling card gave a name and address that were unfamiliar to me. Black-and-white snapshots showed my father and Mutti with a tiny baby. The little one was probably me, for I had been born just six weeks earlier. Why would my parents take a newborn baby on a business trip?

And so, to the third envelope. I felt as if I were playing a game, as if Max had purposely staged a slow exposé in order to confuse or shock me. Inside was my original birth certificate, signed in blue ink by the doctor who'd delivered me. The date of the registration was six weeks after my birth. All the details were correct, with one exception.

Place of birth: Ulm.

That single word shook me to the core. Berlin was my birthplace, or so I'd thought. How could I have been born in Ulm in April when my mother did not travel there until May?

A knock at the door.

'Who's there?'

'It's Georg. Are you all right?'

'Just a minute.' I shoved all the evidence into the safe, rehung the painting, unlocked the door.

'You've been working for hours,' said Georg. 'Feel like lunch?'

'It's freezing outside.'

'Isabell gave me a flask of *Kartoffelsuppe*. It's too much for one. Care to join me?' He opened his satchel. 'Look, we have *Roggenbrot* and some apples too.'

I wiped down the desk with a handtowel, located two clean mugs. The potato soup was hearty and the bread was crusty fresh. Hungrily I ate, for my breakfast had been rudely disposed of some hours earlier.

When my belly was full, I told Georg about my parents' visit to Ulm in the year of my birth. 'Do you know anything about it?'

'Only what Aunt Berry said about family secrets.'

'She implied that your mother would tell you,' I said.

'As you know, that wasn't possible. The only one alive who knew my family was old Father Heinrich, the parish priest. I went to visit him at the presbytery to pay my respects and talk about my sorrow. He said a prayer for us all and gave me a special blessing.'

'And ...?'

'Three weeks ago, I took the liberty of writing to Aunt Berry about your father's death. I also told her about the sad end to my own family—and hers—and asked if she could fill in the gaps.

'It seems that Father Heinrich was harbouring a few secrets of his own. At the age of sixteen, my mother Gertrude had gone to him with a "delicate problem". That was the year before I was born. She was distraught, for she barely knew the boy who'd become her lover, and didn't know how to tell her parents. Father Heinrich advised her to enter the convent. The nuns would look after her until the child was born. Then it would be put up for adoption.

'It seems that Gertrude didn't like this idea at all. She was always a bit of a tearaway. Although she couldn't tell her parents, she trusted Aunt Berry, who was living in Ulm at the time. Aunty agreed to take her in, on one condition: that she marry a good honest man. Ernst Mayer, widowed farmer and devout Catholic, was the only candidate.

'Father Heinrich performed the wedding ceremony. And so, my birth was legitimised. The man I loved and called *Vati* was not my natural father.'

'Is there more to this story then?'

'I think you already know the answer,' he said.

All kinds of improbable scenarios were racing through my mind. Then I looked at him: his fair hair and his blue eyes, his long face and his wiry physique. We were two peas in a pod.

'My parents were poor,' said Georg. 'At the time they could afford only one baby, so Aunt Berry wrote to a close friend in Berlin who'd been unable to bear a child.'

'There was "an opportunity in Ulm". I've read her letter. I thought Aunt Berry meant a business opportunity.' I paused, trying to make sense of it. Eventually it dawned on me. 'So, we are brothers.'

'We are, in fact, twins.'

'You must have known this for ages. Why didn't you tell me?'

'Aunt Berry's letter arrived yesterday; I read it last night. Believe me, this is a shock for me too.' Fiddling with a button on his shirt, he added, 'But I've survived.' He grinned and I knew he was teasing.

As if by telepathy, we pushed back our chairs, stood up and threw our arms around each other. Yes, there were tears, certainly on my part.

'Did you ever find your natural father? I mean *our* father?'

'No. And do you know what? I don't care. Vati was twenty-five years older than my mother. He was kind to her and treated me as his own. I couldn't have asked for a better father.'

'I wish I could have said the same about mine.'

After the revelations of the day, I could only conclude that Max Vogel was a scoundrel of the highest order who'd do anything for money. Although I was not of his blood, I would carry the shame like a sack of coal on my back. Then I remembered Opa, the elder I looked up to, the one who truly loved me. And dear Mutti. Without them to guide me through childhood, my life would have been a complete disaster.

Twenty-four

Reinickendorf: October 2010

'Did you ever forgive Max?' said Kathy.

'To some extent. I forgave him for keeping the adoption a secret. But his association with Nazi war criminals has been hard to accept. Atonement is a better word. Without dragging myself into the mire, I have tried to atone for his actions.'

She shook her head. 'But, as an adult, it must have been a shock to discover that your "parents" were not actually your parents.'

As if stung, Horst sucked air through his teeth. 'Well then, tell me *your* story.'

'I think you already know it. My mother, Maria, was married twice. The first time when she was seventeen to Alice's father, Bruno Zanetti, who died. The second time to Luca Giuliano, my father.'

'And how many years are between Alice and yourself?'

'Thirty-one.'

'That is quite an age gap.'

'I was a change-of-life baby. Quite a surprise, I understand.'

'And when were you born, if you don't mind my asking?'

'Third of August, 1955.'

'In Toowoomba?'

'Yes. Dad was a school principal and Alice worked at the hospital. On her days off, she looked after me and gave Mum a break.'

The questions ceased and Horst's eyes misted with tears.

To fill the awkward silence, Kathy continued talking. 'Towards the end of her life, Alice would ramble on about people and places I never knew. With dementia, early memories stick while later ones vanish like dreams. In her final week on this earth she mentioned your name for the first time. I didn't know if you were real or a figment of her imagination. She told me she was a nurse at "the family camp", which didn't seem to exist. She talked about her honeymoon but she never married. She said she'd had morning sickness and a troubled birth, but she never had children. Dementia is an awful disease for the sufferer and those who care for them. Then she made me promise to find a man called Horst Schuhmacher and tell him that she loved him. I thought you were just another figment of her mind.'

Horst dropped his head into his hands. 'I truly loved her.'

Touching his arm, Kathy said, 'So did I. When I was a child, Alice was like a mother to me. All that changed when I hit my teens.'

Horst hauled himself to his feet. 'I have a photograph for you. I just need to find it. Please bear with me.' Like an old man, he stomped out of the room.

Shortly after, he returned, carrying a jewellery case and a biscuit tin whose lid showed a picture of the Brandenburger Tor on a clear day. He placed the items on the coffee table and prised the lid off the tin. Inside were postcards, photographs, and other bits and pieces from the past. After sifting through the photos, he selected one with a jagged edge. 'I think you will find this interesting.'

The black-and-white photo had been hacked in half with blunt scissors. It featured a young Alice, a wide beach, and a hill fringed with Norfolk pines. Kathy dived into her purse, brought out her photo of Horst and held the two pieces together.

'The perfect fit,' she said.

'Wait, there's writing on the back.'

She flipped the photos. The caption across them was written in her sister's flowing hand.

'Honeymoon suite', Greenmount. November 1954.

It took a moment for the significance to hit. The period between November 1954 and August 1955 was exactly nine months. At the time of her birth, the woman she called Mum would have been pushing fifty. Had she not just said that, as a child, Alice was like a mother to her? Yet, in all these years, she'd never questioned the obvious.

Kathy put her hand to her mouth. 'I … I don't know what to say.'

Never, in her wildest imaginings, did she suspect that Alice's diseased mind could engineer such an elaborate revelation. She had promised to find Horst Schuhmacher, a bootmaker who lived in Berlin, which she had done. In so doing, she had discovered herself.

She leant across the sofa and kissed his cheek. 'Thank you for telling me the truth.'

Her head was spinning, she needed time to process this avalanche of information. In fact, she'd have to rethink her entire life, substituting one set of parents for another. 'How long have you known about me?'

'Less than a week. When you came to the door that first day and introduced yourself as Alice, I was overcome with joy. You sounded like her. I thought it was real. Since then, I've been sorting through the facts. The more we spoke, the surer I became.'

'It all makes sense now. Oh my goodness, I never expected my visit to Berlin to end like this.'

'But it hasn't ended. It has just begun.' With that, he pressed the jewellery case into Kathy's hand. 'This belonged to my mother, Elsa. My *adoptive* mother, to be precise. I would like you to have it.'

She opened the lid. Inside was a dragonfly brooch. Art deco, gold and gleaming with tiny green gemstones.

'I hope you will wear it in honour of your German ancestors.'

'But I can't possibly—'

'I have no other children. Please, take it. Pass it on to your daughter, Stephanie. Perhaps she will come to Berlin one day and meet her grandfather.'

After a pause, Horst continued. 'You must meet Georg and your cousins. I can't wait to see the look on his face. He lives not far from here. It's a wonder you haven't bumped into him. He goes to the Swan Café all the time. And, of course, he looks rather like me. So many things we can do together. The lakes, the museums, the zoo.'

Still puzzling over the shocking turn of events, Kathy examined the little dragonfly in the palm of her hand. There was something about gold that she didn't understand. She raised her head, looked him in the eye, and asked the question. 'Earlier you mentioned atonement for the sins of your father. What did you do?'

'I'll tell you, but only because you are my daughter.' He smiled. 'And only if you promise to keep it a secret forever.'

Kathy crossed her heart. 'I swear to God.'

'Of all the documents and papers in Max's safe, I kept the ones relating to my birth and the family. The second set of ledgers and the Nazi documents, I destroyed. In the fireplace of my living room in the winter of 1955, to be precise. The ashes I took to the cemetery and dumped on Max's grave. Retribution, I suppose.

'The gold was secure in the safe, so I left it there. Honestly, I didn't know what to do with it. It didn't belong to me, and I couldn't think of a respectful way to dispose of such a fortune, stolen from the innocent dead. Remember, too, that Sachsenhausen was in the DDR and I was in the West. Four years after reunification, the site was restored. A memorial and museum were built and the prison gates were opened to the world. When you visited the museum there, did you see the gold?'

She groaned. Tears streamed down her cheeks. 'The dental gold. That was it, wasn't it?'

Slowly he nodded.

When she'd made the promise to Alice to find this imaginary stranger, she'd done so begrudgingly. Her expectations had been zero. A fruitless ramble through the boroughs of Berlin, nothing more.

Thankfully, she'd kept her word.

What if Alice and Horst had married? What if she'd grown up in edgy Berlin, rather than sleepy Toowoomba?

What if …?

Epilogue

Coolangatta: April 2022

On the clifftops above the curve of white sand, Kathy put down the tote bag, rested her elbows on the guard rail, and gazed out across the vast blueness that separated Australia from the rest of the world. The feeling of isolation was so immense that it hurt. Even now, when the three would be united for the first time ever. Through a mist of sorrow, she watched the waves below thrash against the coffee-coloured rocks.

Twelve years had passed since she'd set Alice free. That day the sky was bleak and the ocean was whipped into a fury. Drenched to the bone and with her bare feet swaddled in seafoam, she'd released the ashes to the waves. The location—Coolangatta beach—was not accidental; it had been specified in Alice's will.

Since Kathy's first trip to Berlin, she'd visited Horst three more times. Once with Stephanie. Another with Jack. Again, in March 2022, when Australia reopened its borders after a global pandemic. That time she'd brought him back with her. As his closest living relative—his daughter, lost and found—she'd taken the initiative, a move that would have made Alice proud.

Kathy shouldered the bag and turned away from the wide ocean, walked down the staircase to the beach. She kicked off her shoes, and crossed the dazzling white expanse to where blue water kissed the sand. Little waves fizzed around her feet as she waded towards the rocks. She glanced up, to the site where the old guesthouse used to be. The Norfolk pines stood tall and proud, exactly the same as in the picture of Alice and Horst on 'honeymoon' at that very spot.

On a flat stretch of sand between two towering rocks, she removed a bricklike container from the tote bag. Satisfied that this was exactly the same place as before, she waded into the shallows and gazed out to sea. The circle was complete.

There were no prayers and no tears. Instead, she spoke as if he were there with her. She thanked him for his kindness and honesty, apologised for her absence when he needed her most. Finally, she squatted and released the ashes into the crystal-clear water. Snatched by the swirling currents, the fragments eddied and flowed. She watched until they drifted into that immense glittering pond, until every trace of him had disappeared.

It felt good, it felt right.

The lovers—her parents—were together at last.

Thank you for choosing my book. If you enjoyed the story, please take a moment to leave a rating or a brief review—just a sentence or two—on your bookseller's website or on Goodreads.

Until we meet again, Tschűss.

Author's Note

The Bootmaker of Berlin is a work of fiction inspired by history. The world events, settings, and historical characters are real. The central characters—Kathy, Horst, Alice, and their associates—are creations of my imagination.

Research for this novel was done with the assistance of a Fellowship with the State Library of Queensland (SLQ). I relied heavily on records held by the National Archives of Australia (NAA) and online publications at Trove (National Library of Australia). These primary sources reveal detailed and surprising information about people, internment, and life during wartime. One example is the true story of the Italian School of Babinda, a language school set up by mothers with the assistance of Mussolini's government. The organisers were labelled fascists and interned during the war. Their experiences informed the narratives of Alice and her mother, Maria.

Churchill's 'collar the lot' approach to Germans in the UK, the transportation of internees from Great Britain to Australia, the torpedoing of the *Arandora Star*, and the notorious voyage of the hell-ship *Dunera* are true. The circumstances of civilian men who were captured and interned in Britain and Australia during WWII informed the narratives of Horst, Georg, and Werner.

The 'family camp' at Tatura actually existed, though little of it remains now. I have visited the sites of the four camps and the two war cemeteries, which hold the remains of men and women who died while interned in Australia. Paintings and items made by inmates are displayed at the Irrigation and Wartime Camps Museum at Tatura.

Historical figures and places aside, all of the characters and many of the settings are invented. For example, the Zanettis are an imagined family from the fictional sugarcane town of Currawong near Cairns.

In Berlin, I have roamed the streets of Reinickendorf and Mitte, taking in the grandeur and sorrow of the city. Memorials to the murdered Jews, museums about the divided years, relics of Sachsenhausen and the Wall are simultaneously enlightening and gut-wrenching. I have woven this material into relevant scenes. My intention is to be respectful to innocent people who were tortured or killed in the camps, and to those who survived the horrors of war.

Abbreviations and terms

ABC Australian Broadcasting Commission (1932-1983)

AIF Australian Imperial Force

BBC British Broadcasting Corporation

CAC Civil Aliens Corps

CDS Camp Dressing Station

DDR *Deutsche Demokratische Republik*; East Germany

Il Duce The leader (Italian), Benito Mussolini

Der Führer The leader (German), Adolf Hitler

KaDeWe *Kaufhaus des Westens*, upmarket store in Berlin

Nazi Abbreviation of *National-Sozialist;* members of the Party

Porca miseria Expression of surprise or irritation (Italian)

Pranzo The main meal in the middle of the day (Italian)

Puttana Prostitute, woman of loose morals (Italian)

Stasi *Ministerium für Staatsicherheit*; DDR secret police

Wehrmacht Military forces of Nazi Germany

Ufa-Palast Picture palace near the Berlin Zoo, destroyed in 1943

Acknowledgements

This ambitious writing project was completed during the years of Covid-19, a challenging time for us all. Archival research commenced in 2018-19 with the assistance of a Fellowship with the State Library of Queensland. All site visits were done before travel bans and lockdowns, and were recorded on my camera and in notes.

Many thanks to the knowledge and generosity of librarians, archivists, historians, and volunteers at the State Library of Queensland; the National Archives of Australia, Brisbane; the Queensland Museum; the Tatura Irrigation and Wartime Camps Museum; the Innisfail Museum; the Army Museum South Queensland; the Museum of Nursing History RBWH, Brisbane.

Thank you to the museums and memorials of Berlin, which preserve the history of World War II and the post-war division into East and West. Of particular note are the Sachsenhausen Memorial and Museum at Oranienburg, the Holocaust Memorial, the Kaiser Wilhelm Memorial Church, the Stasi Prison at Hohenschönhausen.

Thank you to beta-readers Lucretia Ackfield, Ruth Bonetti, Diane Clarke, Davide Cottone and Elizabeth Cottone, who gave me honest feedback, along with praise and encouragement, and to the ladies of my book club who have been so positive and supportive of my writing journey.

On a personal note, the project reconnected me with family. My German grandfather migrated to Australia in 1887 and lived here peacefully through both world wars. Thanks, Evon Anderson, for your detailed update of the Fischle family history. In 1942, my Italian father-in-law, a sugarcane farmer and naturalised British citizen, was interned at Loveday, South Australia. Learning of his experiences was the catalyst that drove me to explore social pressures and the political response, which was to banish innocent migrants to barbed-wire prisons.

In Berlin, our guide is our daughter, Elise. As a long-term resident, she has shown us the light and shadow of the city's intriguing past. She is also the designer of this beautiful cover. Her feedback on scenes set in modern Berlin helped my words achieve another level of authenticity. Thank you from the bottom of my heart.

Thank you, my darling Sam, for your support, inspiration, and critique of the manuscript. Above all, thank you for putting up with me all those months when my mind was in another space.

Selected References

Commonwealth of Australia. *Investigation case files, internees.* NAA: BP242/1. Various.

Commonwealth of Australia. *Interpreter's Reports by Lieutenant R. Finzel.* NAA: BP242/1. Q30580. In particular, 'Babinda Fascio'.

Commonwealth of Australia. *Official Visitor's Report - Dated 1st April 1942 - Internment Camp Gaythorne.* NAA: MP508/1, 255/713/27. MP508/1.

Connors, Libby; Finch, Lynette; Saunders, Kay; Taylor, Helen. 1992. *Australia's Frontline: Remembering the 1939 - 45 War.* St Lucia: UQP.

Geissmann, E. & Bridges, Myrtle. 1941. *Geissmann Diary and Bridges Correspondence 1941.* Unpublished. State Library of Qld.

Hammond, Joyce. 1990. *Walls of Wire: Tatura, Rushworth, Murchison.* Victoria: J. Hammond.

Harder, H. 1941. *Diary 1941.* In diaries and papers, 1917-1984. Unpublished. Fryer Library, University of Queensland.

Inglis, Ken; Spark, Seumas; and Winter, Jay. 2018. *Dunera Lives: A Visual History.* Clayton, Victoria: Monash University Publishing.

Monteath, Peter. 2018. *Captured Lives: Australia's Wartime Internment.* Canberra: NLA Publishing.

Ohler, Norman. 2017. *Blitzed: Drugs in Nazi Germany.* UK: Penguin.

Peeters, Joan. *Joan Peeters Diaries 1941-1944.* Unpublished. SLQ.

Peeters (nee Taylor), Joan. *Nursing During the War Years, 1943-1945.* Unpublished. SLQ.

Rees, Laurence. 2020. *Hitler and Stalin.* UK: Penguin Random House.

Spizzica, Mia. (Ed). 2018. *Hidden Lives: War, Internment and Australia's Italians.* Carindale: Glasshouse Books.

Sullivan, James T. 2008. *Beyond All Hate: A wartime story of an internment camp for Japanese in Australia, 1941-46.* Camberwell: James T. Sullivan.

Terranova, Debbie. 2019. *Queensland Women and War: A multicultural perspective of the experiences of female civilians during World War II.* Unpublished. SLQ. Contact the author.